SAVAGE WAR

BY

JASON BORN

WORKS WRITTEN BY JASON BORN

THE LONG FUSE:

QUAKER'S WAR

SAVAGE WAR

LIONS & DEVILS are:

HELL SHALL STIR

DEVILS IN THE BREACH

WHERE DEVILS TREAD

THE NORSEMAN CHRONICLES are:

THE NORSEMAN

PATHS OF THE NORSEMAN

NORSEMAN CHIEF

NORSEMAN RAIDER

NORSEMAN'S OATH

THE WALD CHRONICLES are:

THE WALD

WALD AFIRE

WALD VENGEANCE

STANDALONE:

LEAGUE OF THE LOST FOUNTAIN

COPYRIGHT

ISBN-13: 978-1981857234

ISBN-10: 1981857230

DEDICATION

To

Tom & Diane. Your support has been invaluable.

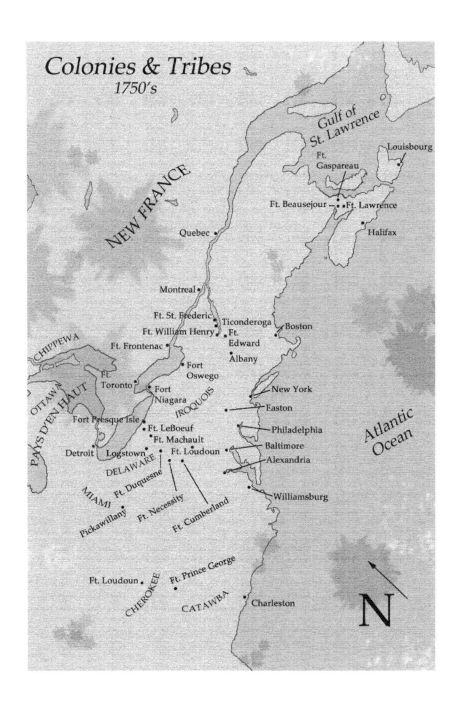

PROLOGUE

You've smelled it. I know you have.

With hairs raised, your tingling skin has felt it. Before your eyes have seen a flash of lightning. Before your ears have heard thunder rumbling.

It's that indescribable change in the scent of the air. The taste of the wind – sweeter than normal. That maddeningly slim variation in pressure. Each of them indicates a coming storm, often long before a single foreboding cloud crests the horizon. You see nothing. Yet, your senses, working at a level above your conscious mind, know a storm is brewing.

In the same way, I knew a storm of mankind's making was more than looming. It had begun bubbling over two years ago. My pregnant wife – she and I had both been sixteen at the time – had been among the first victims. Tahki had been killed for no other reason than pure cruelty. And just two months ago, the boiling pot of war further erupted over its cast iron walls. Its blood-red, gurgling waters doused my comrades and me, while serving under Colonel Washington. We had been the unfortunate recipients of its first great round of destruction. Fort Necessity lay in ruins, destroyed by the French pederasts and a host of Indian allies. Dozens of Pennsylvanians and scores more Virginians and South Carolinians lay dead with lead-shattered bones and now scalp-free skulls.

But not every official in His Majesty's North American colonies was a complete fool. Washington's sad report on those miserable events spurred Governor Dinwiddie to action – well, as much action as a fattened Scotsman in high political office is capable. Mostly, he sent pleading letters to the governors of the other colonies from the safety of his official mansion in Williamsburg, Virginia. He needed funding, a sharing of the coming wartime expenses, he said. Requests went to the crown in London, begging for hard specie and the authority to wage a right and bloody war against the French toads.

For his part, Colonel Washington was left on the shrunken edge of the frontier at Wills Creek. He was in charge of an army of Virginians, though calling it thus would be offensive to the paltriest of armed forces in the world. His men were without food, shoes, clothing, or shelter. If the French decided to attack, Washington's band of misfits would be better able to hold them off with their combined and quite considerable stench than with any show of force. Muskets were in short supply. Powder and shot were hoarded by the quartermaster as if they were the very frankincense and myrrh given to Christ all those years ago.

And that's where I came in. Having just semi-officially left the employ of the wild Irish trader, George Croghan, in favor of the less lucrative and more dangerous work required of George Washington, I found myself stuck in the capital town of Virginia. I had been sent with letters for the governor and the Burgesses. Now I sat around, waiting for replies and directions for my next task.

I hated town life. I hated civilization and its hustle, its pointless bustle. The incessant clippety-clop of hooves on cobblestone streets was as irritating to me as an overly chatty flock of geese waddling beneath my window. People coming. People going. For what?

Even at the edges of towns, out on the farms, there were too many people. That is why I had run away from my family's Pennsylvania farm in the first place. That, and countless disagreements on faith, revenge, and murder. So, the deep Western Wilderness was the place for me.

But there was *one* thing in Williamsburg that was worth enduring all the hob-knobbing gentry and the squalid beggars just arrived from the Mother Country. While buried in the shit and grime and death surrounding Fort Necessity, I had convinced myself that she was more than worth it. I would court Bess Goode. To hell with the French. Curse the Indians – well, the ones allied against our own just cause. Damn war. Damn her stern father. Come hell. Come high water. Bess was going to be my wife.

PART I
PLANS OF MORTALS

CHAPTER ONE
1754 A.D.

Just outside of Williamsburg there is a small wood, mostly insignificant. Within that tiny copse of trees, the land dips down into a shallow glen where a narrow and quite shallow brook naturally drains water from the surrounding fields only after heavy rains. The rest of the year its bottom sits merely damp as if the earth beneath it was only mildly incontinent.

And insignificant or not, that little wood was destined to host a scene that would have lasting consequences for the rest of my life. So, too, the incidents of that intimate setting would even have a broad effect on events and peoples that would never visit its confines. This should serve as a warning to all young men who would demonstrate wisdom enough to heed an older man's advice. *Be careful of the company you keep. And be mindful what you do with that company - especially if one of you is drunk and beautiful and the other lustful and jealous.*

But all in due time.

After swiping a few spokes, and anything else long and resembling a thin club, from the wheelwright's scraps, I headed out through that wood. I jumped the soggy creek and walked through the soft mossy ground that would make a more comfortable bed than most of the real ones in which I had ever slept. Two more minutes of hoofing it brought me into a broad clearing that was skirted with a neat fence. A small herd of heifers and cows and their calves grazed in one corner of the pasture, their mottled brown and white bodies standing in the shade, their tails facing the wind. The herd's bull stood alone and proud at the other end of the clearing, watching his women and children from a distance.

"About time you got here!" said Taeheek. He was a Mohawk from up north around Albany. For simplicity, he usually went by his Christian name which was Tim. A gaggle of other young men and boys stood arrayed behind him in two rough groups. They were a mixture of whites and Indians. Their expressions were serious, matching Tim's.

I waved my wooden prizes as my gang of boys gathered around me. "I got the crosses. Sturdy oak. The better to leave you bruised and bleeding." I began handing out one each to the teens. When they had it in their grasp, they tore off to put the finishing touches on their makeshift weapons as I had instructed them. "It would have been a lot easier if I had some help. It's hard to steal from the wheelwright without a distraction when he and his apprentice are at work in the shop."

Tim, his face streaked with charcoal, shook his own cross. He hadn't needed me to steal one for him because he took his everywhere he went. It was as much a part of him as his musket or tomahawk. "If you and these other dogs came prepared we could have been done already." A few of his fellow Indians, each with a cross crafted by his own hand with its own distinct features, from dangling feathers, to paint, to netting, and much more, pumped their weapons in agreement.

He was baiting me. I chose to ignore him and looked to my new comrades who feverishly worked on their crosses. Some used knives to carve out crude notches or cups in the end. Others used woven twigs and cord or deer sinews. None of their crosses would have any fancy adornment like those of the Indians, but nonetheless they'd perform their expected function. Well, I hoped they'd perform. They'd be put together by hurried hands. They'd be employed during the contest by those same unskilled hands.

Soon enough, my band of warriors gathered behind me, waiting for the fight to begin. In anticipation, each gripped his cross with whitened knuckles in one hand and repeatedly slapped the other end into his opposite, awaiting palm. The repetitive jostling caused the makeshift crook of one lad's stick to fall off into the grass at his feet. A few of the nursing calves stopped sucking from their mothers' teats and lowed, almost laughing at our pathetic force arrayed against a more experienced foe. The calves, as if foreshadowing what we would do, then began racing around, chasing each other, tails elevated and snot flying. The boy bent and began feverishly fixing his cross.

Tim took this as a sign that it was time to begin. He reached into a fist-sized leather pouch dangling from the cord belt at his mostly naked waist. He then pulled out the object that would be the sole focus of every lad in the pasture that afternoon and kept it hidden behind his grip. Though I couldn't see it, I saw plainly that he squeezed it between his palm and fingers as he cocked his arm up and back. "You sailors will need all the help you can get!" He often called whites sailors because of the great merchant vessels filled with spices and manufactured goods that traveled the coasts and oceans. I had never been aboard such a ship. Neither had any of my comrades. "You go first, you sailors!"

He snapped his arm forward and hurled the ball at me. I could tell right away that I was going to be unable to catch it in my basket. And since it was a cardinal sin worthy of a severe beating from the crosses of players on both sides, I did not attempt to catch the fast-moving object with my hand. I stuck out my chest to absorb the throw and decided I would scoop up the ball off the ground a heartbeat later.

The deerskin-covered ball cracked into my sternum with the force of a mule kick. Surprised and in pain, I staggered back two steps, clutching my heart. Tim and his horde were already advancing as I glanced down to examine the ball we had agreed to use. I saw that some of the stitching was new. Tim had obviously replaced the bunched fur that had formed the ball's center that morning with a smooth stone or sanded piece of wood. It might as well have been a hurtling musket ball.

He laughed as he scooped the free ball up in his basket. "Pay attention next time, old friend!" Tim intentionally slowed his pace so that his fellow warriors could catch up and form a protective mob around him. I and my teammates began swirling around the pack of enemy warriors probing for weaknesses. We started by nudging our hips into gaps between opposing players. Every game of *My Little Brother's War*, or *La Crosse*, as the French called it, began with similar genteel considerations. But as I had found out in my first game of La Crosse some years before against the youth of my wife's Miami tribe, the violence escalated from there without fail. Nudges morphed into ramming. Hurt feelings and sore rumps soon spread to the use of elbows to crack ribs. Fists, knees, feet, and of course, the crosses themselves soon joined in as suitable weapons.

The rules were meager in those days. Following even that minimal number proved too difficult for me.

I used my cross to trip up an opposing player. When he crumpled in the grass, I wedged into his place in the roving mob, making a thrust toward Tim. My cross struck his stick and for a flickering moment, the ball danced precariously at the edge of his sinew basket. But he adjusted efficiently, snatching the ball back with a sweeping motion. All the while, he and the mob kept advancing toward their goal, the gate at the end by the heifers. I was stuck in among them, forced to shuffle backwards by their momentum. They mowed down my inexperienced teammates, whose ability to slow, let alone halt, their progress diminished with every step.

A well-placed elbow brought me one step closer to Tim. Only one player now separated us. Tim and his guard noticed me. "You know what to do," Tim encouraged his fellow player. The young man, charcoal streaking vertically from his cheeks down his naked chest like war paint, offered a devilish grin.

I had played La Crosse a few times before. That made me the most experienced member of the team of whites, none of whom had ever heard of the game until we organized it last night. However, Tim and his fellow woodland boys had been schooled with bruised knuckles and wounded pride since they were first weaned from their mothers' tits. As such, I was still considered a novice. I wasn't sure what the devilish grin from Tim's guard meant.

I quickly found out.

He gripped his cross with both hands and quickly raised it as if he meant to jab my snout. I reacted, lifting my cross and tipping my head away from the coming blow. But he had already stopped. His charging knee rammed hard between my legs. A surge of bile raced into my throat. The pain was immediate, direct, and unmistakable to any member of the male of our species. Like a rock dropped from a ledge, I plummeted into the grass.

Moccasins kicked me and stepped on my side as I curled up into a ball and the mob smartly made their way past. I was pressed down into the mud. My eyes were pinched tight in an effort to control the heaving wave of nausea that galloped in my belly. It would earn me no respect from the boys from Williamsburg or our opponents to vomit during the first play. I pursed my lips, wriggling on the ground.

I didn't need to see to know that the Mohawk and his young men had scored a few moments later. Excited cheers and war whoops told me.

When I rolled over onto my back, finally able to stretch out and willing to open my eyes to the sky, Tim's smiling face stared down at me. I reached a hand up for him to haul me to my feet. "Oh, no," he said with a distasteful frown. "I see you come by your frontier nickname honestly." He pointed to my head which felt damp from wallowing in the mud.

"What?" I asked. Though I knew my nickname, I had hoped it had died at Fort Necessity along with the man who had given it to me. I'll not dignify the name by repeating it here. You'll have to read my previous memoir if you wish to find out. Suffice it to say that it had something to do with feces. Tim kept pointing until I sat up on my own and patted the back of my head with my palm. The mud squished. Tim laughed. And I knew why when I looked at the fresh cow manure in my hand.

"Get up on your own," Tim said. "You sailors start with the ball first this time. Maybe with that shit all over you, no one will want to get near you. Your team may actually have a chance to score."

"Ha, ha," I mumbled, climbing up and accepting the ball. I weighed it in my hand. "I thought it was filled with fur."

"It was," Tim agreed with a twinkle in his eye as he led his teammates to the center of the pasture.

"Give 'em hell, Ephraim!" came a shout from the fence. I looked and saw that ol' George Croghan had heard the commotion and come to watch. He'd brought with him several prominent men from town. Already, a table had been dragged from an inn and set up just beyond the pasture. Rum and ale flowed from barrels into thick mugs. An enterprising tavern keeper had brought several casks through the woods and over the creek and, no doubt, charged a hefty premium to his increasing list of buyers. We officially had spectators, a growing jeering audience. "That team of Indians looks tough to beat. You know I hate to lose. Should I bet on them or take the long shot?"

"What are the odds against us right now?" I asked, making my way to our starting positions. It was difficult to stand up straight as my groin throbbed – not in a good way. I gave the ball to the tiniest member of our team and asked him to hold it for a moment. Suddenly proud, he tucked it into the wooden spoon-like end of his cross.

Croghan consulted with several of the newcomers as more gentlemen and even a few women streamed from the woods to watch our impromptu, grand contest. "Ten-to-one!" George exclaimed. "So, should I bet that you'll win?"

We had no chance to win. Our inexperienced team would be lucky to score one goal. At least, those were the rumblings I heard from the wealthy gentlemen who leaned along the fence, wagering.

"What are the odds that we score a goal right here and now?" I asked Croghan. "On our first try?"

He again talked with the men surrounding him. A flurry of Virginia currency notes changed hands as odds were calculated and more bets made. "You haven't even carried the ball in your team's baskets, yet?" Croghan asked. "And these gentlemen want to know if any of your team members has ever played this Indian game before?" He acted like it was exotic to him, though he had seen it played in the Western Wilderness dozens of times. Croghan had even played when he was a younger man.

"Just me," I answered truthfully. "Once or twice."

More betting. Some men even shouted as they waved notes in the air, trying to get someone to take their money for a wager. Connecticut currency traded hands side-by-side with Massachusetts bills. Win or lose, it would be a miracle if anyone could make sense of it.

"The odds of you scoring right now have run the gamut," ol' Croghan shouted in explanation. "Started at five-to-one. Ended at twenty-to-one when everyone realized that none of you really know how to play against the Indians."

"Can we play?" Tim asked, frustrated at the delay caused by the betting, swelling crowd.

"Pipe down!" I scolded. Then I looked at my old boss. He and I had survived many confrontations over the years. "Do you trust me?"

He grinned and saying nothing more to me, set about betting a large wad of notes from his pocket on my team's immediate ability to carry the ball to the other end of the field. It seemed there were suddenly an unlimited number of takers. His currency was mopped up in a flicker of time. No one but the Irishman had faith in us.

I turned and winked at the boy who held the ball. I'm sure he had no idea what I meant by the gesture, but when you've got a secret, it's best to keep it that way. And to the boy's credit, he nodded while whitening his grip on the cross. If he worried about the possible carnage that was coming his way, the boy hid it well.

"Are we playing or not?" Tim barked, exasperated.

It was time to win a bet for ol' George. "With me, lads!" I shouted, throwing my cross down into the grass as I advanced on Tim. My fist struck his chin before his brain even registered that I moved. He staggered back, a swatch of blood coloring his cheek and smearing his charcoal. His fellow warriors dropped their weapons and pounced on me, fists flying. My teammates did likewise and soon, instead of playing a game of La Crosse, an all-out brawl was taking place in the center of a pasture.

Men and women cheered and jeered at us from their spots along the edge. A pair of cows bellowed angrily at the loud disturbance in their normally quiet home. The bull stood, chewing its cud, its head facing us, its ears erect and listening for the approach of any real threat.

And one tiny threat did materialize. Our small player who carried the ball, barely noticeable, for he was scrawny and poorly dressed like the rest, trotted around the massive fist fight. He went, as I had hoped, completely unmolested by Tim's motley team of Indians. They were too busy trying to destroy me. The vigilant bull, however, was another story.

Out of the corner of my eye – the one that wasn't already swollen from Tim's sharp knuckles – I saw the protective bull charge the ball carrier. Snorting, the bull lowered his polled head and raced with a lightning burst of speed.

"Go, boy! Go!" Croghan shouted.

"The child! Get the child!" exclaimed the men who had taken the other side of the bet.

Like a giant club, the bull slashed his knobby head at the last moment. Luckily the boy jumped out of the way – mostly. One of the boy's legs was clipped from behind and he went head-over-heels, tumbling over the creature and landing in the grass. The bull's momentum carried him ten feet beyond the fallen boy.

"Get up!" I shouted. Tim's fist slammed into my cheek. I bounced off another opponent and one of my own players before I fell to the ground.

"Get him!" Tim bellowed when he understood what was happening. He forgot about the fight and ten of his warriors peeled off in pursuit. We tackled some of them and forced them to fight it out. Those who weren't wrestled to the ground were chased by the rest of us, so a looming mass of young men bore down on the boy and the bull.

Each reacted in the way one might expect. The bull, accustomed to scaring off the occasional predator or foolish poacher, saw the odds and became fearful. He blew thick wads of snot from each nostril simultaneously. His head shook so the huge piles of muscle and fat on his neck rolled like waves of grain. Still we came, not to him, but toward the boy. The bull cared not. Just as he began to utter a threatening bellow, he clamped it into a short squeal and raced off, frightened.

The boy sat up dazed.

"The ball!" I shouted, chasing after Tim. "Go!"

The boy gathered his wits, plucked up his cross, and began scanning the thick grass for the prize. Just when his eyes shot wide with excitement, Tim crashed into him with his shoulder. The wooden spoon cross dropped. Ten more men and boys piled onto the waif from behind so the brawl was quickly renewed, perhaps angrier this time. I felt a tinge of sorrow for the battered young boy, but I had a job to do.

I snatched up the cross, scooped the ball, and raced in the direction of the receding bull.

A moment later, we had scored a goal. Croghan's pockets were flush with currency. And the losers were sorely trying to bet on anything and everything in order to win back a portion of their money.

After that, the day went surprisingly well for our team which was made up mostly of poor whites. You see, folks today mistakenly think of our friends, the Indians, as well, *the Indians*. They believe that they are one, if not in tribe, but in purpose. Nothing could be further from the truth, especially in those days. I understood this fact. Tim understood it. And there can be no doubt Croghan knew of the vast differences between the tribes. However, his fellow gentlemen seemed blind to the truth.

I've told you that Tim was a Mohawk from up north. But his team was also made up of Oneida, Abenaki, Catawba, a Cherokee, and young men from at least a half dozen other tribes who happened to be in Williamsburg on business at that time. As such, it was easy for them to begin to blame one another for our sudden success at one goal. Their cohesion broke down. Ancient jealousies, carried from their fathers' fathers' generation, reared their heads. They didn't protect the ball carrier very well. They refused to resort to any trickery, like passing, if it meant one of their rival tribesmen might carry the ball to a goal and glory.

At dusk, we ended the day-long match with an improbable victory. The score was eight to seven. Each goal had felt like it had been the result of a frontal assault on an entrenched enemy. For in a way, it had been. Two of our boys went home crying midway through the day. It probably had something to do with the fact that their forearms dangled grotesquely as if they had an additional joint between their wrist and elbow. One of the Indians on Tim's team lost four of his back teeth when the ball slammed into his jaw. He spat out three of the blunt yellow molars and accidentally swallowed the fourth. After a drink of rum to wash down the blood, he went right on playing.

"I don't care if I never see you again, sailor," Tim called angrily when it was over. He scowled in frustration before heading off with his teammates. But the *team* of Indians disintegrated further after that, each tribesman matching off with his fellows and discarding the rest of the Indians they blamed for the humiliating defeat.

"Same here," I said, cheerily to his back. I was glad to win, but happier still that the abuse had ended.

As the sun set and we limped our way toward the fence, I heard a familiar voice singing a well-known tune. Only it was a voice I'd never expect to be singing that particular song.

> *My dame is sick, and gone to bed.*
> *And I'll go mould my cocklebread!*
> *Up with my heels and down with my head,*
> *And this is the way to mould my cocklebread.*

Of course, I almost blush when I write those words. You know them to be from a bawdy tavern song used by young wenches not known for their modesty. And if it was being sung along the pasture fence, a place where alcohol had been flowing all day long, where the sins of gambling had been practiced in the open, that meant that whoever uttered the words was putting herself in a compromising position.

Despite my exhaustion and bleary eyes, I raced to the fence and scampered over the rails. Many of the older, mature men had already collected their winnings or paid their losings and gone home to their families. Croghan was long gone, probably using a portion of his profits to ply trading contracts from Burgesses in one of the taverns. Still, a gaggle of young men, wanton, lustful, and mostly drunk watched the woman start the song anew. To my horror, she added the actions to match.

Bess' skin was pink from drink. She now sat on top of one end of a long table. Her feet faced the other end. Her knees were drawn up toward her breast and the skirts of her dress were likewise shimmied higher. *Nothing* below her waist, from her calves up to her dark private areas was left to the imagination. After resting for a moment, Bess grabbed her ankles and hoisted them higher, suspending them. The gawking men hooted with glee. In tune with the renewed words from her song, she wobbled to and fro on her buttocks, marching down the length of the table.

Wearied by the time she reached the finish, Bess dropped her legs so they dangled off the nearest end. She panted while resting her elbows on her naked knees. One of her onlookers, his eyes temporarily closed, leaned to plant a kiss on her flushed cheek.

My blood still coursed from a day's worth of simulated war. Rage sprung on me like a thunderclap. With two hands, I took my cross and swung it directly onto that man's nose. Thankfully, the oak landed before his lips had a chance to touch her flesh. The cross cracked in two. His head snapped back, blood poured from his snout. He fell over. The crowd of bystanders stood stunned for a moment.

"My hero!" Bess exclaimed, falling into my arms. Though slight, she weighed a ton. "Did you see what these men were making me do?"

It was clear to me that they were forcing Bess to do nothing, but it was not the time to argue the finer points. While the unconscious man's comrades fell around him, I wrapped Bess' arm around my shoulder and led us both into the copse of trees.

We had gotten a few rods within the woods when the man whose nose I had just broken was revived enough to initiate a chase. His cursing echoed from above. Meanwhile, Bess was completely uncooperative. She staggered and giggled, mumbled and sang. "Cocklebread, cocklebread, cockle, cockle, cocklebread." Bess then halted abruptly on the path. "Ephraim, would you mould my cocklebread?" She burst into a fit of inebriated laughter. Perturbed, I jerked her forward while she snorted merrily.

We soon reached the tiny creek and I thought about leaping it and dragging her up to the main town. But Bess seemed to be losing the ability to stand. She got heavier by the second as she teetered. I knew we would never make it.

It was darker down in the woods with the hills and trees casting their thick shadows. That would work in our favor. I tugged Bess along the side of the creek as the angry voices behind us grew louder. We walked on the soft bed of green moss and made nary a sound. I spun her to face me and set her rump on a rock. Her head swayed to its own happy tune. With one last look,

I smiled wryly and shoved her. "Hey!" she chirped before falling onto the soft earth behind the rock. I jumped after Bess and pulled her feet and skirts down to hide. "What do you think . . .?" she asked.

I slapped my palm over her mouth just as the herd of young men ran along the path and jumped the creek. She bit my hand. I pinched her cheeks. She whined, quietly at first, then louder. "You'll get me killed and maybe worse for you!" I rasped. The thundering men raced up to town, calling out threats to us as they went.

Bess punched me. The first strike didn't hurt, for she found the one spot that hadn't been struck during the game. However, her third, fourth, and fifth wallops felt like the kicks of a draft horse as they landed one after the other on a particularly black and blue bruise on my chest.

I involuntarily let her go. Drunk and not knowing what she did, Bess jumped up to the rock, trying to clamber over. I grabbed her skirts and yanked her back down. She spun and landed on me with a thud, pressing me into the moss and knocking the wind out of me. Moaning, Bess boosted herself onto her elbows on my chest. Like daggers, they poked into another of my bruises. "You're a real pain in the ass, Ephraim!" she said. She then wrinkled her nose. "And you smell like cow dung."

I didn't respond. Instead, I listened for the young men who had been chasing us. I heard nothing but their shouts up at the edge of town. They were spreading out into the streets. We'd made it.

"I said you are a pain in my ass," Bess repeated.

"I'd say the splinters you have from showing everyone your rump will be more painful than anything I've ever done to you," I said.

She scoffed. "Leading me on like that. Sending my heart all a flutter. Then you disappear for, what, six months."

"I was a little occupied," I said. After all, I had been in the middle of the start of a war with the French and a few Indian tribes. "I wrote you letters. You could have written back if you care so much."

Bess' normally large, brown eyes closed lazily. Her breathing became regular and she slept or had passed out. Her forehead slowly settled onto my chest and her arms dropped to my side. I shook my head, chuckling. From what I knew of her father, he would banish Bess to her room for a few years if he ever found out what she'd just done. However, her permissive mother would eventually wear the man down so that Bess would be back to her wild ways soon enough.

Except for a few walks down the public streets of Williamsburg, we had never been this close to one another before. We'd certainly never been left alone. And on that bed of green, I hugged her tightly, stroking her thick hair. She smelled of rum, of course. But I always caught a hint of lavender whenever we strolled together. Now with her hair pressed beneath my nose, she smelled like a full bouquet of the blooming, purple flowers.

Her body was warm against mine. I felt myself stir in a way I hadn't felt since I had been with Tahki, my wife, before she'd been killed. My manhood awakened, pressing up against Bess' belly, only a couple thin layers of fabric between us.

Suddenly self-conscious, I carefully rolled Bess off me to the side. I set her head down on the moss and swept a stray shock of hair from her face. "What am I to do with you, Bess?" I asked quietly while leaning on one hand.

I jerked toward the voices of the men shouting for us. They had come back to the edge of town and the woods. I heard sticks cracking and clothes tearing. "Ouch! Briars! It'll be too dark in there," one called as he obviously retreated back from the copse of trees. "But tomorrow I'll find the cur that busted my nose and teach him a lesson."

"I've got some winnings to spend. To the *Cock and Crown!*" barked another man. It was a rough and tumble tavern at the shadier end of town. Though all patrons would be welcome and served, the *Cock and Crown* attracted a hard scrabble bunch. The fact that these men planned to go there told me that I was not out of the woods just yet. I'd have to keep a low profile for as long as Washington bade me stay in Williamsburg.

When Bess' light touch stroked my arm, I turned to face her. A thin, provocative smile screwed amongst her lips. With the dim light barely making its way into our nook, I saw she blinked coquettishly with bloodshot eyes. One of her hands firmly pulled me down to her. The other pulled her skirts up to her waist. "Unless you want to get caught by those ruffians, you'd better shut up and keep quiet."

We kissed. She tasted like salty sweat and molasses. A rush of electric excitement shot through my entire body. I forgot about the bruises. I forgot about the men who chased us. And I forgot about the dried manure in my hair. The outside world slipped away completely – every problem, every joy, every responsibility. And I'm ashamed to admit it, but I also forgot altogether about my late wife. And I forgot, quite intentionally, that Bess was not yet my bride. I had no business groping her in such a way. But I did.

After a full minute, Bess shoved my face up away from hers. Sweat pooled in the tiny depression above her mouth. Her naked shoulders glistened. "What are you waiting for?" she asked. "We're in the woods. Do what comes natural."

We resumed our youthful, passionate kissing.

And we did what came natural.

CHAPTER TWO

When I awoke the next morning my strong, eighteen-year-old body felt much more like my sixty-four-year-old body does today. Initially, pain, of course, was the most noticeable trait. But what was more disconcerting than the outright agony was that I *noticed* by body at all. Never before could I recall *feeling* my muscles. They, like my joints, had always just worked, flexing when my mind told them to do so. Now, I noticed joints I didn't know I had. Knots of muscles covered my back and arms like a thick hide. My hips and thighs throbbed whenever I moved. I felt bruised bones and stretched tendons that had previously gone completely unnoticed.

At least my head did not ache. I had drunk only one or two – it may have been eight – mugs of rum during the short breaks in the La Crosse contest. Regardless, whether it was a handful or twelve cups of rum, it was not enough to cause a young lad like me harm the following day. It was my body that barely responded, but my mind was sharp.

Looking up at the faint light forming above the tree canopy, I remembered what Bess and I had done. Would she regret it? In many ways, I did. Not because I didn't desire her in that way. I most certainly did. Bess was comely. I was young. The desire was firmly planted in my mind and loins. But I wanted to treat her with respect. I had truly loved Tahki. I would miss her – and still do. A small part of me hoped that Bess would become a fine wife for me and replace the hole left behind in my widower's heart.

The wicked part of my flesh forced a devilish grin as I recalled our activities. Another part of me most certainly did not regret our amorous encounter. I reached down to adjust my loosened trousers, cinching my belt. That other, fleshly part of me was satisfied, sated.

I wondered what Bess' parts, earthly and spiritual, had thought of our union. But that was probably not the best way to start the conversations of a new day. "I bet you have a headache," I said, simultaneously embarrassed and amused as I remembered her antics atop the table.

No answer. She was sleeping. As I should have been. But my mind turned and turned. Though I was a young buffoon, it always spun in those days. It still does today, even as an old buffoon. For instance, tonight I will go to sleep early in the evening when the rest of the world sits down to eat dinner. Unfortunately, my mind, completely refreshed, will stir my body, not rested, awake in the middle of the night. In order to prevent going mad with frantic thoughts, I'll set myself to some task. Then, after working on some minor chore by lantern light for a few hours, I will again grow tired. I will go back to bed around four in the morning and wake up tomorrow before sun-up, my mind already racing on some unsolvable problem. Day-in and day-out, it is the same. All of my mental athletics achieves nothing. You'd think that with all of the thinking I do, I'd be the smartest man in the world. Ha! That claim probably goes to Jefferson. I would have said Adams, but he's too irascible for me to give him such praise. I'm the only one I allow to be so short-tempered without suffering rebuke.

As I rolled over to take a gander at Bess' lovely form, I felt twinges in more of my body. A lump in my arm made itself known. I groaned loudly, loud enough to wake her up.

Had she been there.

I sat up rapidly, regretting it as I was rewarded with what felt like a tear in my hamstring. "Bess," I rasped into the woods, thinking she had gone off to release some of the excess rum that had accumulated in her bladder while she slept. "Bess."

Behind me, I heard a soft set of footsteps approaching me on the mossy forest floor from the other side of the rock. "How's your head?" I asked, unwilling to turn and risk igniting a new bout of pain.

"Terrible," said a male voice.

I spun to see Taeheek, Tim, that is. He had climbed onto the rock and peered down at me. Washed away had been his charcoal. His cross was strung over his back by a cord wrapped over his shoulder and chest. His war hatchet was nestled safely in his belt, next to the pouch containing the La Crosse ball. The butt of Tim's musket rested on the rock near his feet. He gripped the barrel and leaned some of his weight on it, employing the weapon like a crutch. "And my face hurts, my shoulder hurts, everything hurts, you dirty sailor." His features were dour, heaping scorn upon me, but compared to how he had appeared with his war markings during the match, Tim's demeanor appeared almost pleasant.

I gave him a broad smile and noticed that my cheeks ached when they bunched. A soft touch with the end of a finger told me that most of my face was swollen and tender. The only reason I had not noticed my aching head until that point was that the pains everywhere else took precedence. My smile faded in order to relieve this new burst of discomfort.

"Yep," said Tim. "I can't smile either. You hit me pretty hard yesterday. And one of those skunks on your team used his cross like a club. I thought we agreed, no clubbing."

I laughed. It hurt. "We did agree on that."

He frowned further and wagged a finger in my direction. "Listen. We agreed on the fur-lined ball in the morning. You never said it couldn't change its guts before the match."

"Well, I guess some of the rules changed, too," I said, jutting my hand in his direction. "Help me up?"

"No," Tim answered with a wrinkled brow. "I can barely keep myself upright. I don't need another burden."

I sighed and spent a full minute crawling to my feet. Tim, in no hurry to move either, said nothing as he watched lazily.

"Did you see Croghan last night?" I asked.

"Yes," Tim said. "Where were you?"

In answer, I jabbed a thumb over my shoulder and pointed to what had been the bed I had shared with Bess.

"Too drunk to find an inn?" Tim asked, derisively.

"No!" I snapped. I was going to lie and tell him I had only downed a dozen mugs of rum. But he had watched me all the way. "Yes, probably," I then admitted. "But that's not why I was here."

"Why were you sleeping in the open woods? Even my people stopped doing that a few thousand years ago," he added with a thin smile.

"There was Bess. And I, after the game, I broke a guy's nose."

"So, you were hiding," Tim surmised. "A wise choice. That fella's nose you broke went and got drunk himself. Then he and his gang of fellows spent the night searching the town for you. A few of them got locked up in the stockade for disturbing the peace, others for outright fighting. But as far as I know the guy with the nose is still free. He might be surlier today with his hangover adding to his busted face. Come on," he grunted. Normally, he would have hopped off the rock toward the path. This time, like a tribal elder who had long ago lost his balance, he carefully slunk his way down. "Since you didn't show last night, we still have business with Croghan."

I peered around the shallow glen, squinting into the trees. "I really should wait for Bess to return. I need to talk to her."

"Your little Bess went home. I saw her sneaking her way there before sunrise."

Bess was a magnificent liar when it came to spinning a yarn to stay out of trouble. But I didn't know what she could possibly say to her father to steer clear of his wrath for not coming home all night long.

"Let's go," Tim encouraged as he hobbled toward the path. "You'll have plenty of time to propose marriage and make her an honest woman."

"What's that supposed to mean?" I asked, slowly crawling over the rock, my shirt still mostly untucked, my trousers improperly belted and feeling loose.

"Washington sent you here to coordinate supplies with Croghan for his sad army at Wills Creek. When it comes to funding, the Burgesses are slower than sap in a tree before the maple run. I assure you, you'll be here a while."

I caught up to him. "I meant what do you mean about making Bess into an honest woman?"

Tim glanced at me through the corner of his eye as we gingerly crossed the creek and made our way up to town. He began delicately enough. "From the looks of her dress this morning, either she is a restless sleeper, or something else happened to her in these woods."

I'd not let him question Bess' decency. "She had a drink too many yesterday! I stayed here to protect her while she slept. Nothing happened."

"That is what she said when I said hello and asked where to find you," Tim replied.

"See?" I said. We had just emerged from the woods and stood at the edge of the silent town. Not a dog barked. Not a sheep bleated from the nearby meadow. A morning mist was beginning to form. It mixed with the low-hanging, smoky remnants from last night's cooking fires that oozed from chimneys to create a fairly thick fog.

"The lady and the lad doth protest too much, methinks," Tim said, willing to venture a grin despite the bruising that blanketed his face.

I had not known my Hamlet back then. But I was smart enough to know what Tim had implied. "You have called *me* many things," I said, slapping his shoulder with the back of my hand. "But you will not call Bess a liar!"

He looked at me from my head to my toes as if sizing me up for a coming fight. I suddenly prayed that he would simply apologize so we could move on. Win or lose, I didn't think my body was capable of another thrashing.

Tim tipped his head deferentially. "Bess is no liar. I am sorry to suggest otherwise."

I breathed a sigh of relief. "It's fine. Just don't let it happen again." I began marching down the street. "It's early yet, but let's go find Croghan. He'll be plotting out his day in the corner of an inn."

I felt a sharp tug on the back of my shirt. "You might want to be more discreet," Tim said as he yanked.

"What? The guy with the nose?" I asked. "I have you to protect me. Between the two of us, we can take anyone."

Still, Tim held onto my shirt. "That may be true," he allowed, tapping his tomahawk. "But I'm not talking about that. I'm talking about the situation with Bess." His eyes again studied me from top to bottom. He must have really wanted a fight.

My eyes flashed in anger. "I thought I told you to drop it. Nothing happened."

Tim lifted his musket and held up his hands in surrender. "I believe you. I believe you. It's a shame though, really. Even though nothing happened, Bess had to stare at your manhood all night."

"What are you talking about?"

His eyes locked on mine and he pointed downward.

I looked and saw that, indeed, my manhood hung out from my trousers for all the world to see. Scrambling, I shoved it and a shirt tail back in place and cinched up the front of my clothes, adjusting everything along the way. Tim smirked.

"It doesn't mean anything," I grumbled as we resumed our course.

"Oh, no. I'm sure it doesn't," he agreed, chuckling, sarcasm dripping.

"Nothing happened," I insisted.

Only, as you'll see, something did happen. And as with most things in my life, one event collapsed into the next, until finally they all spiraled into a great cataclysmic disaster for much of the world.

But all in due time.

CHAPTER THREE

George Croghan wasn't all wilderness exploits and business dealings. He had actually settled down enough at some point to create a family. I'd met his Indian wife and their children on at least a dozen occasions. The wild Irish trader even owned a place of respite on the frontier, a home, fairly well-appointed for its remote location. I know for a fact, because I had been there many times. Perhaps more than he in the last few years. Most of his time was spent traveling from place to place.

But Tim and I easily located him in one of his more usual haunts. He was eating a fair helping of undercooked bacon and runny eggs at a corner table of *Maude's Cellar*, an inn known for comfortable beds, good food, and privacy for conducting business. He shoveled his breakfast in with energetic vigor. Croghan was always on the move, even when he rested.

"Damn glad I found him," he said between mouthfuls, referring to Tim. "Sad day in heaven and hell when you foolishly decided to leave me and work for Washington, my Quaker boy. You'll be poor, you know. You've got no rich plantation. No land. No wealthy bride. But each man makes his choice." The food went in, was chomped rapidly, but only partially, before being forced down his gullet. "And I can't see you ever having the honor of our friend Colonel Washington. Born old, he must have been. But I've got Tim here. Even better than you, if you don't mind me saying. Scares the Holy Ghost right out of the Burgesses when he sits next to me in meetings. Gives them just a look, he does. Meetings go fast and usually in our favor when he's around. And don't get me started with how well things go out in the wilderness. You had a way with Indian negotiations, Ephraim, I'll tell you that. But Tim here? Why, he's a master." Croghan then wagged a finger of caution at his new employee. "Now don't go getting a proud head, lad, all bloated like. You've got a lot to learn. My armpit knows more than you. And if you ever try to go out on your own, I'll see your suppliers and creditors call in your funds before you complete your first trip."

Unfazed, Tim answered quietly, "Yes, George."

"Don't just *yes, George*, me." Croghan chewed harshly before washing down his latest bite with a generous sip of wine. He studied us both as if he'd just noticed our appearances. "You look like Satan's dung, boys."

Tim and I glanced at each other. I hadn't yet seen myself in a mirror. But if I resembled Tim, it was true that we both appeared to have been beaten to within an inch of our lives. And I don't know if that is what the Devil's feces looked like, as Croghan suggested. "How'd we do?" I asked.

Croghan dropped his fork on his plate with a clatter. After glancing around the room to make sure prying eyes and ears weren't near, he reached down into a pack at his side. "Boys, boys, boys." His smile ran from ear to ear. His eyes were as big as saucers. "For a few moments yesterday, I thought about abandoning my trade altogether. If we could make money this easily with one match, we should make a go of it. Run from one town to the next. In one season, we'd have enough to live in luxury for all our days. Even if the newspapermen got wise to us and began shouting a warning to other cities, we'd make out just fine."

Tim held up a hand to show us. One of his fingers was bent sideways and needed to be corrected and splinted soon or it would end up permanently disfigured. "Sounds like a plan, George, but I don't think your players could last more than one or two games."

Croghan pulled two huge piles of various colonial notes, all in large denominations, from his pack and set it before his plate. He giggled and shoved them across the table top to each of us. "No matter," said the Irishman. "I couldn't stand to live a life of ease. My dear bride of many years would murder me before a week was out. I'd drive her mad. She likes it that I come home, tell her wild stories, get her pregnant, and then run back out into the frontier. The girl likes her privacy, you see? And as crazy as it sounds, I enjoy selling apples, iron, fabric, and flour to settlers, Indians, and soldiers. Now, I had such fun yesterday, I divided up my split between you boys. Besides, what do I need more money for?"

"How much is here?" I asked, leafing through my stack.

"Not enough to keep you fat forever, skinny lad," the Irishman said as a reprimand. "But enough for you to get a little start with that Bess of yours. Make an honest woman out of her."

Tim giggled. "See?"

"Nothing has happened that she needs to be made honest," I insisted.

Croghan fixed me with a disgusted look. "Do you not think the girl's parents and friends weren't frantically searching the streets of Williamsburg for her last night? The fact that Prince George is a loon is a better kept secret. And do you think I don't know she was last seen with you? Do you think half the town doesn't know you broke Alex Braun's nose? They all think you are in the midst of a tug-of-war with him over Bess' heart. The taverns were aflutter with gossip last night. Maybe you and the lady ran off to wed, they said. And it might be best that you do disappear for a while."

"That was Alex Braun?" I asked.

"Do you always go around breaking the snout of someone you don't even know?" George asked. "Saw him meandering around last night. His nose was crooked enough to spook a thief."

"So, it was Braun?"

"That's what I just said," Croghan answered tersely as he returned to the last of his meal. His fork had a mound of soft bacon on the end and he raced it through the egg's yellow slop.

I obviously hadn't recognized Alexander Braun. I had never seen him before. But if you've read my other tales, you know I am wide traveled in these parts and beyond, all the way from the James River to the pays d'en haut. One thing I've discovered is that every town, be it English, French, Chippewa, Delaware, or other, has its bully, a man of sour reputation who would rather spend a night in irons than be found wanting in a challenge of strength. Alex Braun was that man in Williamsburg. He was a brute who wore a chin of stone and carried a will of burning embers inside his body of thick muscle. And I hadn't even given him the respect of making it a challenge. I had bashed his nose in with a stick before he had seen me coming. Retribution would be the only thing on his small mind.

A pair of men walked into the front door of the inn. These newcomers were obviously riders, newly off the trail this morning. Their beards showed at least two days of growth. Their shoes and leather gaiters were splashed with mud. Each wore a streak of mud up the back of his cloak like a stripe, a sure sign that a horse's hooves and snapping tail had done their work while on the oftentimes soggy roads. They glanced around at the handful of patrons who had gathered for breakfast. Not recognizing anyone, they walked to the proprietor behind the bar.

"Your sign needs a fresh coat of paint, ol' timer," said the first man.

The owner frowned, his big jowls sagging. "Why's that?"

The man leaned on the bar. "So patrons can find the place."

"Have I ever seen you around here before?" the proprietor asked suspiciously.

"Nope," answered the man. "From the Northern Neck. Never been here 'til today."

The owner of *Maude's Cellar* scoffed, letting out a puff of air from his big cheeks to show his displeasure at the answer. "Looks like you found the place alright. And without any fresh paint. Now, what do you want?"

The second rider leaned over and patted the owner's arm. "He doesn't mean anything. Pay no attention. We're just looking for…" And his words faded as the two struck up a hushed, though congenial, conversation.

"Maybe you *should* go away for a while," said Tim, agreeing with Croghan. He was serious, in no way calling me a coward. "Braun has a… reputation."

"So I've heard," I muttered, looking away from the newcomers. I had spent the better part of two years hunting down a Frenchman for murdering my wife. Now, just a couple months after he had met his demise, here *I* was suddenly the hunted.

"George!" called the inn's owner, a man whose girth indicated that he obviously enjoyed his own cooking. He was a man who looked nothing like someone who was named Maude, as in *Maude's Cellar*. "These men are looking for that young Quaker lad who used to work for you, Ephraim Weber. Where is he?"

"Who wants to know?" Croghan asked, fixing me with a steady glare that indicated I should keep quiet.

"They say they come from Wills Creek with an important message from Colonel Washington."

"I'm here," I called, tucking my ill-gotten winnings into my shirt. Tim did the same with his. Soldiers or not, they might be the kind that would knock a pair of boys on the head for such an easy windfall.

"You look like hell's refuse, boy!" called the innkeeper as the riders confidently strode over to our table, a track of mud in their wake. "That ain't all wounds left from Fort Necessity is it?"

"No," I said. "Rewarded with just a couple scratches there. And some nightmares."

"Ah," the proprietor said knowingly as he headed toward his kitchen. "Braun was in here last night looking for ya. Must have found you after all! And you must be tough enough to have survived it. Count yourself lucky. The last fella who came to a disagreement with Alex hasn't been seen since. And I'm speakin' no rumor. Folks are pretty sure that man is dead." He threw his hands up in the air before withdrawing behind a woolen curtain. "But no dead body was ever found, so Braun walks free." Pans began clattering. "I'll get you newcomers your breakfast in a wink."

Tim and I scooted our chairs, making room. The riders lifted a pair of small benches from other tables and sat after George indicated they should. Greetings and introductions went around.

"So, can you men speak in front of mere civilians?" George asked with a grin. "Or, is Ephraim here to be given information of a secret variety?"

"Nothing secret," answered the first man. "In fact, it's about as public as can be."

Croghan frowned and leaned back in his chair, packing his pipe with shriveled tobacco leaf. "Nuts," he scoffed. He had, of course, hoped to hear news of an army nature so as to jump ahead of his competitors on supply contracts. There were always a few Burgesses in his back pocket who owed him favors. More often than not, their debts were paid, not out of their own funds, but out of Old Dominion's treasury by way of contracts for blankets or bullets. He'd get nothing like that today.

"Out with it then," I said. "What does the old man want with me?" Colonel Washington was only about twenty-two years of age. But except for his occasional nervousness in the presence of ladies, he acted like a man twice his years. His troops had recently begun calling him the old man.

The first rider resumed, pointing to his quiet compatriot with a thumb. "Zeb here will take over coordinating with Croghan and company for supplies to Wills Creek." He looked to Croghan. "Is that alright with you?"

George puffed on the pipe as he used a candle to light it. His lips puckered. One of his cheeks billowed in and out as clouds of smoke began swirling about him. "Suits me. Why would I care?"

"Don't get all sentimental on losing me, George," I said.

"The colonel said that you have a history of working well with Mr. Weber. He wanted us to make sure his dismissal from Williamsburg won't cause any issues," said the one called Zeb, my replacement.

"Once you run out of fingers and toes, can you keep on counting?" Croghan asked.

"Of course," Zeb answered.

"And you know the difference a'twixt a hogshead and pork bellies?"

Zeb chuckled. "One's a barrel, the other bacon."

"He'll do," Croghan answered, returning his attention to the first rider.

"I know a heck of a lot more than that," I protested to my former employer.

"Keep your skirts down, sonny," Croghan warned.

It was pointless getting upset with George. I had been the one to quit working for him. "What do you mean, my dismissal?" I asked the men.

"There are important matters for you to attend in the interest of defense. You're being sent north, to Albany," the first rider answered. The manner in which he'd said *Albany* indicated that he thought I'd been given ample information to figure out what I was to do in the capital of New York.

The blank look on my face told him I required a more detailed description. "Have you been living under a rock?" the rider asked, brow furrowed.

"Since when?" I asked.

"For these many months."

"Oh," I said calmly. "Is that all, you limp-nutted goat? Well, I was preoccupied cutting a road through the desolate wilderness with Colonel Washington. I was busy fighting the French and Indians at Fort Necessity in a rainstorm that would make a duck cry. And then, after getting our rears handed to us, the survivors limped to Wills Creek without food or water. Since then, I've been working with Croghan and the Burgesses to get badly needed provisions out to Washington's army. And what have you been up to? I don't recognize you from Necessity. You both seem pretty chipper to have suffered those bloody days."

The first rider, glowering, refused to answer. Zeb did so in his place. "We only just signed on a few weeks ago. No sooner got out to Wills Creek than Washington sent us back this way. We've heard from the survivors that Fort Necessity was miserable."

"You don't know the half of it, sonny. And pardon me for not know what you are talking about in Albany. Wait until you have some hot lead piping past your mangy face. We'll see how much time you spend worrying about current events beyond how to survive for the next minute. Now, what's going on in Albany."

The first rider stood angrily as the innkeeper emerged with two steaming plates. He snatched his breakfast and rammed the entire meal down in four bites, clearly burning his tongue in the process. "I'm going out for some air," he said as he paid the surprised proprietor for the meal.

"Not like you to offend folks, George, and send them on their way," said the innkeeper as he set the second plate down before Zeb. It was the same as Croghan's had been, greasy and undercooked, the specialty of *Maude's Cellar*. "Bad for business, you always say."

"Wasn't me," George grinned, puffing. "You know how offensive those Quakers can be."

The innkeeper smiled. "I know this one well enough. He's not like his Pennsylvania kin." He gave me a wink and waddled back to his bar where he resumed polishing dishes.

"Are you going to get some air, too?" Tim asked Zeb.

Zeb ate his breakfast greedily. In his short time in the army, he had probably discovered that the provisions at Wills Creek had not yet caught up with demand. Meals were sparse. "I'm not turning away from a perfectly good slab of meat."

"And are you going to tell Ephraim what he's supposed to do in Albany? Or, do I have to tell him?" Tim asked.

"What do you know?" I growled.

"I read the papers," Tim answered. "You should try it."

I remembered all the reports I'd devoured following my first trip with Washington into the frontier. They'd been the most farcical things I'd ever seen. "Ah, the writers of those papers have wilder imaginations than a five-year-old with too much maple syrup."

"Clearly, I learned enough from them to know about the Albany Congress," Tim retorted.

"Albany Congress? What's that?"

"Colonel Washington wants you to go. He can't get away. There's been an increase in Indian raids on the frontier," said Zeb. "Apparently, all the colonies are sending representatives to Albany in order to coordinate defense against the Canadians, French, and Indians. Well, some of the Indians. No offense," he said to Tim.

"None taken," Tim answered. "Onondaga's been firmly in the camp of our English brothers over the French fathers for many years. As far as I know, the Covenant Chain remains strong. I don't suppose that will change anytime soon." Of course, Tim's Mohawks were one of the original tribes in the Iroquois Confederacy, which was ruled from Onondaga. His was a good guess, based on more than a generation worth of history. But he'd be mostly wrong. For a good long, and bloody time, Tim's prediction would be mostly wrong. None of us knew it then.

"What's that got to do with me?" I asked.

Zeb shrugged, slurping up his egg yolks. "Washington said you'd be a good person to explain to the delegates what's gone on from a military standpoint. Press them for inter-colonial cooperation."

"You know the colonies, lads," Croghan said. "As independent as you and me."

"I can surely do that," I agreed. "But there are a dozen officers who were at Necessity. Their word would carry more clout than mine. My place is around the council fire, not the negotiating table."

"Washington said you have a good relationship with the Indians," said Zeb, nodding. He pointed to Tim with his fork which dripped grease onto the table. "Some Delaware chiefs will be there. Lots of other tribes, too. Most importantly, a representative from Onondaga will participate. He'll speak for the Six Nations."

I shook my head. "He'd have to be resurrected. The Half King is dead. I saw his body in the mud at Fort Necessity." I physically shuddered. "One of the images in my nightmares."

"This one isn't a half king," Zeb said. He finished his meal and still looked hungry. He waved for another from the innkeeper, who gladly trotted back to the kitchen. His pans again clattered behind the curtain. "He's the real deal. They call him Chief Hendrick."

Tim's eyes brightened. "Theyanoguin. My kinsman," he added proudly. "A Mohawk of renown. He wasn't too happy with the English crown during King George's War. Thought more could have been done to help protect Iroquois lands from raids by the Canadians and Abenakis. But he's fair. You'll like him. If he comes to negotiate, he does so in good faith."

My first father-in-law had been Memeskia, a Miami chief known as Old Briton. I figured if I could talk him into allowing me to marry his lovely daughter, I could get along well enough with Chief Hendrick. "Alright," I said.

"You'd best go, too," George said to Tim.

"Why?" he asked.

"Something important is brewing. I've never heard of a time when officials from all thirteen colonies got together to talk of military matters. It's not happened once in a hundred fifty years, not once from Jamestown to Plymouth Rock or beyond. The colonies, you know, are as provincial as the tribes. Don't you think if you want to get paid that I'd better have an ear in those meetings. Quite a lot more than a farthing of money may be committed in those conferences. Can't trust Ephraim here to do my bidding any longer. He's all mucked up with Washington. So, I need you."

Tim was already used to being on the road for Croghan. He took the change in his plans in stride. "Then we'll get some breakfast and I'll get a change of clothes and a cap," Tim said. "Can't scare the colonial delegates by looking too much like a Mohawk." He pointed to the shock of hair, held up tall with bear fat, on the top of his head.

"You'll do no such thing!" Croghan chastised. He was suddenly aghast. "You see, boy? You've got so much to learn. Those haughty delegates, especially from Connecticut, Massachusetts, and Philadelphia will say things in front a simple savage that they'd never say to a properly dressed gentleman. You'll get their secrets, you will. And you'll not use your Christian name."

"Taeheek it is," Tim said with a grin.

"We'll leave later this week, then," I told Zeb. "I've got a couple things to wrap up."

"Washington said you were supposed to leave immediately," Zeb said. "Get your meal and gear and go. Since Washington's been so busy, he found out about it late. The Congress has already begun."

I immediately thought of Bess. As much as I had protested to Tim and to George, I really had to make an honest woman of her. My parents and I disagreed on many aspects of faith. But I was not so wonton that I deemed it appropriate to have my way with a woman and then discard her. She and I needed to be wed, whether or not we'd just created a child. It was the only right thing to do. My heart told me I loved her. Though neither she nor I had ever used the word love to describe our relationship, I believe we both understood the direction we were heading. Besides, it would take more than a single conversation to convince her father to let her marry me, a penniless, part-time soldier. I needed more time.

"Tomorrow afternoon, then," I said in compromise.

Zeb shrugged with one shoulder. "The colonel threatened to hang a soldier for not following orders last week. And that man only used the Lord's name in vain." Colonel Washington was notoriously and legitimately pious. Zeb continued, "But I suppose the old man won't really know if you take an extra day to get going. I certainly won't say anything."

"Thanks, Zeb," I said. "Now for breakfast. I'm starved."

"I think that is the man you're looking for!" came a shout from the door. There stood the rider who had come with Zeb. He was pointing directly at me. Over his shoulder, darkening the threshold was the hulking form of Alex Braun.

His giant fists were balled. His arms and chest were pulled taut. His nose was grossly disfigured and he had two black eyes. And he wore a look of intense displeasure that surpassed even the glares I had received from my father and mother in the days before I'd run away.

"You're dead!" said Alex. And he shoved aside the rider, rushing at me faster than anyone his size should have ever been able to run.

CHAPTER FOUR

"Watch out, Zeb!" I cried as I over-turned the table toward the oncoming bull of a man. Zeb's back had been toward the door. The edge of the table tipped into his lap, sent his chair falling, and followed him all the way down. Both crashed into the shins of Braun, who toppled over. I was blessed with enough time to leap over Croghan and onto the bar. At that moment, a half dozen of Braun's goons swept into the bar, fists up like pugilists. Each man was clearly itching for a fight.

Tim, thinking he was in no danger from the coming scrap, hadn't bothered to move from his seat. He sat there peacefully, waiting patiently for the storm to pass. You see, Tim had come to know enough about me, that in order to save his own hide from time to time, he would have to let some things alone. He incorrectly thought this was one of those times.

Braun climbed onto all fours and noticed him. "Wait. You two are friends?" Braun barked to the Mohawk. "Not only do I have a broken nose, but I'm out three months of wages because of you cheats!"

All focus in the inn had suddenly turned toward Tim, isolated in the corner. Instead of saving myself by running out the back, I hesitated, wondering how I could help my friend. It turned out that I had to do nothing. Braun's followers streamed toward their leader while he reached his mitt over the up-turned table. His efforts were rewarded with a swift crack on the knuckles from the butt of Tim's musket. "Excuse me, George," Tim said politely as he placed a moccasin onto the Irishman's knee to jump after me.

"Report back after your travels, Timmy," was all that Croghan said to his employee. He'd witnessed countless wilderness, tavern, street, and battlefield brawls over his long trading career. There was nothing special in this particular altercation that would cause George any concern. He brushed away a smudge left behind on his breeches from the sole of Tim's moccasin.

"Wait! You were in on it, too, you potato munching geezer?" Braun accused as he recognized George from the prior day's betting. The mad fury in Braun's wild eyes ignited further into a roiling conflagration. Alex rolled up his sleeves and slowly stepped around the table, looming over his latest prey. He seemed to have forgotten about Tim and me. "I suppose you were the ring leader, you drunken paddy."

"Leave him alone," I shouted.

"Be gone!" George commanded us. "Get out of here!"

"But," Tim protested, easily calculating the odds that a middle-aged Irishman would have against a band of young scrappers.

George fixed us with a stern look before he resumed his pipe puffing with Braun standing over him. Croghan was the picture of calm. "I can take care of this cowardly leviathan faster than a Nantucket whaler," he mumbled through the corner of his mouth. "Now run along!"

"You get those two!" Braun ordered his henchmen. "I'll handle this old blowhard."

His gang rapidly closed the distance to the bar. It was one of those rare times for me to demonstrate prudence and discernment. "Good luck!" I shouted to George as Tim and I leapt down. My knees rattled, reminding me of every bruise from yesterday's skirmish. In search of a back exit, Tim led the way through the drawn curtain into the kitchen.

But first we had to get through the rotund proprietor. Tim crashed into him as he obliviously dumped his latest, sloppy concoction onto a tin plate. Innkeeper, Mohawk, grease, eggs, bacon, and pans scattered in all directions. "What in Heaven's name!" the man shouted as he went down. I tripped, headlong, over the entire mess and skidded across the floor and into the closed rear door.

By the time I reached my feet, Tim was already grappling fiercely with two of Braun's men. The mass of arms and legs rolled back and forth over top the supine proprietor, who angrily grunted his displeasure.

"Get out of here, you sailor!" Tim shouted to me in warning. "I can take this bag of scum on my own."

Like a good friend, I quickly tossed my momentary bout of prudence to the wayside and raced into the fray. At this point, the last trio of Alex's men were wedging their way into the crowded kitchen. "You'll get no more service from me, Ephraim Weber!" the innkeeper shouted as I used him as a step to jump over Tim and the others, whose feverish wrestling had taken them under a counter.

I had aimed for the lowest shelf of a bank of open cabinets that surrounded the doorway. I'd snatch a cast iron pan from the innkeeper's stock up by the ceiling and bash Braun's boys to sleep. That is what I had planned anyway. But when my foot securely struck the edge of the lowest shelf, the entire plank broke free. Like a wild cat, I began clawing at the upper shelves to stay upright. My feet cranked to gain traction – anywhere. All my wasted effort succeeded in doing was to rip away more of the shoddily constructed ledges. Rails cracked. Stiles broke. More shelves split in two. Boards flew through the air as I feverishly tugged. The hurtling scraps crashed into storage jars and containers on other sides of the tight quarters. Glass shattered. Crocks exploded. Flour poured onto the counter and floor. Tea leaves fluttered. Lard splattered. Eventually, I fell back onto one of Tim's attackers as the entire room crashed down around us.

For a few moments, I could see nothing but dust. It was as thick as the black powder smoke that lingered following a volley fired by a regiment of the king's finest. Only this cloud carried none of the familiar scents of sulfur and death that always remained after a musket blast. No, this veil carried a mixture of pleasant aromas. I smelled baking bread. Some bottles holding exotic spices from the East Indies had fractured in the crash. I caught whiffs of them, nutmeg and ginger, as well. Sugar was in the air. I smelled fresh-split wood. We'd scattered the chef's woodpile and a few of the arm-sized logs sat next to me.

"What's going on in there?" Croghan shouted from the front room.

I was relieved to hear that he could still speak. Perhaps he hadn't been bragging when he said he could take Braun. "It's under control!" I shouted as I sat up. The haze was just beginning to settle and I saw that two of the three men, who were forcing their way into the kitchen at the time of my accident, lay curled in balls. They rolled and moaned while clutching bleeding wounds on their scalps. A pile of iron pots lay scattered around them.

The third man was not injured, but he had fallen with the rest. He saw me and climbed onto his hands and knees before diving at me. I picked up the heaviest object nearest my hand, a log. I used it to crack his skull. My attacker settled down onto the floor, unmoving.

The man beneath my rump began to wriggle. I struck him in the arm with the log. "Damn you!" he shrieked, wiggling radically to free himself.

Wham! I slammed the log onto his arm again. It was the only part of his body I could reach while still balancing on top of him.

"Ouch!" he screamed. "Stop that!" He tried to roll me off.

Crash! The log cracked into the man's arm again.

"Stop it! Stop it!" he pleaded. His efforts to free himself had halted altogether. Instead, he simply clutched his swelling arm in the palm of his opposite hand. "Just leave me alone!"

"Will *you* leave me alone?" I asked, giggling. A good scrap was often fun, especially when I came out the victor.

"Yes!" he insisted. "Please. Get off."

"Quit horsing around," Tim ordered. I spun to see that he had just finished wrestling with the final man, who now cowered beneath the counter daintily cradling a hand that had at least three broken fingers. "We best get out of here, and fast. Out of Williamsburg altogether. It's official that we've both made an enemy of Braun."

I slowly stood, feeling twice my age. "I need some time. I've got to talk to Bess."

"Go ahead and make an honest woman of her," Tim said. "But we need to head north today."

"Tomorrow," I insisted as we picked up Tim's scattered gear.

"Braun will get you by then. Sure as hell," warned the man whose arm I had just broken.

"Maybe Croghan will convince Braun otherwise," I said to the injured man. I pointed to the limp arm. "Maybe you can tell Alex what happens to people who tangle with Ephraim Weber."

Like a child frightened by the memory of a recurring nightmare, the man's eyes widened and he shook his head vigorously. "I'm not getting between the two of you. I thought *he* was crazy. But you!"

"Today," Tim repeated as he stepped out the back door.

"Alright," I relented. "I'll meet you on the highway north of town later today."

"Fine. You can celebrate your marriage here at the inn when you return from Albany. Maybe things with Braun will have blown over by then," Tim said before rushing off to make his travel preparations.

"Don't think it's going to happen, boy!" said the innkeeper. I turned to see him standing in the center of his kitchen, a disaster radiating all about him, groaning men rolling at his feet. He was covered in what was supposed to be Zeb's second helping of breakfast. A slab of bacon dangled from his elbow. A heavy dousing of flour made him appear like an apparition. "If I didn't think so highly of George Croghan, you'd be in the stockade in a heartbeat! But that doesn't mean I'll ever serve you or that poor little girl you intend to marry. Stay away or I'll be among the first to sick Braun on your tail."

"I'll keep that in mind," I said with a polite tip of my head. I stepped over the threshold into the fenced backyard of the inn where the cook's herb garden wilted with the autumn temperatures.

Then from the front room, George called out again. "You're as fool as a clown on holiday for staying so close, Quaker lad. I delayed Braun as long as I could. But he's headed your way."

Braun came rushing through the curtain, tripped over his men roiling on the floor, and smashed into the innkeeper from behind. The two of them careened to the floor.

And I chuckled while slamming the door closed. A bucket, half-filled with water, sat in the herb garden. I slid it onto the path directly outside the door and ran away as fast as my feet would carry me. After rounding a corner or two, I heard someone clatter over the wooden bucket. The sound of splashing water and Braun's curses made me smile while I kept pumping my legs. It's true that I was terrified by the prospect of getting pummeled by Braun. Yet, I was also utterly exhausted from my activities of the last twenty-four hours, physically and mentally. And so, while running and hobbling, I laughed, almost deliriously, all the way to Bess' home.

CHAPTER FIVE

The town was coming to life for the day. Slaves bustled about for their masters, beginning the day's chores. Laborers opened shops or ignited forges. Hammers began pounding. Hooves began clopping. Whether indentured or free, the reaction of these strangers to me was, in each case, identical. Each offered a queer look at my disheveled, bruised form before consciously stepping to the other side of the street.

I slunk into the narrow alley between the printing office and Bess' home, the one where I'd originally met and inadvertently exposed myself to her. It had been the same place I had also first laid eyes on the man with whom my life had become so entangled – George Washington. The winding green vine that partially blocked a view into the alley from the street was nearly identical to what it had been upon my initial visit. Fading leaves and curled flowers were all that remained of what had clearly been a lush summer bloom. I tucked myself into the alley and crouched low, not yet certain how I would approach Bess or the confrontational situation that was bound to occur with her father.

I ventured a peek into the side window that faced the printing and post office. Through the sagging, pitted glass I saw that the tiny, well-appointed parlor was empty. As was the front hall.

Then Bess' father marched in with her mother in tow. "She'll not be allowed out of our sight until the day she is properly married!" shouted her thin father, who was fastidiously dressed. I ducked out of sight, plastering my back against the clapboard wall below the window. His voice could be plainly heard as he cried. "Then she'll be her husband's problem. I mean, Mary! Think of it! Our daughter willingly spent the entire night out of the house. A common sailor's daughter knows better than that!" He was as lathered as a sorrel after a day of galloping on the trail. "I, I just don't believe it. She's always been headstrong! But, Mary. Can you believe it?" He awaited no answer, but marched away from her. I heard footsteps that sounded like a thick Jutland draft horse as he approached my window. He pressed his hands against the casing, facing the exterior wall of the post office three feet away.

I heard his fingernails dig into the white paint covering the frame. "And then she comes home smelling of alcohol! Alcohol, Mary! What vices can be next? Gambling? Worse?"

"All of what you say is correct, John," said Mary. She was an attractive woman, not yet forty, but with a girth that seemed to fluctuate with the cycles of the moon. "But there is no need to shout about it."

I heard his heels grind as he spun. "I'm not shouting at you!" he shrieked. When I moved to peek again, Bess' father angrily turned to looked out the window a second time. I dropped. He was too agitated to notice me. Blinded with rage.

"Then at whom do you shout?" Mary asked quietly.

Distressed, John tore himself from the window again. "I'm shouting to her! She's up there living in bounty, disregarding all we've taught her. I'm shouting to her!"

"John," Mary began.

"But I *will* shout at you, Mary," John warned. "If you insist on acting as if this is not a calamity."

"Calamity, John?"

"Yes, a calamity, Mary!" John snapped. He sounded like a mocking child. That's when the conversation ended abruptly.

A few moments of silence passed before I got the nerve to twist upright and peek again. By the time I saw the couple through the bluish pane, John and Mary were silently embracing. "I am sorry for shouting, Mary," John said, suddenly calm, but panting as if he'd just run a foot race. "But the girl has a damaged reputation now. The whole town knows we were frantically searching for her last night. We were the last to find out that she had spent the day drinking and gaming and singing and dancing outside a pasture. A pasture! All while watching some savage frontier game filled with violence and cursing. Cursing, Mary."

Mary fixed her husband's gaunt cheeks between her palms. "John, she's grown up in Virginia. And while you and I have tried to live a life of piety, not all in our fine colony do so. There are planters, farmers, hunters, tradesmen, legislators, sailors, soldiers, and hundreds of others who come and go on the streets outside. As much as we don't wish it, they curse, and our daughter will hear such things."

"That doesn't mean she has to speak that way herself." He gently took her by the wrists and held them in place against his cheeks. John was clearly beside himself.

"Did she? I don't recall anyone telling us that Bess was cursing."

"You always defend her. Besides, if she didn't," said John shaking his head and carefully setting Mary's hands at her side. "Then that is about all she did not do. Drinking, carousing." His voice dropped to a whisper. "And I hate to speak it aloud, but I fear she spent the night in the company of that frontier ruffian. Why, he's dressed in buckskins most of the time! A savage."

"Ephraim," said Bess' mother. She spoke my name in a way that made me smile.

"I don't care his name," said John. "What kind of life will he give our daughter. He runs all over with that Irish trader. And the Indians. He's been in battles. Even if we approved of such a match, which we don't, what if he winds up dead from his adventures? Then what? Is that what you want for Bess? To be a young widow?"

"She cares for the boy," Mary said.

"She could just as easily care for a dog, Mary!" John snapped at her. But he quickly clamped his mouth. "Sorry," he added softly. "I only mean that it is up to us to turn her from a silly girl into a strong, just woman."

Mary nodded at her husband and glanced at the large clock standing in the corner. "Unfortunately, John, neither of us wants to admit it, but Bess has turned the corner. She is already a young woman. Now, it is finally a decent hour. I'm sure the governor will see us if we want to have him put a stop to this brutal game that brought on so much wickedness in our city."

John sighed heavily. "Yes, let's go. We'll worry about what to do with Bess once we return." He cocked his elbow out and offered to escort Mary. She smiled and interlaced her arm in his. They made their way from the parlor and paused in the hall. "Have I failed her, Mary? Have I done something that drove her to such behavior?"

Mary patted her husband's slender chest. "You're the model of a father in this modern age. Stern, but loving. All a daughter, and a wife, could hope for."

He nodded. "And you? Can you think of anything that you ever said or did when I was away to make Bess think that such behavior is acceptable?"

"Mr. Goode, I'll not dignify that with a response," Mary said humorlessly. She then craned her head so it faced upwards and, raising her voice, said, "Bess! We go to see Governor Dinwiddie. Your father and I will be back by noon. You'll have just enough time to think things over."

The morning was only just beginning. I nearly jumped for joy at the prospect of so much time alone with Bess. We would make all our arrangements for marriage. And I could still run off to Albany. While I was away on Washington's errand, Bess could then lay the groundwork for her father's approval. The day was turning out better than I had thought it could. Bess would soon be an honest woman, not some cheap harlot. Washington would have his representative at the Congress. And my neck would be safely out of Alex Braun's reach.

"Did you hear your mother?" John asked, his voice raised slightly.

"Yes," Bess squeaked from upstairs. Her voice carried the choked pitch of someone who had recently spent a fair amount of time crying.

The front door to their home opened and the married couple passed out onto their step so I could no longer see them. However, since they were now outside and just around the corner, I could still hear. The door closed and I heard a key rattling in the lock. "What are you doing?" Mary asked.

"Locking this door to be sure that young tramp doesn't wander in while we're gone," John said. "I hear he's been skulking about Williamsburg since Fort Necessity."

"Good idea," Mary whispered. Their footsteps then began crunching their way down the street. "Oh, goodness," she then said. "John, wait here." Her single set of footsteps were already tapping back to the door. "I forgot my coin purse."

"We're not shopping, Mary," John said. "I have a little money if we need something while we're out."

"Wait here. It'll be just a minute." Her key rattled in the lock, she entered, and closed the door behind her. I ducked back down when I saw her enter the parlor.

"What am I going to do with those two women?" John muttered to himself as he paced the street not fifteen feet from where I huddled.

Suddenly, directly above my head, the latch on the window scraped open and the window itself was lifted. I made myself as tiny as I could, pressing myself down against the foundation. I heard the scratch as a small board was wedged into the space to hold up the sash. Something hard clacked immediately against the sill. I shivered in fear, more than I had during my fracas with Braun's goons.

"Ephraim," whispered Bess' mother. "You have a short while to set this right. If you cannot do that while we are gone, I cannot guarantee any further help from me."

I refused to answer.

She continued. "I do love the man I married. And I've had happiness. But I've had to grow to love and respect him. It was not a marriage formed out of fondness from our youth. I do not know how it will turn out for Bess. But I'd like to give my daughter the chance to begin with her heart firmly attached to the man she marries. A woman deserves happiness. Do you understand?"

"Yes," I rasped, not moving to meet the glare I was sure she sent.

And I wanted nothing more than to make Bess a happy wife for the rest of our lives. But I should have remembered Tahki, my first wife, and all that happened to her. We had been happy from the start. And it all came to misery. And Bess' mother, with her twin benefits of age and experience, should have known that happiness was as elusive as snow in July. Here one moment, gone the next.

Her feet clapped across the floor swiftly. "And take care of yourself!" she chided. "When I saw your face in the window, I thought a monster had gotten loose in the town!"

"Yes, ma'am," I whispered.

But she'd already exited her home. The door slammed loudly behind her.

"I thought you got lost," said John. He was close, right on the stoop.

"Couldn't find my purse," Mary said.

"It'll turn up," John said in a soothing manner. He stuck his key in and again locked the front door. "Seems like you lost your key while you were inside, too," he said playfully. "You'd lose your head if it wasn't tied on." The two shared a pleasant chuckle and walked off in the direction of the governor's red brick mansion.

Their footsteps had long since faded before I got up the nerve to stand up and peer into the window. When I did, I saw that the sash was propped up a half inch. On the inside sill rested the key to the front door that Mary had placed there. I greedily snatched it, ready to let myself into their home and sweep my true love into a whirlwind bout of planning for our coming, perhaps secret, wedding.

But before I did go in, I giggled at the thought of Bess' permissive, perhaps overly romantic, mother. There on the side table just beneath the window was her coin purse, in plain sight. She and John might even share a laugh when they saw it. That is, unless John discovered what Mary had actually been doing. He might accuse her of letting a fox into the henhouse.

CHAPTER SIX

I went inside and locked the door behind me, propping the key up on the nearest chair rail. It seemed like a logical place for Mary Goode to have set it when she had entered the home. My first impulse was to bound upstairs to Bess, but I could hear her sniffling and didn't want to frighten her. Instead, I quietly stepped my way up the treads which were worn smooth from years of traffic. One of them squeaked and the muffled sobbing stopped.

"Mother?" she asked, voice wavering. "I thought you'd gone."

"Uh-uh," I said.

"Father?" she asked as she clearly heard my footsteps approaching down the hall. "I'm so sorry. It will never happen again. I found myself caught up in an unfortunate situation. Nothing like it has ever happened. That game, those boys, they led me astray. Never again." I was fairly certain that she was unfairly shifting a lot of the blame.

Her door was ajar. "What about that Ephraim Weber, boy?" I asked in my gruffest tone as I pushed it open. I wore an ear-to-ear grin. "I hear he is quite something."

Bess saw me and, burying her face in her hands, fell onto the bed, sobbing louder than ever. "You must go. You must. If they catch you here, they'll have you arrested for robbery or something. Ephraim, this isn't some backwoods Indian lodge. You cannot just break in."

I rushed to her bed and sat next to her. It seemed almost inappropriately intimate to join her where she slept, even if my motives were pure. Bess peeked out between two fingers and chirped in fear before sliding away. When I reached to her, she recoiled further.

"Hey," I chastised softly. "A few hours ago, you couldn't keep your hands off me. And remember, you let me touch more than your wrist." I quickly discovered that this had not been the correct thing to say.

"Look what you made me do!" she yelled, sitting up to face me. Her face was red and blotchy, her hair disheveled.

"Made you do what?"

She pointed to my crotch. "That! Oh, my, that. We did that. You did that."

I held up my hands, surrendering to her. "I know. I know. It's alright. That's why I'm here."

Bess rolled quickly to the other side of the bed and jumped to the floor, backing against the far wall. "If you've come here for more of that, you can go to hell, Ephraim Weber! With those ideas in your head, I'm sure you will end up there anyway."

"That's not what I meant!" I said defensively.

"It's what you said," she accused. "It's what you did last night!"

"*We* did it," I clarified. Again, that was the wrong response.

She burst into tears, her back sliding down the wall until she was nothing but a curled ball of skirts, tresses, and sobs. "I know. I know. I can't even look at my mother and father. They smelled the alcohol. They suspect…us, what we did. I'm so ashamed."

"So am I," I said softly as I walked around the foot of the bed toward Bess. It was all I could do not to yell at her for acting this way. She hadn't even given me a moment to explain. But then again, Bess had the wrath of parents to worry about. I didn't have such concerns. I'd left them behind years before. Hers, along with their reprimands, were in the here and now. And it was clear she was afraid of the consequences they and God might deal.

"You are?" she sniffed. "Ashamed?"

"Yes," I assured her. I felt a surge of pride at finally hitting on something on which we could agree. At least my words hadn't sent her into renewed fits.

"Why are you ashamed?" Bess cried with a mix of anger and sadness. "What's wrong with me?"

I stopped creeping toward her and stood up tall, hands on my hips. With voice raised and head cocked, I said, "Bess Goode, you listen to me." I continued, speaking over her words when she attempted to interrupt. "I'm ashamed because what we did is an act best kept in the sacrament of marriage, not because I am ashamed to have done it with you in particular. And I came here this morning, not to ravage you in any way! Though even with all that snot on your face and all the injuries peppering my body, I am still tempted."

Bess wiped snot away from beneath her nose with her palm. The action made her look like a child. Well, in many ways we were both still children back then. I had been married and widowed by the age of sixteen. I was now only eighteen and Bess was just a year younger. She studied me from her spot on the floor. "So why did you come if not to get more from an easy young woman?"

"Easy?" I scoffed. "There's nothing easy about you."

She half smiled. "Why are you here? And you look worse than the last time I saw you. That was just an hour or two ago. Is that flour all over your shoulders?"

I moved a step closer and sat on the floor, still an arm's length away. "A lot can happen in a short time when you're Ephraim Weber."

Bess was not amused. "Seriously, Ephraim, why did you come? You broke into my home. My parents will see you arrested, tried, and punished for this. I'm in no position to bargain on your behalf."

"Your mother left the key behind for me. She let me in."

Bess' forehead wrinkled and her chin withdrew back into her neck as she thought. "Let you in? Why would she?" But I didn't even have a chance to answer because her eyes brightened suddenly with excitement. Bess began sobbing again. This time, however, it was for joy and with a smile. She dove across the short distance that separated us and wrapped her arms around my neck. I rolled backward as she planted repeated kisses on my bruised cheek. My head cracked the floor, but I was already in so much pain, it felt like a love tap. "Oh, I knew it all along!" she cried. "You've come to take me away! To marry me. Mother let you in because you told her you'd make me happy! That is all she ever wants for me. Mother works so hard to make me happy. Father works to make me right. He fails so often, you see? But mother? Oh, mother usually succeeds! And she has again! I'm so happy. And I will always be happy. You'll make me happy."

Without warning, Bess sprang up and raced to a large chest of drawers. She tugged out the top one and dumped its contents on the bed. The dovetailed drawer soon found itself discarded on the floor. Soon more empty drawers joined it as the pile of clothes on the bed mounted.

"What are you doing?" I asked as I slowly crawled to my feet, grunting the entire way.

"We're to be married," she explained. "My parents will be back shortly and I need to be gone. We must find the minister and be wed today if I have any hope of happiness. Otherwise, I'll live a life of misery. Misery, Ephraim! Don't you hear? Do you understand? It's either a life of gloom or true happiness. You want to make me happy, don't you? That is why you've come?" Bess frowned only momentarily before she smiled cheerfully while organizing her clothing. "Of course, that's why you've come," Bess sang to herself.

Then she snapped her fingers as if she just remembered something and hurried from the room and down the hall. Stunned, I stayed put. Soon, I heard a great commotion and crashes coming from what must have been her parents' bedroom. Bess then came back toward her room, dragging something heavy across the floorboards of the hall. A massive trunk followed as she backed her way through her door. She made pronounced ruts in the floor where the two sharp feet on one end of the trunk scraped across the wood. Bess dropped the other end heavily when she was near her bed. She tossed the lid open and, instead of carefully setting her clothing in place, she used one extended arm to sweep the heap into the trunk. As quick as a wink, she slammed the lid shut and latched it. "There!" Bess proclaimed. "You'll do those types of things for me once we are married. A lady shouldn't have to drag trunks down a hall."

This was not at all how I had envisioned my proposal to go. "Yes, of course," I stuttered. "But it's a little more complicated than that."

"How could it possibly be more complicated than it already is? Ephraim Weber, you despoiled me. And you must make this right." No longer did she appear the least bit worried. Gone were her tears. Only the blotchiness of her skin remained as a sign of her earlier distress.

The entire house shook suddenly from someone downstairs beating on the front door. It felt like the house had been shoved off its foundation. Bess and I exchanged worried glances before I followed her into the hall. We ran to the front window that sat just above the entry door. On the front stoop was a man, angry and pounding on the door with a fist the size of a puncheon of gunpowder. And it was just as explosive. One of the panels in the door was already breaking away.

"I know you're in there, Ephraim Weber! That's right! I know who you are now!"

"Who is that?" Bess whispered, frightened.

I shook my head in modest disgust. Bess had probably let that man kiss her a time or two while she merrily sang about *cocklebread* and performed the lewd dance to go with it. Not a full day had passed since those events. But rum had a way of erasing memories, good and bad. I'd let Bess forget about that particular incident. "It's Alex Braun," I muttered.

"Alex Braun? His brutish reputation precedes him! You know him? What on earth does he want with you?"

Braun answered for me as a portion of a panel broke into splinters. I watched him force his hand inside to unlock the door. From above, I heard him struggle blindly, cursing about the wood scraping his arm. "I'll kill you, Weber, when I get my hands on you."

CHAPTER SEVEN

It was my job to make sure that Braun never got his hands on me. At that point, I was still young and quite partial to being alive. But today? The way I feel now? Who knows. I might let old Braun, if he were able, pound me to death just to have relief from the monotony that comes with age.

Planting a peck on Bess' flushed cheek, I was surprisingly pleased that Alex had delayed the need for my conversation with her and perhaps even our nuptials. Time would fix our slight misunderstanding. We'd be married once I returned from Albany. What was a few weeks? "I've obviously got to run," I said, shoving all my illicit winnings from our La Crosse match into her hands.

"What? Where?" Apparently, my need to flee hadn't been that obvious to Bess. She looked at the big mix of colonial notes in confusion. It was a small fortune.

"Anywhere would be better than right here, right now," I said. A gaggle of spectators had gathered on the street to watch the belligerent attack the door. A few gentlemen shouted for him to stop. But it would take more than words to curb Braun. I shuffled away from Bess to the top of the steps. From there, I could just see the cracks the attacker was creating in the Goode's entry way door. His forearms were so huge he couldn't reach in past them. I had just a few moments.

"What's wrong with here?" Bess asked, oblivious to the danger I was in, seemingly pleased to sop up my time.

The answer to her question seemed audibly obvious as Braun angrily used his knee to strike the door while he struggled to reach the latch with his fingers. He clearly hadn't given much thought to his first round of ramming. Braun now focused his attention on the panels nearest the knob.

I took three steps downward before pausing and meeting eyes with Bess through the railing. "I'll write. Be back soon."

"Write?" she asked. Bess suddenly looked as lost and forlorn as a big-eyed puppy abandoned by the roadside.

"Yes, write!" I exclaimed just as another broad fist poured through the door. Splinters now littered the front hall. The time for talk had ended. I renewed my flight downstairs while keeping my gaze fixed on the front door. I planned to escape out the back.

Like the driver of a freight wagon, I slammed on my brakes when I was three-quarters of the way down. A single fiery eye stared at me through the latest hole. "You're not going anywhere, Weber," Braun warned.

Then I made a juvenile mistake. I've told you I was still a child myself. "I don't have to go anywhere!" I threatened. "You'll be arrested long before you can break down that door." I didn't feel nearly as confident as the words I spoke. Braun could probably sense that fact, because he chuckled villainously. I then glanced at the chair rail where I had set Mary Goode's key.

Braun's eye followed mine. His hand quickly took the place of his eye. Lacerating his arm, he jammed it through the small hole and had the key in less than a second. "You were saying?" he asked as he shoved the key into the lock and twisted. The door shot open on its hinges, crashing into the wall. Pictures rattled to the floor, glass shattering. Bess shrieked as she looked down at us from upstairs.

I was frozen as Braun's feet slowly crunched over the debris that had just been scattered. "You're trapped," he said with a maniacal gleam in his eye.

I most certainly was trapped. Any move I might make to the front or back and he would have me. Braun was going to enjoy every moment of crushing me. His pace was deliberate.

Bess was in an inconsolable state – not that I had any chance to offer comfort.

"The watchmen are coming!" shouted a few men from the crowd outside. "Hurry! In there!"

"You'll be in the stockade," I warned Braun as he gradually drew near.

"Worth every moment of imprisonment," he said. "Steal from me? Break my nose? You'll pay far worse than what any of those constables can do to me."

I believed him. I was more frightened of Alex Braun than I had been while wading in the blood and entrails at Fort Necessity. I suppose it was because I was all alone and exposed, the only one on which he could focus all his vehement urges. I had been one of hundreds at Washington's first disaster. Quite reflexively, I stepped up and back a step.

Braun guffawed. "Go ahead, Weber," he laughed. Rivulets of blood coursed along his arm, trailing down his fingers, dripping from three of them onto the Goode's floor. "Upstairs or downstairs makes no difference to me."

That gave me an idea. I turned and sprinted to the top of the steps.

"What are you doing, Ephraim?" Bess wailed, stuffing the wad of money between her bosom and the bodice of her dress. "Face him. Are you a man or not? Protect me! A husband would."

"I don't think you have to worry about anything. Besides, he's a little bigger than me," I said, perched at the very top of the steps. And Braun *was* large compared to my very average size. He had six, perhaps eight, stone on me. Well fed, he was.

"That's right," Braun agreed. "I have a size advantage. And the Quaker here doesn't have his little Mohawk friend to defend him. Or, his potato-munching geezer to talk his way out." He began ascending the stairs with the same painfully slow pace. When he squeezed his hand into a fist, blood squeezed between the fingers. "And you don't have anything to worry about little lass. Once we get rid of Weber here, I'm sure you'll show me your *cocklebread* again." His smile was devious.

Bess gasped at the reference. Her hand went to her mouth in horror. "Ephraim!"

"You there! Stop!" shouted a handful of watchmen that poured through the door, muskets drawn. They were accompanied by a single British regular, his smart, red coat in sharp contrast to their worn and mismatched uniforms. Three of them moved to the foot of the steps, preventing any retreat.

"Not just yet," Braun said without looking back. He continued his way toward the top. Braun made a show of rolling up his sleeves.

With worried eyes, the three watchmen looked at me over the foresights set at the end of their barrels. Each was a novice, nervous at confronting the well-known town thug. Their hands trembled. The muzzles inadvertently alternated between pointing at Braun and me. Here I was again, like far too many times in my short life, staring into the blackness of a gun barrel. I noticed everything about their weapons. Their hammers were cocked. I could even see the leather patch that helped hold their flints firmly in place. It would only take one accidental spasm to send the flint falling against the frizzen and then, after a short reaction, a shot of lead hurtling toward my gut.

Enough was enough. It was time to exit. The armed militiamen below would have to protect my bride-to-be, and her *cocklebread*. "Tell your mother I'm sorry about all this!" I shouted to Bess as I spun to face the rear of the house.

After two long strides, I dove, punching my way through the second story window with eyes closed. And I kept them pinched, awaiting the rapidly approaching ground as shattered glass and fractured mullions flecked my face. My breath was held. My body tensed. Though I plummeted like a stone, I briefly felt like a bird.

Then a leather thong on my shoe caught on the window frame as it passed through. I was jerked to a halt in midair for the shortest heartbeat imaginable before I renewed my descent. My feet were the hinges, my body the door. Now upside down, I slammed into the side of the Goode home. The lace on the shoe snapped and down I went, ripping through vines and bouncing off a trellis before my rump crash landed on a heap of squash that Bess had harvested from the family's bountiful garden the day before.

I heard a gun discharge inside. Bess was still shrieking. The British regular began shouting at whomever had shot the musket.

"Quite an exit, sailor!" shouted Taeheek. I looked up to see him mounted on a horse. He pulled mine, fully outfitted for the trail, by the reins. They were just a rod away from me over the short fence that kept rodents out of John and Mary's garden. "I came to warn you that Braun might be coming this way. Looks like he found you."

A scuffle erupted up at the broken window as Braun was shoved and pulled by a growing host of watchmen. He fought wildly against their collective grips, using his elbows like clubs, his head like a mace. The British officer came to the window and pushed the entire mass of fighting men to the side. He leaned out, calling to me, "You, too. Halt."

"Not just yet," I said, parroting Braun. I jumped to my feet and ran to the fence. A day earlier I would have easily leapt it and mounted my horse. This time, aching and fatigued, I gingerly crawled over and into the saddle.

"Come on, grandfather," Taeheek mocked. The officer discharged his pistol and the ball splintered a section of the fence. Tim shook his head at me and spurred his horse while pulling mine after.

"Who is that man?" the redcoat shouted after me.

"I'm sure I don't know, sir," Bess pleaded. "He and this oaf just broke in here in the midst of a wild fight."

And I rested my chest against the horse's neck, giggling. I didn't know whether to be proud of Bess' quick lie or worried that it had come so swiftly.

CHAPTER EIGHT

The ride to the Albany Congress was most uneventful. But I had not ever been in this particular part of the country and so there was one small thing remarkable to me. It was the sight of the countless little Dutch villages dotting the nooks of the Hudson Valley as we plodded upriver. They appeared almost foreign compared to the English, Miami, Delaware, or other settlements I'd passed through thus far in my life. These old Dutch towns, remnants of New Netherland, with their many neat houses of low-slung, gable roofs that were invariably surmounted by aging weather cocks, were straight out of a fairy tale. Their chimney smoke seemed to nestle over them like a low blanket, creating a mysterious fog, out of which my mind could conjure the most amazing trolls, princesses, or knights. In these same towns and somewhat more familiar, however, was the speech patterns of the older folks. These were mildly reminiscent of the German accents from my home in Pennsylvania, though a bit softer.

Our topics of conversations at night around the campfire were typical of all young men since ages past and probably into countless generations of the future. They centered on women, money, and rum. We rounded out our talks by touching on hunting, shooting, the damned French, gambling, dirty Canadians, women, fighting, and women. I chattered nonstop about my forthcoming marriage to Bess. We had a great laugh about my confrontation with Alex Braun in the middle of the Goode home.

And Tim wasn't silent when it came to the fairer and more amiable sex. It turns out that ol' Taeheek was partial to a girl from the upper Hudson area, not far from our destination. Her lineage was as crooked as the rest of us who called the colonies home. She was Mohawk, of course. But she also had an ancestor from the Mahican tribe, which was nearly wiped out by the Mohawks in the Beaver Wars a few generations earlier. Tim said her Mahican lineage made little difference to him. He was more focused on how her hair shined whenever a sunbeam broke through the thick tree canopy above. This mystery girl had Dutch ancestors, too. But most recently, she had a couple English grandparents and, therefore, an English name.

And apparently, this girl even had a smidgeon of French blood left behind from some conniving trapper, which I found disconcerting. When I mentioned my alarm to Tim, he smiled with smitten affection and said, "If all French women had eyes as rich as Anne's, I'd gladly say au revoir to you, you stinking sailor, head north to Montreal and say bonjour to all of them. Maybe even take one of your English ships all the way over to Mother France herself!" Satisfied with his pronouncement, he leaned back on his hands to gaze upon the starry sky, taking in its majestic vastness from our spot in a recently cleared meadow.

"You love this Anne for her shiny hair and rich eyes?" I asked, ridiculing his shallow criteria for selecting a woman.

Without skipping a beat, Tim answered. "They're as rich as a beaver's pelt, I tell you. And a lot of man's blood, in addition to the blood of beavers, has been spilt in the name of its treasured pelt. How much more is Anne worth?"

We both had a chuckle, each reflecting on his then-limited understanding of love in his own way. And in truth, it took but a moment for me to realize how similar Tim and I had been. For the standards I had employed when selecting Tahki as my wife had not been any more meaningful. Her naked calves, sprouting up from tightly cinched moccasins were the first things I had noticed about her. Those legs had been long, slender, and strong. I had then seen her sturdy hands peel the hide off a deer carcass killed by her father. And, if I'm honest, I, too, loved the way Tahki's hair shone when we canoed through a clearing on the Miami River.

Such was the way of youth. It took experience to turn the fantasies and lusts of the smooth flesh into the deep, sacrificing love that came with the wrinkled skin of age. With commitment, even a marriage first laid down on the shakiest of foundations could be corrected into something that had pilings driven deep into bedrock and sitting upon pillars of marble. So, I had no shame in summoning visions of Tahki's cheeks, her neck, her breasts – or her thighs, which poured down from her hips like the twin falls of Niagara.

But while sitting with Tim and fondly recalling Tahki, I failed to envision my wife's eyes. Though I tried, I was unable do it. I remembered loving them, their shape, their hue. But all I could see in my mind were the large brown orbs of Bess, whose eyes were heavenly in my imagination. But they were perplexing as well, for in my dreams they had begun to regard me with indifference. Even worse, in my mind, when Bess looked on me, her glance was accusatory, as if I had somehow mistreated her.

This new set of images upset me, so I changed the subject to one that had also occupied a fair amount of our conversations on the road. Off and on we had speculated wildly on how Croghan had avoided getting killed by Braun in *Maude's Cellar*. As we had for the previous week, we went 'round and 'round that night until we both fell asleep, no closer to an answer.

"Paid him off," Tim suggested, snapping his fingers. It was the next day as we rode into the outskirts of Albany. The Hudson was on our right. It was a beautiful sight with autumn in full swing this far north. We traveled up the road that the locals called Broadway. Indeed, it was fairly broad in those days.

"You haven't worked for George very long if you think he actually gave money to somebody like Braun," I scoffed. "George is generous enough with pay to his men and gifts to his customers. But there's no way he dumped even a counterfeit Queen Anne's farthing into the purse of that wharf rat."

"If you're so smart, what do you think George did to keep his arms intact?" Tim asked as our horses took us past an old Dutch Calvinist Church. A minister was sweeping the front steps and heard the steady clop of our horses' hooves on the short section of road the city fathers had seen fit to pave with stone. He lifted his head with a beaming smile in order to greet us. But his countenance shifted swiftly when he saw my filthy condition, grossly healing wounds, and natively dressed companion. The minister's lips fell into a pinched frown. He merely offered an obligatory wave before becoming the most diligent caretaker his parish had ever seen. With eyes focused on his work, the dust was soon leaping out of the broom's way.

"Croghan's Irish," I suggested with a shrug, paying the stern Calvinist no more attention. Up the hill to the west, an eager lieutenant shouted spirited orders to his drilling regulars. They marched outside of Fort Frederick's walls. In those days, some folks mistakenly called the earth, stone, and wooden stronghold Fort Albany. But I'm sure King George's son, Prince Frederick, for whom it was named, would take offense – not that he ever had or ever would set foot in North America to hear the blunder. "Even Braun's not dumb enough to fight an Irishman after he's had his bacon and wine," I said, expecting a laugh.

"Uh-huh," Tim said, no longer listening. "Watch this," he whispered before raising his voice. "Where's the Albany Congress being held?" He asked the question of a slave woman who carried a basket of eggs in the crook of her arm. She had been heading in the same direction as us and hadn't notice our approach from behind. So, Tim startled her when he pretended to have the thick, drum-like accent of a backwoods Mohawk who had never ventured away from darkest Iroquoia.

The black woman turned abruptly and instinctively covered the basket with her other arm as if we were there to steal from her. The short woolen cloak she wore whirled. Her saggy bonnet nearly flew off. The woman took one look at Tim and recoiled. His earrings dangled. The nose ring that hung above the middle of his lips bobbed as his horse continued on. His hair stood straight up with grease, aided today by a knotted piece of red ribbon and decorated with an eagle feather. She glanced at me and curled her lip in disgust, perhaps noting my stench from the trail, before quickly pointing us further up Broadway. "That way. You'll see all the Indians and gentlemen. Why they let you savages in there is beyond me." She then marched in the direction from which she had come, hurrying to be away from us.

"Why'd you go and scare her like that, Tim?" I asked after we'd continued on. "You speak English better than a redcoat officer! Heck, you're a Presbyterian!"

Tim chuckled. "From here on out I'm Taeheek, remember?" He patted all the weapons that draped around his waist and from his horse. "I'm a warrior with little understanding of the tongue used by you sailors. "Looks like I'm getting just the reaction George had hoped for."

"We haven't even set foot in the congress yet," I protested mildly.

"If that's not the congress, I don't know what is," Taeheek said, pointing to a large building on the right side of the street, about a block ahead.

It was three stories in height with a good many windows surrounding it on each floor. It had a gable roof with a shallow slope that would empty any rain or snow toward the east and west sides. At the top of the peak and in the center sat a cupola which acted as a belfry. I knew it housed a bell for at that moment it began to peal loudly.

The clang of the bell ushered a flurry of activity onto the street. Tavern and inn doors swung open, setting free gentlemen dressed in clothes that ranged from fine to finer in their extravagance. Indians, too, were belched out from the cities' eateries and outhouses. In ever-growing herds, they began to descend on the large building that Taeheek had seen.

We reached the split rail fence that surrounded the building's green yard which was kept neatly shorn by a half dozen sheep that lingered about constantly nibbling. Sliding down from our mounts, we both moaned and stretched as we tied the reins in place.

"Ah, new arrivals from the tribes!" said a voice from behind. Though hospitable on the surface, it betrayed a Philadelphian accent which immediately set me on edge. Philadelphia was by far the largest city in the English colonies in those days. And Philadelphians were proud of their significant stake economically and politically, both in Pennsylvania and all along the seaboard. They acted like they knew it, too. All the time. Even the lowest members of the merchant class walked about with their chins held an inch too high. And the gentlemen who would have been sent to haunt the Albany Congress would no doubt be among the worst offenders when it came to broadcasting their arrogance. "You're here for the congress, no doubt. May I help you become acquainted with our schedule? It can be a bit daunting at the start."

"Don't waste your time. We're smart enough to find our own way around!" I snapped, turning to see a man dressed elegantly, but tastefully. The men who had emerged from all the town's inns worked their way around us, into the gate, and up the walk of the large building. The bell ceased its call as the flock of bleating sheep were chased around to one side of the structure.

"I see. Certainly," the man answered, brushing off my brusque tone with a most affable nature. He was around fifty years of age. His long hair ended at his collar and was somewhat thin with only a slight wave. It was salt and pepper in color, with the volume of salt having only recently overtaken the pepper. The flesh of his face was showing the initial signs of what would be the inexorable slide ever further downward. I could tell he had been of medium build for most of his life, but had begun to put on the softer, puffier weight that chased and usually caught men as they aged. Extending a hand in my direction, he said, "I like young lads who love life. And you obviously do, for you don't squander time. And time, as we all know, is the stuff life is made of."

He thought he was a smart one, wise in his years and reading. I'd show him. "Time is money," I said sarcastically. "Even on the frontier, we've read *Poor Richard's Almanac*."

The man smiled. His eyes brightened. He held his hand out further, which I had yet to take. "Excellent. Good. Many have, I know it! How do you think I'm able to find myself here today?"

"I suppose you came by horse or buggy," I answered drily.

The man laughed pleasantly and, seeing I had no intention of shaking the hand he had offered, stuck it toward Taeheek. "True enough. And you are Mohawk, no doubt. Tall and strong, filled with heart and mind. It's hard for an empty sack to stand upright, you see?"

I groaned. This windbag was tossing out poor versions of quotations from Poor Richard. It was as if the famous almanac had been the only source of wisdom for this Philadelphian.

Taeheek seized the hand and gave a firm, single-stroked shake. He said something like, "Taeheek. Mohawk. Warrior. Good."

The man turned his head curiously upon hearing Taeheek speak, perhaps seeing through the somewhat poor ruse. But he quickly reverted to his good-natured grin. Then, tipping his head slightly to each of us, he said, "It was a pleasure meeting you both.

I shall see you inside presently and look forward to conferring with you on these great and grave issues swirling about His Majesty's colonies. Coordination. Cooperation. These are of the upmost in importance with the threats we face from the French. But, when the sun sets and my head alights upon the pillow, I am pleased to know that we are Englishmen." He gave a friendly glance to Taeheek. "And King George's allies. I know we plough deep while sluggards sleep. Now adieu, my friends. I must be going. God helps those that help themselves." The man turned and immediately fell in with a group of delegates, chatting them up in encouraging tones.

"What a dolt!" I rasped when he'd gone.

Taeheek furrowed his brow. "I liked him," he countered.

"If he wasn't the stupidest man in America, I'm not Ephraim Weber."

"Ephraim Weber?" asked one more new and unfamiliar voice. Yet another middle-aged man approached as the crowd thinned, filtering into the building. Albany seemed to be chock full of wealthy gentleman and Indians who were past their physical primes. "Washington forwarded me a letter indicating you'd represent him at this proceeding. You're late."

I shook the hand he offered. Taeheek did the same. "Obviously, I'm late," I answered. "Does everyone here speak only the obvious?"

The man frowned, confused.

"Well, first him," I said pointing to the poor copy of Poor Richard who now passed into the tall town hall, offering some pithy advice to another set of men. "And now you."

Though I insulted him, the newcomer laughed. Apparently, everyone in Albany was a buffoon, too stupid to realize when someone made fun of him to his face. "I'm Isaac Cotton from Alexandria, Virginia. Come with me," he chuckled, setting his hands upon our shoulders and turning us toward the gate. "If you've thrown my simple mind into the company of that great man, I am most honored. Let us now get you in a conspicuous place to hear and be heard."

I allowed him to propel me forward. "That's a great man?" I asked. "You've not met any other men in your entire life, have you?"

Turning us onto the walk and pausing to shut the gate behind him, Mr. Cotton, mumbled, "Can't let the sheep out." Before asking me a simple question. "You don't know who that man is do you?"

"Why would I care or ever want to?" I asked. "His mind has more hollow spots than a loaf of over-leavened bread. He's just a pompous Philadelphian. And ain't they all?"

"I wouldn't know about that," Mr. Cotton said diplomatically. "I clearly don't have the vast experience *you* do in dealing with men from Philadelphia." Isaac Cotton appeared to be twice my age. And his tone suggested that he did, in fact, know many men from Philadelphia who would not fall into the category in which I had just placed them. "But what I *do* know is that the man you call hollow-minded is the smartest and perhaps the richest, self-made man in all of the colonies of all of the great European empires. He retired at the un-ripened age of forty-two."

"Ha!" I scoffed. "You sound like him! Is everybody at Albany so infatuated with *Poor Richard's Almanac* that you see his likeness everywhere you go?" And as soon as I said it, the truth dawned on me.

Mr. Cotton then said just what I was suddenly thinking. "Why, young Ephraim, that *is* Benjamin Franklin. In the flesh."

CHAPTER NINE

I'd written Bess four letters during our ride north. I'd pen her many more over the coming weeks. And it was to be none other than Benjamin Franklin who would ensure that each of those love letters would arrive in Williamsburg in a good and timely manner.

He was, of course, His Majesty's Deputy Postmaster General. But that was only one small fraction of the life led by the most famous, celebrated, well-liked, and intelligent man the New World had ever seen. It's a well-known story. But we all know people have memories shorter than a nibbled worm dangling on a submerged fish hook. And Mr. Franklin has been dead and gone for several years now. So, for the sake of spinning a complete yarn, I'll summarize it here. Franklin was a runaway apprentice who, through grit and unrivaled ambition, built a publishing empire during his working career.

Had that been the extent of his mark on the world, Franklin would still be considered noteworthy. Yet, since retiring, he now dabbled in the study of all strange and wonderful things in the natural world, discovering and recording a dazzling array of phenomena. To this day, I understand little of what he described. Still he went further. To top it off, Franklin would commercialize his discoveries, successfully peddling things from unconventional stoves to his strange new invention called a lightning rod. As evidenced by my first meeting him in Albany, he also spent much of his considerable energies in the realm of public service, coaxing recalcitrant assemblymen and king's officials to bend to his firm, but invisible, pleasant, will.

And I had treated him in such a way that verified that it was I, not he, who was the imbecile.

"I'm sure Franklin's already forgotten all about it, Sally," Taeheek snickered, trailing Cotton. We snaked our way into the packed hall where gentlemen wheeled-and-dealed for their colonies, and perhaps mostly, themselves. Taeheek had immediately taken to calling me by names other than Ephraim after I had so proudly proclaimed about Franklin, *If that wasn't the stupidest man in America, I'm not Ephraim Weber*. Taeheek's was a humorous gag, but it was quickly wearing thin. He was careful to select only female names for me. "Did you hear what I said, Martha?"

"I hear you well enough, turd," I grumbled.

"As you represent Washington, you two may join the table of Virginia's delegation," Cotton said, not in the least bit interested in the ribbing going back and forth between his two new colleagues. Like a sturdy ship's prow, he led us through the crowd, slicing a path.

I was quick to note that Taeheek and I were among the youngest in attendance. Many an elderly fellow looked down his nose at our youthful and shoddy appearances. I was certainly the filthiest in the hall that day, but Taeheek was a close second. That's what over a week on the road, riding through downpours, sleeping on hillsides does to you.

As we squeezed among the ranks of men, who whispered in hushed conversations where more than a few chiefs traded away ancestral lands for their own aggrandizement, Taeheek received more than his share of curious glances. Even those Indian representatives gave my friend the cold shoulder. The Six Nations had sent dozens of delegates, since one of the goals of the assembly was to reaffirm the Covenant Chain between the Iroquois and the British Crown.

These confederates dotted the room. But I also saw Delaware and Shawnee warriors. Even the southern tribes had sent men to observe the proceedings and their important outcome. And to a man, these chiefs and experienced warriors were more appropriately dressed for the occasion than either Tim or me. Their tribal accoutrements such as tattoos, piercings, jewelry, and decorative tomahawks were accented with clothes that would have been natural sights on gentlemen in any fashionable colonial city. They wore soft white shirts with snug collars that were covered by long-sleeved coats complete with rows of shiny buttons and ruffled lace at the cuffs. They even wore shoes and stockings and colorful breeches.

Around their necks, most of them displayed silver gorgets that had been given to them by representatives of King George at previous gatherings. Many of the ornamental gorgets had the same image of a sun overlooking an Englishman and an Indian making peace. The pair smoked a ceremonial pipe while sitting around a council fire. Other gorgets had etchings of bears or stags or arrows or hills. Still more had carvings of native flowers intertwined among dense vines.

Gorgets worn by a few of the tribesmen had the royal arms of Great Britain flaunted boldly. The fact that this depiction was worn by Indians implied the decorative armor had been seized from dead British regulars at some previous battle. It served as a clear warning as to the still deadly power hidden among the recently quiet tribes.

I did see one, and only one, gorget that was shockingly unique. It was astonishing, really. If marching around in a room full of English colonial citizens with a gorget pilfered from the dead was bold, then whoever donned this singular design was brash indeed. It was worn by a grizzled warrior with a grotesque scar running from the left corner of his mouth all the way to his ear. The wound was ancient and healed, but it was wide and curving so the man appeared to have a freakishly large smile that never went away. Even when the rest of his face frowned, he was left with a complicated, perhaps confused, look because of the permanent, macabre grin. His frame indicated that he may have cut a handsome figure in his youth, but today he was ugly – ugly from a difficult life and the wars he'd seen. He was at least seven decades old. Yet, it was the gorget that I first noticed. It made me blush when I thought of this man walking through a town of mixed company. On the gorget, for all to see, a completely disrobed Indian woman bent over at the waist and clutched a tree. Her teats dangled toward the ground like a cow's udder. From behind the woman, a celebrating warrior, his arms held high, mounted her in a way that left little to the imagination.

This image was still emblazoned on my mind's eye when, in time, we settled to our places. "Did you notice my kinsman among the Iroquois delegation?" Tim whispered into my ear.

"Which one?" I asked. "There must have been a dozen Mohawk warriors alone."

"The big scar," he answered, using a finger to draw a curve from his mouth to his ear.

"Oh, the vulgar gorget," I said.

One corner of Tim's mouth rose into a tiny, mischievous smile. "There is that, yes. I guess he likes to keep you sailors guessing. Just like me."

The hubbub of deals and counter-deals rumbled to a close when Franklin stood from the table of Pennsylvanians. Though it was my home country, I felt no nostalgia for it and gave no thought to being situated with the Virginians. As a matter of fact, a few hundred Virginians had fought bravely next to me in the mud and blood of Fort Necessity. Many had died miserable deaths. They had proven themselves as capable, brave souls. And Virginian or not, that type of sacrifice was good enough for me.

Out of deference to the practical and wise Franklin, all conversations ceased by the time he opened his mouth to speak.

"Learned representatives," he began. His tone was not pompous as was that of most men preparing to make a great oration. He was conversational, friendly. He reminded me of a tender father who employed reason and kindness with firm temerity to instruct his children. We were his little ones. But despite thinking the man an idiot moments earlier, I didn't mind being under his tutelage. "For many days while here in the hallowed Stadt Huys of Albany, we have been like the inexperienced and slightly awkward bachelor attending a ball." He paused to allow the image to sink in before chuckling to himself. "Though he dances the night away, grasping hands and sharing glances with many a young maid, he forgets the ultimate purpose for his presence at the event." Franklin leaned casually against the Pennsylvania table. "He is there to find a woman, to woo a wife, to consummate a deal!"

The room giggled politely along with him and he went on. "Even the married men at such a gathering are there to transact business. They talk to acquaintances about shipments or lending, rum, taxes, or politics. But these married men would also be smart to keep their wives happy. To dance with them. To lock eyes with them and affirm their commitment. Otherwise, and sadly I can guarantee this from personal experience, when he comes to bed after putting the horse in the stable, he will find that, like the awkward bachelor, he will have no success in consummating any type of deal with his most intimate of business partners."

The room, full of seasoned men, laughed louder. I laughed along with them, though I had not yet experienced that which Franklin discussed. I was too young. Tahki and I had been too green and we had both always been ready to consummate our relationship. No fatigue was great enough. No disagreement lasted. But as I write this, with many decades in my wake and several wives buried before me, I know all too well of what Franklin joked. A woman, a wife, that most intimate of business partners, must be wooed, loved, and nurtured. She must be romanced with stories, no matter how many winter seasons the marriage has survived.

"With our chatter here in Albany, we have danced, and danced some more. I've talked so much about topics that lie so far from the heart of the matter that my feet ache. We have traded horses and land, trinkets and tributary with our Iroquois brethren. I'll bet the honorable Reverend Woodridge and his partner in crime, Mr. Lydius, the somewhat infamous sutler from New York, have dumped many pipes worth of rum down theirs and their Indian friends' gullets to secure a Wyoming Valley land deal."

Lydius *was* a sutler. But was also a smuggler. It was quite common knowledge that he illegally transported goods from Albany to Montreal. In doing so, he violated a few dozen of His Majesty's commercial activity laws, an affront especially egregious during this time of war. Though Lydius was never prosecuted, because he knew with whom to share his ill-gotten profits. Customs officers, magistrates, and perhaps even a governor were rumored to drink from his sluicing trough. And so, everyone knew that John Henry Lydius was a common crook. But it was something else to call a man out in a large gathering.

I glanced toward the New York table to see if the shadowy one-eyed pirate was there. I was not disappointed. He sat in the second row of chairs, away from the main delegates. He raised a small glass of rum in a silent toast and then with his one good eye, winked at a batch of Oneida Indians behind him. They shared a quiet chuckle, remembering hours of inebriated bliss that may have already led to striking a land deal on the upper Susquehanna.

If and when it was completed, Lydius and these chiefs would be enriched at the expense of the Delaware Indians who resided in the valley. As such, Lydius was in a congenial mood. He let Franklin's insult roll right off his back. Completely unflustered and comfortably smug, he then returned his cycloptic attention back to the speaker.

Franklin, too, had paused to see the reaction from Lydius. If Franklin had been disappointed, he made no indication. "All these swirling land deals are something that will need to be further discussed at some point. Pennsylvania, Connecticut, the Delaware, and the Iroquois have a vested interest in the area. But our contract between the English and the Iroquois, the Covenant Chain, is secure for now. And I am not here to talk any more about these side issues. You'd not stand for it, I'm sure." Looking around at the faces of the men, I realized that, in truth, most had come to Albany with the goal of haggling over land with the Iroquois as their chief aim. They'd prefer if Franklin talked about nothing else. He'd not oblige them.

Franklin stood from where he was leaning on the desk. Not a tall man, he straightened himself to his full height and walked somewhat stiff-legged to a spot on the floor where he could best be seen by all. "Gentlemen. The French have moved aggressively into areas that are clearly within our borders. The Iroquois are threatened. Pennsylvania is bloodied. And Virginia has lost many of her fine sons to a recent battle in the wilderness. We've heard the rumors about Colonel Washington's mighty struggle." He pointed to the tables of other colonies. "And you, New York. You, Massachusetts. You, Connecticut. You. And you. And you." He went on down the list. "If you think that this problem is localized to just your cousins in Pennsylvania and Virginia, you are mistaken. It is grave, indeed. It is a boil that will no longer fester. It will burst, spreading like a pox, until we've all suffered the deprivations of French aggression."

He began fumbling in his inner coat pocket as he continued with his discourse. "We must unite. We must approve the Plan of Union that I have repeatedly submitted for your consideration over these many days. This new body, this Union, will be led by a President-General appointed by our king. But it will also have a legislature elected by you with the power to tax only for our mutual defense."

The room mumbled with mild disapproval at this proposal. You see, since their founding, each colony had been formed in a separate manner, with separate goals, and separate proclivities. They'd been run autonomously, with only the mildest of coordination. Suggesting a union was akin to suggesting that the French, the Swiss, the Italians, and other diverse peoples and powers unite into some strange European Union – preposterous on its face.

Yet here was Franklin, a renowned thinker and doer, proposing just that. Had it been anyone else, the room would have erupted into a furious battle. The speaker would have been mocked, shouted into submission and sent packing in shame, his head down, his tail tucked between his legs.

As the murmuring ebbed, from his inner pocket Franklin pulled out a large piece of newsprint that had been folded into a manageable size. The portion shown to us was blank, but the faint imprint of words or images on the hidden side of the page could barely be discerned. With the thumb and forefinger on each hand, he held it before his chest. The still-folded piece dangled. Franklin scrutinized the mysterious document for several full heartbeats.

"Lunacy, you may think of what I ask," he acknowledged with a self-deprecating grin. "Let the Pennsylvanians die for their country, you may say. Let Virginians do the same. Why should boys from New Jersey be called upon to fight for the concerns of others? But I don't wish a large-scale war with France any more than you. I hope for learning, prosperity, and peace. And I believe that by approving my Plan of Union, we will have peace. It will be the reason that the bloodshed stops with the recent disaster in Pennsylvania's wilderness."

"The reports I've heard was that Fort Necessity was erected in Virginia's wilderness," Mr. Cotton politely corrected Franklin. There had long been disagreements between the colonies of Old Dominion and Penn's Woods about which had rightful claim to what. Their respective charters were broad indeed when it came to western expansion.

Franklin bowed his head with formal civility toward our table. "A discussion for another time, Mr. Cotton." He paused a moment to recapture his thoughts. Franklin then cleared his throat and went on. "Separately, our English colonies *cannot* successfully fight the might of the Canadians and their Mother France. But together, I believe our sheer size, wealth, and numbers of able warriors will bring the French to the bargaining table. By coming together as one, we will *not* have to fight. So, I urge you to approve my plan. Do so today in order to save a generation of men and women from the poverty and destruction that comes with war." Franklin fiddled with his fingers to get a fresh grip on the newsprint. "And keep in mind that you may delay, but time will not."

He snapped his wrists and pulled apart his hands. What had been a folded, unseen page, unfurled. Franklin lifted it over his head and slowly turned so everyone in the room could see his banner. If the words of his speech had not been clear enough, the image he displayed was indeed. After all, as Poor Richard himself may have uttered, *Well done is better than well said.*

And he had done well.

If I hadn't already held Benjamin Franklin in high esteem, I did after that. And my admiration for him would only grow throughout the years. In comparison, I respected Washington greatly. But I cannot say I, or anyone else save his wife, loved him in any sense of the word. Washington, at that time, desired no love from his men. He was guided by honor above all else. But, like a compass needle to the north, Franklin drew others to him. His personality, his charm, his intelligence was captivating. And he was wise. And dare I say prophetic in a way that perhaps even he hadn't realized that day up in Albany.

On his large newspaper was printed a flag no one had ever seen before. Though since then, it has become as common as a Queen Anne's penny. His flag was bordered on the outside by two lines, the outermost thick and dark, the inner one thin. A coiled snake, its tongue flickering out in a threatening fashion, occupied the majority of the field. But the snake appeared to be less than menacing, at least any longer. It was chopped into bits, eight pieces to be precise. The severed head was labeled New

England. Then, the dismembered portions of its sliced body were marked from New York all the way down to South Carolina at the tail. Finally, to make everything clear for even the most obtuse of his viewers, below the snake, in bold, capital letters was the phrase, *JOIN, or DIE.*

FRANKLIN'S PLAN OF UNION
ALBANY CONGRESS, 1754

CHAPTER TEN

Days ran into weeks. My letters to Bess became more resolved than ever. I expressed my love and my devotion to her more freely with each page. In fact, one letter alone ran to five long sheets. Only one of the pages was dedicated to all that went on in Albany – the personalities, the intrigue, the arguing, bickering, and downright stubbornness of these high-born gentlemen and their Indian counterparts. No. Most of the words that flowed from my pen had their origin in my heart. I don't know if what I said was poetic, or not. It's not that I attempted to be clever. My goal was honesty. I was a rural, lovelorn lad with limited education expressing his feelings to a well-to-do town girl as best he could. Pure and simple. Or, perhaps Quixotic and daft.

But I had no idea if Bess appreciated the sentiments I laid bare. Though I was now writing to her at the end of each day and dropping letters in the royal post almost as frequently, I received no reply. None. Nothing arrived from Bess that expressed relief when I had explained to her we had made it to Albany without incident. There was no astonished reply when I confessed that I had talked down to *the* Benjamin Franklin.

Eventually, I panicked when her silent distance became unbearable to me. I even broke all semblance of decency and wrote a short inquiry to Mary Goode, Bess' mother. I apologized for the misunderstanding and the mess that followed after I entered her home in pursuit of Bess' hand. But the matriarch's marked silence was as notable as the daughter's. Mary, too, must have been afflicted by the same mute malady that had settled on Bess. They both seemed unable, or unwilling, to communicate.

Or, perhaps they were prohibited. Only for a moment did I consider writing to Mr. Goode. From our first meeting, he had made it clear I was to stay away from his daughter. And if he had forbidden either of the women in his life to enter into correspondence with me, any plea that landed in his lap would serve only to isolate my would-be bride even further.

So, since it never occurred to me that the mail just did not get through – that was one of the reasons Mr. Franklin was so popular, his service ran very effectively – I resolved myself to waiting until my travels again took me to Williamsburg. Then I would rekindle my courtship with Bess. Our wedding, secret or not, would be followed by a life of siring children and traveling far and wide in the service of Washington. Or perhaps Croghan, once again, would take me on. I had been thinking more on that subject of late.

"Croghan will be pleased with me," Taeheek bragged. We often settled into one of the busy taverns for dinner and drinks after the congress let out. Working for Washington, who himself was paid only the most nominal of wages by the stingy Burgesses, was far from lucrative. And since I had impetuously left all my La Crosse winnings with Bess, I was forced to rely on my friend's generosity for my food and lodging. Even without cheating others with our game, Tim was paid well, as I had been, by Croghan. A single man with no property, he had money to spare and gladly shared it. However, it placed me in his debt. And it only encouraged him to taunt me more. "Listen, Cora, I'll bet you never came to him with information like I have to give him. This illiterate savage routine is genius."

"What do you have?" I asked, at the moment preferring to show no reaction to his repeated use of women's names for me. I had alternated between wrestling him to the ground, to total disinterest. Neither extreme, nor anything in between, seemed to dissuade him. He was a good friend.

"I know he's made most of his wealth by trading with his wife's people, my fellow Indians. But I also know George likes the odd military contract when he can get it. Heck, you know that even though Fort Necessity was a complete disaster for you and Washington, Croghan was paid handsomely for the provisions he sent."

"Your point?" I asked. I was tired of hearing about Fort Necessity. As are you, I'm sure. It was on everyone's lips. Yet, none of the men dispatched to Albany seemed to use it the way I had wanted. Rumors of its horrors should have served as warnings to spur the delegates to accept the Plan of Union. Instead, they spoke about the tragedy with near giddy delight, like it was a made-up tale told in a pamphlet printed in London for their personal entertainment. Well, it wasn't. Real men had died. Their brains had been bashed in. Their innards had fallen into the muck. Lead and sickness had drained away all their vigor. English lands, wealth, and pride had been ceded to the Frogs.

Besides, all anyone in the English-speaking world talked about was Fort Necessity. Fort Necessity this. Fort Necessity that. It was as if the incident had been all that happened over the past two years. The gossipers and newspapermen – often one and the same – made hardly any mention of our resounding victory at the Battle of Jumonville's Glen. But the victory had come *before* the defeat. Men's memories were short, indeed.

"My point, Catherine, is that by standing around and looking like an ignorant pagan, the delegation from Massachusetts let me in on their plans for next year's campaigning season. All I did when they politely requested I give them their privacy was to grunt in a confused manner. Satisfied I could do them no harm, they said no more on that subject. But they talked at length about their engagements next summer. Governor Shirley will send out two or maybe three expeditions to the north against the Canadians. Each of them will need provisions. And I don't think Croghan would mind one bit shifting his focus eastward for a few years. Especially if it means selling more blankets and bacon."

"So, Massachusetts means to attack the French? They are uniting for the defense of Pennsylvania and Virginia after all? Even without a formal Plan of Union?" I asked. As soon as I said it, I wished I hadn't.

"You really are like a young woman. You're more at home in a parlor playing cards and reading novels, aren't you?" Tim asked. Of course, he knew I was more than comfortable living in the woods, having spent the better part of my life in its hollows. "To ask such a question! You think Massachusetts cares one lick about Virginia? Massachusetts cares about Massachusetts. And to be more specific, Governor Shirley of Massachusetts cares about Governor Shirley and his position in Massachusetts."

"I know. I know," I mumbled. "He probably wants to take land from the Canadians for his own settlers, expanding his own wealth and influence here and back home in the Mother Country."

"Bullseye!" Tim said, poking me roughly with a finger.

"I guess I just hoped that Franklin's plea would be heeded."

"Even after the initial excitement around his flag, have you seen any indication of success in all these meetings?" he asked.

"No," I muttered. The propensity of men to act on that which will benefit themselves and no others was why I had originally gravitated to commerce rather than public service. At least by their actions of buying and selling in trade, even the most selfish of motives was usually over-shadowed by the need to satisfy a customer. But Washington's selfless devotion and nobility had swayed me. His integrity had convinced me that serving the public was not destined to be a frustrating endeavor. But I hadn't been in his presence for many weeks. I could feel his influence on me waning. I again thought about asking Croghan for my old job. At that moment, I didn't consider what might happen to Tim's role in the trading empire. I also did not consider that perhaps Croghan wouldn't want me back.

"Then tomorrow you'd better be ready," Tim warned. "You serve Washington. You're no longer an Indian trader. You represent the Virginia militia. Do you think it might be wise to bathe and clean your clothes tonight?"

I had been informed by Mr. Cotton that tomorrow I would speak to the congress about Fort Necessity. I would personally describe its horrors. I'd tell of the immense threat coming to all of us from the French. I'd remind them of the importance of our Indian allies – King Shingas and his fellow Delaware had told me they wanted the French out. And I'd convey Colonel Washington's wishes. Even though the colonel had been on the losing end this past summer, he was still quite famous and his opinions respected due to the printing of the journal he'd kept during his first celebrated trip into the Western Wilderness. He so desperately wanted that union for a strong and mutual defense.

"Maybe I should take after your savage routine," I said. "The delegates might take more pity on me if they see me dressed in my normal rough buckskins when I get up to speak."

"Perhaps," Tim allowed, clearly not believing it. "But by looking like the fool in their eyes, *I'm* getting them to talk. *You* don't want to look the fool while you speak. You want them to respect you."

He was right, of course. I stood to prepare for the next morning. As I could not afford to pay a local lady to perform the task, I had laundry to do. I had a letter to write to Bess. Maybe I'd tell her that I considered returning to a safer and more profitable profession. Would that get her father to allow her to write back?

"Oh," Tim said. "I almost forgot. Word is that there's a big fella with a busted-up nose poking around for you in the Albany taverns. Do you suppose it's that mutual friend of yours and Bess'?"

"Braun," I growled. Just what I needed. A vindictive beast chasing me over the countryside.

"That's what I thought, too. He'll be carrying a lot of anger if his nose is still misshapen and he served time in the Williamsburg stockade. Here," Tim added, sliding a few pennies across the table to me. "Don't skimp on the soap. You need it."

"So do you," I grumbled. But I pocketed his gift, nonetheless, and headed for the door.

"Keep an eye over your shoulder," Tim warned as I exited.

But there was nothing to worry about.

I made it quickly to my room without incident. That night, I washed my clothes along with my own body in the single tub owned by the tavern in which we stayed. While sitting in the rapidly cooling water, I began tossing around ideas for my talk the next day. With no preparation, my speech at Logstown a few years earlier had gotten the Indians to agree to support an English fort at the Forks of Ohio. Well, now that fort was destroyed and the French lived there. How much more important was this speech? How much better could it sway the listeners if I actually prepared?

While my clothes dripped dry hanging from a cord in my room that night, I sketched out several ideas. I logically laid out my case, Washington's case, sure to drop his name more than once. I appealed to their pocketbooks, personally and provincially. Croghan had always told me gentlemen loved their portfolios more than their wives. Therefore, it wasn't their heartstrings I meant to pluck. It was the tone of their coins, slipping through their fingers and bouncing down the street, I intended to play.

By the time I was done speaking the next morning, each delegate would clamor to be the first to vote in favor of the Plan of Union.

I set my stack of pages at the corner of the desk in the room, blew out the candle, and opened a window to allow the cool autumn air to enter. Then I went to bed. I had not written to Bess, for I did not have the energy. And I had given no more thought to working for Croghan. Appealing to these learned men, as I had in my writing, reminded me of the good I thought a man could do in the service of others. It reminded me of what I admired about Washington and what his steadfast countenance brought out in me.

I would make him proud of me in the morning.

CHAPTER ELEVEN

I was aroused from a dream just before dawn, surprised to see that the fireplace flared bright. It had been mere embers when I had turned in. And no one had entered the room to restoke its flames during the night. Rubbing the crust from my eyes, I sat up just as the temporary flash died back down and eventually disappeared altogether. Smoke then curled lazily up through the flue. The mystery blaze, whatever it had been, was fully extinguished.

Throughout the city, delegates would slowly be rousing themselves. All were experienced merchants and politicians and so none, even if they planned to speak today, would be as nervous as I. As soon as my feet hit the floor, I poured water into the basin at the dry sink and began grooming. My whiskers, such as they were, were scraped away. My hair, wiry and unruly, was shaped into some semblance of control.

I had one shirt that was somewhat presentable for such an occasion. I plucked it from the drying line and put it on, quickly noticing that there was a hole in the elbow I should have mended last evening. As I had no fashionable coat to cover it, I was relieved that Providence had sent the brief flare in the fireplace to awaken me early. Knowing I had time to spare, I plunked down on the bed with my sewing kit and gradually pulled the hole closed with thread. At least with the tear fixed, I'd not have to wear my old buckskin jacket. Its mud splatters and blood stains left behind by many a hunt and a few wars might prove too chilling for the delegates at such an early hour.

Next, I slid into my lone pair of cotton breeches, newly laundered and, to my delight, smelling quite renewed. The soap I had purchased with the money borrowed from Taeheek had worked wonders on the them as well as my flesh. Fresh socks, tied garters, and polished shoes followed. My only belt was rough and worn, but I would not leave it behind. It not only kept my drawers in place, but it held my knife and its sheath at the ready. Besides, I'd complete my "dress" outfit with a newly cleaned hunter green waistcoat that would extend just over the shabby belt.

After cinching my bright blue stock tie in a neat knot around my neck, I set about brushing clean the nap of my cocked hat.

When I was at last assembled and the sun had crested outside, I noticed myself in the wavy mirror. I was no Virginia planter, Philadelphian merchant, or Boston preacher, but I would do. It would be my irrefutable argument that swayed the assembly. Not my presentation of it.

I turned to gather my notes from the corner of the desk and stopped in my tracks. The speech was gone. My heart leapt into my throat as I scrambled to peer under the chair, desk, and even the bed. Panic set in as each second ticked by without finding the missing pages. I dug through my belongings, behind my patchwork-assembled Brown Bess and the heap of my other weapons. I tossed my war hatchet over my shoulder. It clattered onto the floorboards. The ornate French pistol I had inherited from my deceased wife joined it. I tore off the bed covers and threw the pillow to the ground in search of the most important words I had ever written. In short, I looked everywhere the tiny room had to offer. But the speech was nowhere to be found.

Perhaps someone had entered my chamber, I wondered, massaging my temples. My mind turned on all sorts of conspiracies. Someone from another colony was against Washington and, therefore the Plan of Union. They hated Franklin. They hated me. Braun had stolen my speech in order to exact his revenge. It's amazing how many different ogres one's mind can conjure in a half a minute.

But the door was bolted from the inside. I know because I checked it – twice in those frustrating moments. There had been no conspiracy to prevent what was, in my mind, to be the most brilliant oration ever given – by me anyway.

Returning to the desk, I plopped down in the chair. I closed my eyes to mentally retrace my steps from the night before. I was certain that I had set my finished product right on the corner of the desk.

I reached out my palm and set it where the pile had been as if that might help me now locate it. And believe it or not, it did.

Beneath the sleeve of my shirt, a ripple of goosebumps cascaded along my extended arm. My eyes shot open. I watched the small hairs on my exposed wrist stand on end. I felt the hairs beneath my pristine shirt do the same thing. There was a fall breeze blowing in through the open window. It was faint, but cool, frigid almost, and caused me to shiver.

I raised my palm toward the draft and felt the direction it blew. As a test, I gathered up a few sheets of blank paper and set it in the same corner of the desk. One-by-one, as if an invisible hand carefully peeled them back, the pages lifted free and fluttered in the air. I let them flitter as they slowly drifted along a path which guided me to the missing speech.

Less than a heartbeat later I crouched at the hearth. Clearly, the last thing that had burned in the fireplace was not a fat log or even a twig. The remnants of brittle, black pages littered the tops of the coals. The unburnt corners of several of the sheets remained. I could see portions of my messy handwriting, mocking me, but nothing of worth remained. My superbly clear, dare I say, inspired, speech had vanished.

At first my shoulders sagged in defeat. I didn't lament the fate of the king's empire or Washington's army. No. I fretted about my pride and reputation. But only briefly. Then I stood up and kicked the brick of the chimney, scuffing the shoes I had polished the previous evening. Next, I took at least a full minute to march around the room, cursing my misfortune. It was during my pounding strut that Tim knocked on the door. "I'm busy!" I snapped.

"I'll see you there, Primrose," Tim said to the door, laughing. "What's his problem?" he muttered to himself as he left. I cursed him and his woman's name game under my breath. But at that moment I strangely recalled how much I liked the name Primrose – just not for me.

Washington! His resolute, unsmiling, somber, tanned, young face burst into my brain. Sitting as he was with a sad, defeated army out on the frontier, he was counting on me to succeed. Even these delegates were counting on me to rally them to provide a defense. They just didn't know it – yet. And what would the colonel do if faced with the same circumstances? Would he mope?

And because I knew the man then as you know him now, no answer was required. It was obvious.

I raced to the desk and assembled my writing instruments and the last of my blank pages. I took a deep breath, dipped the nib into the well and set the quill to the page, expecting the words to fly as freely as they had the previous night. But my inspiration was gone. I could hardly recall the ingenious phrasing I had employed the night before. I remembered only that somehow these important delegates would save and make money if they supported Franklin's grand plan. I heard a clock from the hallway ticking away loudly. No words sprang from my pen. The only thing that poured onto the page was ink as it seeped from the nib that now wandered aimlessly.

Alright, I thought. Just begin anew.

Gentlemen, I wrote beneath the large blotch of ink. It was a good start. It was something.

Then I heard the bell above the Stadt Huys peel. Barking dogs and the height of the sun outside told me I had wasted a full hour while accomplishing nothing.

Damn it, I muttered. Standing, I wadded up the useless paper and tossed it into the fireplace. I watched it for a full minute. First, two little trails of smoke snaked their way out from under it. Then the smoke became thicker as the paper blackened and curled. At last it burst into flames with a whoosh.

Utterly frustrated, I glanced around the room in search of true inspiration. Perhaps Mr. Cotton could delay for another day. But, I dreaded the thought of disappointing Washington. And even though I didn't really know Franklin, who can say they would ever look forward to embarrassing himself with one so famous in the audience? I willed myself to think as I scanned for ideas.

It was a drab room. I couldn't afford a nicer one, even if there were any to be had in Albany. As such, I noticed only three things in my austere surroundings. First, I saw the book gifted to me by Washington, *Dialogues of Seneca the Younger*. Though the colonel had implored me to read it, I had yet to crack open the heavy tome. Now, I figured, might be a good time to search the wealth that was rumored to be amongst its pages. Next, I laid eyes on my fighting gear – a powder horn, a pouch of lead balls, my tomahawk, Tahki's French pistol, the battered Brown Bess, and a few other sundries. Thirdly, I saw the basin where I had washed up that morning.

And I had my inspiration. It was a rough idea, but would have to work. Gathering up the items I now required for my impassioned oration, I raced to the hall, arriving just as the last clang from the belfry died on the morning air.

CHAPTER TWELVE

"I thank the congress for granting this most gracious gift to Virginia," Isaac Cotton was saying as I entered at the back of the packed hall. He must have been stalling for time, for I was scheduled to start off the day's speeches without any preamble. Cotton fixed me with a decidedly unhappy glare as he watched me bump through a standing-room-only crowd. I then dropped all my paraphernalia with a crash and I was soon found rutting among the onlooker's feet on a quest of clumsy retrieval. Cotton quickly resumed his discourse. "It is clearly out of the mutual respect you all have for the most famous of *my* countrymen, Colonel Washington, that you acquiesce to our unusual request. But," he paused when I at last burst through the front row of men into the center of the room. My Brown Bess slipped from my grasp. It slammed to the floor. The lock knocked a cleft into the oak boards about the size of a shilling. I was making a terrible racket. Nothing like the dignified entry I had planned out the night before. Gentlemen expressed their mirth in the usual manner.

Mr. Cotton, obviously an unflappable public speaker, went right on talking, hardly noting the chuckles from his audience as I again gathered my gear and began stacking it on the table assigned to the Virginia delegation. "But I'm certain that you'll find the information contained in Mr. Weber's speech to be useful as deliberations of the Plan of Union conclude and the vote is taken. He comes to us at the direct request of Colonel Washington himself."

Tim, that is, Taeheek, in his best uninformed persona, clapped loudly. Whether it was to buy time for me or in honor of Washington's request, I know not. I do know however, that he was the only one applauding. The rest couldn't take their eyes off me and had likely not heard a word offered by Cotton. For his part, the experienced Virginia delegate sank back into his chair, obviously praying that my floor time was not going to be excruciatingly slow political suicide for him.

"Ahem," I said, gathering my wits. I smoothed out my green waistcoat and tugged at the stock tie, which suddenly felt too tight. "Thank you, Mr. Cotton." I tried to remember all that I wanted to say in opening. The notes I had made the night before even contained a humorous anecdote about the first time I'd met Tahki. Or, had I decided to talk about Croghan? Either way, I couldn't figure out the right way to begin. "Yes," I mumbled nervously. One of my fingers fell onto the hole in my shirt I'd sewn that morning. I anxiously picked at a loose thread.

"Must be a cat skulking around here with an extra tongue!" Lydius called out from the New York table. The Oneida he'd been cavorting with and employing to take advantage of other tribesmen, gathered around behind him. "Cause this lad's missing one!" His sycophants first, and then the room, erupted in a flurry of uncomfortable giggles at my expense. One man in particular, unseen by me, was laughing in fits. Had I ever heard a lion, I should think its roar would have been tamer.

And if I'm honest, I would have thought Lydius funny had he directed his barb at anyone else. But I had faced tougher crowds – veritable armies bent on running me through. I defiantly balled my sweaty palms and held them at my side. "Powder!" I exclaimed, still unsure how to start. The word echoed over their quickly fading chuckles. The momentarily stunned crowd watched me, warily. "Powder!" I shouted even louder, slamming a fist on the Virginia table, rattling my goods. "Bring the powder!"

Chief Hendrick, Tim's kinsman, watched me with quiet interest from his spot at the center of the official delegation sent from Onondaga. Their table was right next to New York's. And though he made me feel self-conscious, I carried on with my illustration. I lifted my powder horn from where I'd slung its leather cord over my shoulder, holding it aloft to show everyone in the room. Biting my lip in frustration at what I knew I was about to do and the risks I took, I lifted my Bess and primed her pan, careful to sprinkle the powder in plain sight of everyone. I added a silent prayer for Providence to see me through what was to come.

"Mr. Weber," Cotton said quietly but firmly. "I thought the weapons you brought in were to be props. The congress would prefer you not load them."

"The only one who could possibly be in any danger is me!" I answered as I dropped the butt onto the floor, dumped a measure of powder into the muzzle, stuffed in wading and a ball, and then packed it all tightly with the ramrod. The room fell completely silent when I half-cocked the hammer and set the Bess onto the table.

"Now, as a part of my demonstration, I'll require the use of several more guns," I called.

"Mr. Weber," Cotton warned. "I'm certain that Colonel Washington did not send you here to endanger anyone."

"Mr. Washington sent me here to demonstrate what we faced from the French on the western frontier and I intend to do so!" I snapped. "Now, pass the guns forward!" I ordered as I deliberately loaded Tahki's ornate French pistol in the same methodical manner I had loaded my Bess.

At least eight guns came forward – one rifle, four Indian muskets which were adorned with feathers, a pair of well-polished gentleman's muskets, and one pistol. There were many more guns in the room, but their owners were more selective in choosing with whom they shared. I loaded each of them using my powder. But I packed in the shot and ramrods provided by the original owners. I then slapped the last one down next to the Bess, nodding in approval of my own work. I thought my dangerous weapons cache was good.

"I've got business to attend to," Lydius called out. "Apparently, you gentlemen have the time to devote to this farce. But I do not! I call on the president of this congress to release us to the bushes so that the real meat may be discussed." He had more side dealings to which to attend.

"Mr. Lydius!" I shouted angrily. I did not know any more about the man than what I've already shared with you. But he had made a joke out of me and spoken out of turn. It felt right to single him out. "You will get your ragged, one-eyed self up here this instant! You have just volunteered to take part in my experiment."

"Mr. Weber!" Cotton exclaimed in horror. I guess he wasn't as unflappable as I had thought. "You will sit down this instant. You are no longer permitted to speak for the Virginia delegation." He turned to the New York table, meeting Lydius' gaze. "I offer humble apologies to the gentlemen of *your* great country, sirs."

"But I do not!" I shrieked. "And I shall not cease my activities. Colonel Washington demands it! Not only do I aim to show just how ineffectual our response will be if we remain disunited, but I intend to demonstrate just what a cowardly thief Mr. Lydius happens to be. Now get up here you swindling crook!"

Lydius stood abruptly. "You, sir, will take back your words or pay the price!"

Satisfied, I rested my hands upon my hips and meandered in a broad circle. I noted that Tim watched me with confused fascination, perhaps considering that I'd lost my mind. And from the Pennsylvania table, Benjamin Franklin observed me while leaning his chin in one palm. I swear he had an amused grin on his face. The rest of the audience murmured.

My silence spurred Lydius to further heights of anger. "I said that you will renounce your slight, you cur, or I will meet you in a duel at this very moment, behind this very building! And I call on all these men to be my seconds. None would dare serve as a second to a scoundrel such as you!"

"I'll be your second!" came a call from the back. That someone began shoving his way through the crowd to join us at the center.

"He'll need no second!" I shouted, spinning on my heel to face Lydius. "Have I made you angry?" I asked quite sarcastically.

"If you have to ask the question, you share your intelligence with a snail!" he barked.

I slowly walked over to the New York delegation so that just two feet separated us. After scanning the table, I pointed to a pewter mug resting in front of the shady sutler. It was half-filled with rum, obviously Lydius' drink of choice, regardless the time of day. From an artistic standpoint the mug was attractive. It was highly decorated with the image of a town nestled in a scenic valley, complete with a bridge and the workings of industry such as a mill and an armory. It wasn't worth a fortune, but it was the priciest item within reach. WITHDRAWN

I snatched it up and drank its remaining contents before Lydius could do anything. However, I did have to jump back a step to outrun a paw he swung in my direction. "Is this yours?" I asked, mocking him.

"You know it is! You impertinent pig!"

"Then I propose," I called loudly for all to hear. "That you, Mr. Lydius, step forward to the Virginia table. I will position myself and one other volunteer at the opposite end of the room. Using the weapons I have so clearly and properly loaded, if you can drop me before I arrive at your side, you may retake your precious mug. Pluck it off my dead body. If you do not, the mug will remain securely in my hands."

"But you stole it!" he proclaimed.

"The offer will be withdrawn shortly!" I shouted. "Defend your honor and your property, sir, or return to whatever cave you crawled out of!"

Lydius shoved the table at his fellow delegates as he rushed around it toward the Virginians. His fellow New Yorkers and the scoundrel Iroquois he'd been negotiating with watched him go with minor horror mixed with amusement. Lydius dropped his hand onto the nearest loaded pistol. I slapped it roughly back down onto the table. "Ah, ah, ah," I chastised him. "Let's make a contest of it. Wait until I remove myself to the other end of the room."

"You'll not be permitted any weapons?" Lydius shouted.

"Just my blades," I sang, holding up my war hatchet and knife. I turned and ambled across the floor, the cup dangling from a buttonhole. "Taeheek, you'll join me for this game of La Crosse."

"La Crosse?" Cotton asked as Tim rose to his feet. "What game?"

"La Crosse," I answered smugly. "It's an Indian game with a French name, sir."

"Mr. Weber, you'll cease!" Cotton proclaimed. "I'll inform Colonel Washington of your behavior."

"Do inform him," I coldly goaded Cotton.

Tim pulled off his gaming cross and employed it like a weapon in one hand. In the other he gripped his tomahawk and came to stand next to me. "Like this?" he asked in a patently dumb accent. He grinned, not knowing what I had planned, but trusting me, nonetheless.

"Like that," I said, nodding. "Now, Mr. Lydius, the impotent goat, will have all the time he wishes to raise those weapons, aim them, and shoot each one of us in turn." I craned to face the delegations to my rear. "Yes, gentlemen," I encouraged. "You'll want to scramble. There is a chance Lydius' aim is as poor as his business practices." From his table, Franklin rose slowly, chuckling merrily as he moved. The other delegates moved with a more pronounced haste.

"Lydius still requires a second!" shouted the man who had elbowed his way forward. "You've got one, Weber. He deserves one." The way he called my name had a familiar ring to it. I glanced toward the voice. The man wore an evil smile beneath a badly disfigured snout.

Alex Braun had caught up with me.

CHAPTER THIRTEEN

"I don't need a second," Lydius shouted proudly, beating his chest.

Braun pressed forward to the Virginia table and glared down at the smaller, one-eyed man. Everyone was smaller than Braun. "Like it or not, you've got one," he growled.

Lydius, preferring to see the giant as an ally, stepped aside with the pistol. Braun wasted no time in selecting the rifle for its accuracy.

"Dead or alive, you'll pay for any damage done to the Stadt Huys, Mr. Weber!" warned another of the New York delegation.

"Why, I have no money! Alive or dead," I laughed. "My salary, like that of Washington himself, is paid for by a House of Burgesses that only negotiates themselves raises with any regularity."

Cotton's face fell into his hands in shame.

"I'll pay for any of the damage!" Lydius exclaimed. He held the pistol in his hand. "And the expense will be worth it. There'll only be two worthless pools of blood to mop up."

I took my first deliberate step forward. "You may fire when ready, Lydius, you fish-stinking turd! Or will you go first, Alexander Braun, you brainless oaf?"

Without delay, they raised their guns and peered down the sights. They had forgotten Taeheek existed. Both men looked squarely at my forehead. It was not the first time I had looked down the barrel of guns. It wouldn't be the last.

And they depressed their triggers.

CHAPTER FOURTEEN

Their flints struck the frizzens and slapped downward with a click. There was no telltale primary explosion in the pan. There was certainly no din from the rear of the barrel or sparkling burst from the front. I threw my shoulders back and puffed my chest outward. Lydius looked at the side of the gun in confusion as the crowd of onlookers oohed and aahed as if we had been part of a traveling spectacle. The frustrated sutler threw the pistol to the floor.

"Hey that's my gun!" called a man from the crowd.

"And the taxpayer's floor!" said a New York delegate.

"Shut up! The both of you." Lydius shouted.

Braun was just as livid. He grabbed the spent rifle by the muzzle, spun around once, and launched it at me. I ducked. It narrowly avoided clunking my head as it dashed into Pennsylvania's table behind, scattering inkwells and documents.

"You see, gentlemen," I said calmly as Taeheek and I deliberately stepped forward with our weapons at the ready. "Mr. Lydius' quest is an honorable one. You need not worry about Mr. Braun's problems. In either case, the sorry dogs have been reprimanded by me, their better. They have been verbally assaulted on a public stage. Lydius has even had his property stolen without the slightest provocation." I flicked the mug. It made a little ding like a bell.

"And I'll get it back," Lydius said, lofting one of the donated muskets. Hardly aiming, he pulled the trigger. This time the pan gave a little spark, but nothing more erupted from the gun.

In a burst of fear, my heart almost leapt out of its chest, but I kept on walking toward the threat. "You may try to get the cup back," I said, my brow breaking out in a cold sweat. I suddenly realized that my haphazardly assembled plan had more flaws than a Quaker's quilt. "But you will fail."

"I watched you load these," Lydius said as shoved the musket to the floor. He studied the outside of the remaining guns that lined the table. Lydius then peeked into one of the loaded pans to be certain he wasn't crazy. "And you're no magician!"

"No," I agreed. "But nor are you. None of us can conjure victory where all the elements of defeat are already assembled."

"What are you talking about?" Lydius asked, his mind clouded with anger.

"Shoot us! Quickly!" Taeheek demanded.

Lydius wanted to oblige. But Braun pushed him away from the table. The brute from Williamsburg hoisted a gun, this time aiming it at the Mohawk's face. Tim's eyes blinked when the flint struck the frizzen. But once again the pan merely sputtered. The muzzle remained silent.

In short succession, Braun used and discarded gun after gun. And gun after gun after gun failed to stop us. While Braun was busy breaking one of the butts over his knee, Lydius snuck behind him and gathered up the last of the loaded weapons.

That is when, at last, we stood next to Lydius, who pressed the muzzle of Tahki's pistol firmly against my green waistcoat. I had once used the gun on my own quest for revenge. I hoped that Lydius would be as unsuccessful as I had been. He shook with rage. "You intentionally fouled your own powder! You cheated!"

"Did I?" I asked, loud enough for every member of the gaping audience to hear. "Or, did I just demonstrate what it was like for those of us under Colonel Washington's command at Fort Necessity? Like Mr. Lydius, we, noble Englishmen, were publicly humiliated by the French over a period of time. Like Lydius, we warned His Most Christian Majesty of France in the sternest, but most diplomatic of terms, to cease operations in the lands of the Ohio, which clearly belong to Great Britain. And also like Mr. Lydius, we had our property wrongfully seized. Even now, the French rest on grounds cleared by my hand, my ax. They sit in a great fort where the seeds of an English stockade used to live."

Lydius still pressed the muzzle into the fabric of my waistcoat, but had decided to listen to what was, at last, the point of my oration. He was, after all, a delegate sent by New York. Meanwhile, Braun's chest heaved in anger as he stood behind Lydius. The huge Virginian gritted his teeth.

I stamped my foot loudly. "When the French took over the Forks of Ohio by force, we could no longer stand idle. We're

Englishmen! Men of Virginia, Pennsylvania, and even South Carolina risked their lives for a cause that must unite us today. Under Washington and with little hope for resupply or wages or relief, we marched into the great and wild hazards to meet the enemy. We cut our own rutted, muddy road as we went! Did we get extra powder? No! Did we get provisions? Once. And that was out of the goodness of George Croghan's heart. What we got from our home countries was silence or delayed letters expressing regrets."

"The French and the Delaware Indians drastically outnumbered us. Still we went, because that is what an Englishman will do." I pointed toward Lydius. "It is what we do whether we come from the Mother Country or from our own countries: Virginia, New York, and so on."

"Like Lydius here, we fought in unfair conditions against an organized foe. Our powder stores were fouled by weather and lack of resupply. Still, we met the enemy." I held the mug aloft. "And we lost. We lost lives, scores of young men, and our property." I stepped away from the angry New Yorker and again hung the mug by sticking the tail of the handle through one of my button loops. "And we, like Lydius, will continue to lose to the French and Canadians if we insist on facing them in a piecemeal fashion. Let me tell you, I have seen Pennsylvania men die. I have watched Virginians and even one or two from New Jersey bleed. They all died the same, crying while clawing at the inside parts of their body that had spilled outside. Different countries or not, we must support Franklin's Plan of Union. Our legislators must provide resources to Washington and other valiant commanders like him. Otherwise, the language spoken in the next Albany Congress will be French! To that I say, *mon Dieu*!"

Had a cricket dared to creak, I could have heard it in that suddenly hushed all.

"Or," Franklin said quietly into that calm. He was about to show just how prescient he could be. "Our Mother Country will stop allowing us to manage our own affairs and will send someone who will unite us by force! I dare say the latter may be worse than the former." The rich printer gave me an approving nod.

And the room erupted into a storm of words. Important men shouted important notions of honor. Many of them decried Virginia's lack of adequately provisioning Washington. Cotton and the rest of his Virginian's defended vigorously, criticizing the other colonies for their utter lack of support, militarily or financially. Both camps were correct. That had been the entire point of the Plan of Union which, for good or bad, was now entering a period of vigorous debate.

After clapping Taeheek on the shoulder to express my gratitude for his bravery, I turned to see that Lydius had lowered the weapon. He even smiled. "You are an arrogant little prick," Lydius said as the shouting carried on. "But aren't all Virginians?"

"Pennsylvania is my home country," I corrected him. All around us gentlemen, heretofore thoughtful and refined, had been awakened by my demonstration of England's feckless lack of power. Or was it Franklin's simple warning of British intervention that had these Americans agitated so?

"A Quaker fighting in a war? No wonder Washington lost," Lydius said with a good-natured chuckle. He extended a hand for his mug. "But I'd say you make a fair, though unconventional, point for union. All's forgiven. I'll take the cup."

I looked down to where the mug dangled by the tail of its handle. "I'm afraid not," I said. "You didn't drop me by the time I reached you. By the rules we agreed upon, it's mine, fair and square."

Lydius didn't lose his pleasant grin. Shaking his head in disbelief, he said. "I figured you'd be the type with little brains and big thieving mitts. Chummy as you are with these Injuns."

"Yep," I agreed with a smile.

"Uh-huh," Tim agreed, wearing an equally stupid grin.

Braun muscled Tahki's pistol from Lydius' hand while advancing on me. "And by those same rules I have one more chance to retrieve this man's property." Without warning, Braun rammed the muzzle of Tahki's pistol into my chest and squeezed the trigger at the same time. The whack alone felt like it cracked my sternum.

But my troubles didn't end there. To my horror, as I fell back, the pan of the pistol flashed brightly. Braun's instantly wicked face was illuminated. The intense flare brightened Lydius' surprised expression, too. In the agonizing full second that followed the blaze, I said at least a dozen prayers.

You see, Lydius was correct that I had fouled my own gunpowder with water from my washbasin. But I couldn't be too generous with the liquid, or else the powder would have clumped and never flowed into place. Any eye in the audience, even an inexperienced one, would have noticed that something was amiss. As such, the longer the merely damp powder sat unused, even if it had been packed inside a gun, the better chance it had in erupting.

And I heard the second, louder burst from deep within the barrel. It started as a sputter and ended with a bang.

A fraction of a heartbeat later, I felt the ball slam into my chest with what felt like the force of a thousand cannons.

CHAPTER FIFTEEN

"How do you feel, Amelia?" Tim asked me. It was the evening after my rather painful demonstration. We sat at a front corner table in a tavern called *Beverwijck*, which was the former name of Albany. Through a small window, I could see the painted image of a beaver balancing mugs of ale on his broad, flattened tail hanging over the door. The sign slowly creaked whenever a small gust of wind would catch it. At the moment, listening to its sound was better than listening to my friend.

"I'm asking, will you live? What do you think, Louisa?" Tim said.

"I think you should shut your mouth," I warned. Since the congress had broken up for the day, Tim had worked very hard to come up with a litany of new nicknames for me, never repeating a woman's name.

"Oh, settle down," Tim said. "Don't be so sensitive or I will think you deserve your new names. I just want to know how you feel. Are you alright?"

With the tips of my fingers, I tentatively touched the spot on my chest that had been struck by the ball. Obviously, I had survived. My fashionable vest and best shirt had holes torn in them from the impact and sparks of burning powder. But my skin had nary a scratch. I was, however, left with a grotesque black and blue and green blemish that grew to the circumference of a pumpkin by day's end.

"You're lucky the powder in the barrel took so long to burn. And only half of it ignited," Tim said. "Otherwise, you would have made a mess all over their Stadt Huys floor. And I would have had to pay to clean it up."

"Thanks for your genuine concern," I muttered. "But don't worry. I'll live."

"Oh, that is a relief, Dorothy," Tim laughed.

"Leave him alone, Taeheek," said his Mohawk kinsman, Theyanoguin, better known as Chief Hendrick. He shared the table with us while eating a hearty portion of boiled venison and carrots. Even he tired of Tim's antics. But the chief's personality wasn't absent humor. For, whenever the tavern maid would come by to replenish his drink, he would flick the lewd gorget he wore as a not-so-subtle taunt. Experienced in working with less than desirable clientele, the woman rolled her eyes and, after topping him off, would amble away chuckling. Hendrick would laugh with her while nibbling his bread.

Tim patted the top of my head like I was a puppy. "Aw, she deserves the attention."

I swatted his hand away. I was in pain and downright woozy. The delegates had debated Franklin's Plan of Union fiercely while I recovered in a corner under the suspect care of a quack doctor. He drained my blood of the bad *humors* caused by the ball slamming into my chest. I was left weakened, but alive. By the time I was again upright, the votes had been tallied and the plan's approval complete. It was a blurry-eyed victory that, I dare say, could not have been achieved without my outlandish display.

But my painful triumph was countered by financial defeat. Lydius had plucked his pewter mug up from off the floor amidst the chaos before disappearing into the bushes, as he called them. Therefore, I was left without any suitable clothing, save my wilderness wear, and without the proper compensation of a pewter mug I could sell.

For Braun's part, I'd been told that a constable had come and taken him away for deliberately shooting me. That officer quickly discovered that at least three of his colleagues would be required to place the fearsome Braun in irons. But the constable's perseverance eventually paid off.

It was the second time an encounter with me had resulted in Braun's arrest. Though I seemed to be the one getting injured of late, I hoped he had learned his lesson and would just leave me alone. But, as I've learned since then, the best laid plans of mice and men...

I glanced back onto the street. "That must be them now," I said.

Hendrick leaned across his plate to peer through the rippled glass. "That's them," he confirmed. The old chief settled into his chair and used his sleeve to wipe away unseen crumbs from his face. He dusted off his coat and sat up straight, his chin held high as the door swung inward. "This will be the most important discussion held at the congress, boys. I want no distractions."

It seemed to me that Franklin's plea for union had been the most important issue percolating in Albany. Yet, if significance was to be judged by what everyone discussed when the congress wasn't in session, it was business, pounds and pence, that mattered most.

From behind the heavy old door, two men emerged. The first was tall, lean and handsome – a dashing figure every man might hope to be. He was more fetching than Washington, but with less of a military bearing. The flickering candlelight did nothing to take away from his refined features. I recalled seeing him sitting at the New York delegation nearby Lydius, but outside his cadre of swilling bargainers. He smiled instantly upon setting eyes on Hendrick and set a determined course for our table.

The second newcomer followed behind. I had heard that he was, like me, a Pennsylvanian. And like the first, this man was thin, but with none of the vigor. He appeared sickly with pronounced cheekbones and hollowed out caverns for eyes. The first was perhaps forty. The second had survived sixty winters, barely survived, it seemed.

"Chief Hendrick," said the first man, gripping firmly the hand offered to him by the Mohawk chief. He spoke with an Irish accent like my old boss, Croghan. Hendrick rose from his seat and the pair embraced affectionately, patting each other's back. They then went back and forth, speaking in the Mohawk dialect of the Iroquoian tongue. With Taeheek as a friend and many other Indian acquaintances from the north, I knew some of the language. But this newcomer was proficient indeed. I could tell the pair had been allies for a long time. With a shared, rolling laugh, they ended a fond memory that involved a runaway horse and a deep creek. I did not pick up the other details that made the story remarkable.

"Boys," Hendrick said to us. "This is William Johnson, a neighbor and friend, whom I would gladly trust with my life."

"We're just negotiating a deal that everyone wants, Theyanoguin," Johnson said. "I should hope we risk neither life nor limb."

Hendrick showed his teeth with a wide grin. Corresponding to the area beneath the brutal scar, several of the tiny nuggets of ivory had been knocked out long ago. The left side of his mouth was defined by bleak darkness. In contrast, the right side was filled with clean yellow teeth, like kernels of dried corn. "This is my kinsman, Taeheek."

Taeheek shook Johnson's hand vigorously. "Good," he said with stoicism.

Hendrick gave his relative a suspicious glance and added, "You can call him, Tim. It's his Christian name."

"Very pleasant to meet you, Tim," said Johnson.

"Likewise, sir," Tim added, swiftly defeated at his game of pretending to be an illiterate savage. Apparently, Hendrick wanted nothing but honesty in the coming discussions. I elbowed Tim in the ribs. It felt good for him to get a dose after giving it to me all day.

"And this is Ephraim Weber," Hendrick continued.

"Oh, I'm familiar with the boy," Johnson said enthusiastically. He shook my hand. "I heard his tale of woe while sitting in the Stadt Huys today. After he told what happened to Washington and the lads at Fort Necessity, I could not help but think that Franklin's bold Plan of Union would do anything but succeed. Then you went and got yourself shot! What political theatrics! You guaranteed that the plan passed with resounding success. Now, it only needs to be approved by the legislatures of the colonies. Then we won't need to have some arrogant British general sent over here." Johnson then leaned in, looking me in the eye. "'Twas a grim affair, lad. Grim. I'm surprised you are even willing to stay in Washington's employ after such adventures. I would think you would have gone running off to Croghan. A relatively safer business, Indian trading."

"You know George Croghan?" I asked, though I obviously had.

"All Irishmen know one another!" he exclaimed. "The Irish must stick together, you see." Johnson gave me a wink. "It's easier to watch over the English."

He stepped to the side, setting a hand on his companion's bony shoulder in order to bring him to the front. "Chief Hendrick, this is Conrad Weiser. You often said that if I knew of an honest man capable of negotiating a land transaction that I should introduce you. Well, here is that man. The Pennsylvania Assembly has granted him sweeping authority to transact business that is in the best interests of all parties. He has the full faith of Governor Morris down in Philadelphia."

"Good to meet you," Weiser said in the thickest of German accents. "Ich bin geehrt."

"I'm honored as well," Hendrick said with a bow, surprising me with his ability to decipher the German phrase. A polyglot. A warrior. A leader. There was more to the Mohawk chief than met the eye. He swept a hand over the table. "Sit."

After settling into our places and more food coming from a kitchen, that was busy filling the orders of hungry delegates, Hendrick leaned with one elbow on the table. The other he had cocked behind him with his hand placed on the chair's armrest. "Before we begin, I must get something off my chest."

"Please," Johnson said.

"Ja," Weiser agreed, eyeing the gorget somewhat suspiciously. Though sickly in his physical appearance, Mr. Weiser appeared fastidious in dress and manner. He folded his lean hands and listened to what the chief had to say.

Hendrick tapped his disgusting scar with a single finger. "I do not wish to receive a matching one of these. And I don't wish for any of my Mohawk or English brothers to welcome such a prize. Forget the French for right now. I worry more about my own. Your own. So, if we agree to something, it must be fair under any and all scrutiny that will certainly come from my people and yours."

"Of course," Johnson said.

"Ja," Weiser said, nodding. "I must answer to the royal governor. He and the assembly will bless any transaction with ample examination."

Hendrick studied his longtime friend and Weiser. "I believe you both. But what about all the other seething intrigue performed away from the congress. Out here in the bushes, as they say, the diplomacy is of a liquid variety. It is a fluid frontier, with the boundary lines running across the map faster than the rum."

Johnson opened his mouth to protest, but Weiser settled him with a firm grip. "Ja. Ja. You speak of Lydius and his attempted theft of the Wyoming Valley. Even now they rest in a tavern across the street, carousing and stealing. He is a creeping urchin, eine Schlange. And several of the lesser chiefs from the Oneida that he easily plies with rum are no better. They sell away the lands of the Delaware for heaps of hard currency, to be sure. But it is money that will go only to them and their spending on an extravagant lifestyle. If the Lydius deal goes through as the rumors say, those drunken chiefs will share none of it with the Delaware. That's what happens when you negotiate with crooks from New York and Connecticut."

"On the other hand," Weiser continued, glancing at one of his hands for effect. "Pennsylvania has been *the only* colony with a history of the fairest relations with the Indians. We have no standing militia. I intend to keep that tradition alive, a military unnecessary. And I pray you do as well. I'll not deal with anyone who would sell out his people for narrow, personal gain."

"I'd never sell out my people," Hendrick insisted, maintaining his calm. "And only *I* speak with authority that comes from Onondaga and the Tree of Great Peace."

Old Weiser poked the tabletop with his rigid fore finger, tapping again and again to emphasize his point. "Yes, but will you sell out the Delaware, one of the tribes that you speak for today? Like those Oneida chiefs I mentioned, you represent the Iroquois League. And you are a steward for your children, the Delaware. Would sell them out for your own gain? History has shown that for hardly any treasure at all most men happily sell that which is not theirs."

Hendrick folded his arms at his chest and leaned back. I prepared for him to erupt in anger at the accusation. Instead, he clicked his tongue in his cheek before adding, "He is good," to Johnson.

"I knew you would like one another," Johnson said with a smile.

"Like has nothing to do with it," Weiser answered in dispute. He was exacting in his words as well as his dress. "Fairness. Mutual benefit. Those are what we intend to use in barter. I am not here to be liked by anyone." It was refreshing to see an older man who managed to maintain some of the earnest passions from a youth he'd so long ago left behind. Then again, perhaps he was just like every other crusty elder I'd ever met.

Hendrick smiled even more at the sickly looking German. He clapped Weiser on the back with enough force to snap him in half. "But I do like you! What's not to like!"

"Ja," Weiser said, shifting uneasily in his seat from all the extra attention. "Das ist gut. But we do not have time for pleasantries. Let us complete and publish our negotiations before word of Lydius' maneuvering gets out beyond these valleys. News of his outright theft will create a firestorm throughout the Indian lands. As a result, our bargain, no matter how fair it is in reality, will be forgotten, disregarded amidst the Indian war that is sure to follow."

At Pickawillany, I had seen what a few score of angry Catawba and Ottawa Indians could do to an unguarded village. At Fort Necessity, I had witnessed what a couple hundred incensed Delaware could do when their anxieties were stoked by French propaganda. In both cases, blood had sloshed over the countryside, English blood. And if news of a theft of the Wyoming Valley reached the area around Fort Duquesne, even those Indians who were completely unaffected by the terms would rise up.

No. It wouldn't be a mere uprising. And we wouldn't be at war against just the French. We'd be at war with the French *and* the Indians, all of them. I glanced at Hendrick and Tim. Most of the Indians, anyway.

Hendrick turned sober, though his scar still made him smile. He sighed heavily. "It is time to create a lasting peace between our peoples. Here at Albany we have extended the Covenant Chain between the Iroquois and Britain to a true union in the spirit of Franklin's audacious plan. Our pact, our sale, should we reach an agreement, may further that peace, extending a mutual trust down through generations. And then no blood must be shed on any side, today or tomorrow. The French will be compelled to sue for manageable peace."

"Here. Here," Johnson said, raising his glass.

Without further discussion, we downed our rum. The negotiations began. Honestly, openly Weiser offered terms, protections, weapons, hunting rights, and manufactured goods to the Iroquois, but also to the Delaware men and women affected by the sale. Openly, honestly Chief Hendrick accepted, turned down, or modified proposals, adding some of his own with regard to timelines and boundaries.

And they went long into the night. The tavern slowly emptied of other patrons. Candles burned low and were replaced. The proprietor went to bed. The last maid went home. Even the tavern across the street where Lydius plied his evil brand of barter eventually faded to black. Thus ignored, our little table was all that remained occupied, busy.

And the two men, a Mohawk bargaining for the Delaware and a German negotiating on behalf of an English colony, heroically continued on into the next morning. Sunlight replaced the short, nearly extinguished candles. The innkeeper came down. The maid returned to work. The belfry of the Stadt Huys echoed with the sound of a clapper striking iron as the congress was set to reconvene.

And, to both parties, after many pages of many versions littered the floor, the negotiations were at last considered a tremendous success, fair to all. On behalf of the Delaware people, Hendrick, a hallowed chief of Onondaga, had agreed to sell the lands west of the Alleghenies to Pennsylvania – not Connecticut, not New York, not Virginia. That stretch of wilderness would officially become a part of Penn's Woods. He promised to help his English brothers take back the Forks of Ohio, which the French had so deviously stolen from us just a few months earlier. Once the Forks were again under English protection and open to commerce, Chief Hendrick would convey the good news to his wards, the Delaware people. They'd be permitted to hunt in the area surrounding the Forks, but white traders and settlers would be permitted to emigrate. In exchange for money and heaps of goods, the Delaware people, all the Indian peoples, could then be certain that everything west of this purchase was their domain – as long as they prevented the French from taking control.

And it was a fair bargain.

At the time, we all knew it was in everyone's best interest – white and Indian. I would have bet that even my old nemesis, Shingas, the self-proclaimed Delaware king would have difficulty finding fault. Everyone around that table considered it ironclad, with enough detailed assurances to pacify the most reluctant assemblyman or Indian warrior.

And, before you use hindsight to protest, it was impossible to think that any more land would ever be required by the tiny colony of Pennsylvania, or any of its coastbound cousins.

But, as you'll see, the negotiations were too little, too late to stop the momentum that had already begun forming years before. As I said in my last tale, our prior actions had been the spark that lit a fuse of destruction that could not be snuffed out. The bargain struck by Hendrick and Weiser would do nothing to staunch the blood that would run red.

Lydius and his final liquid dealings had been printed on broadsides that very night. While we talked and others slept, the posters had been plastered on doors and shop walls. Word of mouth carried the news from one town, one Indian village to the next.

Hendrick was furious.

The Delaware would be enraged.

PART II
FEATS OF PROVIDENCE

CHAPTER SIXTEEN
1755 A.D.

Curse John Henry Lydius and men like him. For eternity, his ilk has been a blemish on the earth. They've bestowed a bad name on all merchants, traders, and common peddlers who would prefer to carry out their affairs with honor, decency, and, of course, profit. With oozing derision, I call him a sutler. Younger folks act like sutler is just another word for a victualer. They're wrong. A sutler sold things that others couldn't or, more than likely, wouldn't dream of hawking. Lydius did it with his smuggled goods. He did it with Delaware lands.

And with my Quaker upbringing, I happen to know that the word sutler comes from an old Dutch word that meant *one who does the dirty work*. Indeed, Lydius and his labors were filthy.

But damn him and those wicked Oneida chiefs, who sat around tables and on blankets outside Fort Frederick at Albany swilling pungent brew. They concocted something even more odious than the liquor they swigged. With their detestable contracts, they didn't just sell land for temporary riches. No. They dealt in one commodity only. The only product men of their sort were capable of manufacturing. The only crop, were they ploughman, their type was able to sow. You know the good of which I speak. Magere Hein. La Mort. That is, Death.

For the wintery months that followed the Albany Congress, whispers of Indian raids began to spread eastward. A single family burned out here. A cluster of homes torched there, the men slaughtered. The women, too, were killed unless they went along willingly to be adopted into the attacking tribes. In the next logical step of what the Indians called a Mourning War, most of the white children were taken. I had heard of young boy who had seized his father's musket after he'd been killed in an attack. The Delaware and Shawnee warriors who continued their assaults showed the lad no quarter. Summarily slaughtered. Scalped for a trophy, proof of an heroic deed performed in the name of the tribe.

The numbers of settlers killed was still low – perhaps two dozen. But I hated Lydius because of it. It was the furor caused by his bald swindling that set the pieces in motion. His theft was water to a wheel, wind to a mill. It caused the most distant mechanisms in the chain of cogs to spin to the will of its force. Sure, there was already talk that the legislatures of the colonies Lydius represented might nullify his singular achievement. But the bloodletting had begun in drips, drops, and drabs. And the colonies most affected, Virginia and Pennsylvania, could do next to nothing about it because the Plan of Union had so miserably failed.

That's right, it ultimately, definitively failed. As a result of my excruciating theatrics, the Plan of Union had passed in Albany. But not a single legislature, not the Burgesses in Virginia, not the General Court in Massachusetts had voted in its favor. Most of the lazy lawmakers saw fit to avoid taking up the matter for debate altogether. Pompous, genteel bastards living in distant wealth, unaffected by the trials felt on the frontier from the French and the Indians.

Back then, I was getting surlier by the moment. Just recalling the events today in my infirm years, even decades removed, sets my heart aflutter – and not in the good way that a happy young lass still can. Our failure to band together meant the crown back in London would have to take the burden of defending the colonies into its own hands. The seizure of power would be performed gladly, inefficiently, and heavy-handedly, to be sure.

And to top it off, I prayed for misfortune to fall upon Alexander Braun. The tight joints between my sternum and ribs creaked and ached with every move in the exact spot he'd shot me with my dead wife's pistol. If only a plague might strike Braun! I was to be forever tormented by his assault. Damn me for being so foolish as to have handed him the chance to shoot me. To this day, any cough, even in the mildest form of a chest cold, racks me to the core with pain. It gets worse by the month.

Damn the representatives at the Congress of 1754 for being so careless as to allow John Lydius the freedom to create such havoc. Damn the constable of Williamsburg for ever having released Braun into the public.

Damn Bess! Damn it!

Dozens of letters had swept from my heart to my hand and into Franklin's postal service. From there they may have wound up on Hades stoop for all I knew. I was nineteen, at the tail end of those years when every fleck to those fragile strings of love felt like a stab deep within the soul. When it came to Bess, I believed myself to be in Hell. The love I had fostered for her felt most unrequited. As such, over time my letters slowly evolved from heartfelt expressions of devotion and even some tastefully phrased lust to those of a jilted lover. By the end of those many months where she had yet to respond, I had begun to heap scorn onto her father. For three letters straight, I accused John Goode of putting a stop our romance. In the next letter, I added her mother into the mix, accusing Mary of preventing our love out of spite for what happened between Alex Braun and I in her once-tidy home.

I now sat bare chested in my breeches in Alexandria, Virginia. Washington was somewhere in the city. He had kept me busy running between supply depots and our base at Wills Creek throughout the winter. We had made no moves to protect the western settlers from Indian incursion with our army during those frigid months. Our loitering was not indolence. It was because we were entirely unable to anything else. A flock of geese could have wiped us out with their shit and bills had they attacked us at that point. Between the malnutrition, disease, and lack of military supplies – we did not deserve to be called an army.

It was morning, before yet another critical meeting. All, yes all, of the royal governors from His Majesty King George's American colonies were present. These were important men. Essential in their own eyes, in the king's eyes, and in the eyes of their colonies. They were powerful. They were rich. They were, for the most part, used to getting what they wanted with the right amount of pressure and diplomacy. Some were arrogant.

And each of these significant men were summoned to Alexandria like he was a liveried house slave called upon to clean a mess. They were given no options, no choice, no possibility to send someone else in their stead. There was no acceptable excuse for absence. The governors had been called with a minimum amount of notice to make it to the meeting on time – two weeks. As such, those who had to travel the greatest distance – Governor Shirley from Massachusetts and Governor Reynolds from Georgia – must have had to jump into their coaches within a day of receiving the summons.

And if these royally appointed men felt like they were to be treated as subordinates, that is because they *were* to be treated as such. They were viewed as such. They were beneath the man who called them. He could order any royal governor, any independent legislature, about as he saw fit. And he meant to exercise his authority.

Just thinking about the arrival of this new interloper from London sent me into a quiet fury. I placed my pen onto the paper to begin writing to Bess. This was to be my first letter in which I'd assault her lack of action personally. And in the mood that gripped me at the moment, the tone was likely to be exacting and cold. Piercing. If my previous missives had not driven her away completely, this one would do the trick.

I didn't want to be rid of Bess. However, she did need to know the pain I felt. And, at nineteen, I was willing to inflict the figurative knife upon her myself. I had lost one wife to war. It seems I would lose another before I even had her, to spite. Oh, well.

"Firecrackers, lad!" shouted Croghan. Without knocking, he had burst into my room, which was upstairs in a shady Alexandria tavern. "I thought I'd find you here putting pen to paper. You spill more ink than ol' Jonny Swift when he scratched out Gulliver!"

"It's a letter to Bess," I said, turning on my stool.

"Confound it! Of course, it's a letter to Bess. You'd hardly be able to write a lick if you didn't write to that lady. What makes you think you have anything in common with a well-to-do lass from Williamsburg, Virginia. You are a farm boy from Pennsylvania who lives to be out in the wilderness. Find yourself an Indian bride. I found mine many a year ago. And look how happy we are."

"I had Tahki," I said quietly. We'd been happy.

"Boy," Croghan said, easing his tone as he shuffled in. "Fine girl, she was. Lovely. Hard worker. Loved her father, too, I did. God rest his soul, ol' Memeskia, Old Briton. But they've been gone for three years now. You've mourned. And there's honor in that. But it's time to move on."

My focus returned to the page where I'd written a few harsh lines. I started where I'd left off. "I thought I had moved on. Maybe I have. Bess was, *is* to be my wife."

Croghan's presence loomed over my shoulder. His shadow fell on the page.

He reached around me and crumpled up my letter. I swiped at him, but missed. "I don't think the girl is right for ya. But I don't think you want to be known for talking to anyone of the fairer sex in such an angry manner."

"Give it back, George," I ordered.

Croghan stuffed it in his pocket. "No time."

I glanced outside. The sun was just cresting over the Potomac onto the buildings of Alexandria, sending their long shadows out toward the dominion of Lord Fairfax. "It's early. We have plenty of time."

"Uh-uh," Croghan said, gathering my things for me. I still had not replaced my vest and shirt that had the bullet holes. I had no money to do so. Yet, the rips and burns had been mended, somewhat. "We need to go. Money will be flowing. It always is to those with a nose. Hurry." He held up my shirt and studied it. "You need to invest in a new wardrobe, lad. You didn't dress this shabbily when you and I were out trading at the Forks of Ohio."

"Put it down, you old Irishman," I said.

He slung the shirt at my face. "Put it on, you stubborn German. We've been summoned."

"I know. That's why we're all here." I put the shirt on.

"No, you lovelorn puppy. We, all of us have been ordered to attend a meeting *right now*. The general is here and waiting is not his strong suit."

I rolled my eyes. "Don't tell me that Governor Dinwiddie has elevated Colonel Washington to a general now."

"I won't, because he didn't. *The* general is here. The one sent from the king to take charge of the defense of *all* the colonies."

"I know *that* general is here. He's here because the colonial legislatures all failed to pass Franklin's Plan of Union. Mother England doesn't think we care to defend ourselves. But his meeting isn't scheduled to begin until after the noon hour."

"Well, *that* general has decided to set his schedule to his liking, not yours, mine, or any subservient royal governor. The meeting won't be a meeting. It sounds more like we are going to a briefing where he'll dictate expectations to us. It starts in minutes."

I glanced at the letter bulging from his pocket. Croghan patted it. "With or without the summons, you'll not get this piece of poppycock back."

"Not yet, anyway," I grumbled as I finished dressing. I slid into my shoes. "Oh, I never asked you. How did you escape from *Maude's Cellar* unharmed by Alex Braun? Taeheek and I have a bet."

"What's the wager?" he asked, immediately thinking of the business aspect of the bet.

"One shilling, three pence," I said. "The longer we talk about it, the higher the bet goes."

George eyed my ragged wardrobe. "Do you even have that much to your name?"

"No," I admitted, cinching my belt.

"Then let the wager get up to at least a full guinea. I'll whisper to you my secret and we'll split the money."

"You're a turd, George," I muttered.

Croghan smiled. "Ah, but a fresh Irish turd, as clean as a crisp whistle." He donned his hat and flung the door open. "I'll take that as an agreement. Now then, let's go meet this General Braddock."

And the name Braddock would go down in history, ever ringing on the lips of Americans. He wasn't mentioned in hymns or songs of praise. No, he would be cursed in the most somber of dirges, fit for the funeral procession he was to lead.

CHAPTER SEVENTEEN

In February, Braddock had arrived in Williamsburg to confer with Dinwiddie about the events of the Battles of Jumonville Glen and Fort Necessity. By the time of the Alexandria meeting he'd been in America for about four months and had traveled to several of the other leading cities. Rumors soon spread that he had been less than pleased with the reception and cooperation he had received on his visits. Royal governors, serving at the behest of the king, were expected to be firmly in his camp. The colonial legislatures, in his mind serving the governors, were meant to quickly fall in line. He bristled when reality proved otherwise. Therefore, rather than cater to intractable provincials, he gave up the tour and settled in Alexandria, waiting for us to come to him.

A major in the king's regular army, specifically the 44th Regiment of Foot, stood in the center of the packed room by the time Croghan and I arrived. His red coat was rich. The yellow of his out-turned cuffs and lapels shone in the morning light streaming through the windows. Low at his waist, he wore a sword with a handsome hilt.

"Governors and guests," he began with audible disdain for those he addressed. "By the grace of God, His Majesty George II King of Great Britain and Ireland, Defender of the Faith, Arch Treasurer and Prince-Elector of the Holy Roman Empire, and Duke of Brunswick-Luneburg has heard your distress of these past months. He wishes for nothing but the prosperity and safety of his citizens. Therefore, our great king has dispatched a most able, most loyal servant of the crown to remedy the situation and set it again on a right course. This leader, from the moment of receiving his commission until he himself deems the job complete and reports thus to the king, shall serve as your commander-in-chief over *all* matters. I am certain you will find him up to the task of subduing every manner of insurrection on this continent." The way the major said the last, it was clear he viewed the American leadership gathered around him as a part of the problem. "I give you Major General Edward Braddock, most recently of the Coldstream Regiment of Foot Guards." He bowed and backed away from his place, joining a line of like-uniformed soldiers at the side.

Standing at the rear as we were, I could not lay eyes on the general. But I did hear the legs of a chair scrape slowly and then the methodical, confident clack of boots walking across the planked wood floor of the quiet room. Then I watched a diminutive soldier turn into view between the shoulders of two men in front of us. The general, perhaps sixty years of age, fixed his audience with a stern, silent glare.

One of the men immediately in front of me craned back and whispered, "Prepare to hear what a general from our beloved Mother Country has to say, Mr. Weber. How he'll take command. How he'll inspire us. How he'll turn our colonial troops into fit soldiers. How he'll deploy us to maximum effect. How he'll devise an undefeatable strategy."

It was Colonel Washington. And he wasn't whispering. I'd been told he was a sickly young man, with plenty of pneumonia and pleurisy to go around. His maladies had left his voice forever hollow chested. It was a struggle for him to shout with any volume at all.

Surprised that I hadn't noticed the tall, athletic form right in front of me, I said only, "Yes, sir, Colonel Washington, sir." He was in his mid-twenties and commanded nothing but the utmost respect simply by his graceful demeanor.

"It shall be an *honor* for us to serve him," Washington said enthusiastically, returning to face the front of the room after giving Croghan a polite acknowledgement. And honor, for the colonel, was more highly prized than anything this world had to offer.

"Yes, sir," I said to the colonel's back, at the top of which rested a shock of his long reddish brown hair, which had been pulled back in the accepted military form.

"I am most displeased," General Braddock began. His Scotsman's attitude came out naked for all to hear in a thick, rolling brogue. Braddock's heavily powdered wig sat atop his gray hair like a new fallen snow alighting upon a gnarled mountain. His chin was not double, but certainly one and a half. Despite his Lilliputian stature, the general's shoulders showed that he had seen physical labors in his day. He appeared physically fit for duty – at least as much one of his age and proportions could possibly look.

He crossed his arms in front of his chest and the little man slowly paced, not saying another word as if he was allowing his anger to sink into the heads and hearts of his little children. I would say he play-acted out a scene for maximum effect. But from what I could see, his heated anger was real, vitriolic. It was all the general could do to contain and channel it into anything other than wrath fully unleashed.

"Savages have shed blood," he went on. "The French have taken land from our king and sowed dishonor over your *colonial* soldiers." He said the word colonial as if referring to a sickening plague. "Your good king sends me here, to these desolate shores in order to usher in the return of civilization." With a derisive wave of a hand he indicated in the general direction of a window. "Well, as much civilization as is possible in such a landscape."

"The Exchequer, which is funded by the hardscrabble, taxpaying citizens of England, Scotland, Wales, and Ireland, has sent a chest of hard coins to fund this operation. And then I arrive and find nothing but a gaggle of hens, clucking o'er a broken egg, wondering which of you might gobble the yolk. None of you governors has been able to convince your stingy legislatures to appropriate even one farthing to our cause. Nothing!" His voice raced into a shrill shout at the end, which he immediately cut off. He breathed, gathering his calm.

"Furthermore, I find that merchants from every major or minor port, alleyway, and town are illegally trading with the French pigs at Louisbourg and Montreal. Smuggling to the enemy! Feeding Louis' soldiers with bacon, stocking his ammunition." Braddock's anger was again creeping, ready to get the better of him. Before it did so, the general paused, resuming his silent pacing, while still chastising us as surely as if he did so with words.

A hand tapped my shoulder. Turning, I saw William Johnson, Chief Hendrick's old friend, who had just arrived. "Sounds like I've missed some cannon fire," he whispered. "Glad I'm not the fodder."

"Father's scolding his lads," Croghan said out of the corner of his mouth. Still Braddock paced, his ears turning from pale, to red, to pink, and back to pale again as he relaxed his stirring emotions. Then Croghan added, "I hope he does more than rebuke these peacocks today. Campaigning season is near upon us. Or else, I've wasted a good many months cozying up to Governor Shirley for military contracts that may never be necessary."

"You can take it out of Tim's hide," I muttered.

"But he's out earning me profits. And you're close by," Croghan quipped. "I'll take it out on you."

Braddock resumed his dress down. "In short, the lot of you have been insubordinate in the most grievous of manners at the most heinous of times. You bicker like siblings with one another. Even within your own legislatures, you harangue to no end. Against the purposes of the king!" He bit his lip in frustration.

"Ephraim," Johnson said during yet another moment of silence. I felt a poke in my ribs. Looking down, I saw that he held a sealed letter. "A messenger was calling for you outside. I took this in your stead."

"Thank you," I said, plucking the folded pages from his grip.

"See there?" Croghan said. "All this *woe-is-me* business for nothing. Oh, you're lucky I wouldn't let you send that letter. At last, your little Bess has answered your forlorn cries."

I turned the letter over and saw that it was addressed to me in care of the Alexandria postal service. I realized I had never seen Bess' handwriting before. The script was polished, but not overly ornate or ostentatious.

"Best tuck it away for a later reading, lad," Croghan advised. "You've waited this long. Might as well not spoil the moment by mixing it with a boiling Scot." I took a lingering, longing look at the sealed letter and tucked into a pocket of my waistcoat.

"No matter!" the general said. "I care not to list your faults any longer. For the fault lies with me, your commander-in-chief. I mistakenly thought that I would treat you all as equal subjects of the crown during these dark days. No longer will I repeat this error. You will take my orders and faithfully execute them to the satisfaction of your king. There can be no discussion. I'll not debase myself."

The faces of the governors and other leading figures around the room could not have been more plain as to what they thought of Braddock's speech. A more dour bunch had never been seen.

"Governors, you will inform your legislatures of their share of expenses." He pointed to the officer who had introduced him. "The major has copies of all the figures for each of you. They are not up for debate or negotiation. Have I made myself clear to you?"

With as much confidence as he could muster after such a verbal beating, Governor Morris of my home country of Pennsylvania asked, "The amounts, General Braddock, come from the king and Exchequer?"

Braddock fixed Morris with a frustrated glare, his green eyes turning a fiery shade of orange. "The figures are the result of *my* calculations as to the cost of the coming campaigns where we will wipe France off the map of America. As I am here at the king's pleasure, placed in this position by his hand, *yes*, the amounts are from him." He stamped the floor like a steed.

A few unhappy mumblings rolled around the crowd. I had not dealt directly with any of the elected bodies of men that passed laws for the colonies. But I knew that none of them, as individuals and as groups, appreciated having terms of any sort dictated to them. It violated all that their self-governing sovereignty allowed, going all the way back to the Pilgrims. These governors, royal or not, would find the task they'd just been handed exceedingly difficult.

"Am I clear?" Braddock spat. A wad of spittle literally leapt from his lips. "Do you understand?"

"Perfectly, sir." This was Dinwiddie from Virginia. He was another Scot, though much more plush and rotund than Braddock. Hearing another version of his native brogue set the general at ease.

"Thank you, governor," Braddock said, tipping his head politely. One-by-one he then fixed his eyes on the governors to convey just how critical he deemed their compliance. "And thank you for your time, gentlemen. You may return to your posts and await further instructions."

He referred to their *posts* in the full military sense of the word.

"Excuse me, General Braddock, sir," came a soft whisper from the crowd as the general moved away.

Braddock stopped and cocked his head, not sure if he heard someone speak. Was the building settling?

"General Braddock, will you take questions about the coming military campaign? There is abundant activity of late. And as much as it is beneath your station to quell rumors, there has also been ample speculation as to the aim of the thrust."

Braddock returned to the center of the hall and looked through the crowd for his petitioner. "And you are?"

"Lieutenant Colonel George Washington of the Virginia militia, sir," said Washington, stepping from his spot near the rear to one in the front.

"Ah, the famous journal," Braddock said. "I've read this, you see. The frigid wilderness. The hostile Indians. The perilous rivers. I've read the accounts. The battles – one successful, one…" His voice faded off. It was clear that regardless of Washington's worldwide fame, Braddock viewed him as just another colonial trooper with less sense than a jack rabbit. "What exactly is your question, colonel?"

"Sir," Washington began. "There is talk about an expedition in the north led by the honorable Governor Shirley. But I have heard fairly specific rumors of perhaps a few more. As I and my militia will be honored to take part in anything transpiring in our fair country, would you be so kind as to remove confusion."

Braddock nodded slowly. "I see," he muttered. "First, Colonel Washington, I appreciate the directness of your question. Less so, however, do I appreciate the quiet level at which you deliver it, forcing me to heed each of your words as if my life depended upon it."

Washington's jaw clenched in anger. I had seen his temper once or twice. He had one, no matter what people say today. He was a jealous, sometimes exceedingly proud man. But the colonel had learned this fact about himself at a young age. He constantly struggled to master his passions. And more times than not, Washington succeeded.

"I'll be plain in my answer as is clearly required by you men from America." Braddock again paced the room slowly, his boots clipping smartly with each step. "As we speak, Admiral Boscawen is leading a blockade of the Gulf of St. Lawrence. He will starve the enemy of provisions."

"And the land, sir?" Washington asked.

"Patience," Braddock answered. "For the list is long and complete. First, I have approved of Governor Shirley's plan. He will personally command regulars, the 50th and 51st regiments. They will leave from Albany and take Fort Niagara at the head of Lake Ontario."

Croghan gave me a wink. "Looks like my time wooing the governor was not wasted. Young Taeheek deserves a raise."

The governors standing beside Shirley patted his back for receiving the great honor.

"Second," continued the general. "William Johnson will lead an expedition of Mohawk warriors and provincial men drawn from New England and New York. I have much sympathy for him as he in charge of such inferior soldiers. If they could be called even that. Based upon his reputation, I have further named Mr. Johnson as the crown's sole Superintendent of Indian Affairs. No longer will your individual colonies be permitted to wrangle with the savages and one another. He is your sole contact."

This brought grumbles from the crowd. No one liked having his authority usurped.

"Did you know this?" Croghan asked Johnson.

"Found out same as you," Johnson said. "Care to be my lieutenant? I'll need someone who has connections to the tribes to the south of New York."

"I'll get back to you," Croghan answered with all of the caginess I would expect of the expert trader.

"And the objective of Mr. Johnson's expedition?" Washington asked.

"I thought I told you to speak up, man," Braddock chided, before moving into his answer. "I have little hope of its actual success, but we must occupy the heathens in the north as accomplices so they do not descend upon us as enemies. But I do not worry. This campaign is secondary to our overall strategy. They will march to Lake Champlain and seize Fort St. Frederic at Crown Point."

"Another chance for contracts," I whispered to Croghan.

"Ah, the governors will all be tripping over one another to set their own high prices to supply the Mohawk's. Kickbacks, you see. I'll leave that one to Johnson to figure out."

"Thanks, George," Mr. Johnson whispered.

"And a third land expedition is already approved as well. Using provincial soldiers, it will leave Boston to eradicate two French forts in Nova Scotia. Again, this is of an ancillary nature, hence the inferior troops. Details will be sent to its commander. It doesn't concern any of you men here. Satisfied, Colonel Washington?" he asked, quite sarcastically and expecting no answer.

"Well, actually no, sir," came the breathy reply. It was Braddock's turn to clench his jaw. The flesh of his face flared red. But the colonel was undeterred. "You've listed one sea campaign and three land attacks. Two of the land assaults you acknowledge to be supplemental. The third, the attack on Fort Niagara is important to be sure, but it does nothing to relieve the most immediate attack and threat upon English civilians and the king's lands. What about Fort Duquesne at the Forks of Ohio?"

Braddock considered the upstart colonel for a full minute. In that time, his countenance shifted from extreme displeasure to one of minor admiration. The general glanced at his faithful major at the side and asked, "Shall I tell the precocious colonel?" he asked with a smile.

"Your prerogative, sir," the major answered, stone-faced.

"Yes," Braddock mused. He more firmly fixed a genuine grin on his face. It was narrow, but demonstrated true pleasure. "You have perceived a great flaw in the plans I've laid out for you, Colonel Washington. Better than these *royal* governors, I'll say. But I haven't told you everything. The attack on Fort Duquesne I leave to the best and brightest of His Majesties men, the fighting foot of the 44th and 48th. And by way of Wills Creek, the track you took I'm told, I will lead them to destroy all that King Louis, in his impudence, has built." The general glanced at the clock in the corner and added, "So by Christmas the French in Quebec will be starving due to the naval blockade. Their main supply point at Niagara to the west will be vacant. And I will have lopped off Louis' grasping fingers at the Forks of Ohio. And we will again have peace."

In fact, applause broke out quite spontaneously among the men who had spent the better part of the meeting murdering the general with daggers sent by their eyes. Now these men cheered. For nothing could unite disparate Englishmen like the prospect of drowning the French in their own blood.

And Braddock basked in the glow.

CHAPTER EIGHTEEN

The general disappeared immediately following his Alexandria oration, allowing no chance for any further rebuttal or questions. After passing out the itemized listing of funds required from the colonies, his brilliantly coated officers vanished likewise. The governors were left to their own devices. Most strolled out of Alexandria's humble hall in spirited negotiations over who would supply what to which of the four armies in question. Forgotten were the long list of affronts by the blunt general. Guineas glittered in the men's eyes. Victory percolated in their souls.

Washington, Johnson, Croghan, and I formed a small cadre as we filed out onto the street. I was, by far, the most shabbily dressed among them.

"Too ambitious!" Croghan lilted.

I glanced around, looking for a reasonable opportunity to disappear myself and read Bess' letter. It was burning a hole in the pocket of my waistcoat. I reached a finger in just to feel the paper. To think that a week earlier, Bess' hand had grazed the page.

"I agree," Johnson said. "It's not necessarily the number of campaigns that is the problem."

"Says an Irishman who's never had to supply a single army before!" Croghan interrupted. "You wait until these colonies and their merchants and farmers try to start provisioning those ravenous marchers! If the boys in red don't go hungry, plenty of townsfolk will."

"That's not what I meant, George," Johnson said in defense. "I mean that from a military standpoint, these campaigns sound more like they were decided upon across an ocean over a map in some room at Westminster."

"Because they likely were," Washington breathed. He had taken the lead, striding with his long legs and driving us toward an unknown end. Like soldiers under his command, we unquestioningly followed. "I happen to know that General Braddock consulted no one of a local nature as to the rigors of any of the coming campaigns. He's issued orders without seeking any advice." He peered at me through the corner of his eye. "And if you are about finished gallivanting along the seaboard towns in search of amusement, Mr. Weber, we will return to the army post haste."

I stopped feeling Bess' letter with my finger and dropped my hand from the pocket. You know that I was not entertaining myself those many months. Bess was the only reason I cared to spend five minutes in any of the towns in the east. Otherwise, I'd rather brave the elements out west. No, during my time of exile from the tree canopy, I had performed whatever chores Washington had directed. The colonel knew the truth of the matter, too. But such was the life of a young man without rank or privilege. I was the butt of every joke.

"You sound fairly relaxed in the face of a potential strategic blunder, Colonel Washington," Johnson observed. "I imagine that your Virginia militia will be called upon to support the general's regular regiments."

The colonel nodded. "They will. But I hope to leave the command to another."

Croghan stopped. Had it been I who said something so surprising, he would have jerked at the tail of my coat. Washington was spared such an attack. "But you were made for soldiering!" Then he crinkled his nose while fixing me with an accusing stare. "And you stole one of my best workers! Who will Weber follow if not you?"

"Fear not, Mr. Croghan," Washington whispered as he pivoted on his heels. "Mr. Weber will continue to follow me."

"Colonel," I began, thinking that perhaps at least some of my problems with Bess had just been solved. "If you don't intend to ride west with the army, I'd prefer to leave the employ of Virginia altogether. I had meant to follow you, but I don't think plantation or town life is for me."

One of Washington's faint grins set in just one corner of his mouth. Despite his military air, the colonel was not without mirth. He was toying with me. "Nor are they for me at the moment. I assure you, Mr. Weber, that come this evening we will ride west out to where the army gathers for the expedition to the Forks of Ohio."

"Surely you don't go in some support capacity," Croghan said. "A man of your experience and stature cannot simply walk away from a military life."

"I do not walk away, sir," Washington answered. He resumed his course. We toddled after. "But I do hope to go in support. In anticipation of the general's blunder, I have sent a letter to Governor Dinwiddie, requesting a temporary release from his service. Simultaneously, I penned a letter to General Braddock. He may be reading it even now. In it I've asked to serve on his staff as a volunteer, for no pay. When the requests are granted, as I am certain they will be, you, Mr. Weber, will accompany me in the general's direct service. You will be an aide to an aide."

"For no pay?" I asked, knowing the answer.

The colonel again glanced at me. "I am able to personally loan you a small amount to better provision yourself if that will help. Your clothes, for instance. Your old Brown Bess that I will pretend you did not come by illegally."

"It's legal enough!" It wasn't. George had bought the parts from a source who smuggled them from the Tower Armory in London. "And I don't need your charity," I snapped.

With eyebrows raised, he peeked down at me.

"No thank you, sir," I said, clearing my throat. Washington could convey his extreme disappointment with a simple stare from his pale gray-blue eyes. But he could also do so by more agitated means if forced by the situation. I'd leave it to others to spur his wrath.

"Very well," Washington said, cheerily for him.

"So, if you expect to ride next to Braddock at the head of his army, won't you suffer from his strategic missteps as much as any?" Johnson asked. "Won't my expedition suffer likewise?"

Washington confidently shook his head. He was young. If young Virginian gentlemen had anything, they had confidence. It was a singular shared trait. Well, that and owning slaves and wallowing in debt, among others. "No, sir, Mr. Johnson. Your Mohawks and colonial troops will have you. I expect no suffering. You are an expert in the affairs of our Indian neighbors. You have lived among them and on the northern frontier for many years. They will benefit from your insight and experience."

Johnson smiled at the younger man, who thought it appropriate to lecture his elder. "I see," he mused. "And Braddock, who knows nothing of the distances involved on a continent such as ours, of the hazards, unfordable creeks, and on and on, will have *you* with him."

Washington had a twinkle in his eye. It was pleasant to see. He'd been exceptionally melancholy following the horrors of Fort Necessity. "As a volunteer, I will have only to listen to General Braddock, but everyone else will have to listen to me. And he will have Mr. Weber. We have both traveled to the Forks multiple times. I will advise General Braddock on the terrain, the local customs of the indigenous peoples, the route to take, which creeks to ford, which brooks to bridge. In exchange, I will receive an invaluable lesson on command and on military campaign from a master. And, as a result of the successful outcome and my part in it, I hope to receive a commission in His Majesty's regular army, which is something exceedingly difficult for a colonial."

"They look at us like we are barnacles," Croghan agreed.

"But what will *I* get out of it?" I asked. I knew that the most likely consequence of my tempting fate once again and riding to the Forks with an army was to be my own death.

"Pride and honor for serving your king," Washington said, not in the least bit in jest. "And I shall receive the same."

Johnson stopped in the street. Likewise, we padded to a halt next to him. Washington did so only after taking three more broad steps. Mr. Johnson then mused, "The expeditions to Niagara and Fort Duquesne are key. Mine and the attack on Nova Scotia are less important."

"But that Nova Scotia one sounds ripe for supply," Croghan said. "Those boys will need supplies enough to keep them alive on ships until they disembark. And if they mean to march, which is a crazy idea, they'll need all the more."

"Leave the business back east to somebody else this time, George," Johnson suggested. "You were at Necessity. You know what a trial it was. You don't want that to happen again."

Croghan felt his patriotism was being tested. "Of course not," he stammered. "What does that have to do with me?"

"I asked you earlier if you would like to serve as my lieutenant of Indian relations," Johnson explained. "You're a natural choice. You've got the connections. Now, the more we talk about the coming fight, the more important that becomes. Braddock has no understanding of the tribes. Perhaps he's seen one Indian in a sketch in his entire life. You and your relationships with the tribes out west will be paramount. Your trading extends all the way into the Ohio Valley."

"Beyond!" Croghan corrected, mildly perturbed. "I've traded away in the pays d'en haut!"

"Exactly," Johnson said. "I'm not asking. I'm telling you. You'll be my lieutenant. I can make it an official order by asking Braddock to command it," he warned.

Croghan's face soured. "I don't need any more heat from that Scotsman. You win. I'll be your lieutenant."

Johnson fixed him with a handsome smile. "Thank you, George. Your king thanks you."

"Now you speak for an English king," Croghan rasped. "What is Ireland coming to?"

"We are all Englishmen," Washington reminded him.

"Yes, yes. What am I to do?" Croghan asked Johnson.

The Indian Superintendent assumed his commanding role. "George, you ride with Colonel Washington and Ephraim. Stay close to the general. Send wampum belts ahead of the column. Call conferences along the march. Kindle a hundred council fires if you must. Perhaps by the time you reach Fort Duquesne, you will have doubled the size of your army with the Delaware and the Shawnee on your side."

Croghan scoffed. "I'll do it. And I can gather up the remnants of the Iroquois Half King's old followers. They still respect me. But, otherwise, the chances don't look good. That bastard Lydius from your home country of New York has set the frontier on edge. Shingas, the Delaware king, won't be in a peaceful mood."

"I know," Johnson said, his mind turning. He was bright. His eyes showed an innate intelligence. "That is why I'm running back to the north. I'll stoke the council fires among the Iroquois for my own expedition to Champlain. But first I'll ask Chief Hendrick to come to your aid. I have a great enough relationship with the other Mohawk chiefs to afford to go without Hendrick's mighty influence."

"The chief is a good man," I said for Washington's benefit. "I was there when he negotiated with Weiser. That was a fair deal."

"It was," Johnson said in agreement. "Hendrick has reaffirmed our alliance with the Iroquois. He is the only one who can hope to persuade the subordinate tribes in his flock to join in the Covenant Chain."

Washington was not pleased. His experience with the so-called Iroquois control over the minor tribes was still fresh. All that had gone wrong with our own march westward the previous year in order to retake Duquesne had been the result of a conniving Iroquois Half King. Well, some of the blame could be laid at my feet and my lust for revenge upon my wife's killer. But that is another part of another story.

"So, I'll need to be wary of General Braddock's strategy, Mr. Weber's friendships with Indians, and a Mohawk chief?" the colonel asked. "I run a nursery?"

Johnson shook his head. "I have known Hendrick for twenty years. He is rock solid."

Washington didn't try to hide his incredulity. He glanced at Croghan. "And how long were you friends with our dear departed Chief Tanaghrisson, the Half King?"

Croghan might have studied his shoes in shame if he were another man. "Longer!" he exclaimed. "The damn fool was to be trusted in everything. Until the end, that is! It was like a fever came over him."

Washington fixed Johnson with a firm stare. "Well, then, it sounds like Chief Hendrick will need to be monitored as much as the general and Mr. Weber."

I didn't enjoy being lobbed in with a traitor and an arrogant British general. But none of my fellow plotters would care a lick to hear a protest from me. I was sorely out of place. I always felt out of place among men. That is one of the reasons I longed for the great wilderness, mosquitoes and all. At least there would be fewer men looking over my shoulder, judging my actions, inactions.

"Perhaps, so," Johnson agreed, moving to hurry in the other direction. I suppose we had agreed upon plans and it was now only a matter of seeing them carried out. He paused. "But Hendrick and George remain your best hopes of at least quelling the current harsh feelings along both sides of the frontier. Even if they cannot become allies, at least the Delaware may not prove to be enemies."

"Shingas told me to my face at Great Meadows that he hoped to become allies of his English brothers," I said.

"Do not talk to me of King Shingas," Washington muttered. "I watched him lead his warriors in the killing of many of my men at Fort Necessity. And of the looting of our baggage train afterward."

"Good day, gentlemen," Johnson said, wishing to avoid a skirmish involving our personal histories. "I have a lot of work to do. Good luck." He raced away.

And with Braddock's overly ambitious plans, we would need plenty of luck.

"And Providence," Washington said aloud, as if he had heard my thoughts.

"And wampum will help," Croghan added, before the three of us dashed off to prepare for a drive westward. "Loads of wampum."

CHAPTER NINETEEN

It was not until that evening, by firelight on the road to Wills Creek that I was finally ready to dig out the letter from Bess. Washington and Croghan had settled into a small inn along the trail. I, of course, had no money for such luxuries and, therefore, squatted in the corner of a farmer's pasture. Croghan had offered to share his room with me, but I already owed his employee, Taeheek, money. Besides, I owed Croghan an unpayable debt for pulling me out of obscurity and hiring me when I was but a skinny runaway with nothing to show but potential. To be in a man's debt was to be in servitude. That was one rare point of view I had inherited from my father and still cherished. And I, like so many of my persecuted ancestors who had fled the Old World, desired freedom above all else.

The drizzling rain that had pestered the last hour of our day's journey paused sufficiently for me to finally pull out Bess' note. I relished the moment, leaning toward the sputtering fire in order to study the way she had written my name. I found her script to be bold. That made sense, as Bess, especially as a young woman of her era, was exceptionally daring. But I was surprised to divine a raw, untapped intellect hidden among the way she curved the *E* of my given name, the sharp way she formed the *W* of my family name. It is not that I had thought her senseless before this moment. It is merely that her God-given wits had not been a feature I had ever taken the time to notice. Her smile. Her chin. Her other womanly charms. Those I had seen. But also, her humor. Her impetuousness. Her way with flowering plants of all kinds.

But I could study the way Bess had written my name for only so long. I was quickly reminded that there was a serious matter at hand. Why had it taken many months for her to write? Especially, when it seemed so clear that I was to be her husband, she my wife.

I broke the utilitarian wax seal and unfolded the page.

My heart leapt with excitement when I noticed the date that it had been penned. The letter was weeks old! She *had* been writing to me. But somehow the letters had consistently been lost.

A feeling of relief swept over my body. That is, until I remembered that I had been steadily growing more irksome in the tone of my letters to her. Then suddenly, relief reigned once again. At least Croghan had forbidden me from sending the letter at the point I had been the most peeved.

I took a closer look at the page as the odd raindrop splatted from above. She'd written it from Philadelphia, which she'd abbreviated as Philad. I'd sent all of my post to Williamsburg. Perhaps none of my letters had gotten to her! All my worry and fretting for nothing. Had Bess been away from home with her father on extended business? Was Franklin's postal service vastly over-rated?

I could no longer take the anticipation and so leapt headlong into her correspondence.

My Dear Mr. Weber,

Your exertions of late were so very appreciated. The zeal with which you demonstrated your passions was surprising and endearing. I find myself musing about your methods to this day. I am saddened, however, that your efforts and mine and those of better men were so easily thwarted by the capricious actions of others. I fear these short-sighted men will be our bane for years to come, perhaps not coming home to roost for decades or more. But I remained heartened that there exist men of a younger generation who have not forgotten what our forefathers have sacrificed to build an industrious civilization in this once harsh land. Taming a wilderness and crafting a society require action. Taking a bullet for one's beliefs is a supreme example of such action – foolhardy, yes, but what a display! I only wish our Plan of Union had gathered the proper support as a result of your injuries. In part, I am losing hope. I am afraid that a Confederation of these English Colonies will never be possible unless Parliament imposes one. – And I hope they will!

Yours,
B. Franklin

I worked for the most respected soldier in America. Now, I had received a letter from the most-liked man in America.

But Bess had not written to me.

I wadded up Franklin's kind note, stuffing it into my pack. Then, I promptly pulled out my writing instruments. Awkwardly perched over the fire, and with my disposition as dreary as the weather, I wrote Bess one more letter.

Without Croghan on hand to temper my words, and if she ever read it, there can be no doubt it would be our last chance at correspondence.

CHAPTER TWENTY

A few days later our party found itself in Fredericktown, Maryland, a tiny crossroads that could barely contain the ego of General Braddock, let alone his large train of personal baggage, serving staff, retinue of officers, and, to my astonishment, his own personal train of whores. He had arrived some hours after us. And like us, he was on his way to Wills Creek. But because of his apparent and excessive needs, he was forced to travel at a slower pace.

Word of Braddock's arrival preceded him, however. Upon hearing the news, Washington became anxious to confirm his personal place on the general's staff. The colonel was not a hectic man by nature, he was actually quite subdued despite his boundless energy. But it was all Croghan and I could do to get Colonel Washington to sit still while we waited for the coming of the commander-in-chief. And even when we heard the great rumble of the train enter town, George and I held the eager colonel at bay to allow the general time to settle in.

But before long, the colonel's enthusiasm prevailed. He and I left Croghan behind at his favorite place of business, a tavern. There, in addition to nursing a glass of Madeira, Croghan prepared requests and assembled belts of wampum in order to smooth our way through the possibly hostile Indian country of the Alleghenies. He planned for our first council fire to be kindled at Wills Creek, calling on everyone in the tribes with whom he had a relationship. And, temporarily thwarted in his east coast military supply contracts due to his new role as lieutenant of Indian relations, Croghan had also sent back for Tim. Taeheek was currently his most reliable employee after I had left and was expected to catch the train in a week or two.

Meanwhile, I skipped along behind the colonel like a young lad following after his father. Though we were so very close in age, I was forever to be perceived by others and myself as many years his junior, and most often as his *inferior* in more measures than mere age. He was tall, straight, and carried himself gracefully. Every manner he exhibited had been self-taught and practiced until each had become second nature. I, on the other hand, was of average height and build. If any feature was remarkable in any way, it was my face. It was marred by several small scars left behind from the many battles and scraps I was accumulating in my thus-far short life. I often misspoke. Frequently, I appeared rude or crude, even when my intentions were the complete opposite.

"What a delight!" exclaimed Benjamin Franklin. He emerged from one of his post offices, just as Washington and I walked by on the street. "Ephraim Weber! My, do you get around. And so robust. Shot in the chest just months ago and now marching down the street next to a remarkable military figure! Ah, the bloom of youth!" He sucked a huge swath of air in through his nostrils as if youth was a scent to be enjoyed.

With surprising energy, he trotted down the steps and took the hand I gladly offered, shaking it vigorously.

"Shot in the chest?" Washington asked warily. "Please tell me that is some new patter being employed in the north."

I had not told him about the near fatal ending of my speech. Such a tale would do nothing to improve my already fragile reputation in the colonel's eyes. He had been aware of the Plan of Union's success in Albany – and its ultimate failure in the legislatures – for months. However, my messages to him had said only that my account of our trials and my plea for union had caused a great uproar of backing in the Stadt Huys. This partial truth was accurate enough.

"There might have been an incident," I began, always afraid to disappoint the colonel. "But, you'll want to meet an acquaintance of mine. Colonel Washington, may I introduce Benjamin Franklin of Philadelphia."

The two men bowed with exacting politeness before Franklin offered his hand, which Washington took into his firm grasp. "Benjamin Franklin in the flesh," Washington breathed with a shake of his head. I could see that the usual staid colonel was struck in the presence of such celebrity. The young southern gentleman had spent his short lifetime hobnobbing with wealthy men. But even then, Franklin was in a league all by himself.

"Lieutenant Colonel George Washington!" Franklin said, with nearly as much wonder. "I have been told I was ambitious as a young man. But mark my words, you, sir, shall put me to shame."

The colonel blushed. And under the extra attention he stammered. "Ambition? Nay, sir. I, uh. It's my country. My Virginia I serve."

Franklin immediately noticed the young officer's awkwardness and changed the subject. "But to say that Mr. Weber and I are acquaintances is a gross understatement. If two men, bound to so valiant a cause as a union of these colonies, carry that burden on our hearts so profoundly, I dare say we are more than friends. We are brothers."

Washington fixed me with an incredulous glare. He was constantly surprised to learn that though I was among the simplest lads in the world, I somehow had a way of making friends with men at the highest levels of importance. It had been that way with the now-dead Half King. It's how I had connived my way into Croghan's employ. It was even how I had entered the colonel's inner circle of close collaborators. Despite my impetuous actions and my desire to flee from people altogether, I made friends. Washington would soon come to expect it.

"Yes, Mr. Franklin," answered the colonel. "We are all brothers in purpose when it comes to defending these colonies. Self interest in our home nations means we must be attentive to the defense of His Majesty's other countries."

"Another day, perhaps," Franklin allowed. "We won't soon get another chance after our failure at Albany. Now tell me. To where do you gentlemen stride with such purpose?"

"Major General Braddock has arrived in town," Washington said. "We have military business to address."

"Fortuitous!" Franklin said with a shake of his fist. I liked him. He was unlike any of the other rich men I had ever met. He was always optimistic. With cunning and compromise, everything was possible. "I have an appointment with the general myself. Perhaps right after yours."

Embarrassed, Washington suddenly fidgeted without moving. It is possible to do so. Just imagine someone perfectly postured, but anxiously twitching his muscles just below the loosest parts of his clothing. "We have no appointment, Mr. Franklin," he admitted.

"Join me on mine, then. Do you care to accompany me?"

"Of course, sir," Washington said. And we resumed our walk, three rather than two.

"What do you need to talk to General Braddock about?" I asked.

Franklin giggled to himself. "I'm not exactly sure yet."

"He summoned you?" I asked. "He has a habit of doing that to important men."

"So I've heard," Franklin said. "No. I've come to meet with him. I have an appointment."

"You made an appointment and don't know why?" I asked.

"Quit prying into another man's business, Mr. Weber," Washington chastised.

"Fair instruction to the lad, colonel. But it's alright," Franklin answered easily. "I know only that some of the general's feathers have been ruffled by his dealings in America. And nobody has more trouble flying right than a British general when his feathers are improperly fluffed. I've come to help smooth them back into place. But other than that, I'm not sure what I can offer."

And we continued on, traveling at a slightly slower pace as Franklin seemed happy to absorb as much of the visit with the young officer as he could. He peppered the colonel with questions about our adventures over the previous two years. Washington, not prone to long dissertations, would answer efficiently and respectfully. The colonel was slow to make friends and, therefore, I was shocked to see him laugh once or twice when Franklin rephrased a part of the tale in a more humorous way.

"You fell in a frigid river and this lad had to save you?" Franklin asked.

Washington was enjoying himself. After fixing me with a wily look that I had never before seen, he said, "If only it could have been someone else."

"I dare say that someone else might have let you drown!" Franklin laughed.

We joined him. Even though he was right. Most men, after having been led into the icy wilderness and nearly killed a few times, would not have been so eager to save the man responsible.

There was only one possible location for the general's temporary quarters. And that was at the largest personal residence in Fredericktown. It belonged to a miller who'd become wealthy by way of his three-story gristmill operations set somewhere along the Monocacy River. He packed cornmeal and refined flour, shipping his goods locally and throughout the world. His house was tall and easy to see, poking up through trees. Our assumption gained credibility when we saw military activity in the yard surrounding the home. It was readily confirmed when, upon approaching the front stoop, the general's angry brogue shook the windows on the ground level.

"All of them are thieves," he grumbled to a subordinate. "Every last one is a smuggler. These Americans are the most ungrateful batch of stag turds I've ever had the displeasure of laying eyes on! Their colonial colors ought to be currencies rather than flags. I mean to go out there and lash the lot of them. It might take a year, but I'll have every man from Boston to Charleston whipped."

"Yes, sir," said a patient officer, who was in the room with the general. "We are short scores of wagons for our army's march to Duquesne. Do you think we should leave behind some of your, I mean, *our* personal baggage to make room?"

"Shall I knock?" I asked my two companions on the front step.

"Shh," Washington and Franklin said in unison. Long before I had ever considered the concepts, each man was familiar with the art of reconnaissance and intelligence gathering before an important meeting or battle.

"I'll not adjust *my* needs! And don't remind me!" Braddock continued on. "It's an ominous beginning when the governors and legislatures must be beaten like unruly children *and* my quartermaster fails to gather adequate transportation! Sir John is as good for nothing as these backwoods colonials. A few months in country and he's as traitorous as the rest."

Washington and Franklin raised their eyebrows while sharing a knowing glance. It wasn't the first and wouldn't be the last time that they'd hear about the inferiority of Americans from men raised in Britain or on the continent of Europe.

"I've heard enough. I know what I must do to smooth out the peacock. You may knock now, Ephraim," Franklin said.

Washington nodded his approval. "And my purpose will help."

I rapped loudly.

"See who is here to bother me!" Braddock ordered.

"It is likely your meeting with Franklin, sir," said his officer.

"Who?" the general asked.

"His Majesty's Deputy Postmaster General."

"Oh, fine," Braddock sighed. "I suppose he wants something from me. Everyone else on this side of the ocean seems to need something. It's not enough that I will destroy the savages and their French and Canadian enemies. Hell! Bring him in."

A moment later we were led into the miller's finely appointed office, which he'd vacated to the general. Braddock was seated behind a desk that was piled with maps, letters, supply lists, and bills. In short, it was just a fraction of the correspondence that would be created during his campaign. Braddock rose from his place and gestured to chairs. "Tis an honor to meet you, Mr. Franklin. Sit. And, you," he said to Washington. "The Virginia colonel from Fort Necessity."

"Washington, sir."

"Sit, please," Braddock said pleasantly enough. They, and the general, did so. I was ignored by all, left standing behind the colonel, next to the general's assistant.

"I'm afraid I stand at the precipice of the most extensive military operation ever conducted on North American soil," Braddock boasted. "You must appreciate that I am burdened with planning this and coordinating with the other campaigns. And so, the efficiency of a widow's mail in Philadelphia is not my chief concern at the moment. But, if there is anything I can do to assist you, I will. But let us get down to the foundation of the matter, shall we?" He stamped his foot below the desk to emphasize his point. The unlit candles on the desk jiggled.

"Yes, general," Franklin said, a friendly smile perched on his face. "It is the time of year when locating a wagon is terrifically difficult in these parts. I'm afraid I have taken it upon myself to fall into my old printer's ways. You see, I've had broadsides drawn up in your name, sir. None have been distributed because I await your permission, of course. They call for the delivery of 150 wagons, teams, packhorses, and teamsters. On the pages, I've offered generous terms to those willing to participate. This is, I'm sure, something you would do in any case. However, if an inadequate number of carts descends upon your army to assist with your successful recovery of our king's territories, I'm afraid I've taken some poetic license. You see, I've threatened that your quartermaster would come to Pennsylvania and seize whatever he needs by force." He winked at the general. "I plan to post the broadsides in townhalls, taverns, and even on trees." Franklin, an expert in every possible art, especially persuasion, paused and studied the general. "But if you do not need the publicity, or if I've misstated your will, I'll have them destroyed."

Braddock and his officer exchanged a surprised glance. "No," the general said, feigning deep reflection. "It will be good to have excess capacity for hauling. We might be able to put a few more wagons and teamsters to good use."

"And the expense is already taken care of," Franklin added.

I thought Braddock was going to fall over backward. He was stunned. "Pardon me, sir. Did you say there was no cost to the army for the printing service you offer?"

Franklin gestured to the heaps of papers and parchments stacked on the desk. "It is clear you have enough to worry about, general. It is just one small way that I and the other members of the Pennsylvania General Assembly hope to send you into the wilderness knowing you have our deepest gratitude and respect."

Braddock smiled broadly. "I know it now, sir. Is there anything I can do for you, at all?"

"There is one thing, general," Franklin said, almost sheepishly.

Braddock's genuine smile faded. He waved his hand as if to say, *here comes the real request – and it will be costly.*

"You will soon be traveling in areas that have scarcely seen contact from any human, let alone Englishmen," Franklin said. "I'd like to ensure your messages and dispatches are efficiently carried through my postal service so that you are not burdened with their management. To whom shall I speak about coordinating?"

Franklin had again surprised the general. "I. Well, sir." Braddock smacked the desk cheerfully. One of the candles tipped off the edge. The stick broke when it struck the floor. "The major here can arrange that with you. Thank you, Mr. Franklin. Thank you. Are you sure there is nothing I can do for you today?"

"Not today, general, but you may do something for me in the coming months," Franklin answered. "Achieve victory so that my country may once again be at peace."

"Certainly," the general said. "It will be my honor. I'll take the Frogs by the throat and smash their bellies with my heel."

"Very good. But I realize that I've fibbed to you, sir," Franklin said, feigning self-disappointment. "I do have a request for you today. Would you hear from Colonel Washington on some important military business? That is all I ask."

Braddock leaned back in his chair, relaxed. He fixed his steely eyes on the colonel, who would not melt under such scrutiny. Washington's mother was the first general he'd ever known. Braddock said, "I thought I heard more than enough on military matters from this man at our conference in Alexandria. But this morning my assistant told me that I received a request of some nature from you, colonel." He pointed to the cluttered desk. "I have yet to sift through the mess in order to deal with it. There are a hundred Virginia officers writing to me to ask for royal commissions. I hope that is not what you wish me to address."

That is exactly what Washington's end goal was. He wanted the respect that came with serving King George II directly in the army. But the colonel was quickly developing his political savvy.

"No, General Braddock," Washington claimed. "I have now found myself in the vicinity of Fort Duquesne twice. I dare say I have traveled there more frequently than most any man."

He hadn't. I had been through the area at least a dozen times. But I was not an officer. I was a runaway. Croghan, too, had been there countless times. But he was a lowly Indian trader.

Washington continued. "I wish to volunteer my time and my experience to serve at your side as an aide-de-camp. The only payment I require shall not cost our king one farthing. I hope to witness how a commander with your reputation goes about securing victory."

Braddock laughed merrily. It was a deep laugh for one so small.

Washington frowned, his ego instantly bruised.

"Where have you gentlemen been these past months?" Braddock went on laughing. "Franklin and Washington! Who's ever heard of you? Had I met you before now, I would not have been forced to describe the king's American subjects in such harsh terms in my letters to London. You see here, major? I knew there would be examples of colonials worth defending on our travels. I was just saying that before they came in. Didn't I tell you that?"

"Yes, sir," the major said. He glanced at me from the corner of his eye. I shrugged.

"So, you'll accept me on your staff, general?" Washington asked, clearly hoping to hear the general say the words.

"Accept you? I welcome you. I invite you. I'll give you your own whore if you want! I've got two aides-de-camp already. But they'll be as worthless as tits on a bull! One is the son of Governor Shirley. If he's ever been outside of Boston, I myself am the son of a whore."

To my knowledge, he was not the son of a whore.

Washington shifted in his seat, uncomfortable with such open talk about harlots. "Yes, thank you. I'll gladly offer my services in any way I can. The company of a woman will not be necessary, sir."

"Speak for yourself!" said the general, laughing. Then he noticed Washington's discomfort. He held up a calming hand. "You will do fine, lad. Fine. Just don't be surprised at what follows a proper baggage train of the regular army. That's all I ask. Now, if you'll excuse me."

All three men stood and exchanged handshakes. The major stepped to the side in order to usher us out.

"Oh, there is something else I should tell you," Franklin said, turning in the threshold.

"Any wisdom you have to offer, will be gladly received," said the general, in an all-around convivial manner.

"My countrymen on the frontier have been attacked lately. The Delaware and Shawnee have been upset by some illegal dealings that took place in Albany between some drunken Oneida chiefs and a man called Lydius."

"I am aware of the attacks," the general said, properly somber.

"I knew you would be. My request is that you do all in your power to defuse the situation. I've heard Mr. Croghan shall accompany you as an Indian diplomat. He is knowledgeable. His advice may avert British casualties and save the lives of Pennsylvanian farmers."

Braddock grinned and stepped around the desk. He was a head shorter than Washington. And the top of his wig came only to the end of Franklin's snout. The general placed a pudgy hand on the postmaster's shoulder and pulled him closer in a gesture of fondness. It appeared that he comforted a child who had awakened, screaming from a nightmare. "Savages may indeed be a formidable enemy to your raw American militia." The general chuckled. "But upon the king's regular and disciplined troops, sir, it is impossible they should make any impression at all." He swept his hand slowly over the room. "If any brutes should raise a hand to us, they'll be gleaned as simply as wheat by the scythe." With a pat on the shoulder he retired behind the desk. "No need to fret, Mr. Franklin."

"No, sir. Thank you," said Franklin, sounding full of confidence.

After stepping outside, the three of us were silent while the door closed and we put some distance between us and the miller's house. "Was there not a company of regulars with you at Fort

Necessity, Colonel Washington?" Franklin asked when we were out of earshot of the many officers who came and went.

Washington nodded soberly. "From South Carolina, under Mackay."

"And were they able to glean the Delaware like wheat from the field?"

"I need not answer that, sir. You are well read." Those men, bright red, woolen coats or not, had died like the rest. Every paper had reported the gory details.

"Then I pray you'll be able to talk some sense into the general as the campaign progresses. Otherwise, he may be making a mistake by dismissing the importance of the tribesmen."

"As his fellow Scotsmen say, *many mickles make a muckle*," Washington mused. "I am hopeful that his small mistakes don't add up to a big one."

"That is why you are along, I'm sure," Franklin assured us. It was more hope than unbridled conviction. "Now. I must be off to have those broadsides printed. You'll need those wagons for the long march."

"I thought you said the broadsides were ready to distribute," I said.

"No, no, son. It was something I came up with at the time to prevent the mickles of my legislatures from making a muckle with the general. Good day, sirs." He tipped his hat.

"Good day," Washington and I answered in unison.

After Franklin had turned the corner to return to the printing and post office, Washington observed, "A capable man." It was an understatement, to be sure. But coming from the colonel, it was meant as the highest of compliments.

"Yes, colonel," I agreed, my mind still turning on mistakes, mickles, and muckles.

"Gather your belongings. I shall meet you back here, presently," the colonel said. Washington then raced away to the inn in order to collect his gear and encamp with the general's men. I obediently departed for the sorry tent I had erected at the edge of town. On my walk, I mused about many questions.

You see, I didn't know with any certainty what a mickle was. But I remembered facing hundreds of muskets blasting away at us the prior year. And if those enemy guns were a host of tiny mickles, I, too, hoped that Braddock would not make them into a big muckle.

CHAPTER TWENTY-ONE

Three weeks after our meeting with Braddock, we were well into the construction of a sizable fort at Wills Creek. Well, it wasn't really at the old trading outpost owned by the Ohio Company and Croghan. The original settlement had been minimal. It had consisted of a few sturdy log houses that could be securely locked to protect provisions as they came and went. There was one building that acted as a sort of general store. Again, it was more of a thick-walled stockade. Finally, there were a handful of shoddy homes that peppered the nearby woods. These housed itinerant traders and their families. When Washington's army had come through initially and then returned after Necessity, we had cut a clearing in order to pitch tents. Braddock would not allow such a slapdash post to serve at the trailhead of his march to certain victory and notoriety.

The general sent us floating to the north side of the Potomac, into that narrow strip of territory most maps agreed belonged under the jurisdiction of Maryland. There, just a few hundred yards from Wills Creek, we built a log fort on a fairly even promontory. Its palisade walls were made of brawny trees that extended above the ground level to the height of two tall men. As no threat from massed artillery or a French army was expected this far east, the plans did not call for massive ditches, earthen escarpments, fortified bastions, or ravelins. It was christened Fort Cumberland by Braddock in a salute to the *Butcher of Cumberland* himself, Prince William – one of the king's sons.

The ranks of men and materiel gathering at the new fort swelled by the day. Provincial troops, which the general spent most of his free time disparaging, arrived from Virginia, Maryland, and North Carolina. They were promptly put to work on menial chores alongside the other colonials already onsite, thereby permitting the regulars to perform tasks more fitting for soldiers.

The redcoats drilled, marched, surveyed, and drilled some more. I remember gazing from my spot on the fort's construction site out to where they exercised. Their red coats and white breeches were accented with glinting bayonets. They looked utterly precise. I thought that their long, thin lines were almost pretty against the gloomy black-green of the vast wilderness beyond.

I also remember wondering what they practiced *for*. Not that it was improper for respectable soldiers to drill. But I could count on one finger the number of places with enough open ground between here and Fort Duquesne where they could stretch out their forces in such a linear manner. And I had no doubt that the French army would employ similar European battle tactics if they could.

If they could.

And I knew they could *not*. The forest beyond Wills Creek – sorry, Fort Cumberland – was dense in those days. Dense. Thick. Wild. Endless. Shaded. Untamed by anyone. Travelers today, with firm dirt roads, sometimes as wide as a rod, on which to ride, can hardly appreciate what we encountered back in '55. It wasn't just the enemy's bullets, or the sickness, or the lack of supplies, or the endless boredom – interrupted by hours of torturous pain and loss. No. It was the trees and bushes and ravines and mountainous terrain themselves. Even if our human enemies never materialized, our geographic ones would prove formidable.

But, I had been a quasi-soldier long enough. Upon seeing the redcoats and their pointless mastery of linear battle tactics, I simply shrugged and returned my back to its strenuous tasks.

"Phoebe!" came a shout from outside the palisade. In addition to men, women were arriving at the burgeoning camp. As they do for today's armies, they would clean the laundry and perform mending for the officers and enlisted soldiers. Most all of the women were the wives of those serving the army or its sundry forces. There were some women who were not united in marriage, however. Dozens of these had been brought in by the British officers and caused a stir, if not outright shock, among the Americans. Braddock and his officers, though married themselves in most instances, were unashamedly open about their use of whores. These unmarried women had their own set of tents in a well-marked section of the camp – remarkably close to the officers they were there to serve. I am ashamed to say that even a few of the American men who could afford such a thing, were soon seen leaving these lairs of ill repute, wearing tousled clothing and satisfied grins.

"Weber!" came the shout from below. "Phoebe Weber!"

I rolled my eyes and peered down to see Tim. He wore a grin, not from visiting any of the popular tents of iniquity, but from his incessant jest. "Good to see you, Phoebe!" he said.

"When did you get here, Taeheek?" I asked, less than enthused that he was so ready to continue his name-calling.

"Just now," he said.

"Come on up," I said with a wave of my arm. "Give me a hand with this wall walk."

"Can't," Tim called. "I was sent to gather you."

"For what?" I sighed. Though, in truth, I would appreciate the break from my labors.

"I don't know," he answered with a bright smile. "When I arrived with Chief Hendrick, Croghan thought it best to set up a council right away." The tribesmen from the west had begun descending upon us in answer to the dozens of wampum belts George had sent ahead. "Braddock agreed. Washington wants you there."

"Why me?" I asked, handing my wooden mallet to a nearby man.

"How should I know?"

"Because the colonel probably told you." I turned and momentarily lost sight of Tim. I climbed down the ladder inside the fort while Taeheek circled toward the gate. "So, why am I to go to a council meeting?" I asked when our paths again crossed.

Tim extended his hand. I took it, remembering that he was a good friend, despite how much he aggravated me. With his free hand he set a finger my sternum. "All healed?"

It actually still hurt fiercely, especially when someone touched it. But I gritted my teeth and said, "It's good. Are we going to have a council fire down by the river?"

We turned and walked side-by-side. "No," he answered. "Braddock said he wants everyone to come to him outside his great tent."

"Makes sense," I muttered. "Makes him feel important when everyone jumps at his command."

"Just another sailor," Taeheek said cheerily. "Like you."

"Shut up," I grumbled. "I'm nothing like Braddock." More and more supplies were coming in on the road from the east. But among the packhorses and wagons bulging with supplies, there were several that were empty of cargo.

"Why the empty wagons?" Tim asked, noting the train.

"Franklin concocted a threatening story to get my fellow Pennsylvanians to contribute teams to the war effort. Looks like it's working. Those must be the first to arrive." We paused on the slope for several minutes and observed them streaming in. The road was so congested, a red-coated regular was sent to direct traffic. In its own, temporary way Fort Cumberland had become the heart of a bustling London market. Laden carts were sent to the fort or to the camp. Empty carts and pack animals were sent to the quartermaster to receive instructions. They'd likely be sent back the way they'd come with orders to gather a host of prescribed goods from depots and port cities on the coast.

"Isn't he supposed to be in jail?" Taeheek asked a few seconds later.

I furrowed my brow. "Franklin? What are you talking about?"

"No. Him." He pointed toward a dray driven by a young man with large muscles. He swore loudly and whipped his beasts of burden with incessant fervor. The cart he guided was stacked with hogsheads filled with something liquid. They sloshed and sweated in the sun. Below a worn cocked hat, I could see that the driver's nose was fully healed, but permanently disfigured.

"Just what I need," I sighed.

In between curses, Braun glanced around the mass of activity. When he looked up the hill in our direction, we both spun on our heels and pretended to walk the other direction. Tim and I were soon absorbed into the bustle and I was fairly certain we'd gone unnoticed. At that moment, my entire hope was that the brute would deliver his goods and then return to the city-lined coast to gather up more. If he did not, it would be exceptionally hard to avoid him for an entire campaign. And I feared that Braun wasn't yet finished exacting his revenge.

Several moments of play acting later, Taeheek and I resumed our original course down the slope. Braun's dray had been sent into the camp by the traffic redcoat. We followed at a safe distance behind, waiting for Braun to turn to the right or the left in order to deliver his goods to this regiment or that. But he didn't. Right toward the center of the sea of tents he ambled, cursing and spitting for no real purpose other than to exhaust pent up energy. If he continued on his path, he would wind up in the very spot where the council was to be held.

Braun yelled to his oxen, "Whoa, you sons of bitches!" But I didn't duck away quick enough when he turned to check his load. Braun noticed me right away. He smiled fiendishly. "As I live and breathe!" he exclaimed. "If it's not my long-lost pal, Ephraim Weber! We've got some unfinished business."

My first inclination was to run. I was no coward. If you've read my previous tale you know this to be true. But there was no victory – win or lose – in fighting a giant among the general's tents and those of his favorite harlots. A victory would find me on trial. A loss would find me, well, maybe, dead. I preferred better odds.

"Just tell Washington you couldn't find me," I whispered to Taeheek. "It'll be my fault that I missed the council fire." I turned and made it three full paces away.

"Shit-for-brains!" called a familiar voice from the large area cleared at the center of the tent encampment. "Why do you flee? Have I frightened you?"

I froze. Among the last times I had heard that voice, its owner had bragged about giving me the dead and mutilated body of one of my friends as a gift. The voice's owner had fought alongside those sending down a hail of shot from the heights around Fort Necessity. I am certain that his experienced musket had killed at least several of my comrades.

"Shit-for-brains!" he shouted again. It was a nickname bestowed upon me by that dead friend of mine when he was very much alive. I had thought, I had hoped rather, that I had heard the last of it.

"Shit-for-brains?" Taeheek asked. With his constant use of women's names for me, Tim had forgotten this particularly unpleasant frontier moniker. "Is he talking to you?"

"Yes. You know he is," I said, returning to Tim's side. "Why didn't you tell me Shingas was here?"

"Is that his name?" Tim asked. He was forever feigning ignorance. It could be a part of his charm. But at the moment, I found it infuriating.

"You know it is!" I snapped.

"No," Tim corrected. "Washington just said that you needed to come talk to some Delaware king."

"Then why didn't you at least tell me that much?"

"What difference does it make?" Tim asked.

"Come Shit-for-brains!" Shingas called. His tone was friendly compared to the last time we'd met. "If you wish me to forget your past transgressions and those of Conotocarius, we've much to discuss." Conotocarius was the name the tribesmen had given to Washington.

"Ephraim Weber, you Shit-for-brains!" called Croghan, coming into view with a dozen Delaware, Shawnee, and Mingo warriors in tow. "Get over here. Washington sent for you an hour ago. What do you want? A fife and drum to welcome you in?"

"An hour ago?" I asked Taeheek.

With a happily guilty look plastered on his face, he answered, "I may have gotten side-tracked by a game of dice."

"Yep, Shit-for-brains," Braun interrupted. He unloaded the hogsheads from his wagon. He plucked each one up as if it was no heavier than a sack of air. "Join us." His invitation was filled with silent, menacing undertones.

"Damn it!" I mumbled, sucking in a deep breath as I surveyed the scene. My mind could conjure no possible ending for the meeting that did not result in my being beaten by Braun or scalped by Shingas.

Tim gripped my shoulder firmly. "Don't worry, Shit-for-brains. I'll go with you. I can protect you." He tapped the many weapons that dangled from every available cord over his shoulders or around his waist.

And I wished that I at least had my tarnished Brown Bess or Tahki's pistol. But they sat unused in the tent I shared with five other men. I did have my hatchet and knife, though. I wasn't a big man, but I could be deadly enough with my blades.

Tim had stepped toward the center of camp where a fire was being kindled. Soldiers and warriors congregated in clumps. I hesitated. Taeheek reached back as if he meant to take my hand and guide me. In the most condescending manner possible, he said, "Don't be frightened, Shit-for-brains. I'm here to help."

I actually had more than my knife and my tomahawk. I was also blessed with an obnoxious companion. Together, they would have to do.

And I had the return of a nickname better forgotten.

And I realized that Phoebe, Sally, Cora, or any number of other women's names weren't such bad monikers after all.

CHAPTER TWENTY-TWO

Braun was an idiot. At least I thought so back then. But he was not lacking all sense. He'd been able to learn a lesson from his blatant attack on me in the Albany Congress. Patience. When it became clear that he wouldn't lash out and pounce upon me in front of so many well-armed Indian, colonial, and English warriors, I began to relax. Besides, Braun's attention was elsewhere. He was already tapping his hogsheads, serving out cup after cup of wine to the council's grateful attendees.

"Courtesy of John Henry Lydius," he would say with a bow of his head whenever someone asked who had provided the luxury. "Plenty more coming, too. John Henry Lydius," he repeated. "Fellow colonial. Loyal subject of the crown. Friend to the Indian."

Lydius' reputation was, of course, that of a scoundrel. But once Braun had gone around the great circle of chiefs, warriors, officers, government representatives, traders, and other clingers, only three individuals were wary enough to decline his hospitality. One was me. I was a little afraid Braun would slip arsenic into my cup. Another who passed on the offer was Croghan. What would it look like if he accepted the drink from a rival trader who had recently stolen Indian lands? And the last to refuse was King Shingas, who angrily curled his lip upon hearing the name of the infamous land thief.

"I'll not drink that rascal's wine," Croghan muttered when Tim and I approached.

Tim wasn't so discriminating. "But it's good, George," he said, smacking his lips. "And free."

"Nothing's free. Lydius and that Braun are up to no good!" Croghan snapped. "I'd think my employee would be a little more dedicated to my wishes."

"Hard to turn away free wine," Tim said, unshaken. "If it upsets you, I suppose you could have brought in your own beforehand."

Croghan growled like an angry bear. "That's your job. Maybe my praises of you were too soon in coming. Ephraim would have never let a villain like Lydius get a leg up out in my territory."

"Ephraim who?" Taeheek asked wearing a devious grin. "Oh, Shit-for-brains."

"Pipe down," Croghan complained. He groaned as he crouched into a seated position on the ground around the growing fire. Tim and I dropped down on his right and left sides as other attendees slowly filed into place. "Do you know how many runners I sent ahead, out to the tribes? Do you know how many letters I've written? How many belts of wampum I've delivered? All at my own expense. I worked my tail off assembling this meeting for the safety of everybody here and the general's good fortune. Now, Braun and Lydius are scratching at a sore that hasn't even scabbed over yet. And where the hell is Braddock? What is he doing?" Croghan peered around the center of the camp, his eyes at last falling on the old general's great tent. "Probably whoring away in there even now."

In a way, Croghan was right. Just his camp geography was wrong.

From directly behind us, we heard a rapidly growing crescendo of rhythmic grunting. The slap of naked flesh accompanied each grunt, which corresponded to the sound of a pair of love-makers thrusting themselves against a straw-packed mattress. At last, the Scotsman groaned in pleasure. "Oh, now that's a good lass," he breathed, releasing the words in a whoosh. Turning my gaze from the massive canopy under which the general normally stayed, I saw behind me a relatively large tent with the flap closed so that none of the interior could be seen. Less than a minute later, I heard belts and buckles clattering as the general clothed himself. I heard him loudly kiss his harlot. Where his lips were planted, I don't know. "I wish it weren't so, my dear," he said affectionately. "But I've got savages to attend to. Please rest yourself this afternoon. And see you are clean for dinner. We shall share a table together in my tent." He planted another warm kiss somewhere upon her and the tent flap shot open and closed as he marched out like a man half his age. I was able to glimpse only one naked arm of a woman who was curled up on a bed of rather generous proportions given our distance from civilization. It was just one of many explanations for the monstrous baggage train that we had dragged this far.

"What are you gaping at, lad?" Braddock snapped when he saw me craning around. "Where's Washington?"

"Here, sir," came the hollow reply from the opposite side of the fire. He sat on a log next to Shingas, a position which surprised me given their mutual distrust. But the colonel had learned a lot about diplomacy since his first trek into the wilderness two years prior. From where I sat, their dialogue had not appeared overly convivial. However, he and the Delaware chief looked well on their way to mending fences.

Also across the way sat Taeheek's kinsman. Adjacent to the self-proclaimed Delaware king, Chief Hendrick rested on patch of blanket that cushioned the hard log. Hendrick held in his hand a ceremonial pipe in anticipation that an agreement could be struck by all present and then sealed with a mutual smoke. I had witnessed and been a part of such a ceremony on several occasions through the years. It was considered a sacred way to ensure a lasting, binding trust.

Braddock took one look at the ancient and storied Mohawk chief. The general's disdain was impossible to masquerade. And he made no attempt to do so as he began the meeting. "I initially thought Mr. Johnson had some small amount of sense when he sent along the Croghan fellow." At the general's feet, Croghan's lips curled. He prepared to bite his flaming Irish tongue for what might come next. Unaware, the general paid the old trader no attention as he sauntered away from his love nest. "It helps our army keep up appearances when we have a dedicated liaison to the savages. I take it these wampum belts I've heard of are supposed to mean something to the primitives. But I'll be damned if I am going to waste more than an hour of my life on this march consulting with the heathens at every turn." Braddock pointed at the colonel. "I am on this continent because your assemblies cannot figure out how to coordinate a defense. I am here today merely as a courtesy to you and Mr. Franklin for your generous assistance, Mr. Washington. Make it worth my while."

"Mr. Franklin is an elder who gathers around the great council fire in Philadelphia. He sends greetings from his country," the colonel explained to the tribesmen. "The governor of Virginia and even the King of England across the great waters hold our allies in the forests in the highest of regard. Today's council will surely clear the way for the safe passage of our army. No longer shall the French hold sway where they are not welcome. We shall liberate the Forks and its inhabitants," Washington claimed boldly.

"Liberate or conquer. I don't care which," Braddock said, already bored. He stopped his uninterested meandering when a large shadow fell upon him.

"Compliments of John Henry Lydius," Braun interrupted, handing the general a glass of wine.

Braddock was momentarily startled. "Lydius, huh?" Yet, he took the glass, inspected Braun, and then downed it in one gulp. You could almost see his chest and mood warm from the alcohol. "My activities," he said, laughing at his euphemism for intercourse with a whore. "They've worked up a thirst within me, good man. Keep the wine coming." He snapped his fingers.

Braun bowed, striding to the nearest barrel. "Yes, sir," he said. "Mr. Lydius is happy to provide all you need. This entire wagon and its contents are at your disposal, free of charge."

The fact that Lydius and Braun so obviously worked in coordination, sent Croghan into a muttering diatribe that might only have been decipherable by some Celtic priestess of yore. And she might have blushed in mixed company.

General Braddock consumed three more glasses before he had settled at what might be called the head of the circle of dignitaries. With the fifth glass in his hand, his face began to pinken and his irritated features softened. He nursed this one. "I do not see why there is such strife over a man such as Mr. Lydius when he is so obviously generous with his wares."

"Lydius pours liquor down the gullets of generals to win favor. And he does the same for Iroquois dogs to get them to sell land that is not theirs!" King Shingas barked.

"Not all Iroquois," Chief Hendrick quietly corrected the much younger man. "Certain members of the Oneida broke the trust between our peoples. No others." If he was offended by the Iroquois remark, Hendrick showed no indication of it. He merely set a gentle hand on the Delaware chief's forearm in order to calm him.

Shingas sloughed off the touch. "The protection over us that we once granted to the Iroquois Confederacy is broken. We no longer need them to talk to the English for us. We do that on our own. The Six Nations are no longer our fathers. They are to act as our brothers."

Every complexity, minor or major, of the intertribal relationships and how they, in turn, related to the colonies was lost to Braddock. And he had no interest in learning. After sipping the wine and resting the glass upon his knee, the general sighed, "Colonel Washington, I have other matters to attend to. I grow weary from hearing half-clothed savages bicker among themselves. Will you straighten out these *friends* of yours?"

"Conotocarius, the Destroyer of Villages, is no friend," Shingas shouted. Perhaps ten voices grunted in agreement. They sat directly behind the Delaware king and were all his kin or from Shawnee tribes. "But neither are the French!" This time, as many as fifty Indian voices called out in agreement, loudly and for ten full seconds. All the tribes represented, from Mingo to Mohawk, concurred with an unexpected distrust of the French. It was a fortuitous turn of events. We had only to seize upon it in that moment.

Shingas continued. "And that is the only reason I am here today. The French drove my English brothers away from the Forks of Ohio. It is true. I did nothing to prevent this. Some might say that I and my people provided aid to the French. I'll not argue. But despite my frustration with my brothers, the English, my French fathers have not acted as they should. They have not provided gifts to their children, the Delaware. They have raised their hand to strike at us and rain down discipline. They've failed to mediate conflicts among their children as a good father does. They build a fort many times larger than the outpost my English brothers planted at the Forks. The French mean to conquer us. To rule us. We are here to strike a bargain with the King of England."

"What the hell is a Conotocarius?" Braddock growled. Out of all that Shingas had said, that was the one thing the old general had noticed.

"It's a name given to my great-grandfather by the Susquehanna Indians, general," Washington whispered. "They've seen fit to bestow it upon me as well."

"Destroyer of Villages, eh?" the Scotsman asked, a sneer of approval on his face. "But I don't think we'll be needing your services anytime soon, colonel." Raising his glass, the general pointed around at the busy camp and growing fort. "No savage would be foolish enough to raise a hand to our army. Therefore, we won't have any villages to raze." He winked. "The threat of doing so is enough to keep them in line."

Washington shifted uncomfortably in his seat. There had been times in our first forays into the woods over the previous years when the colonel had been somewhat tone deaf to the complaints and needs of the Indians. But to his credit he was a good student, learning much in a short time. Most of the lessons had been paid for with blood, so he was sure to heed them now. "Yes, sir, general. There have been times when Chief Shingas has been an adversary. There have been times when I was not certain. However, I do think it is a fine omen that he has accepted Mr. Croghan's invitation today. Were he our enemy, he and his people would have refused. There is room to talk. And that is why we share this seat around this fire. We are a great deliberative body."

Shingas pinched his mouth closed. He appeared stern, but nodded his approval of the colonel's sentiments.

"My Delaware children feel they have been wronged by *certain* Iroquois and *certain* whites," Chief Hendrick began. It was an important first step for such a high-ranking member of Onondaga to extend an olive branch to the wayward Delaware. He gripped the ceremonial pipe firmly in front of his chest. "We must assure our fellow Indians that we value them. Given the rumors of Lydius' land theft sweeping the countryside, they are right to feel attacked." There was wisdom in Hendrick's approach.

"They are not right to feel attacked!" Braddock yelled. "For they have not been assaulted in any manner. On the contrary, I have heard they slather themselves in grease and paint before creeping onto farms. They then scalp and kill settlers who have come peacefully from other parts of His Majesty's colonies. The *only* item we have to discuss and agree upon around this fire is that such activity will cease this instant!" He threw his empty glass of wine into the blaze, which, after flaring briefly, seemed to shrink as the collective temperament of the circle cooled. Braun, already schooled in Lydius' liquid diplomacy, scrambled to retrieve another. "And I'll not hear any more about Lydius' deal. That is between the savages themselves and the colonies. Perhaps the new Superintendent of Indian Affairs will investigate. But I am here to drive the French away from lands rightfully belonging to the King of Great Britain."

Puzzled by the general's explosion, Chief Hendrick studied Braddock with penetrating eyes.

"Yes, general," Washington breathed. He always held himself, his emotions in check. In public settings he was the most controlled man I have ever witnessed. And I consider battlefields, debates, and Indian councils to be public forums. But George Washington, especially in his younger days, had a boiling temper that vibrated just below the surface. To me it seemed a single scuff could send it bursting forth. I doubt any other human being around that fire noticed that day, but I saw his eyes flash with rage. The skin of the colonel's neck grew taut. His jaw clenched. It is a testament to his great temper that he constantly fought so hard against it. "Chief Shingas and I have our differences, as I've suggested. But we have a common goal to be rid of the French. Ought we not hear what they and the rightful Iroquois spokesman have to say before making pronouncements that may be premature?"

"Premature? I've already heard them," Braddock said. Quite the opposite of the colonel, the general made a show of his failed attempts to remain calm. "They wish to have the French gone. Well, if they would just return to their huts and villages, we will take care of the situation for them! I'm telling them to get out of the way!"

"Sir," I ventured, completely foolishly. But short of the Indians themselves and Croghan, I was the white man with the most experience in the woodlands and with the tribes. "It's not that simple. We came here to Wills Creek on decent roads by America's standards. Well, those trails disappear from here on out. All that we have to travel on is a crude path that Colonel Washington hacked out last year. There is another hundred miles of virgin wilderness in front of us."

"Lad!" Braddock snarled. "*Nothing* in my wake remains *virgin*." A few of his regular officers chuckled at the reference. The small general sat up taller, proud of himself.

"General Braddock," Croghan said, trying a different tack. "The boy means that our march over those long miles can be peaceful or filled with fighting warriors who've grown up in these woods."

"What do you think you are doing?" Braddock shouted, staring at Croghan, Tim, and I.

"Trying to help build an alliance against the French," Croghan retorted.

"Not you, you dirty son of an Irish whore!" Braddock called. He pointed over our heads. "You, there! What do you think you're doing?"

All eyes fell on a colonial officer who was in the process of ducking into the whore's tent behind us. Being called out by the general caused him to freeze. He dropped the flap and slowly turned. He was young, perhaps in his mid-twenties. His coat showed him as a gentleman officer from North Carolina. He attempted levity. "General, I've been told that the occupant of this particular tent is gifted in the healing arts. I've got an unspeakable pain I hope she is able to cure."

The general's aides, except Washington, giggled like school lads. Braddock was not amused. "Who told you that?" he barked.

The Carolina man cleared his throat. His mirth faded. "A compatriot, sir."

"From where?" the general grilled him, standing to his full, unsubstantial height.

"North Carolina, sir. A friend of mine from back home. Like me, he commands a company of provincial troops."

The general cut him off. "Doctor!" he shrieked, scanning the circle. "Bring a doctor here. Doctor James!" His startled officers raced around until they pulled a middle-aged man wearing spectacles into the fray. The duration of the search was less than a minute. "What took you so long, doctor?" Braddock yelled, the wine was fully in his system now. His face was flush. His anger flowed.

"I came as quickly as I could."

"I am not a tyrant, but I can be if I must! If you insist. Let this be a lesson to you. All of you." The general marched toward us, scattering officers and Indians in the process. Tim and I rolled out of his way. Braddock stopped with his nose at the chin of the Carolinian. "Go. And don't ever come back here. Do you understand?"

"Yes, sir," the emasculated officer said. He shrunk away like a sick animal.

"Doctor, I want every woman in this camp who is not married to be given a full examination so that I may be assured that they remain healthy."

"Every woman, sir?" the Doctor James asked, blinking behind his glasses.

"Every unmarried woman, man! I find out that these Americans have been skulking around my whores! There's no telling where these colonials have been, what they've been doing, and with whom. Who knows what types of maladies they've picked up in their relations with the indigenous population of women. Even many of the white women are savages at this point."

"Sir, I'm sure I could see that you are comfortable with any woman with whom you've, ahem, spent time," the doctor offered. Even this early in the campaign, the doctor would be busy setting broken bones and treating the ever-present intestinal maladies that accompanied armies on the march.

"I am a commander, sir!" the general barked. "The welfare of my officers and men is paramount. That, and victory. I cannot have His Majesty's regular soldiers of foot hampered by an illness gotten from the savages by way of the colonials."

"No, sir," the doctor relented. "There's a small company of regulars who have not adjusted well to their new home. In order to cease the spread of the malaise, I'm considering a quarantine. Doctor Craik and I will be able to begin the examinations of the women in the morning."

"You'll begin them now," the general countered through gritted teeth. "You'll start with the young lady in this tent. Once you are satisfied that she is innocuous, send her to me. Then work your way outward among the other women of the camp."

"Yes, sir," Doctor James answered, defeated.

"Well, go gather your instruments!" the general snapped.

After the doctor was away, Braddock raised his chin and strode toward the fire. Every participant was stunned silent. The tribesmen burned with rage. The American officers were offended. Washington was embarrassed. The regular officers, apparently used to the general's behavior, betrayed no emotion. They stood like toy carvings made of wood.

"I believe that is enough talk for today," General Braddock said after a long while. "I believe I've made my point."

Hendrick clasped his ornate ceremonial pipe in both hands, raising it in order to bring it down across a knee. A shattered peace pipe could be interpreted in only one manner. The colonel saw the motion and reached across Shingas to grab the Mohawk before he made so bold a move. He succeeded at the last possible second.

"But, general," Washington began, still clutching Hendrick's suspended arm.

It would do no good. Braddock slowly retired to his tent, paying no attention to the growing hubbub around the fire. His tent flapped closed.

"Give the general time," Washington cautioned Hendrick. The old chief nodded reluctantly before bringing the peace pipe carefully to his lap.

It was going to be a long march.

CHAPTER TWENTY-THREE

Washington could be persuasive. The Lord knows that with few words he convinced me to follow him from one dangerous and unprofitable situation to the next. True to his nature, the colonel encouraged Hendrick to stay with the army following the disastrous exhibition by Braddock around the council fire. And it served the interests of both the Iroquois and the English to demonstrate a united front in matters of the lesser tribes. In turn, Hendrick, by the sheer force of his reputation, inspired Chief Shingas and his fellow Delaware to remain. As a result of their collective actions, a week after the failed council, the population of tribesmen in the camp had actually increased. Entire families consisting of warriors, women, and children descended upon our army encamped at Fort Cumberland. Mingo, Delaware, Shawnee, even a few Wyandot from the pays d'en haut came hoping for, if not expecting, a grand treaty to be struck between all the tribes and their English brothers. The French seizure of the Forks had done something no Indian chief had ever been able to do. It had united the tribes. All Braddock had to do was take advantage of the opportunity that had magically fallen in his lap.

Days went by. I was occupied by putting the finishing touches on the fort with the other colonial troops. When I wasn't heaving logs or pounding pegs, I was avoiding the path of Braun, who seemed to have plenty of money placed in his pocket to purchase all manners of liquor for the general and his staff. Lydius clearly felt it worth most any expense to keep the king's highest-ranking representative, Braddock, from looking into the shady purchase he'd made in Albany.

But not all was bad. Thus far, I'd been successful at evading any of the revenge that I still anticipated to receive from Braun. And I was becoming sprier every day. Other than permanent scars and memories, my wounds from jumping through windows, getting shot, and playing La Crosse had all finally healed. I was a new man. My muscles were not robust, but they grew with my labors and as I transformed from a boy in his teens to one on the cusp of entering his third decade. If I lived that long, I reminded myself.

But eventually, the toil on the fort was done. A small company of provincials was assigned the task of garrison duty, leaving regulars with the rigors of fighting the French. And for the most part, my fellow colonists didn't complain about such a boring task. Every one of them had other options for work and pay. Avoiding a musket ball to the face was something their loved ones back home would appreciate.

Road builders had scattered out in front of us. With axes, saws, and oxen, they had widened the path for a full mile on toward our destination at the confluence of the Ohio. The construction crew still had about ninety-nine miles to go over the harshest territory. Nonetheless, and at last, we were set to march today.

"We cannot accompany you to Fort Duquesne without an agreement of some sort," Shingas pleaded with Washington. The Indian had shown great restraint in the preceding days, occupied with hosting his family and significant members of the other tribes. But as the army's column had begun to assemble, he could wait no longer. Shingas was forced to seek out Washington. The pair now walked through the heart of the camp along with Chief Hendrick. The site was busy with workers disassembling its canopies and poles, piling items into Franklin's Pennsylvanian wagons, and then the wagons into a line. The Delaware king held a rolled-up piece of parchment in one hand. He used it to gesture as if it was as important as the sentiment he conveyed. Behind them a score of chiefs and warriors and I followed. One Indian, a Mohawk by his dress and freshly greased hair, was a newcomer whom I didn't recognize.

"I understand, Chief Shingas," Washington said. "That is why we go to the general now."

"King Shingas," the Delaware insisted.

"Of course, King Shingas," Washington readily agreed. The colonel deemed his task too important to dip into the waters of semantics.

Shingas saw that there had been no ill intention in the colonel's choice of titles. The Delaware sighed, "The delay of the march has been a good thing. It has given me time. And I have come to believe what Chief Hendrick says about the Lydius land theft. And I believe what you say, that it may be overturned or at least renegotiated. But my people need more. We must have assurances from your general. He has given us nothing. Not even another council meeting. Does he not understand that we are willing?"

"I have known many Scotsmen in my life," Chief Hendrick opined. "My best friend is the Irishman, Johnson. They are similar peoples. Their temperaments can run hot as a kettle or cold as a stream from one minute to the next. But I believe that with the map you carry to him, General Braddock will be able to finally appreciate your good intentions. He is new to American soil." It was a kind sentiment meant for the general who had angered so many by his aloof treatment of the tribes.

Shingas opened his palm and studied the rolled, worn sheet. "It is a fine gesture that you've given this to me," he said. "You could have benefited from your own hard work."

Hendrick smiled and patted the younger chief on the shoulder. Glancing at the new Mohawk behind, he said, "I am too old to have secreted it out myself. It was Moses the Song who did the dangerous work."

Shingas stopped. The entire procession halted around him. He extended a hand to the man who must have been Moses. "Then I thank you for risking your life to get this map to me today."

Moses answered simply, "Anything to be rid of the French and their Catholicism."

Apparently, he was devoutly Protestant.

And I had not seen or heard of any map. It seemed I was the only one in the dark about the small scrap of parchment.

"We were fortunate to have had Hendrick send Moses in," Washington said, resuming his course so that the rest renewed theirs as well. We went toward the regular officer's section of the camp. Their tents would be down, but it was where we expected to find the general and his closest advisors loitering. Especially, if their strumpets, who had all been deemed in reasonable health by the doctors, remained behind as well.

"You will need to receive the gratitude that comes along with a vital document such as this," Hendrick said. "Much more than I or my people."

"The general had best see wisdom in becoming friends with the Delaware," Shingas warned.

The giggle and cackle of ladies welcomed us to the center of a camp that was empty of structures. The general sat upon his beast, a white Arabian. Several ladies were perched on horses around him like he was a sultan in a Turkish court. Another half dozen ladies walked away from us. A moment later they climbed into the back of a covered wagon, to be hauled around like common war materiel. I suppose they were.

A few British officers and the general's other two aides-de-camp filled out the nearest ranks of the growing column that extended a mile in either direction. One of the aides was the spitting image of Governor William Shirley of Massachusetts. He was, in fact, William Junior, the governor's eldest son. Junior grinned lustfully in the saddle as his gelding pranced around an attractive lady's horse while the lady laughed as if they flirted in a city garden.

"I'm glad you've finally decided to arrive, Washington," Braddock said, winking at one of his girls. "Though had you come earlier, I'm certain your forceful nature would have scared my little pets." He gently caressed a woman's cheek. She coquettishly tipped her face away, which made the general reach a little farther.

In those days, Washington was flummoxed in the presence of ladies, regardless of their station. "General, I, uh," he mumbled. This would change as he aged and became more confident in social settings, but at Fort Cumberland in the summer of '55, he was as articulate as a mule.

"But you've come to your post and that is the mark of a fine soldier, sir," Braddock said. He was in good spirits from his many weeks of amorous activities and the prospect of military success against Britain's fiercest enemy, France.

"I've brought King Shingas with news, sir," Washington said.

"King, huh?" Braddock said, chuckling. "News? I've got something to share with him, too."

"This cannot wait, general," Washington argued. "It is the utmost of importance."

"Then by all means," the general said, granting Shingas the floor with a broad sweep of his newly gloved mitt. He peeked to yet another of his bevy and added mockingly, "*Utmost of importance.*" He said it with a hollow whisper that was extraordinarily similar to Washington's naturally empty voice. The general's mannerisms, encouraged by the flirtatious women, were more akin to those of a boy one-sixth his age.

Shingas held the rolled parchment up to Braddock, who plucked it away and unwound it. Neither the Delaware king nor the general said anything while the latter studied whatever was on the page. "Humph," Braddock said to himself. For once, his officers were able to tear their attention from the women. Curious, they guided their beasts closer to the general in order to peer over his shoulder, just as he added, "A good hand. Nice detail."

"And accurate," Shingas assured him. "I give it to you as a token of the goodwill of my people." The Delaware then acknowledged Moses and Hendrick with a curt nod. "I have worked with my Mohawk brothers to gather this for you." Though he had done nothing to get whatever it was, it was a fine augury to see him grant credit to two members of the Iroquois League.

Braddock carefully rolled the page back the way it had been. The faces of the Indians and Washington proved they expected a complimentary reply from the general. They waited.

They'd have to wait a long time.

"What is it you want from me, Mr. Washington?" Braddock asked. "You said Shingas here had something urgent."

"He did, sir," Washington protested. "The map. The diagram. Perhaps take another look."

"Oh, I see," Braddock said, condescension dripping. He stuck his hand out with the page set gently between his thumb and first finger. A heartbeat later, it was falling to the ground.

"General Braddock," Washington gasped, astonished. Even the general's ladies had felt a chill in the meeting and had begun to draw away from him.

"*General Braddock* is right," the general retorted. "His Majesty the King of Great Britain has sent me here to right what you've got wrong, Mr. Washington. You seem a likeable man with good qualities, if not too serious. But you have much to learn about war, sir. It is still my honor to tutor you in its arts."

"But the plan. You've just discarded a vital piece of intelligence," Hendrick said.

"I'm sure all sorts of conniving things are done in your wilderness north of Albany, Chief Hendrick," Braddock answered. "And how much more so in the even less civilized marches of the Forks. But this army does not resort to chicanery or treachery. We will march with haste to Fort Duquesne. There I will, in manly terms, beseech its commandant to surrender. I expect, that in an equally manly way, he will decline. And so will begin the slow, inexorable siege where his walls, no matter how stout, will be reduced to rubble. His soldiers, no matter how hearty, will succumb to devastation, disease, and death. And England will once again, and rightfully so, be masters over all her dominions. Britannia shall rule."

Shingas was past being angry. He actually appeared saddened. For he had seen war and he had a suspicion that one was coming his way, no matter which side he chose. "General," he said, nearly exasperated. "You will have our cooperation. But it is clear you intend to skip any formal council with my people. Please just tell me that my British brothers do not mean to control the region that we've so recently come to occupy."

That seemed a reasonable bone for the general to offer in return for Shingas' support. That had been the official agreement all along – from the time of the Logstown Council through Hendrick's latest negotiations. The English would build a fort to protect trade and the Indians. No more.

The general would not relent. He gazed down his nose, making it appear long and narrow behind his pudgy chin and a half. Slowly, he said, "The English should inhabit and inherit the Ohio Country."

Shingas, proud warrior, was crushed. I had known him to bluster. I had seen him fight with the tenacity of a bear. But he didn't want to fight now. He wanted an agreement for the long-term safety of his people. While his braves muttered angrily behind him, he tried yet again. "General, please tell me that Indians friendly to your king may live and hunt there to support families so they don't have to flee into the arms of the French."

It was a plea. It wasn't a threat. But the general took it as the latter. "You think you will switch sides to the Frogs? I'll tell you this," said the fiery Scot. "No savage should inherit *any* of the land!"

Shingas' temporary weakness fled. He stood taller, righteously indignant. "I have tried to work with you. I have tried to make a lasting peace with you."

"I am not here for peace," Braddock countered, gruffer than ever. "I come to wage war against the enemies of my king. Now, I wish you would not be counted in their number. But only you may decide." He ended the declaration with bared teeth, his upper lip quivering like a wolf on the prowl.

I understood enough of the Delaware tongue to know what the warriors behind Shingas wanted him to do. It involved stripping the general from his horse and flaying him open, eating or mutilating various body parts. But Shingas was smart enough to know that just this one army of Britain numbered some two thousand souls, plus whores. His Delaware warriors, when united with the Shawnee, might comprise a few hundred. And that was the total upper limit to his strength. Shingas needed a bargain. Almost anything.

"You say we are not your enemy," Shingas said.

"Your decision," Braddock answered. He glanced ahead to where the van of the column was beginning its march. It would be several moments before we began to move into the woods.

"I do not wish to fight my English brothers," Shingas said, relenting, his shoulders sagging.

"Fine," Braddock said cheerfully. Victorious, he screwed up tall in his saddle.

There had been no assurances, but war seemed to have been averted. "You will find yourself rewarded for taking up the hatchet with His Majesty the King of Great Britain," Hendrick said to Shingas. "Even through disagreements, I have known him to be a generous brother."

"Yes," Washington agreed. Despite the pompous attitude of the general, a calm had at last descended upon the impromptu conference. "With your help, we will again free the Forks."

"Stop," Braddock insisted. "There will be no Indian hatchet. There will be no help from Shingas and his Delaware or whomever. I do not need their help and I have no doubt of driving the French and any Indian allies away forever."

Dumbfounded. That is what I was. That was the feeling held by everyone. I think even the whores had a better grasp of the implications of upsetting the tribes than did the general. But he wasn't yet done. "That reminds me. I'd prefer if all of you just returned to your villages. I suppose I understand that I require a handful of savages to guide me to Duquesne. But since we've come to such a fair agreement just now, I am willing to be flexible in my demands. If you insist on following along with our train, I ask that you have your women depart immediately. Their presence causes too much commotion. They cause the eyes of my soldiers to wander."

Flabbergasted. I think that sounds more astonished than dumbfounded. For I was. I looked to the general's previously frisky women, whose entire purpose was to attract the gazes, coins, and other things from young soldiers. None would meet my eye, as if being associated with Braddock was suddenly more shameful than their chosen profession.

Braddock snapped his reins upon his Arabian's withers. "Catch up, Washington," he ordered as he joined in to the long procession. Shirley Junior and the others followed along, leaving us standing behind.

No one said a thing. There was nothing to be said.

When they'd gone up the path a piece and after many of the baggage wagons had rattled by, I stooped to gather up the curled plan discarded by Braddock. Unrolling it I saw writing running in all directions in the margins of a diagram. The diagram was of a fort with four bastions and two ravelins. There were labels and lines going all over the page. It showed detail down to the smallest degree, including barrack locations and powder storage. A discussion of blind spots from the embrasures was included and a summary of troop strength, garrison diet, and shift changes.

"The key to Fort Duquesne," Washington said from directly behind. He had startled me.

When I looked up from the map I saw that the rear guard of the column was already marching past. I had been lost in thought for a long while.

"Where's Shingas?" I asked, seeing the two of us were alone.

"Gone," Washington said.

"Home?" I asked.

Washington shook his head. "Into the arms of the French, I'd say."

That wasn't a surprise. "And Chief Hendrick?"

The colonel gestured with his nose. "Ahead with army. He'll ride scout for much of the mission."

"But he's not from these parts. And no disrespect intended, but he's old."

Washington agreed. "Which is why you, Croghan, and I will also find ourselves ahead of the van as we draw away from Fort Cumberland." He laughed to himself with gallows humor. "We do have seven Mingo warriors and probably your friend Taeheek. They've decided to stay. You cannot say we've alienated the entire continent."

I looked again at the map. "It seems a waste."

Washington stuck out his hand. I set the diagram into his large palm. "It will be a long march," he added. "I will have many opportunities to convince the general to use what he calls chicanery." He tucked the map into his coat pocket.

"How did Hendrick know that Moses the Song could get the map?" I thought about the handwriting. It was made by a practiced hand holding a quality pen. "Who made it?"

Washington smiled sadly. "You know who made it. We've got a man on the inside of Fort Duquesne. You know him quite well."

I racked my brain. I didn't know we had a spy. Then it hit me. "Van Braam!"

"And Captain Stobo," Washington added. "They've been prisoners of the French at Duquesne since last summer. I had Hendrick send Moses ahead in search of them. He was able to make contact with Van Braam and Stobo. While they couldn't get away, they could give me all the details of the new fort. But the two brave souls have paid a price. Moses tells me they were discovered as they smuggled out the note. The map is free, but Van Braam and Stobo have been banished to Quebec." He patted his coat pocket. "But there is still hope, Mr. Weber. I shall do my duty. You shall do yours."

He strode off to gather his horse and join his place in the column. I felt a heavy weight had been on my shoulders a moment earlier. But Washington with his cautious optimism, had removed it. Even his patting had reminded me of his utter confidence on our first mission to the wilderness when he carried a letter to the French from Dinwiddie. That had been another foolish, deadly undertaking. And somehow, we had survived.

So, with lowered expectations, I prayed for a similar outcome for Braddock's expedition.

CHAPTER TWENTY-FOUR

A week later we had traveled only thirty-five miles! And I would say that is a pathetic pace if only it hadn't slowed further. On day eight we passed through just two miles of swamp. I think I slept a mere mile away from my last resting place after day nine. When the wilder rivers and mountains came, I knew our rate of passage would only decrease. A crippled tortoise moved faster. In fact, one did. He passed us walking backward.

The road workers toiled from sunup to sundown felling trees and clearing a path for eight-inch howitzers and a string of twelve-pound cannons. In some cases, they used the crude trail blazed by Washington's sad army the prior year, widening and firming its base. In others, these men had to cut an entirely new route laid out by scouts and engineers. I was pleased not to be in the ranks of those poor road workers. As May slid into June, three men died from exhaustion the first week alone. Five of their beasts of burden keeled over as well. The flesh of the animals was quickly roasted, efficiently supplementing our walking stock. The bodies of the men were buried along the side of the path with little ceremony.

My knowledge of the region allowed me some modest autonomy. I alternated between riding at the head of the long column with Croghan and Hendrick and scouting out far ahead or to the sides of the march. On a morning in early June, I was a quarter mile away from the army on the right front flank. Tim and a handful of provincial soldiers accompanied me. When I was in the van, I usually traveled on horseback. But in the thick wilderness where no path even existed, we treaded on foot.

"Shh," I hissed as we crept through a dense section of gnarled vines and briars. A storm had taken down a pair of trees many years earlier and created a rare opportunity for sunrays to fall to the forest floor, creating the thick new growth.

"Listen, Quaker boy," said Zeb, one of the Virginians who had originally come to Williamsburg and sent me north to Albany. His services back east were no longer required and so he had joined the march. "I'm not saying anything that we aren't all thinking. I bet Taeheek here would toss a few shillings at those whores if they'd have him."

"I'm to be married," Tim answered, his eyes trained through the branches. "Anne's her name."

"All the more reason to visit their tents," Zeb continued. He was in the middle of our pack. I led. "Sometimes you don't even have to go to the tents. Braddock has so many carriages in the train that some of the girls will conduct business while we are still on the march. It's like riding a green filly."

I hated braggarts. "What do you know?" I asked, leading us around a particularly impenetrable mass of brush. Like me, he couldn't afford to fix his tattered clothes. I doubted he had an extra penny to spend on the cheapest, toothless harlot.

Unfazed, the Virginian went on. "The boys and I pooled our resources and were still short. We found a girl willing to work on partial credit." He giggled. "Can you believe that?"

I couldn't. Strumpets weren't educated. But they weren't stupid. Like the rest of us, they performed chores for money. I remember wondering when I would again get paid. Perhaps, I was the stupid one.

"Shh," I insisted, listening intently. I pointed to Taeheek and indicated he should curve his path to the left. He nodded and slowly peeled away.

It was the fourth time we'd decided to split up that morning. Each of the prior occasions we'd found nothing, just a tapping woodpecker or shuffling squirrel. Zeb had grown heedless. "But I hear there's a gal in the camp that is too pricey for anyone. Only the general himself can afford her. He now keeps her to himself. Can you imagine what kind of girl is worth so much that only a general can keep her?"

Perhaps ten feet away, Tim peeked over his shoulder. "No amount of money in the world could make me want to see that old bastard naked, let alone huffing and pawing around on top of anyone. She's not paid enough to let his stinking sweat drip off his nose onto her tits as far as I'm concerned."

Zeb snorted in laughter.

"Shut up, you two," I said. "Follow Tim," I added to the Virginian.

Zeb went on laughing, but obediently ducked under a limb and closed the gap between he and Tim. He was a braggart, but I probably didn't hate him. As you can see, my emotions ran hot and cold when I was a youth. I'd like to tell you that they've mellowed with age. I'd like to tell you that, but alas.

The rest of our provincial scouts were all men who had lived on the frontier. They were familiar with backwoods living and silently followed me.

"What's her name?" Tim whispered. "The expensive harlot?"

Zeb guffawed. "See? He's curious. I told you old Taeheek would want to go a whorin'! Who cares what a whore's name is?"

"I said, shut up!" I scolded them. I saw a glint of light reflect from behind a thorn bush on my left. I didn't wait for more confirmation. "Down!" I yelled.

It was too late.

I heard a single war whoop. In answer, a cacophony of muskets erupted from within the dense thicket and from around the other side. Bark splattered as errant balls smashed into oaks. Tim spun, his musket falling from his hand, as I took a knee behind a tree. Zeb, for all his worthless bluster, was a good soldier. He ducked low and raced the three steps to where Tim had fallen, jerking him behind a decaying log. Tim clutched his ribs, but waved with a crimson palm, assuring me he was alive.

Before our attackers swarmed over us to slice off our scalps, it was time to show them we had fight left in us. "Return fire!" I ordered. "At will." Our small group began answering with smattering gunfire.

I hiked the butt of my Brown Bess to my shoulder and pressed my cheek against the stock's comb before wheeling around the tree, searching for a target. All I saw was smoke and leaves. I heard the telltale sound of powder and shot being pounded in place as the enemy reloaded. Squinting, I saw what looked like an arm go up and then throw down a ramrod. Its owner would be pressed against the nearest tree. I had no shot worth taking and hoped that my fellow soldiers weren't wasting precious ammunition shooting at ghosts.

Brazenly, I leaned out further to the right, sweeping my muzzle to the left. A batch of thick, lingering smoke told me that the largest concentration of warriors was hidden behind the shroud. Behind me, my fellow provincials had unloaded their muskets in a helter-skelter manner. They reloaded. One fired. Then another. More reloading. Likewise, musket fire from the attackers now came in a disordered fashion. Still I scanned for something worth aiming at.

I saw it. Him, rather.

Standing tall above the thickest smoke was Shingas. He began shouting orders in his native tongue, picking out targets for his kneeling warriors. He had not yet seen me. For a moment, as the cloud of smoke grew, shifted, and drifted, I had a window of opportunity. I could kill the Delaware king.

Bringing my hammer to full cock, I gazed down the length of the barrel. My right thumb wrapped around the small of the stock as my forefinger felt the face of the trigger. I had a perfect target. He was no more than twenty paces away. His naked chest, adorned with paint, faced me, broad and strong. Even with my sometimes-inaccurate weapon, Shingas would be dead with just a flex of the tiniest of my muscles. It would almost be effortless.

I heard a grunt behind me. I shouldn't have craned back to see what happened but I did. A provincial lay at my feet, felled by a musket ball in his neck. He was dead before he hit the dirt.

"Damn Delaware," shouted Tim. He had managed to prop himself on one side and shoot, rather ineffectually. Zeb had formed a protective cordon around the side of the wounded Mohawk by rolling a lone stone in place. He crouched next to Tim, firing and watching over him like a mother hen.

I returned my gaze to the battlefield where smoke grew thicker. Shingas, if he was still in place, was veiled by the fog. I silently cursed myself for not taking the initiative when I had the chance. I had yet to fire my weapon in the battle.

Then a breeze fluttered through the trees. The uppermost section of the cloud swirled down upon itself and rolled away. There was Shingas, standing proud in the same place. He pointed to our flank opposite the dense briars, ordering a portion of his men to attack with tomahawks.

I couldn't let that happen. I leveled my Bess, took aim, and...

Didn't fire. Instead, I whistled loudly. "Shingas! I see you!"

His head jerked to the side and for a few heartbeats time stopped. I could have. I should have shot him. Instead, I jerked my head to the side, indicating he should leave.

"Hold," he called to his Delaware warriors who had already begun running toward our left flank. "Retreat!" he ordered. Good braves though they were, I heard much cursing and questioning as his warriors fell in behind their chief, who was already running swiftly through the woods. "This was your one warning. I owe you nothing, Shit-for-brains!" he called after.

And then fifty guns exploded from behind me. My ears rang and hissed. Spinning around, I saw the real reason Shingas had fled so quickly. He was not honoring some bond we held from our shared history. No. A company of red bedecked British regulars had come to the sound of our battle.

"What happened here?" asked a somber, befuddled looking captain. He held up a hand to prevent his company from pursuing the disappearing shadows.

My ears hummed. I cupped my hand over them as I stood. "Ambush," I answered, gathering my gear. "We drove them off."

The captain looked down at the dead provincial at our feet, using his toe to nudge the man. He then glanced over at Tim, who was upright. Beneath his blue-checked linen shirt Tim had found a six-inch laceration left from the ball. It had entered his skin at a shallow angle, rattled – and probably broken – one of his ribs, before tearing out the back. Zeb used a long swatch of cloth to wrap the wound while Tim swore profusely at the pain, employing words his soon-to-be Presbyterian bride would blush upon hearing.

"It almost sounded as if you let them go," the captain accused, surveying the scene. I had. What can I say? It's hard to shoot someone you know and hold in respect. My fellow combatants wouldn't care. They were just happy the fight had stopped, no matter the reason. "I'd think *we* drove off the ambush, sir. And isn't that what you are supposed to be doing out here? Making sure the column isn't ambushed."

"I'd say we did that quite successfully, captain…"

"Gates," he said as if I should have heard of him. "Horatio Gates." It was a name that all Americans would come to know, but not for more than twenty years. Arrogant son-of-a-bitch. But I get ahead of myself.

"Captain Gates," I said. "By the smoke, I'd say there were no more than a dozen warriors."

"And do you have any idea who it was?" he asked. "A French patrol."

"Delaware Indians," Tim answered.

"Chief Shingas was among them," I added.

"Shingas?" Gates asked. "The Delaware king? Why, he was in our camp at Cumberland just a week ago."

"He was," I answered.

"Traitorous savages," Gates muttered. "Fought the Mi'kmaq and their damned Wabanaki Confederacy at Chignecto. It's the same everywhere." We all had our own personal stories of relationships with the Indians turning bloody. It's what happened when two different cultures came into contact.

"Maybe," I said. "Or maybe our good general made it impossible for Shingas to do anything other than fall under the protection of his French fathers."

Gates was conceited beyond measure. But he could see right away that it was beneath an officer of his caliber to argue with the likes of me. "Bury this man," he said of the provincial soldier. A glance sent two of his infantry men digging in their packs for their small shovels. They tossed them on the ground for us to use. "When you're done, report what has happened to the general. We'll take over the scouting duties for the remainder of the day."

I shrugged, thinking his sharp, red coated lads looked like ripe targets amidst the greens and browns of the wilderness. "Suit yourself."

Without further discussion, they slowly marched away on a course similar to the one we had originally set. Their job was not to eliminate every tiny force of hostile Indians, but to protect the main column for our advance to the Forks of Ohio.

Tim reclined on the log he'd hidden behind during the fight, shutting his eyes to help control the pain. The rest of us found a place on the forest floor with the fewest roots snaking over it from the towering trees above. It was a pastoral place tucked into one side of the briar mass.

Then, alternating between sitting silently out of respect for the dead, or digging, nearly an hour passed by. Not a word was said, for it was the first dead body of a man seen by some of the younger ones. Hell. I was a younger one at that point. Unfortunately, I'd already seen a lifetime's worth of dead men and women, starting with my murdered older sister when I was five. I've laid eyes on many more since.

Unseen and in the distance, we heard Braddock's great army continuing on. Teamsters called to their beasts. Wheels crashed up and over stray roots or rocks. Chains rattled. The occasional whip cracked. The van was long gone. Even the main body had passed. It was now the baggage train of heavy carriages and rear guard that slowly creaked by, echoing through the trees.

Nearer to us, the wild animals started to make their tentative returns to an area they had fled when our battle had erupted. Thinking all was safe, a curious black-capped chickadee flapped to a halt next to us. It soon began its indicative *whoo-who* song as if we were nowhere to be found or just a part of the scenery. The bird remained, singing brightly, when I stood and helped the others drag the body and lower it into the grave.

Those of us with hats each set them to our hearts and silently mourned the man whose name I had known back then, but cannot remember now. I have seen so much death, so many men culled by the hand of Providence. He was but one more.

When I opened my lips to order the grave be filled, Zeb slapped his hand over my mouth. Before I had a chance to smack him across the face, he pointed into the woods beyond the thick briars in the direction from which we'd come. There, skulking toward the main column, was Shingas. He was cunning, deserving of his warrior reputation. With a hunch that our army's scouts had moved on, he had returned to probe the rear of the march. This time, however, he had with him not a dozen men. I stopped counting at fifty.

The entire train itself was not in danger from so small a force. But Shingas and the others could easily attack the baggage, kill dozens, and make off with badly needed stores. And the five of us were the only ones in any position to stop them.

Donning our cocked hats, we shook Taeheek awake. Then our small platoon hefted our weapons and stealthily ran on a course parallel to Shingas.

And I had no real idea what to do.

CHAPTER TWENTY-FIVE

Like most of my life, I made up the details of our pursuit as we went along. Familiar with every ravine and rabbit hole, Shingas, however, needed no real planning. He and his men raced with amazing speed through the forest, making the same level of noise as a few scattering deer. They communicated with an occasional whistle, whisper, or hoot. On the other hand, we were afraid to utter a word. As such, it was a challenge for us to gain ground with any cohesion. Nonetheless, we did manage to keep up and keep secret.

Confident that they hadn't been discovered and without taking a glance backward, the Delaware attackers began to fan out. The din of the army became louder. Its dust and stench followed closely behind the noise, hovering like a pall beneath the tree canopy. The sweat of human and beast mixed with the fumes of animal waste. The skulking Indians crawled and crept closer to the army's path, which ran a rod's length below the grade of the woods down a gentle slope. They used some of the trees, recently felled by our road workers and shoved up the hill, as cover. One-by-one our foes found their hidden shooting positions and nodded to Shingas, who took a spot in the center behind a boulder.

We had seconds to act.

Some thirty yards off the right rear flank of Shingas and his warriors, I dropped to my knee. Tim, needing no direction, dropped next to me with a small grunt. His shirt and bandage were blanketed with red. But the blood was no longer seeping and had begun to dry. Both good signs. Zeb took a knee on my left while the other two scouts stood tall, bunched up behind us. Without any order, we all leveled our muskets at whomever we could see.

I gave my shrillest war whoop and our muskets snapped and then burst to action, spitting flames and shot out the muzzles. My Bess kicked into my shoulder like a draft horse. An instant later, through her smoke, I saw my target topple forward out of view. To his side, I watched at least two more Delaware fall, wounded. I slammed Bess' butt into the earth and began the process of reloading. My comrades did the same with their muskets.

On my left and a second later, Zeb's face exploded in a burst of blood, bones, and brains. I was splattered with a thick coat of the ghoulish paint. The seventy-five caliber blast shoved Zeb limp against the legs of one of our standing men. His focus, however, stayed on the task of feverish reloading, more for self-preservation than any great courage. Bullets ripped the ground and brush around us as the Indians turned the focus of their attack.

We couldn't see the army down on the newly built road. But we could hear them in between the thunderous cracks of the battle we'd begun. Warned of the attack by our premature discharge, a Virginian officer shouted orders to the rearguard of his fellow countrymen. A drummer beat out his version of what he heard. The musician would be a boy of about thirteen, likely releasing a firkin's worth of piss into his breeches. "Platoon. Fire by rolling rank!" called the officer. *Tappity-tap* went the drum. *Boom, boom, boom. Boom, boom, boom.* It was a rough, stuttering volley, not the artful blasts set off by His Majesty's regulars, for the rearguard was just provincials. Nonetheless, musket balls crashed into the fallen log cover of the Indians on the ridge and up into the leaves of the tree canopy.

We'd successfully alerted the army. Now it was their job to drive the invaders away. Then, I was suddenly terrified that Shingas would order an immediate retreat – right through us. There would be no way for any of us to survive their swiping club and tomahawk blows if that happened.

I raised my weapon into firing position, but hesitated, preferring to keep a shot ready in case I was charged. Fortunately, the Delaware king disregarded our tiny lot, preferring to inflict as much damage as possible on the column. Raising his war hatchet and giving a shrill call of his own, he leapt over the boulder he had used for shelter. His warriors followed on his heels. And a heartbeat later, we were abandoned in the forest.

"Come!" Taeheek rasped, his bloodlust up from battle. He hiked his musket and ran to the small ridge just deserted by the Indians. After glancing toward the mangled form of Zeb, I, and the rest, joined.

We dove against the cover overlooking the army column. A few warriors lay next to us slowly bleeding to death from our own shooting and that of the platoons below. Close to a dozen tattooed and war-painted Delaware lay scattered over the short hill down to the road. They'd been killed at close range by the fire from the Virginians. More than a score of the Indians, led by Shingas, were fiercely engaged in hand-to-hand combat with the rearguard. Bayonets sang. Men cried out. Many more soldiers raced to the fracas from the main body of troops some distance ahead. Finally, a brace of Delaware warriors had pulled away from the rest. These two climbed into the back of a wagon to pilfer goods and kill its unarmed driver.

The entire scene was shocking in its brutality. But it was the small clash in the wagon that gave me a start. "No!" I screamed.

With the musket muzzles of my team flashing next to me, I jumped down the hill and ran headlong toward the wagon. I jumped over several bodies just as the first invader of the cart had pinned down the driver on his back. The fearless warrior's long knife was perched over the Pennsylvanian's eye as they grappled, struggling to see who had the most strength at that moment in time. I already knew which of them would win. And it wouldn't be the teamster.

Unless I acted. I slammed to a halt and raised my Bess. She felt sweet in my hands, almost as good as the real live Bess. I said an infinitely short prayer for accuracy and unleashed her fury. My shot was not fatal to the Indian. I had aimed high to avoid killing the driver. The ball skidded over the Indian's back, ripping a gash that probably plucked out a chunk of his vertebrae. He arched in pain and fell off the wagoner, who scampered up and over the other side of his cart. I dropped Bess into the dust – I didn't own a bayonet – and jerked my tomahawk free, advancing.

The second Delaware warrior at the wagon saw my approach. After I'd taken down his friend, he turned on me, sprinting. We closed the gap with one another with breakneck speed, clashing. We fought like dogs, like cocks in a pen. His hatchet against mine. My sinews against his. Fists and nails. Knees and elbows. Foreheads and jaws. We employed everything we had in a draining battle that was not heroic or pretty. It was horrible, brutal.

He rolled me over onto my back and straddled my chest, raising his tomahawk swiftly. I saw his teeth, though he didn't smile. He clenched them, red lines of blood outlining each yellow tooth. I was a hair's breadth from death.

When a tiny blinding flash bolted across the sky. A deerskin-covered stone had bounced off his temple. He momentarily looked away from me. Then came another flash, this one *whooshing*. The Delaware's head snapped so his ear awkwardly rested on one of his shoulders. He grew heavier as his weight sunk onto my ribcage. The warrior then sat on me motionless, his surprised face staring at me with grotesque lifelessness. His bladder had just begun releasing its urine, when a foot wearing a moccasin kicked the body to the side.

Tim had his La Crosse club settled on his shoulder. A smear of the Delaware's blood decorated the basket. He grinned as he scooped up the hard ball from the ground. "You must really love eating to nearly get killed protecting a wagon full of salted port, Rebekah." At least he hadn't called me, Shit-for-brains.

"It's Ephraim. Ephraim," I insisted, slowly climbing to my feet. Then I remembered why I had raced to action in the first place. I spun to see the wagon, but the attacker I'd shot had already fled. Looking around, I saw that the entirety of the short battle had ended. Shingas and more than a score of warriors were disappearing into the woods without pursuit. Braddock, Washington, and an entire regiment of heavy infantry rumbled in. The general barked orders, riding regally up and down the column. Washington cut a straight line to the Virginian officer who had commanded the rearguard. The colonel's interview about the incident commenced immediately.

"So, we heard them whoop, but their first shots didn't fall anywhere among us. We were fortunate," the officer reported.

"That was us," I said, limping over. "We saw them approach and called out a warning. We shot at them from behind to give you time."

"Good thinking," said the officer.

Washington, from atop his charger, gave me an approving nod. "Well done, Mr. Weber."

"Ephraim Weber?" asked a familiar voice from my distant past.

I was not surprised, for I knew who it was. I had seen him during the battle. Turning back to the wagon, I saw the young and terrified driver peering over the sideboards. "Yes, it's me," I answered simply.

"You saved my life," the teamster gasped. "I thought you were dead," he squeaked.

"I know," I said with a shrug. "I like it that way." I actually didn't like it that way. I was too young to understand the value that came with anonymity. Back then I still wanted my share of renown for all my exploits, good and bad.

Washington gave me a sideways glance. "Do you know everyone on this continent, Mr. Weber?"

I didn't.

Nodding, I said, "Yes, colonel. And that fart-in-the-wind hiding on the other side of the wagon is my brother. One of them, anyway. Last I knew, I had four. Four?" I asked my younger brother, Caleb.

"Four," Caleb confirmed. "But we have a new sister since you left. With you that means there are five boys and three girls. Eight in all."

"There were nine of us," I hissed. "Four girls."

His forehead crinkled. "I think I should remember how many sisters I have."

He obviously didn't. "Never mind," I said, remembering the anger I held toward my parents and why I'd run away in the first place. As if accepting the tragedy of the murder of their oldest daughter with nary a peep of justice wasn't enough of an affront. They had to go and bottle up every mention, every indication that I'd ever had an older sister. My younger siblings never knew. Well, I knew. And I'd never forget.

And I never have.

CHAPTER TWENTY-SIX

If fateful decisions had thus far been made on our expedition, there were more to come. Everything, every action in my life, seemed to sprout up from a choice that I made in some mundane circumstance. Events tumbled out of control from a decision as trivial as bathing or not. Eating the bacon or the bread or both. Tying a kerchief around my neck with the knot on the right, the center, or the left. Somehow every small decision added up, leading me on some cascading path. I've quit trying to ascertain too much detail. Accurately predicting the outcomes of my actions and those of others has had little positive effect on my life. It has been best to keep my mind clear and operate in the moment. So, what exactly was the ill-fated decree produced on this particular night, I cannot say. I know only that one was made.

As aide to one of the general's aides, I went along with Colonel Washington to Braddock's tent the night following the ambush of the rearguard. It was a large structure made of thick sailcloth pulled taut over more posts than trees in a small forest. He had the tent divided into two rooms. An enormous meeting and dining area at the front housed a long, imported table. And a second chamber rested behind an opaque screen. The rear room contained the general's desk, allowing for privacy as he wrote letters and orders. The back section also held trunks of his clothing and had ample space for his bed. A small flap at the rear of the structure allowed for quick and discreet ingress or egress of his presumably well-compensated whores.

As usual, we had come just a moment early. Washington was always punctual, thinking it a mark of respect to appear at any engagement exactly on time. This trait endeared him to most of his superiors, Braddock included.

Though the table was mostly empty now, once the officer corps arrived, there would not be enough seats for me to sit. I stood behind the colonel, tapping my foot to a tavern tune that twirled about in my mind. Anything to stave off boredom as the required attendees filed in.

"Swept them away today, eh, Washington?" the general said, making conversation.

Croghan punched his way into the tent. He was followed by the Captain Gates I had met in the woods earlier in the day. From his place at the head of the table, Braddock acknowledged each newcomer with a curt nod. His eyes silently told them which seat to take.

"Yes, I believe we were fortunate to have employed experienced woodsmen as scouts," the colonel answered. "Keen eyes and quick thinking saved many lives."

The quartermaster breezed in through the flap. He was swearing loudly to another officer, but not out of anger. Sir John was just one of those men who peppered his speech with profanities. Well, the number of choice terms he actually inserted was considerably more than a dash. He employed curse words like a sweet-toothed baker used sugar. Four lettered varieties appeared to be his favorite. He went on with his swearing even after sitting, but was respectful enough of the general's ongoing conversation to lower his tone. Lieutenant Colonel Gage, one of the commanders from the vanguard regiments and the officer who had been sucked into the curse-laden conversation, quickly found his spot. Several majors and a few more captains arrived at the meeting thereafter.

"Aye," the general agreed. "Even so, those Virginians at the rear drove the savages away effectively enough." It was a rare compliment given to provincial troops. All eyes on the table gave Braddock a second glance to be sure he hadn't been replaced by a changeling. Even Sir John, the quartermaster, paused mid-curse to raise his eyebrows in surprise.

"Thank you," said Washington, speaking for the captain who had commanded the rear. "Four good men gave their lives in the rear today. It sounds as if another two may die of their wounds yet tonight."

"And my two scouts died," I reminded the colonel.

Braddock gave me a frosty glare for speaking out of turn. But Washington took it as intended. "So, we may have lost a total of eight brave soldiers," the colonel summarized.

"Regrettable," the general allowed with a dismissive wave in the air. "But we've preserved the column. I note the cowardly savages made certain to avoid my regulars. Their effective command and training would have sent the painted bastards to hell quicker than a slick trout slips through the hands."

Ah, I thought, there were the usual sentiments of the general. His regulars were worth three provincials any day.

"All told, how many of the foxes did we kill today?" Braddock asked.

Washington, after briefly struggling to control his rage at one more attack on the abilities of his fellow colonists, pulled a small note from his fob pocket. "Twenty-six on and around the road. Seven on the ridge. And...it looks like four at the first meeting between Mr. Weber and the Delaware."

Horatio Gates cleared his throat.

"You have something to add, captain?" Braddock asked.

"We saved Mr. Weber's inexperienced scouts from certain catastrophe. I am confident our single volley dropped more than a score of the rascals," Gates said with all the sincerity of a Jesuit missionary. He almost convinced me. Almost. I know we killed no more than the four cited by Washington. Gates hadn't even bothered to walk over to Shingas' lines and peruse the remains of the battle.

"Fifty-seven!" Braddock said. It was really thirty-seven. "I shall round it to seventy since we know many of the savages will die out in the woods from the wounds we've given them."

"A fair assumption," Gates said. "I was happy to be of service." Self-serving ass.

Washington neatly folded the page that tallied the casualties and replaced it into his fob pocket. He spent a full five seconds silently judging Horatio Gates across the table.

Braddock rapped his knuckles on the tabletop indicating he was ready to begin with the business portion of the war council. "I am most displeased by the progress we make." He looked at the poor officer in charge of the road making crews and waited for an explanation.

"This country is most inhospitable, general," said the tired man. "Even the roughest regions of your homeland, in Scotland, have paths that approach roads. I'm afraid we start from scratch in this wilderness."

"I've given you tools. Cut down some trees," the general explained. "Push them to the side."

"The men do so, general. Nonstop," answered the road's engineer. "But we must make the trail wide enough for our baggage and carriages. The base must be firm enough to carry our howitzers and cannons. If we don't tear out or cover up the roots, the spokes of our wheels would shatter and our beasts would come up lame or worse."

"Is there anything we can do to improve our transportation?" Braddock asked the collection of officers.

Sir John huffed. "There's nothing that can be done in this godforsaken land to improve anything. It's a shithole, sir. Bleak as a privy lacking a supply of old newsprint. But I've got you all the wagons and supplies you needed." He hadn't. Most of the wagons and teams came as a result of Franklin's manufactured plea. "We have to accept it. Our train just takes up space and requires finesse. Like screwing a good whore, sir." His eyes sparkled beneath raised eyebrows.

Braddock wasn't in the mood to joke about his harlots. "Suggestions?"

"General, sir," said Croghan. "You and the men may think of this region as hell on earth. But it's my home. I've traveled these hills and valleys, taking goods to and fro for decades. I know the march can be done in a manner that is quicker than our current pace."

"Well, speak up. Don't create the suspense," Braddock demanded. "This isn't the theater."

"Packhorses," Croghan answered, cutting to the chase.

"Packhorses? We've got hundreds of them."

"Double the number and eliminate a majority of the wagon train by commandeering most of the teams as pack animals," Croghan explained. "Your foresters will cut in half the number of trees that must be felled. They'll save time hauling earth to create a base. And the column itself will suddenly spring along."

Braddock frowned, the outside corners of his bushy eyebrows scrunching down to his cheeks. Folding his arms and leaning back in his chair, he growled in displeasure.

"It's a fine idea, sir," said Washington. "We ought to employ Mr. Croghan's plan with tomorrow's march. Furthermore, general, sir, we may increase our speed of advance even more."

"Go on," Braddock prodded, hoping for some other solution.

"Send back the heaviest baggage, not just the unnecessary wagons. The excess luggage will be safe with a minimal guard. Those of us still advancing will draw the entire focus of any ambushes planned by the French or Delaware. Also, sir, we must quit building bridges over every river we cross. There will be time to circle back and do so after we've successfully taken the Forks."

"Except for good cause, a British army doesn't swim through a river like a common savage," Braddock growled.

"It's a good cause to move swiftly, sir," Washington answered.

Unconvinced, Braddock asked. "Is there nothing else you can think of?" He scanned his officers.

But he hadn't paid me any attention. "You could send back the howitzers and cannon, too," I offered.

"What's this provincial prick doing here?" Sir John asked.

The general paid his quartermaster no heed. Instead, he leaned forward on the table, perturbed. "And just how many times have you faced the French in battle, you green lad?" It was a rhetorical question. I should have known.

I looked up at the sailcloth ceiling as I counted on my fingers. "At least three, sir. More if you count the times I've fought against their Indian allies. How about you?"

The general's face turned cherry red. For all his experience, he had never fought in open battle against the French. Though I had heard he'd been on the losing end of a siege carried out by the French in the last war.

It was Washington's turn to clear his throat. "The boy has a suggestion, sir. The terrain is not suited to the transport of heavy artillery. We will save much time by forgetting them altogether."

"And how do you propose we breach the walls of Fort Duquesne?" This time it was Captain Gates, coming to his general's aid.

"I've been to the Forks more than once," Washington said, a slight admonition to the other officers in the tent. "If the French have been fortunate enough to bring in a pair of cannon, that would be miraculous. In any case, an army of this size will easily starve them out and hold off any reinforcements that can possibly arrive in time. A formal siege with cannonade may be unnecessary. If an old-fashioned escalade is required," the colonel patted his pocket that still held the map of Duquesne drawn by Stobo. "We know just how to launch it."

Braddock clicked his tongue, contemplating the new idea. He then rested back in his seat, forgetting all about me, or the fact that it was I who proposed getting rid of the artillery. "Gentlemen, Mr. Washington has made some fine suggestions. But given his inexperience in true war, they require refinement. We will *delay* the approach of several of the howitzers and cannons."

"Delay?" asked Sir John. "What in the pope's ass does that mean?"

Braddock slowly stood from his seat, preparing to lecture us in the manner he had condescendingly addressed the royal governors in Alexandria. We were his pupils, none of us considered stars. "Each of you has failed to come close enough to the proper solution to our quandary." He reached both hands to assure his wig was secure, twisted it a finger's breadth, and then proceeded. "I'll just explain what needs to be done starting tomorrow. I cannot delay any longer." The general glanced through the opaque screen toward his unseen bed. "I've got an appointment that I must keep."

He went on. "We will split our army in two." I didn't like the sound of that. Halving the number troops available at any time seemed like an efficient way to get carved to minces.

"The slower column will take along most of the baggage. Not all," he added with a finger of warning. "It will carry some of the artillery, those howitzers and cannons that some of you have lamented. It will also be the source for the majority of our road improvement operations. This column will be permitted to travel at the current sluggish pace without affecting our campaign in the slightest."

"If the slow column continues to advance into enemy-held territory," Croghan asked. "Won't it need to be guarded?"

Braddock wasn't the least bit flummoxed. "Of course. Moving slowly, it may invite attack from the savages. Recall, they picked out our baggage today. But also remember that we are swimming in provincial soldiers. We don't need so many. Nearly half our troop strength can guard the support column and we'll *still* be saddled with a gaggle of colonials along with my regulars in the front column. Those undertrained Virginians proved today that even *they* can drive away a band of ill-led barbarians."

Warily, Washington asked, "And the front column?"

"Shall be called our flying column," Braddock announced triumphantly. He drove a fist into his open palm. "No longer will we slog through just a mile a day. The van of our regulars and scouts will run four, perhaps eight, miles before settling into camp. I've studied the maps you drew of the area, Mr. Washington. My compliments. They are quite detailed. I'm confident we can be at the Forks in less than a month's time. And then, if we must ford the Monongahela at the last minute to surprise and drive the French away, that is a tactical adjustment I am willing to make."

"Do you think it wise, sir?" asked Captain Gates, hesitantly. "Our forces could become separated enough that one would not be able to support the other."

"I'm counting on it," Braddock said boldly. "If we are within a day's ride of the support column, my plan has failed." He glared at each man in turn. "It shall not fail."

Lieutenant Colonel Thomas Gage, who had remained silent thus far, finally spoke. "It's a fine compromise, general. You've taken the suggestions of the locals regarding speed and terrain and mixed it with the experience of better men." Waiting for a decision to be announced and then proclaiming your faith in it, was a sure way for advancement. And this particular peacock was destined for advancement and infamy at helping to start another war. More on that will come in one of my later records.

Better men? I wondered, but said nothing. Nor did Washington. It was clear from the slight twitch in the colonel's head that he gave the older man a curious look.

"It's settled then," the general said, fluffing his shirt cuff beneath his coat in order to make himself more presentable to his night's companion. "Make the alterations necessary to our order of march, Mr. Washington. Colonel Gage will assist if you have any questions."

"I should not think I do have any questions," Washington said, calmly. "You require all the regular regiments in the flying column, supported by a small number of provincial troops. All but the barest necessities shall be in the support column at the rear."

Braddock placed a hand to his chin, thinking. "On second thought, speak to Sir John about what baggage is most necessary. He'll guide you properly." He disappeared around his screen. "You may send for the lady now," he said to an unseen attendant.

"Yes, sir," said a man's voice. The rear flap opened and the junior soldier scampered away.

The party of officers and Croghan began to break up, filing away from the table and out the front flap, held open by a Welsh servant who bid everyone a cheery goodnight.

"Could be a fair bit of trouble," Captain Gates whispered to Washington as he stood and left. This one phrase was enough to bring him back into my good graces, if only for the moment. "Good evening, sirs," he said to the other retiring officers.

Colonel Gage groaned as he stood. "Sounds like I'm off the hook playing nursemaid to an aide," he said referring to Washington, whose muscles bristled beneath his coat. "I'm going to bed. I'll need the rest. My vanguard will finally be making good time tomorrow." He swept out into the camp, whistling.

Sir John, the quartermaster, sat at the table with Washington. The colonel glanced toward the screen. Behind it, Braddock hummed like a lucky youth anticipating a certain excitement on his wedding night. Washington asked Sir John, "Shall we find a place that affords both..." he hesitated. "Both parties more privacy?"

Sir John smirked. "What I have to say won't take but a moment. The general and the lady will have their privacy for their..." It was his turn to hesitate.

"Activities," Washington said, finishing the thought in a tactful manner.

"Hell, no," Sir John said. "I'm sure the general will be spitting and grunting the whole time he's ploughing the lass. There's nothing as genteel as *activities* going on anywhere around that bed."

Braddock had overheard. He chuckled. "Get to your point, Sir John," he ordered.

The quartermaster did. "I know my general. If he says flying column, he means for us to fly. But that doesn't mean we jog around naked like the savages we've tamed. Make sure you provide enough of those provincial guards to watch over a dozen carriages for his personal baggage."

"And the whores, Sir John," Braddock said, unabashedly. "I've decided I want a horse for my favorite personal female company to ride. Her conversation in particular brings me much pleasure and I'd like to continue it during the day's march. Oh, and be sure to allow that Braun fellow, Lydius' man, to join us in the flying column. His wares are most welcomed after I'm parched."

"Yes, sir," Sir John said. "You heard the general. Don't skimp on the baggage, or his other personal needs." The quartermaster rose and waited impatiently at the closed flap of the tent. "What in hell are you waiting for?" he snapped to the Welsh attendant who stood outside. "Open the damn door."

Knuckles grabbed the edge and the flap opened. Sir John slipped through without a second glance.

"Hold that!" Washington curtly ordered the Welshman. The colonel stood, looked at me, exasperation covering his face, and said, "Come. We've got work to do."

"Good evening, Mr. Washington," Braddock called cheerily over the screen.

The colonel was not in the mood to answer. I responded for him. "Good evening, sir." And I ducked out after Washington.

Twenty feet later, his strides had only grown longer. He had his hands balled into fists at his sides and the colonel breathed loudly through his nose. He was as cross as I'd ever seen him. "They don't value provincial soldiers," he muttered. "Fine! At least give us a chance to show ourselves worthy. They won't take our advice about the map of Fort Duquesne. Fine. Allow me time to persuade. They will not heed even Captain Gates' warning about splitting our forces or Croghan's suggesting of eliminating carts altogether or mine about not bridging every creek along the way. Fine. Fine. Fine. I disagree, but fine!" He muttered in garbled tones for a few more moments before slowing and eventually coming to a halt. The colonel pressed a hand to his belly and winced.

"What is it, sir?" I asked. Despite his hollow voice, I had always seen him in the picture of health. "Are you alright?"

"Yes. I've got a strong constitution. I've seen enough of sickness in my life to know this is nothing. Just anxious to succeed." He bit his lip against some affliction and straightened up to his normal, perfect posture. "But now I must organize carriages and a personal mount for..." his voice dropped. "Trollops. Its unseemly."

I was less proper in my manners than the colonel. But even to me, the general and his staff's outright acceptance of whoring struck me as strange. Maybe worrisome. I suppose it had something to do with the fact that half of the colonies were populated by folks fed up with the hypocrisy of the Church in England and had left to plant their own, purer versions. "It is," I agreed. "And when Croghan finds out that one of the wagons especially requested was the one from Lydius, he'll go into a fit."

Washington pinched his eyes shut, while swallowing hard. His hand again shot up to his belly as if he'd been struck by a sudden bout of pain. "Shall I fetch Dr. James?" I asked. "He's been busy. Some of the men have fevers. And I've heard there's a tremor of dysentery about. But I'm sure he'll spare a moment."

"No. I'm fine. I did not eat my usual dinner. I'll be right by tomorrow's march." Then the pain passed or he was able to master it. Breathing easier, the colonel relaxed and pulled out a folded letter from one of his coat pockets. "And to top it off, I've got to deal with these issues!" He handed me the page.

George Washington was slow to make friends. If he had any at all in his entire life other than the woman who was to his become future bride, I'm sure I was not counted among them. But after knowing the young Virginian for two years, and after traversing the country with him now three times, I was about to get only the slightest glimpse into a personal life he shared with no one.

"Read the demands at the end," he told me as I unfolded the note.

I scanned to the bottom of the paper and read aloud, "*At your earliest convenience fetch me a Dutch servant. The last I had was merely adequate. I expect you to know better. And, more importantly, bring some butter. Your Mother. Mary Ball Washington.*" Confused, I slowly refolded the piece just as Washington gathered it back. His features indicated that he regretted succumbing to the impulse to share his family life with me.

But then his frustration won over. "Can you believe it?" he asked, tucking the letter away. "I am on campaign in hostile territory, passing through a place that was nearly my own grave a year ago where there is nary a civilized human being, let alone a mercantile. And my mother thinks it appropriate to tell me to find her a servant and some butter. Butter!" he hissed.

I thought of my own mother. "Mothers can be demanding," I said. "What do you mean to do?"

"Humph!" he said. "After I organize the general's strumpets into a proper and safe order for our march tomorrow, I shall respond to my mother's most irrational demands. The honorable woman will know from her dutiful son that both of her requirements will have to go unfilled for the moment as I am in a part of the country where they are impossible to obtain." He sighed. "These are the days I wish to speak to my dear Lawrence. A better man than I. He would know what to do."

Lawrence was Washington's older half-brother. He'd raised the colonel after the death of their father. Lawrence had even held Washington's position in the army before his death just a few years ago. My Washington looked up to the departed Washington in deep reverence.

"Mr. Weber," Washington said. He was rapidly shaking off his moment of pain and melancholy. "You've done well today. You'll find yourself busy enough scouting in the weeks to come.

I've decided I don't need your assistance tonight. Retire to your own brother and visit. Do not allow those fraternal bonds to break."

My brother and I weren't terribly close. We weren't enemies though. "Alright, sir," I said. I then pointed to his stomach. "Take care of that."

He smiled thinly as was his way. Though unlined and unravaged by time, his smooth complexion carried a weight beyond his current responsibilities. I think he worried about things that he didn't even know he worried about, things that hadn't happened. Campaigns, armies, and battles to come. "Thank you, Mr. Weber, I will. And since I am in charge of making the order of the march, I'll make sure your brother's wagon is in the flying column so you can keep an eye on him. It appeared like you have a strong desire to protect him."

I did. He needed it. "Thank you," I said.

And I retired, leaving Washington completely vexed with his abdomen and his general. As far as I remember, I hadn't offered him a salute that night. I never saluted the colonel by grasping my hat's brim or tipping it. After all, I never wore a uniform beyond my own buckskins or a coarse set of breeches. I was hardly a soldier in any sense. But I was resourceful and dedicated. In that, he and I just had an understanding.

CHAPTER TWENTY-SEVEN

After much asking around the encampment, I eventually found Caleb enjoying a small fire among a group of other teamsters. Sparks danced into the black night sky as one of the drivers played with a stick in the burning logs. Around the blaze, curses and lies rolled from their lips like waves against a beach. While exchanging their stories, the cadre of handlers shared a generous portion of salted pork that they'd pilfered from the back of Caleb's wagon. Based on Sir John's slapdash treatment of his quartermaster duties, no one would be the wiser. I was, therefore, happy to accept when they offered me a crackling slab from their frypan.

"Hot!" I breathed around a mouthful that sat sizzling on my tongue. "Good."

"Some of it might be from father's hogs," Caleb said proudly. "When he saw the broadsides calling for Pennsylvanian teamsters, he sent me. *Was the loyal thing to do for the king*, he said. But he also sent along a half-dozen fatties to market."

"I imagine the army will pay handsomely for your services and the meat," I said, feeling a layer of skin slough off the roof of my mouth and tongue. It would be three days until anything tasted normal again. Not that the flavors of trail meals were all that enticing in the first place.

"Father told me not to accept any pay for the team, wagon, or the hogs. *Just make sure they feed ya*. That's what he said."

"Humph," I muttered. "Sounds like him. Lets you slave away for someone else."

"What do you mean?" Caleb asked. He was an innocent kid who seemed to ignore or not notice the bad in most people. Except for the occasional trance put on me by the fairer sex, I had never suffered from this particular affliction.

I didn't want to fight with the first member of my family on whom I had set eyes in over five years. Or was it six? Perhaps I had been gone from the farm for as many as seven or eight years by then. With my traversing the wilderness for Croghan since I was as thin as a blade of grass and about as tall, I had lost track. "Nothing," I said, waving it off. "Good for him. Pa's giving to the cause. How about you? You willing to give your life for king and country?"

This had caught Caleb off guard. "Uh, I suppose. But I'd rather not," he stammered.

I tugged my knife from my belt. It was a good one, sharp, with a good temper. And among the best pieces of any equipment I owned. Certainly better than my Brown Bess, which was cobbled together from a dozen stolen parts. "You'd better have some protection out here. The Delaware are in a state."

Caleb didn't even lift a finger to take the gift. "I'm alright, Ephraim. Don't need it. We've always had good relations with the Indians. I bet there are seven Delaware families coming to our church these days."

I laughed out loud. "Tell that to one who is racing toward you in full paint and bloodlust. I'm sure he'll be in a discriminating mood." I snapped my fingers. "Oh, right. That very thing happened today. How did that work out for you?"

Caleb quietly watched the fire burn, temporarily lost in thought. He probably wished that I'd not come to visit. "You know I can't take the knife, Ephraim" he said calmly. "Even though you abandoned your family and your faith doesn't mean I have to."

It looked like I'd be arguing anyway. "I didn't abandon anyone!" I hissed. "Is that what they told you? They abandoned me. You think pa is high and mighty. You think ma is the picture of virtue. Well they ain't! They left me out to dry after what happened to Trudie."

He shook his head in disgust, folding his thin arms at his chest. "I was too young and don't remember much about you, brother. But that's just how ma and pa described you. Hot-tempered. I don't know who Trudie is or what that has to do with you running away when mother and father needed you," Caleb said, fixing me with a glare. His fellow teamsters had decided to move away from the fire as our conversation grew heated enough to warm the entire Western Wilderness.

"Ha!" I exclaimed. "You don't know anything because they won't tell you anything. That's why you didn't even know if I was still alive. They probably never told you I wrote to them."

His surprise proved that I'd guessed correctly. Caleb shook his head.

"I did. A bunch of times. But the last time was a few years ago now. Got frustrated when I realized they'd never write me back. And so, my letters became sporadic. I stopped wasting my time entirely when they didn't even say congratulations after I got married."

"You're married?" He sized up my pathetic kit and probably wondered how I'd ever afford a wife. Just a couple years prior, as the son-in-law to a powerful Miami chief, I had been on my way to becoming a prosperous trader. Even now, I could still become one if I ever gave up following Washington and this cause against the French. But I hated the French too much to stop trying to kill them.

"Not anymore," I growled. I returned to my pork, picking and chewing. It was cooling. It was probably delicious but I couldn't taste it. My raw tongue was numb. I threw the plate onto the ground, suddenly not hungry.

"What happened to your wife?" Caleb asked quietly.

My first inclination was to snap. But then I remembered that even as a young child he had been caring. Though Caleb was two years my junior, he'd often find me stewing in the barn over some minor issue. A few minutes of talking and I was usually fully mended. He had always been a good brother. My issue was not with him. I sighed. "She was killed right in front of me."

His hand covered his mouth. "Oh. I'm sorry, Ephraim. I didn't know."

"Ya," I said quietly. "They never told you about a good many things." We sat silently for a long while. It was how brothers communicated.

"Your wife's name was Trudie?" he asked at last. Apparently, we had not been communicating as effectively as I had thought.

Like a lightning bolt, anger raced through my blood. But I managed to keep it in check. For that, Washington might have been proud of me. "No," I said sadly. "Her name was Tahki."

"Indian?" he asked.

"Miami," I answered, nodding. "Murdered by a French officer at Pickawillany."

"I guess that might make you want to take up the hatchet," he said thoughtfully. It was a fairly understanding sentiment coming from a fellow Quaker.

"It did. And I did."

Caleb's brow furrowed. "Revenge? You killed him?"

It was a long story. "No. But he's dead now."

"The Justice of Providence," he whispered. It was a little high and mighty, right out of father's toolkit. But Caleb meant it. And, in a way, I believed it, too.

"Yes," I muttered. "But that's all behind me, now. I've got a new woman to woo. Once this campaign is all done, I'll go back to Williamsburg and get married."

Caleb brightened. It was a genuine smile. "Good for you. Her name?"

"Bess," I said confidently. Then I remembered that the last letter I'd written to her had been harsh. "But I've got some fences to mend. I don't think she's happy with me away all the time."

Caleb twisted on his seat and rustled in a pack. He produced a box of writing instruments and paper. "If you haven't written to her, you're welcome to my gear. I've written to the family every day. You should do the same for Bess. With Franklin's mail system, it'll almost be like she's right here with you."

I chuckled. Caleb would never believe that I had met Benjamin Franklin and counted him as a friend. "It's a good idea," I said. "I'll write to her tonight and tell her all about my day. I'm sure she'll love the blood and death especially."

"You're not making fun of me, are you?" Caleb asked.

I held up my hands in surrender. "A little," I said, smiling. "But I will write to her about today. I promise." And I meant it. He was right. I had no reason not to – other than my own pride. It was time to abandon my personal arrogance in favor of a future with Bess. There was something about getting shot at and seeing men drop around me that had put me in a forgiving mood.

"Speaking of today," Caleb began. "Wasn't the colonel you were talking to on the road George Washington?"

I had a lot of stories to tell Caleb. He'd believe almost none of them since my name had so conspicuously been left from all accounts of the events over the previous three years. The men listed in the newspaper stories had become famous. I had remained anonymous and penniless. But I grinned as I thought about exactly where to start my tale. "Ya. I'm sort of Washington's helper. I track for him. I scout. I procure goods. All kinds of stuff. I do whatever he tells me when he says, *excuse me, Mr. Weber*." I said the last bit with my best imitation of Washington's proper but hollow-chested whisper.

"Mr. Weber?" came a gruff voice not five feet from behind me.

Caleb and I spun to see a band of men had been walking past our fire among the tents, livestock, and wagons of camp. "Yes?" we both asked.

One of the men peeled away from the group and approached. I did not need to see his battered face illuminated by the firelight. His enormous form told me all I needed to know.

"If it's not Ephraim Weber," said Alex Braun with feigned pleasure. He glanced around the area. "And not a single officer in sight to protect you from the thrashing you deserve. I spent more time in irons and you'll pay for it."

CHAPTER TWENTY-EIGHT

I'd like to tell you that Caleb and I joined forces with the other teamsters and sent Braun and his fellow batch of drivers scurrying away. Instead, I'll tell you the truth.

"Listen!" I said, jumping up and scooting away. I was smart enough not to draw my weapons. Washington would have me hanged if I killed a man in camp. And Braun didn't tug out his knife. He was large enough that he wouldn't need any help in pummeling me. "Alex, listen. I was just protecting Bess. You were drunk. She was drunk. Things got out of hand and in some way, you got what you deserved."

He stepped over the log I'd been sitting on and into the firelight. I grimaced. His mangled, shadowed nose was positively hideous in the dark. Perhaps he'd gotten a little more than he deserved.

Rolling up his sleeves, Braun said, "Oh, were you drunk? Was it just a drunken brawl in which you got the better of me?"

I glanced at Caleb who had sensibly backed away. His fellow drivers just watched. They'd not shed any blood for me. Holding up my hands, I said, "You know I wasn't. I just came from the La Crosse game. I misunderstood what was going on. That's all. I thought you were going to have your way with Bess."

He snorted. "Of course, I was. Who wouldn't?" Braun kept inching closer, corralling me toward a set of parked wagons so I couldn't outrun him. Speed was my only chance of survival.

"Well, maybe you didn't know that she and I are to be married," I said as calmly as possible. Just the thought of him climbing onto my Bess, filled me with rage. But I attempted to set my emotions aside. It was another instance when Washington, had he ever been aware, would have found reason to praise my self-control.

Braun stopped. For an instant I thought I had gotten through to him. Our long-term misunderstanding had come to an end. Shooting me in Albany had been satisfaction enough. He stood up tall and craned around to his gang of teamsters. "This fella thinks that the town harlot in Williamsburg is going to marry him."

As one would expect, his sycophants laughed. I, too, would have laughed had the shoe been on someone else's foot. "Take it back, Braun," I instructed. "Just because she chose me over everybody else doesn't mean you need to be cruel."

He scoffed. "Can't believe it." Braun waved me off like I was refuse. "You're sadder than I thought. Not worth my time. You'll get your due soon enough. More pain than I can give you." Braun turned to leave.

"Apologize, Alex," I demanded.

Braun halted. "Settle down," he said, again stepping toward me. "You've got some fire. That's good. But I ain't going to apologize. Just consider us even. You'll see what I mean soon enough."

"Damn it!" I muttered. I could foresee the outcome of what I was about to do. And I did it anyway. Like a wildcat, I dove onto Braun. I scratched, kicked, and pawed.

It was no contest. He didn't even topple over from my momentum. Instead, he fixed his wrench-like hands around my shoulders while I squirmed. Braun walked me to the nearest wagon and slammed my back against it. What happened next felt like an hour of thumping. I think Braun punched me from my waist to my crown a dozen times. The pounding lasted no more than thirty seconds. When he was done, I was left coughing in the dust.

"And now we are again even," Braun said, walking confidently away. "Maybe this time you'll listen."

Caleb rushed to my side when the coast was clear. He helped prop me up against the uncomfortable spokes of the wagon. "That wasn't too bright, Ephraim," he said, dabbing at a cut that Braun's knuckle had torn in my cheek. "I'm sure this Bess is worth defending, but they were just words."

"Sure," I muttered. I tasted the iron of my own blood. Apparently, a burned tongue can still discern some flavors. Then I giggled, thinking just how correct Caleb had been. I was not very bright to attack Braun when he was about to let me off the hook. It's hard to explain the feelings I had back then to someone who has never had them. But when I was young, I had a fire in my belly to right every wrong. And I would do so with as much violence as it took. I suppose it began after what happened to Trudie, the sister Caleb didn't even know he had. I struggled against his attention to stand.

Caleb shoved me down. "Just stay here until morning. You're in no condition to go anywhere."

Against his wishes, I used him like a crutch, climbing up his body until I wobbled on my feet next to him. "Sure. Sure, Caleb." I patted his shoulder in the most patronizing way possible and stepped away. "See you tomorrow," I said, setting one hand over the other along the sideboards of the wagon. "You and your bacon will be in the flying column."

"Flying column?" Caleb asked.

"I have to keep an eye on you somehow," I muttered. Then I laughed. A sprinkle of blood leaked from one of my nostrils. I could hardly protect myself from myself.

He gave voice to my thoughts. "You seem like the one who needs protecting."

"See you in the morning, little brother. You'll be in the first column protected by His Majesty's finest. And me."

"What are you saying?" he asked.

I ignored him and staggered into the camp. Like my father when I'd run away, Caleb made no attempt to pursue.

Some hours later I was awakened by the clatter of pots and pans not a yard away from where I slept. My eyes crept open, each lid weighing a solid ton.

It was still dark, but the camp was coming to life for the early march. Conversations began to hum with the rumor of the splitting of the army. Tents were collapsed. Animals were fed. Breakfasts were fixed.

Again, with the clattering. And so unbelievably close. A pan was set roughly onto a grate over a smoky fire. Someone, a novice, had tossed green logs onto the previous night's embers and tried to coax heat from them. "Stupid goat!" the woman grumbled about her neophyte set-up. She crouched not two feet from me. Her rump faced me, but was hidden behind her skirts, which hung down to my face level in the dirt. "Of all the damn stupid things," she groused under her breath. Even through my headache, I could hear that she had the voice of a young woman. Though I couldn't see her face, I imagined she was pretty.

The smoke thickened and blew directly toward her. She coughed, waving her hand. When it cleared, the woman snatched the pot handle with a cloth and proceeded to repeatedly slam it against the cooking grate. Her cursing matched time with the slaps. My head felt like it was rattling inside a massive bell.

"Is everything going well out there?" called a voice from the tent beyond the fire. I noticed that the sailcloth shroud was well lit from the inside. Its occupants must have pooled their monies to buy a lantern.

The pot beating, thankfully, stopped. But my head continued its painful thumping. "Yes," answered the woman, not allowing any of the frustration to show. "Water for tea will be ready in a moment."

"Ah, thank you, my pet," came the reply. It was a rolling Scottish accent. Braddock. "I'm going to meet with my officers at the head of the column. Bring in the water. I'll be back afore the rooster crows. Together, we'll break the fast at the table before jumping off."

"Be right there," she said cheerfully as her benefactor walked through his great tent to exit via his front door. So, I had passed out behind the general's tent. And I was looking up the rump of one of his trollops – maybe his favorite. This was one of those instances when Washington would not be proud of me.

I glanced past her and saw that the dawn was not far off. But I judged that I had perhaps a half hour to rest before loping to my horse for the day's ride. I closed my eyes, not caring a lick about the general and his damnable activities. I wanted only respite.

The prostitute began coughing again. I attempted to ignore the commotion, but it went on and on. "Like working in a smokehouse," she complained. "Stinks." Again, she coughed.

It did stink. She had found the wettest, greenest wood.

"Putrid," she muttered. "I'd rather be slapped in the face with a codfish."

The image struck me as funny. "I should think a woman of your chosen profession is used to men striking you in the face with their codfishes."

"Whoa!" she shrieked, jumping over the source of the smoke, the grate, the pot, and all. She spun to face me and peered into the low light that was in no way aided by her poor attempt at fire building. "Who said that?"

"I did," I mumbled, slowly sitting up and realizing that I'd covered myself with a tarp during the night. No wonder she hadn't yet seen me. I looked like rubbish. Felt that way, too.

The woman backed up, prodding the air with a stick. "Don't get any ideas," she warned. "I only have to say a word and the general's personal guards will come to my aid."

"You've nothing to fear, lass," I croaked, crawling first to my hands and knees and then to my feet. I was wobbly, but I slowly steadied. "Even if I wanted to play morning games with you, I'm in no shape for the sport."

She slowly lowered the stick. "And you won't do me any violence?"

"Not to a lady, never," I said, with a fair amount of chivalry. And it was the truth. "Besides I'm a Quaker. But what in the hell I'm doing out here following Washington around when I should be in Williamsburg getting married is more than I can say."

The camp continued waking up around us. More sounds and signs of life abounded. But the woman had fallen silent. I'd say she was frozen as if fear had suddenly grabbed a hold.

It was best if I just left. No sense in getting in trouble for pissing on Braddock's territory when I hadn't even been granted the pleasure in doing so. "I'll leave you to it, then," I said backing away. "And find some dry wood."

She said nothing in response. I tipped my head rather curtly, then picked up the pace.

"Ephraim?" said the woman. "Ephraim Weber from Pennsylvania?"

And something about the way she said my name was familiar, if not pleasant.

I pulled up sharply on the path. "Bess?"

CHAPTER TWENTY-NINE

"I wondered if you'd be here," Bess said after I had hobbled over. "I've seen Colonel Washington racing about the camp for weeks and know wherever he is, you follow."

I stood dumbfounded in the choking smoke from the green logs while studying her in the steadily growing light. To me she was as bright, shining, and beautiful as ever. But behind her big brown eyes there was an introspective sadness that I'd never before noticed.

"Say something," she demanded after I had gaped at her in shock for some moments.

Where could I start? "Heck ya, I'm here," I said. "This is an English army meant to beat the living shit out of the French and I'll do that any chance I get. But you?" I pointed to her and the fire and the tent. Oh, my goodness, the tent! The images of what went on in Braddock's tent were too painful to consider. "What?" I gasped.

Her features had initially moved from startled to softness. Now, with my one simple question, they raced straight to bitterness. "Don't judge me!" she barked.

Bess was spirited, which was one of the things I loved about her. But sometimes she just drove me crazy. "I," I began. Of course, I would judge her. The woman I had considered marrying turned out to be the favorite harlot of an aging general and possibly of a hundred other men as well. It was too much. But I'd not judge her – yet. I was plain confused. "I haven't gotten that far."

"You will," she said. "Everybody gets there eventually."

I would. Probably, at least. "Just tell me what you're doing here," I said.

"What else was I to do?" she asked.

I could think of a lot of things. "Why didn't you answer my letters?"

"You wrote?" she asked, suddenly not as sure.

"All the time!" I said. "Not once did you write back. Did your father hide my letters?"

Her lip had begun to quiver. She bit it. And the pain from where her teeth dug in quickly kept her wits sharp. "Probably. But you never came back to Williamsburg. I thought we were to be married. But you got into my dress in the woods and so you were done."

"It's not like that at all," I protested.

"What else was I to think?" Bess asked.

I suppose she had a point. I had left within hours of our time together. And with no letters to speak of, she jumped to a logical conclusion. "Alright. But you must know that I wrote you. I intended to marry you. But I was in Albany, then coordinating for Washington and Croghan. Then I was in Alexandria and then on this march. I kept writing." Not exactly. I had stopped in frustration a while back. But Bess would never know about that white lie.

She huffed before crouching to the fire. "I have work to do." Her hands rolled the smoldering green logs off the embers. Boiling sap and water bubbled from the sawed ends of the logs. Bess began hunting through a small pile of split wood that some young soldier had set nearby.

"Here," I said, bending to select one. "This one should spark right up. And this one, too."

"Thank you," Bess said, not bothering to look at me. She tended to the fire. With careful placement and a little stirring the logs ignited with scarcely any smoke.

"There," I said with encouragement, trying anything to be friendly.

"Maybe the general can pin a medal on your chest for heroics," she said sarcastically. "The good Lord know you men congratulate one another for mediocrity."

"What did I do?" I snapped.

"I was alone. And then I was completely abandoned because of you."

I threw my hands into the air. "I don't get it."

"And you never will."

"But prostitution, Bess. Harlotry? How did you ever make the leap from the daughter of a prosperous Williamsburg professional to a harlot? All within a year's time."

"That's easy," she said resentfully. "There was an all-out brawl in my home between two men. The constables came. A redcoat was there. Then some more. Braun was arrested. You dove out the window and escaped. My father came home. He was embarrassed and horrified at what happened. After a couple weeks, I was just getting him to settle down. That's when he found the stack of money you gave me before you left." She paused.

"So?" I asked. "Isn't that a good thing? I wanted you to have it. I was trying to support you. I've gone without proper clothes and slept under damp rocks for a year because I gave you everything I had."

Her anger was briefly checked. But quickly found its full stride. "I was sitting in our parlor with my mother when he came downstairs carrying the box I'd hidden it in. He held the currency out in accusation. He accused me of being a whore."

"But you weren't," I protested.

"No! I wasn't. Not then," she snapped. "Hey! What did you say in your letters?"

I shrugged. "I told you I loved you. I wanted to marry you. I missed you."

"Did you say anything about us having sex?"

Guilty. "I think I mentioned it. But not in any lewd way. I just said that I'd make you the most honest woman in the colonies."

Bess shook her head. "Then you *did* cause all this. Father said he had proof that I'd had sex for money. It must have been your letters that he intercepted. My father would have turned me out right then and there had mother not intervened."

"But *something* happened. You're here with the general. What happened?"

"Humph," she said. "What's done is done. Two months later I was living on my own with my money gone. The only place that would take me in was a whorehouse in Philadelphia."

"What? That makes no sense!" I snapped.

"It's what happened. Get used to the idea. I had to. Now you had best get going before the general returns." She set the water pot back on the grate.

I grabbed her arm impetuously. "Come with me, Bess."

"For what?" She jerked free.

I wasn't exactly sure. "I'll take care of you. Um, at least you won't have to do this anymore."

"What do you mean you'll take care of me?"

I hadn't thought this all the way through. "We'll get married. There's more than one reverend among the army. We can be married by tonight. Yes. Let's do that!" The more I said it, the more I liked the idea.

"You'd marry a woman that half the army knows to be the favorite whore of an old general?"

I wish she had stopped reminding me. "I, uh," I stuttered. When I swallowed it felt like an entire frog went down. "Yes."

Bess sighed heavily. "I believe you, Ephraim. For all your faults, you're a good man. But I can't. It won't work. It can't work."

"Bess, that's not a reason."

"Don't worry. Edward is a gentleman. He takes very good care of me."

"Edward?" I asked. "General Braddock is married. He has a family."

"For now, he takes care of me."

"But," I protested.

"I've become a harlot, Ephraim. And though it wasn't your intention, you helped make me one. I'll not soon forgive you."

"Forgive *me*?" I shouted, pounding my chest.

"Please leave, Ephraim, before this gets ugly."

"It'll get ugly no matter what!" I yelled, seizing her arm. My heat was rising something fierce. I stepped closer. "Think! It doesn't have to be this way. Come with me now!"

"You!" shouted Braddock, barging out of the rear door of his tent like a bull. "Step away."

I turned to face him. The old man cocked his arm and let his fist smash into my nose. Already sufficiently abused by Braun, a feather could have destroyed me. I went down into a heap.

"Has he harmed you, my pet?" Braddock asked as I rolled in the dirt.

"No," Bess said quickly.

"Good. I'll have him in irons. He'll hang before we move out. I cannot have a woman assaulted in my army," Braddock said.

"No, Edward," said Bess. Looking up, I saw that she clung to him. "It was a misunderstanding. He, he saw me coming in and out of your tent. This young man thought I was stealing from his general's personal stores. He confronted me. That's all."

"But he had a hold of you. It appeared rough to me."

"No. He just said he'd hold me until he could turn me in to a British regular." She was always an excellent liar when under pressure. Bess had been lying since the moment we'd met.

"Is this true?" Braddock asked.

I grunted, rolling up to my feet. "If she says so."

Bess gave me a perturbed look. She must have thought I was not helping her prevent me from dancing the hempen jig.

"Aren't you Washington's man?" Braddock asked. "I just saw you in my tent last night. What in the hell happened to you?"

I was bruised and swollen from Braun. Braddock's punch had set my nose bleeding again. I glanced at myself up and down. "You pack one heck of a wallop, sir."

Braddock shook his head and cocked his arm – thankfully, not to hit me. Bess interlaced hers in his. "Report to your post, soldier," the general ordered. "You and your savages keep my flying column protected. Report any French or Indian activity." He and Bess walked toward his tent. They chatted easily about the morning weather as if the incident had never happened.

And I did what I've always done. Without understanding a lick of what was happening in the world going on around me, I straggled off to safely guide an army into battle.

"Won't it be delightful to ride side-by-side today?" Braddock asked, ushering her through the flap.

"It will warm my heart," Bess answered. To my ears her tone rang as false as wooden teeth. But he heard something entirely different.

And the general and his mistress giggled like young lovers.

CHAPTER THIRTY

The flying column flew.

By the end of the first day, our rearguard had lost sight of the front elements of the support column. The small company of road builders attached to the flying column performed only the most basic of clearing, mostly nipping branches or cutting down saplings to blaze a curling road that curved in and around the enormous trees. The heavy felling, hauling, smoothing, and bridge building would be left to the secondary column. As a result of the hasty pace, a few wagon axles shattered as they rattled over rough terrain, but the general felt happy to abandon them to be mopped up by his larger gang of workers, who would be along in the coming days. For a regular army marching overland in virgin territory, our flying column gobbled up the miles. Braddock seemed the military virtuoso. For a time.

I'd see him sitting atop his white charger often. He was never found in the vanguard, a position I expected a proper commander to maintain. On the contrary, the general rode amidst the main body of marching soldiers and among his still-sizable personal baggage train. The playthings of his officer corps, the harlots, and their comely wares jiggled aboard many of the carts.

Bess, on the other hand, rode sidesaddle on a mare with an easy gait. Her flesh covered in a tasteful shawl, she was forever at the general's side, smiling and laughing along with him as he told her stories of his decades of military adventures. For Braddock's part, he was smitten. And I couldn't say I blamed him. Having the attention and affection of a young woman like Bess was a balm against all the world's ills, all the harms done to one over the years. Still, I gritted my teeth whenever I trotted past the sickening sight.

Wagons filled with gunpowder jangled along immediately in front of Braddock and his favorite paramour. So did short lines of packhorses and bacon carts – like that of my brother Caleb – that carried foodstuffs for quick access by the men in the van. Directly behind the general, Alex Braun quenched the thirst of the officers using Lydius' wine, pouring out disparaging stories of Chief Hendrick and the treaty he'd concluded with as much frequency as the Madeira. Day-by-day Braddock became more of a vocal supporter of Lydius and his theft. Day-by-day Braddock became more alienated from the handful of Indians we had left. As a result, day-by-day stories spread into the nearby villages that ours was an army of conquest, meant to wrench the Forks from the hands of the French *and* Delaware directly into the grip of any of a number of the colonies and the king.

On a basis even more frequent than daily, scores of regulars who had been shipped in from Mother England fell ill. Our host of local diseases would have their way until the men fully succumbed or became immune. Doctors James and Craik were busier than ever. Dysentery hadn't yet begun to rage, but I had been around sloppy marching camps long enough to know that it was only a matter of time. Stout men would grow weaker and paler by the hour. Many would shit themselves to death within days.

I was particularly concerned about Colonel Washington. He had ridden alongside the general and Bess with his jaw firm and lips tight for a week after the formation of the flying column. Knowing the colonel's sensibilities regarding propriety, it was as plain as day to see he was beside himself. His frustration bubbled from the blatant display of infidelity on behalf of Braddock. Still, it was Washington's physical countenance that caused me the greatest worry. At first, I noticed him stooping in the saddle – something he never, ever did. Then, when taking orders from the colonel around a night's campfire, I noticed his cheekbones were excessively pronounced, his eyes sunken.

"Have you spoken with Dr. James," I had asked him that evening.

"No need," Washington had assured me.

He had been wrong. Now I jogged next to a covered wagon, my Brown Bess in one hand, tomahawk in another as I prepared to take over my shift on the flanks.

"Be wary," Washington warned weakly. He reclined on a straw mattress in the wagon. Though it was mid-summer and the day's heat was coming on with ferocity, the colonel was under three blankets. He shivered. He sweated. Doctor James had bled him that morning. "Oh, if only we could have made them allies," the colonel lamented. "Shingas and his Delaware will not just sit back."

They hadn't. "Three attacks on the flying column in the last week," I reminded him. Washington was finding it difficult to concentrate as his condition worsened. I had reported to him about the ambushes we'd suffered at least twice before.

"Has the general decided to pause then?" he asked, just as he had the previous evening. I did not like the look of him. I had seen many men die from hatchet wounds, musket balls, and shrapnel. But I'd seen far more army men die from diarrhea. Washington looked just like all the rest at that moment. "Strength in numbers. Will he let the support column join us at least?"

"No," I said. Washington had been against bringing so much of the supplies and wagons. But under the circumstances he thought it better to move as a complete and overpowering force rather than invite attacks. "With each report I give him about an ambush on our flanks, the general smiles. He sweeps his hand and flutters his fingers. *We are the scythe. They are the grass.* That's what he says."

Washington moaned. He'd told me of his great headaches, like an awl slowly grinding into his skull. One struck at that moment. "He's emboldened by little successes," the colonel said weakly. "I know a thing or two about that. It will be the death of him."

I patted the colonel's silver-spurred boot beneath the thick layers of covers. Even though he was incapacitated, he insisted on being fully dressed as befitted an officer. His sword, propped up against the cart's sideboards in its scabbard, clattered. It was at the ready, for Washington was prepared to rise and defend if a force of Indians reached this portion of the train. "We'll be alright," I assured him with more conviction than I actually felt. "Braddock has allowed us to send out five hundred men in flanking columns into the wilderness around the flying column's supplies. Two-fifty on each side."

"Oh, why would Providence bring me this far only to see my life end in this wretched manner?" Washington lamented, shivering greatly. "I've survived childhood disease. I've outlived family. You alone ·preserved my life twice out here in the wilderness. And for this? I've long believed Providence had stretched out a path of destiny for me. There could be no other explanation as to why I am still among the living. I guess I was wrong. My life will be of no more consequence than the next man's." He groaned, grabbing his belly beneath the blankets and twisting himself into a ball. In profile, I could see his temples clearly. His chin had become almost pointy. Never a man with excessive flab, I'd guess that he'd lost well over a stone's worth of weight.

I thought he might be dead by the time I returned from my scouting. That's when Doctor James rode up from the rear. "His condition is no better, I see," he said, peering into the bouncing wagon from his moving horse. He pulled a small packet from his coat pocket and leaned down to me. "Mix this with water. Not too much liquid, mind you. I don't want to aggravate the bowels. But make sure the colonel drinks it all down."

I took the soft packet which was made of brown folded paper. It had a label that said, Dr. James' Fever Powder. There was even a price at the bottom. Its cost was two shillings, six pence. "What is it?" I asked. As today, there were many so-called cures back then that did more harm than good.

"A powder of excellent quality and potency. It cures many maladies, from gout and scurvy to distemper in cattle," the doctor answered quite proudly.

Tearing open one end, I sniffed the contents of the pack. "Smells like lemon." I had seen and eaten lemons once before. Croghan had received a shipment in and laughed as his young helpers' faces writhed as we had sampled them.

"Close. It's a lime phosphate. That portion of the recipe does little more than improve the flavor so the patient will actually finish the dose," said Doctor James just as Washington was droning from pain. "But the secret ingredient that does the real work is an oxide of antimony. But you mustn't tell anyone or else every quack in the country will have their own, harmful version."

I wouldn't tell anyone because I had no idea what antimony was. "No, sir," I answered as I jumped aboard the tilting wagon.

"Good lad," said the doctor as he trotted ahead to tend another of his growing list of patients.

A single musket shot echoed suddenly in the distance. My head, and the heads of all the drivers and their teams around me, craned to the left as the sound of the sole shot bounced off hills before dying away. The colonel's teeth chattered. He, too, turned to look in the initial direction of the blast.

"Attack?" he asked, just as the cart dropped out from under us when its wheels rolled into a giant hole. The colonel gasped when he crashed back into place.

"Maybe not," I said, struggling to dip a cup into the small pail of water sloshing in the cart. It could have been an accident. Then a few more shots rang out. Then another dozen or more sounded, all at once. It wasn't a hunting party, that much was sure. "Well, probably," I added.

"Careful," Washington warned. "I'd hate to lose you."

It was an endearing sentiment. But I attributed it to his illness and fevers. "I have to nurse you before I go bounding off anywhere," I answered. "The Delaware will have melted back into the forest by the time I'm able to get there." I dumped half of the water I'd retrieved in the cup back into the pail. Doctor James had said not too much liquid. Why a man shouldn't drink more water when he had diarrhea was beyond me. Seemed to make sense that he'd better replace what he'd already lost. But I wasn't a doctor and didn't have the training. I suppose the good doctor thought that if the water didn't go in, it couldn't come out. *An ounce of prevention is worth a pound of cure* – or so said the inestimable Benjamin Franklin.

The command of *Column Halt* then rolled down the train from officer to officer as the distant fighting on the left raged. Our driver tugged hard on the reins to avoid bumping those in front and the wagon jerked to a stop. I nearly dumped out Doctor James' precious powder. More shouts and orders echoed about as regulars and provincials were hustled into formations to protect the train in case the clash found its way to our doorstep.

I closed my eyes in order to focus my ears into the dark wilderness. Though I couldn't make out any of the calls from the battle, men in the woods shouted what could only be curses at one another. Indians shrieked their blood-curdling war whoops. It was certainly an ambush.

I dumped the powder into the cup and swirled it around. "Here," I said, lifting the colonel's head onto my knee. "Doctor says you need this."

Washington's pale, grayish blue eyes fluttered in acknowledgment. He opened his parched lips when I set the rim of the cup to them. His face crinkled as he drank. "Tastes like Doctor James' Powder," he breathed when the deed was done. "I shall be recovered in no time."

At that moment, I said a prayer that the colonel would simply survive the day, let alone fully recover.

"Weber!" shouted an officer whose shadow approached the wagon on horseback. "We have physicians and women who take care of the sick." I gently set Washington's head onto the mattress. "Weber!" repeated the surly man.

I looked up to see Captain Gates. He was displeased with me. "I thought you were to be on the flank scouting!" he said. "Keeping us abreast of the situation!"

"On my way there now," I answered, leaping from the static wagon. Washington had quickly faded to sleep and knew nothing of what went on around him. I glanced back just to make sure the covers still lifted and fell with his breathing. They did.

"I told you to gather those savage friends of yours," Gates growled as he curbed his horse.

"Taeheek and Moses the Song," I said. Captain Gates didn't seem to care about their names. And Moses was not a friend of mine, per se, but he was a Mohawk like Tim and had begun joining us on scouting parties.

Gates turned on his horse as the fight in the woods carried on. It was a long one compared to the other ambushes we'd suffered. Most had been over after two volleys. I counted at least three for this particular fight, with loads of sporadic back-and-forth to match. The captain angrily waved toward the vanguard. Moses and Tim, weapons in hand, emerged from the crowd and jogged toward me. "I've found them for you," Gates hissed. "Now get out there and find out what is happening. Is it a full ambush? Is it the French? You Americans are the most unruly batch of animals I've ever had the misfortune of knowing. Now get! The column wastes time!"

I've said he was an arrogant ass. My sentiment holds.

"Come on, sailor," Tim said, beckoning me with a jerk of his head before I could say anything to the captain I'd regret.

Without another word, I fell in with Moses the Song and Taeheek. We raced out past the line of red-coated soldiers who stood fence-like facing the bleak forest, guarding the train from a danger they did not yet understand.

And while a threat wasn't imminent, they'd know soon enough.

CHAPTER THIRTY-ONE

Just five minutes later we arrived at the scene, winded from running. When we jumped out of the bushes, the frightened British regulars at the rear of the skirmish and nearest the main column spun around with their muskets fully cocked. It was only a litany of English curses from all three of us that kept them from dropping my two Indian cohorts and me.

It sounded as if the main fighting had creaked to a halt. Only the occasional musket cracked and, though the smell of sulfur hung in the air, the smoke had begun to clear.

What met our eyes was disquieting. A rough, but mostly tight line of His Majesty's soldiers followed the hilly terrain in either direction. But it was punctuated by large gaps. The ground in those openings was littered with wounded men, crawling back toward the column. Many cried and moaned, looking at their quaking hands, which were covered in their own blood.

The officer in charge had already begun surveying the damage. A few men began carrying the dead and wounded out of the way as the flanking column soon started reassembling for the march.

"What happened here?" I asked the officer. "The general wants to know."

"Nothing we couldn't handle," the officer bragged. "I'd guess this is the biggest attack yet that we've suffered. Over a hundred of the savages. But we held fast and drove them away." He looked at a scribbled note in his hand. "We've suffered eight killed. Three times that wounded. But the creatures were unable to get in among us with their hatchets. Our lines held."

"Over a hundred?" Moses asked. That was a lot of men for Shingas to get together for just a small ambush. The Delaware usually operated in smaller bands.

"Maybe more," the officer said. "But you can tell the general that his column can march on. We have the situation under control."

I nodded. "You'd best send that word yourself. We've been told to scout out further afield," I lied. Neither Moses nor

Taeheek contradicted me. For we shared the same prickling suspicions.

"Very well," said the officer. "We've all got orders to follow." And he continued to organize his men. He efficiently barked orders, sending several runners to the flying column with news. They also carried instructions to gather stretchers in order to collect the dead and wounded.

Meanwhile, my two Mohawk companions and I ducked further into the forest away from the main and flanking columns.

The first thing we came across was the bodies of Delaware and Shawnee. We didn't take the time to count them, but a safe bet was a score of dead. The young British officer had not been bragging. His regulars had given worse than they'd received. But that wasn't what worried us.

"We'd best track them," Moses suggested.

We had no provisions for a long trek. But our forest senses had been piqued. "We should," I agreed.

Tim gently patted his healing ribs. "A quick run will make these good, Sally." Without further discussion, it was settled. We'd pursue the ambushers. And at least I was again referred to as a woman's name rather than my other, less-favored moniker.

We found that the retreating tribesmen had made no attempt to hide their path or their numbers. And why would they? General Braddock and his Englishmen clearly had one goal in mind, to attack Fort Duquesne. They'd never once sent a patrol in pursuit of the ambushing Delaware. Therefore, we followed after them with ease.

"Since leaving Fort Cumberland and with every passing mile, the Delaware attack with greater numbers," Moses mused as we raced down a ravine, through a trickling creek and up the other side.

"Is it because their numbers are truly growing?" Tim asked, huffing more than he would have liked to admit.

"Or, is it because we are simply in the heart of their territory?" I asked. "As more and more are bloodied from all those redcoats, fewer Delaware may decide to chase after death. Maybe they'll stay home as Braddock told them."

"We shall see soon enough," Moses said.

And he was correct. For after just three rugged miles of running and two hours' time, we were required to slow our pace. The forest ahead had become quiet. Birds did not chirp. Squirrels did not rustle. The wind was hushed. It was the type of quiet that indicated men were lurking about, many men.

On our bellies, we shrunk onto the earth and crawled along the last three rods until we came to the edge of a hillside clearing. There, we observed an impromptu conference taking place without any formal council fire – lessening the chance Braddock's army would spot it. On one side was the band of Indians who had just attacked the column, obvious because many of the wounded were being tended by women and healers. The injured lay in a long line at one end of the clearing moaning and clutching at gaping bullet holes. Shingas and his lesser chiefs sat on blankets in the center of the clearing. They wore stern faces and war paint.

The other delegation to the conference consisted of a half-dozen Frenchmen and Canadians. One of the Canadians was a young officer of the troupes de la marine. By his posture it was plain that he was full of vigor and plenty of piss. He sat in the center, his white coat with blue turnouts as well as his dust-colored breeches making which king he served blatantly obvious. However, the rest of his clothing was unique for a white man in the service of His Most Christian King Louis. He had no shirt on beneath the coat. His strong, lean chest was naked and marked with parallel lines painted on in an alternating pattern of black charcoal and red clay. He wore a necklace of shells around his neck. A tomahawk hung from his belt. And he did not wear a hat upon his head, unusual for an officer. His long hair was pulled back into a queue. Half his face was painted solid red. The other half was his normal, tanned flesh.

"King Shingas," the officer said. I spoke decent French, but Taeheek whispered a clearer translation for me. "Your fathers, the French, are very pleased with your aid thus far. But still, the English dogs continue on."

"My people have sacrificed much, Captain Beaujeu" Shingas said, pointing over his shoulder at the wounded with a thumb. His French was superb. "Our father can expect no more from his children."

"What? No more?" asked the captain. "Will you let your father meet the enemy alone?" He shrugged. "I am sure to beat him without aid. But how much sweeter it is to have one's sons with him at the time of victory."

"And yet my French fathers do not venture out past their walls to join his children in fighting the English general," Shingas accused.

Captain Beaujeu stood, his shell necklace jingling. He tapped his naked chest passionately and raised his hand to the sky. "I, like you King Shingas, was born on these shores. My first home was among the walls of Montreal. But my travel has been broad as I served Our Most Christian Majesty. I am called Hyacinthe, named after a magnificent deep blue flower. In that way, I am like the blue sky, always over you, always watching you, and forever caring for you, no matter what clouds may cover. A father cherishes his children even when they are away and he is required to stay home at the Forks."

"And he is blessed with the name, Daniel," said a gray-bearded Jesuit missionary who sat to the captain's right. He was clad in black robes with a line of ebony buttons running from his neck to his ankles. His collar was large and white. An unadorned wooden cross the size of a man's hand hung from a leather cord around his neck.

"And you will say that like the Almighty God protected Daniel from lions, so will our father protect us from the teeth of the English," Shingas said.

Captain Beaujeu tugged out his tomahawk. "I am no God. I am like you. Flesh and bone. I put my faith in steel and shot. Like you."

"Then will you come out from behind your walls?" Shingas asked. "Or, after we have suffered, will you burn down and flee your fort as the huge army of my English brothers comes?"

"We may have no choice but to retreat," Beaujeu allowed. Though the sentiments were unwelcome by his bloodied Indian allies, his candor was met with nods of approval. "If the entirety of General Braddock's army descends upon us at once, we cannot be supplied in time to hold them off. A siege would be worthless. We will be forced to withdraw."

"Braddock's army remains split in two," Shingas said.

"I thought you said you have been unable to get close to the main column since they've placed flankers," Beaujeu countered.

"Our scouts have been close enough," Shingas insisted. "Braddock's column is at half strength."

"Then the numbers are more evenly matched," Beaujeu said.

"Then you will not flee and leave my people to suffer under the wrath of the English?" Shingas asked. "Their general will want revenge for the destruction and death we have heaped upon them."

"How many hours separates the rear support column from Braddock's flying column?" Beaujeu asked, probing. He strode around in a small circle, his mind racing with possible strategies.

"Not hours. Days," Shingas stated. "More than two days are between them. It may be as many as four."

Beaujeu's eyebrows raised. He and the missionary shared a pleased glance as the captain answered. "Then we *will* leave our walls. I will lead an army of French and Canadians. We will not go out in retreat. We will advance. Attack. Soon. When the English least expect it. Will you join us? Will your people fight alongside us in one final blow?"

Shingas had little choice. Once he had abandoned Braddock, he'd been forced to throw his lot in with the French. But he sighed for a single moment while his commitment wavered. Then he said, softly and boldly, "We will."

A smile curled beneath the Canadian's nose. He was a fighter by nature, that much was plain. His chosen profession suited him. "And how many additional warriors may we expect? You have scores of wounded."

Shingas sighed. "The bodies of many warriors litter the wilderness and this meadow. A new generation of orphans and widows have been created. But we must come to our father's assistance. He will not fight alone under any circumstances. A child must support his father. He shall have more than six hundred braves."

Beaujeu gasped, his head tilting to examine Shingas for sarcasm. "That many?" And it was a huge number. The Delaware and Shawnee in the area were settled very sparsely in tiny towns with populations that usually numbered in the dozens.

But Chief Shingas had not been bragging. He wore the weight of responsibility with proud dignity. He stuck his chin in the air. "In your name have I hearkened all the chiefs. They agree to answer your call to lift the hatchet. I am free to tell you that we will send every available warrior against the English so that peace may come to the Forks, once and for all. When shall we assemble?"

Beaujeu grinned, offering a hand of friendship to the Delaware chief. "Immediately, King Shingas. With your help, we will sortie soon enough."

"And the English shall suffer as they did last year at their Fort Necessity," Shingas proclaimed. "Their Iroquois sheep will bleed."

CHAPTER THIRTY-TWO

The council began to break up after the exchange.

"We'd better warn Braddock," Moses whispered from our place in the bushes. "If it's true, that's a lot more Delaware than we've ever seen in one place."

"Good luck," I said. "He won't take advice from anyone."

"What if you tell Washington?" Taeheek suggested.

"Wouldn't do any good. Besides, the colonel is half dead," I said. It sounded callous when I said it and when I wrote it in my tale. I didn't mean it in such a way.

"What about proof?" Moses said.

"Like what?" I asked.

He turned to peer back toward the council where the Indians were carrying their injured in the opposite direction. Captain Beaujeu lingered in the center with his fellow Canadians and Frenchmen, discussing their next move. "I haven't gotten that far," Moses admitted.

Shingas and his Indians entered the far woods, the shadows instantly gobbling them up so no sign remained. The small party of Canadians walked in a direction that was perpendicular to the Delaware. At the end of the meadow to our right, I saw their grazing horses, which were tied off on branches.

"Attack the French and take back a body?" Tim offered. "That would prove what we saw."

"If we make too much noise, Shingas will be back here before we stole one horse and its rider," Moses warned.

Tim grunted his agreement.

We helplessly watched the French party climb into their saddles. But when Beaujeu led the party into the woods, the Jesuit called ahead to him, "Je vais rattraper. C'est ma vessie. Il est vieux." The old man slowly tugged his reins so his beast walked toward us. He was in no hurry, glancing up at the picturesque summer sky that was so common in the Alleghenies.

"Be ready," I whispered, tugging out my tomahawk. "Somebody's got to piss."

"You'll kill a priest?" Tim asked aghast.

"No," I scolded. "I'll just encourage him to come along."

Moses and Tim nodded, the first pulling his hatchet, the latter clasping his gaming cross. The missionary climbed down from his horse and dropped its reins, confident the beast would not wander. He ducked through a bare spot in the thicket at the edge of the forest and entered about ten yards from our position. As he walked, he began hiking up his robes. Soon his bare rump was perched over a fallen log and he deposited more than just urine.

After just a moment of hand signals, Tim and Moses slowly retraced the path we'd used to sneak in. I, on the other hand, picked my way forward into the clearing. The priest softly hummed while performing his duty. It seemed a shame to fall upon a man while he was in such a compromising position, but it couldn't be helped. I chattered like a chipmunk when I was in position. Taeheek answered with a similar call.

"Qui est là?" asked the missionary. I couldn't see him. Perhaps ten seconds passed before he repeated his question, this time worry in his toné. I heard him hastily finishing his business and snapping his robes into place.

"Bonjour père!" Tim called suddenly.

"Eh!" the missionary shouted in surprise. But then he calmed as I had hoped he would. "Oh, mes enfants," he said, relieved, recognizing my comrades as Indians. "Tu es en retard."

He thought they were late for the council meeting. They'd have to work fast. Any Frenchman with a few weeks of experience in the wilderness would quickly be able to tell the difference between the accepted dress of Delaware compared to Mohawk.

"Mon Dieu!" the missionary exclaimed. My fellow scouts hadn't approached fast enough. I heard the old man's feet pounding toward me. He plunged through the briars and saw me blocking his path to his munching horse. The priest glanced at the hatchet in my hand. His hands shot up in surrender. Then he grunted and fell forward into the dirt. His horse saw the plight of his master. Its head and ears shot erect before it cantered off a second later.

"What did you do that for?" I asked Tim.

Tim slung his cross over his shoulder after employing it against the missionary. He shrugged. "I didn't like the looks of him."

I studied the unconscious old man. He was robust for his age, but didn't appear to be any threat to three experienced warriors.

Perturbed, Moses shoved Tim as he passed. "Now you'll have to carry him."

"Why me?" Tim asked.

Moses slid the tomahawk into his belt and gathered up his musket from the bushes. I did the same and pointed to where the horse had disappeared into the wilderness. "Because you're the one who chased away the chestnut."

CHAPTER THIRTY-THREE

Another day passed as we carried and then dragged our uncooperative captive to the flying column. But other than hunger and lost sleep, the time passed by without any significant events. If the French had sent someone looking for their vanished priest, they'd not found our scent.

It was the next evening that we were granted an audience with the general. I asked that Croghan and Chief Hendrick accompany the Jesuit and me, thinking that their age might better convince the commander to heed my warning. Moses and Taeheek, on the other hand, and for obvious reasons, were happy to bow out from enduring a gathering with Braddock.

"Colonel Washington!" I exclaimed, after ducking into the general's tent. He sat in a chair at Braddock's large table. His rear rested on a plump pillow. Despite his wasted countenance, the colonel sat up tall. His blue uniform with its red turned-out cuffs, normally fitted perfectly, engulfed him like he was a boy wearing his father's clothes. "You should rest."

"I should do my duty," Washington retorted, nearly exhausted by the effort. Then he extended an unsteady hand in greeting. "Thank you for looking after me during my illness."

I shook the hand. It was still large, with a broad distance from one end of his knuckles to the other, but now the muscle and flesh had wasted, leaving it a bony remnant of its former self. His skin felt, and he looked, like he was still quite ill. "Anything for you, colonel." And I meant it.

The missionary followed close behind and ducked into the tent after me. I had freed him from his bonds after he had promised not to flee. His alert eyes quickly scanned his surroundings, noting the furniture and lanterns, before they landed upon Washington. "Oh," he gasped at the obviously sick individual. The priest crossed himself and offered a prayer for the colonel. He probably prayed for himself, too, since we all knew that it took but one man with dysentery to set off a wildfire of the malady among others.

"Wait here, my pet," said Braddock from behind his screen. I then heard him brazenly peck his favorite harlot, my former betrothed, with a lingering kiss – I prayed it was upon her forehead. "So, this is the Catholic Frog-lover!" the general said as he sauntered into view while adjusting his waistcoat. "Can he speak the rightful king's tongue? Or do I have to stoop and haver?"

"I can't get him to speak English, if he does," I answered. Our communication had been entirely in halting French.

"I speak English well enough," the missionary answered, taking it upon himself to sit in a chair at the head of the table nearest the tent door. He clasped his hands and rested them and his elbows on the table, looking none too pleased. "And I would like an explanation for the treatment I have received at the hands of this ruffian."

"In time," Braddock assured him as he found his seat opposite the missionary. "Bats! Washington?" he exclaimed when he finally looked at the colonel. "When my aide said you had returned, I assumed you were recovered."

"I am fit for duty, sir," Washington whispered, teetering in the chair.

"All the same, another day of rest in the cart," the general commanded.

"I think not," Washington said. And then, in order to soften his blatant disobedience, he added, "If it pleases you, sir."

"No, it doesn't. But I can see there is no discouraging you. Though you are plainly a gentleman, you are little different from your fellow colonists. Barely able to obey the simplest of orders."

The colonel's eyes flared. Yet, Washington bit his tongue.

Croghan and Hendrick arrived in the tent at that point and Braddock pointed them to their places. For once, since seating was available, I was also permitted a chair at the table.

"We are nearly upon the doorstep of Fort Duquesne," Braddock began. "I have little time for dawdling and needless meetings. This had better be good."

He still seemed to have plenty of free moments for harlotry. "I'm told the missionary can corroborate information from Mr. Weber's recent outing," said Washington.

"What is it all about?" the general said.

I told him my tale of pursuing the Delaware and all that we had heard while we eavesdropped on the Indian council. I was careful to explain the extraordinary numbers of the enemy Shingas had claimed.

"Six hundred Delaware cannot be right, lad," Croghan said when I was finished. "That would be every available warrior in the region." He had been invited in order to reinforce my version of events, not call it into question.

"And I've never known the Delaware to be so united behind anyone, let alone this so-called King Shingas," Chief Hendrick added. Strike two for me.

"But it is true," I insisted. "Moses, Taeheek, and I heard it all. There's a Canadian captain who is scheming with the Delaware."

"And you bring me this priest as proof of what you say," Braddock surmised. "Even if you are correct, what makes you think he would be foolish, or traitorous, enough to divulge the plans of our enemy?" When the general asked it that way, I felt silly for having struggled to drag the missionary this far. "Besides, we are not at war with the clergy – no matter how misguided they may be in their faith." The general stared straight at my captive and added, "I apologize, sir, for any mistreatment you received at the hands of this lad."

"I thank you, General Braddock," he said. "May I return to my flock?"

The general held up a hand of caution. "I'm afraid not. You are here now. You will ride with us until we have liberated the Forks. But as a man of the cloth, I will take your word that you do not intend to escape."

"If it is not your wish that I leave," he answered.

"Then you will walk freely among our column," the general granted.

"Thank you," the missionary said.

"Your name, sir?" Washington asked.

"Father Denys Baron, colonel," came the reply.

Braddock smiled with formal politeness. "Welcome to our army, Father Baron. Now, as to this lad's story of many hundreds of wild Indians joining in with the French on some sortie outside

Fort Duquesne's walls, am I to believe it. Will it happen soon? I doubt you will tell me the truth. But you understand it is my duty to inquire."

Baron fixed me with a frustrated glare. He reached an arm over his shoulder and rubbed the spot that Tim had clubbed so hard. I swallowed, preparing myself for his lie that would make me the fool.

"Your Pennsylvanian, this ruffian, is quite correct," Baron said. In surprise, everyone in the tent sat up a little straighter.

"About what, exactly?" Braddock asked, leaning forward with an unconvinced look on his face.

"All of it," Baron answered simply.

"See?" I said, a little too childlike. "They're betting on us being split. We need to wait for the rest of the army to catch up. Then, when the French and Delaware come, we can meet them with force."

"Hush," Braddock scolded me. "Can you elaborate, Father Baron?"

"I could, but he's told you everything. Certainly, you are too sophisticated to endure bland repetition," Baron said.

"No, Father Baron," Braddock said, miffed. "That will be enough. You are dismissed if you have nothing of note to add."

"Only that your suffering will occur sooner than later. But I do not know the day or time. *Like a thief in the night*, as they say." Then, nodding toward Washington, the missionary said earnestly, "Then I will retire to the wagon and bed of straw I've been allotted for rest. But first, may I pray over this man and the battle that is to come?"

Uncomfortable, Braddock waved his hand. "If you insist. Make it quick."

Baron did not hesitate. He stood, closed his eyes, and clasped his hands in front of the large cross on his chest. "Beloved Mother Mary, heal this colonel. Make his body youthful and strong once again. How much more fitting it is for a soldier to die from wounds in battle than from wasting disease. And I praise you, in your wisdom, for the victory that will come at the Forks of Ohio. It will be most surprising to these Englishmen as they are defeated by men from my poor country of Canada and the savage souls from these woods. Let no amount of soaring morale aid them. Make their fifes, their drums, fall mute. Fortify the ramparts of my French fathers. Make our lilies bloom. Harvest the souls of your English children. Amen."

His eyes sprang open, carrying a mischievous glint. He looked like a youth who had just gotten away with something unexpected. Seeing that no one cared to echo his *Amen*, Baron smiled, bowed his head courteously, and then left without another word.

"Nothing to worry about," Braddock said as the tent flap still waved. "I've no doubt Mr. Weber heard what he says he heard. But it was a show for his benefit. It's meant to frighten us. Why would they allow Father Baron to be captured? Why not pursue Weber? Why else would the good father come in here and say such things? It's all a clever ruse meant to confuse us. There is no grand, united ambush in place. Our fifes, drums, *and guns* will certainly not fall silent."

"Even so," Croghan muttered slowly. I saw a change in heart coming upon my old boss. "It would be tricky to get that many Delaware Indians in one place working together. But it's not impossible. Maybe we should heed the lad's advice. Await the support column. Why tempt fate?"

Hendrick was nodding in agreement, at least partially convinced by the rude missionary. "While we wait, we can send more scouts ahead to look into our enemy's movements. Perhaps scout in force. At least we would not march into a trap."

"Don't you see?" Braddock said. He shook his snow-capped head in disbelief at our callow gullibility. "That is just what the Frogs want to happen. They want us to dither. That gives the garrison at Duquesne time to be resupplied and supplemented with additional men. They hope to wait out our siege, thinking we'll have to return eastward before winter strikes. It's a bluff I might consider were I in their position. I'll not give them the chance. We move swiftly. This changes nothing. Your Washington agrees. He advocated a quick march. We've done just that."

The colonel cleared his throat. "General, I did hope for a rapid march, but with a full army. In light of this news, I recommend that we tarry for some days right where we are. When the support column catches us, we can resume a more methodical march, without the worry of being outnumbered at any point."

"Noted," Braddock said crisply, his fingers rapping the table in quick, repetitive succession. He craned his neck over his shoulder. "Wine, my pet. A glass of that from Lydius for me. I'll hardly be able to sleep tonight without it. And I do not want to disturb you from your slumber."

"Yes, Edward," Bess said sweetly.

"Now, I suppose we are finished with this episode. I've made my plans clear. We march with haste to the fort. If the French are foolish enough to remain, we hem them in. The Forks will be in our hands by the end of July. Next year we will roll up to the lakes. The year after, we will descend upon the Marquis Duquesne in Quebec. Father Baron and His Most Christian Majesty may pray all they want to the Virgin Mary, but Britannia means to rule this hemisphere."

Bess, fully and delightfully clothed, came around the screen carrying a glass of wine. Her hair was held back with deep green ribbons that made her appear sweet and younger than she really was. She labored hard at not meeting my eye when I dipped and bobbed my head to force it. When Bess set the glass on the table for Braddock, he affectionately touched her soft hand. "Thank you, darling," he said. "Now, run along. I'll retire shortly."

"Don't be too long, Edward," said Bess, confidently. She, at last, lifted her large brown eyes and met my stare. I was surprised that Bess now made no effort to look away. Her face was stern. As I wondered what she was thinking, Bess set a hand upon the general's shoulder. Leaning over, she kissed him warmly on his forehead. Her eyes watched me defiantly.

Braddock's face blushed with schoolboy excitement. Bess spun around and walked confidently back to the bedroom, master of her new domain. Washington looked as sick as I felt. I know what my problem was. But whether Washington's immediate ailment was the lingering dysentery or the unabashed impropriety of his general, I cannot say.

"As you see, I have other tasks to which I must attend," said Braddock as he took his first sip of wine. He turned to Croghan and Hendrick, who had ridden at the head of the army for most of the trek. "How many days to go?"

The pair checked with one another. "Three days until the last crossing of the Monongahela," said Hendrick.

"Good," the general said, standing. "And you'll take us upriver from the forks? I mean to surprise them from the land side. I don't intend to cross a river under their guns."

Croghan nodded. "I've soaked up a good many years in these woods. I know a firm place to ford the Monongahela ten miles up from Duquesne. Unless you don't want British regulars getting their boots wet," he added.

The general sipped his wine, not taking the bait. "Oh, Irishman, you think you are so witty. My men will ford that river, no matter its width. We'll fall upon the French and whatever savages they have in their employ. Hell. I may be back in your eastern towns, such as they are, by autumn. Perhaps I may be in London by Christmas. And good evening to you. I shall see you on the morning's march."

"General, sir," I ventured before he had moved an inch. Then I jumped right in, knowing that if I waited for permission to speak, it would not come. For, like the general, I, too, would have been in a hurry to recline with Bess rather than talk with men. "I've been thinking about how our regulars on the flank defended against the last ambush."

Braddock was exasperated. To his credit he held his simmering anger in check. "I've heard the report. They did an exemplary job, I'd say. Held fast. Loaded the bastards with lead. Good leadership. Good obedience. Something my colonial cousins could learn from."

"Yes. Well. If we do happen to meet a host of Indians like Father Baron and I warn of, perhaps you should consider other tactics," I said.

For ten solid seconds, the general was speechless. "Change tactics to match what unclothed savages are doing?" Braddock asked, aghast. "Why not use clubs and stone-tipped arrows?"

Washington came alive. As much as he could in his condition. "Mr. Weber has a point. If we are faced with a huge number of Indian warriors, we ought to consider breaking into skirmishing parties, rather than standing in line form."

"Now I know you are too ill, Mr. Washington," Braddock said. "My regulars have trained to follow the orders of their officers under the most strenuous of conditions. Blasts. Explosions. Blood. Death. They ignore it all. They obey without hesitation, without question. A single word from my mouth is carried by a chain of officers and drumbeats to the men within a heartbeat. Linear battle, line form, as you call it, is the only way to employ a host of muskets. As such, these regulars send a massive hail of shot into the enemy with such rapidity that even the best trained opponent will flee after the second volley. Nay, sir. We will not break up cohesion. We will not split the very heart of our strength, that is, our lines."

Braddock finished his drink and fixed his wig as if the actions were an exclamation point. "While I do not believe that the savages have put together such a force, I welcome their arrival. For it is pure folly! I will meet any enemy the world over in open combat. In fact, we have. And the proof is in the pudding. We are soon to be masters of the world."

"But these woods are not open combat," I countered. "No matter the location, if we fight any battle that is not the siege you dream of, it will be in dense wilderness. If you cannot see what is plain, you are as dense as these forests."

The general wrinkled his nose. He wagged a finger. "Forty lashes to you for such an offense!" Braddock glanced to his left, contemplating Washington as the one to administer the punishment. But he quickly reconsidered, given the colonel's weakened condition. "You!" he growled to Croghan. "See it done! Does anyone else care to tempt me?"

"Edward, dear," Bess called. "I'm having trouble with a button. Will you please help?"

Braddock's breathing slowly settled. He smiled. "Coming, my pet. Good evening, gentlemen," he added tersely. And he was gone.

After that, we couldn't leave quickly enough. Washington refused my assistance as he struggled to climb from his chair. He lifted the pillow and switched its position from his rump to his belly. He hugged it tightly as he walked, wavering, through the exit. "I trust you'll have a restful evening after your flogging, Mr. Weber," he said, tired and defeated, when we emerged outside. "The general may sleep soundly with his woman and wine, but I will worry about an ambush and our preparedness. You and I have seen wilderness warfare." Then, while hobbling away, he grumbled to himself about arrogant army regulars, which was, ironically, still the position he most coveted for himself.

"I suppose we should get this over with," I said to Croghan.

My old employer scoffed. "I don't follow that Scotsman's orders. I'm here at the behest of Mr. Johnson. Besides, that old crust will have forgotten all about you once he lays eyes on his little sweetheart." But his face quickly showed guilt. "I'm sorry for saying that. I see it was your old Bess, Ephraim. I don't think I want to know what happened."

"Good," I sighed. "Because I know as little about women as I do about generals."

Hendrick patted my shoulder, chuckling. "They are two of the most complicated things you'll ever encounter. One is just a man, but elevated by his own actions or his connections. In either case, he comes to think his words are God-inspired. The other is a woman." He tapped his lewdly decorated gorget. "No further description is necessary. Because we could speak for days about the mysteries of a woman and still she would have a power over us that we cannot comprehend. But take heart, young man. You know a good many things. Among them, you know to be on the lookout for hundreds of Indians, French, and Canadians as you scout."

"You think Shingas can gather that many?" I asked. "I didn't believe it when I first heard it. Now I'm not sure."

Hendrick shrugged. Perhaps it was his immense age that made him unconcerned about a possible attack. "We'll know in a few days' time."

And we would.

CHAPTER THIRTY-FOUR

Perhaps you've come to notice that sometimes I wondered about chains of events and their outcomes. Had I never won all that money in the La Crosse match or struck Alex Braun across his face, would Bess never have been along on Braddock's march? Would Braun not have been at the Albany Congress to shoot me? Would Franklin's arguments alone, aside from my theatrics, been better equipped to convince the multitude of colonial legislatures to vote for the Plan of Union? And had even just a few colonies approved the plan that came out of Albany, would Braddock never have been sent? And would the Delaware Indians never have been so offended since the fiery Scot would have still been in Europe? And on and on.

No matter. Success in our campaign, despite my misgivings, was in the offing.

Three days had passed by uneventfully since our meeting with Braddock and Father Baron. The miles sluiced past and I'm sure we drew further away from the support column. The omens, for men prone to believe in such auguries, were good. Not a single ambush occurred – small or grand. Apparently, Shingas had not delivered all the Indians he had promised. Beaujeu would have to flee the Forks. Furthermore, nothing – not hangnails, dysentery, or hemorrhoids – slowed our progress. Positive rumors percolated. Word spread from the regulars to the provincials that the Delaware, bloodied several times over from their previous attacks, had decided to leave us alone. We were a prickly porcupine, better left undisturbed. And so it was that spirits were high as we dipped our toes into the Monongahela ten miles upriver from the Forks. The day was hot, in the middle of mid-summer, July 9, 1755.

Father Baron had borrowed a horse from a rare Catholic officer in our ranks. The fearless missionary often rode in the vanguard, visiting with Croghan, Hendrick, or even me. If he was worried about getting caught in a crossfire, he showed no concern. I had come to find out that he was not a horrible person. He had a quick wit. He was earnest, but not overly pious, in his faith. And if I'm honest, I, too, would have been upset if I'd been clubbed on the head by Tim's gaming cross.

But I wasn't in the vanguard as I crossed northward over the river. I wasn't even on a scouting patrol. Braddock insisted that his scouts be rotated frequently so that fresh eyes were always on the lookout – an enlightened opinion, I thought. But when I wasn't actively occupied, I was often left bored, hemmed in someplace within the mile-long column. On that particular summer day, I rode alongside my brother's bacon wagon.

"The other drivers say that we'll hear explosions anytime now. The French will blow up their powder magazine just to prevent us from getting at it," Caleb said.

"Maybe," I allowed. It was funny how a boy who had never before seen an army had suddenly become an expert. In truth, the teamsters from Pennsylvania all just repeated what they'd heard said by the provincial soldiers, who, as I've mentioned, just echoed what the regulars had uttered. The regulars took their cues from their officers, who parroted the thoughts of the general.

"I know you've spent a good deal of time out here since you ran away," Caleb said. "But maybe the general knows more than you think. He's led armies for more years than we've been on this earth, put together!"

"Maybe," I said, not convinced, as my horse splashed through the running waters. Caleb's wagon danced as its wheels slowly rolled over unseen rocks and into gullies hidden by the muddy river. "I guess Shingas couldn't get together all the men he'd promised the Canadian, Captain Beaujeu."

"Guess not," Caleb said. My younger brother sounded relieved. He had no desire to be involved in a battle of any kind. I'm sure he had visions of the Weber family hearth and sitting next to it by autumn. He'd joined the long march in order to obey a command given by our father. Father, in turn, had answered Franklin's broadsides only so he could demonstrate our Quaker family's patriotism – a nagging question that always dogged pacifists. It was all another example of those chains of events that caused my mind to turn over and again.

"And I heard Beaujeu tell Shingas that if his Indians didn't bring enough help, he would burn Fort Duquesne and retreat north as we drew near. I suppose we had better have our ears perked up to listen for the explosions," I said.

Water splashed next to me as someone approached rapidly in the hip-deep river. I turned, expecting to see a rider. Instead, I had to peer down and saw a woman on foot. She held her heavy skirts up. The action did little to keep them dry. Her bodice was cut low so that the ample tops of her breasts, glistening with sweat and tanned from the summer sun, bounced as she struggled in the water. From my vantage point I could see the skin down between them. "You might want to walk further back," I warned her. "We're getting close to the Fort."

"Nah," she said with an accent that put her from the Mother Country. "The good general says us girls should be about comforting the men in this time of victory. Expects eruptions from the fort up ahead. How about you? Care to have me help anything erupt from you?"

It was one of the general's bevy of strumpets. She wasn't the comeliest of women. But none of her customers on this train were much to look at either. I certainly had no desire to become one of her clients. Despite my intense interest in the fairer sex and want for adventure, I hadn't completely abandoned my faithful upbringing. "I don't think so," I said.

When I glanced toward Caleb, his eyes were the size of dinner plates. He couldn't peel his gaze from her jiggling chest. "You might want to drop back and seek elsewhere," I added to the woman.

"What? You don't have the coins?" she asked, eyeing my shabby kit. She quickly shifted her wandering glances over to young Caleb, who was more presentable than me in almost all respects.

"It's not that," I said. Though, in truth, I had accumulated only a few pennies in the past year.

From behind, we heard a sudden laugh. It was sharp, though pleasant. I craned in my saddle to see that Bess rode her beast just behind Alex Braun's wine cart. She was ever always right next to Braddock. He must have shared something particularly witty with her. The general was all smiles. Bess dabbed at a happy tear.

Washington rode next to the general and his other aides-de-camp. Unlike the colonel, the other two aides had not fallen ill during the journey. They were the picture of what handsome soldiers ought to be. William Shirley, Jr., though not as naturally monumental in his carriage as Washington, did his best to look the part with a feather in his cap and shoulders pulled back. The colonel, on the other hand, sat on a pillow, wincing whenever his sore rump bounced in the saddle a little harder than usual. He'd recovered a portion of his color, but was frighteningly thin. Like Shirley, he sat up tall in the saddle. Unlike young Shirley, however, the colonel couldn't bear to take part in the banter between the general and his mistress. Washington would frequently peer in any direction, into the forest, along the river, anywhere, as long as it was away from the unfaithfulness that was on full display.

Meanwhile, the old Scot and young Virginian appeared to truly adore one another. It baffled me, but there they were in plain sight, enjoying one another's company. Bess was beautiful to me. More than ever. I'm ashamed to admit it, but I think another man's interest in her, inflated her already lofty value in my eyes.

"Oh, that one," said the trollop who struggled in the water below. She had turned to look at Bess, too. "If you can't afford me, lad. You certainly can't afford her." Then the wet harlot put on a prim and proper accent with a high, mocking voice to match. "She's the general's favorite."

"Why don't you just go bother somebody else," I said to the woman.

"She's everybody's favorite," the harlot said with disgust. "And with a cute face like that, who can blame the men. But give it time. This world. This occupation will fade that bloom as sure as the autumn chill."

"You don't know anything about Bess," I said. I tried to meet the woman's gaze with a stern look. I wished she would just leave.

"And you do?" she retorted.

I swallowed. Without knowing it, the harlot was cutting to the core of the problem. I was naïve in the ways of women. Together, my first wife and I had been blissfully ignorant of the world. "I thought I did," I answered quietly.

"Oh my!" she exclaimed as we made our way slowly through the second half of the wide river. The water had reached the bottom of her bosom. "You're the one! You're the one who is smitten with her."

"What do you know," I said. I had had enough. Turning to Caleb, I added, "I'll ride ahead."

After clicking my cheek and spurring my horse, the whore answered. "I know plenty, lad. Unlike you brutish men, women talk to one another. I was there when she came to us in Philadelphia all swollen with child."

I curbed my horse. "What did you say?"

She rolled her eyes and kept moving past. The weight of the water tugged down her dress so that the top half of one of her nipples was visible. She noticed that Caleb and I noticed. Yet she did nothing to cover herself. "You heard what I said. I was there when the sad, rich girl showed up pregnant. I guess rich or not, a girl is just a whore to a man. Her daddy and mommy threw her out. She had nowhere to go. So, my employer took her in. Hate to admit it, but she took to it all like a fish to water. She earned her keep, if you know what I mean."

I think I did. "Shut up!"

Alex Braun, who drove the wagon immediately behind Caleb, had been listening. I'm sure he'd enjoyed every bit. Now, he laughed from down deep in his belly. "Weber! You're too much. All worried about the one harlot you can't have! You look like you'll explode with the wait. Come now. You've obviously got no money. I'll pay the lady at your feet. It won't even be a loan. Consider it a gift. In camp tonight, just let her do her work."

"Bess isn't a whore," I insisted.

Braun and the harlot in the river shared a glance and then broke out laughing. "Darling," said the prostitute to Braun. "This one is in such bad straits that I'd best give him a plug for half price. It's for the public good. He's like to explode."

"Suits my wallet just fine," Braun giggled.

I looked back in the distance to Bess, who met my glance as if she had known we were talking about her. She sat on her beast with her legs and skirts pulled up so that she remained dry. "Bess is pregnant?" I asked just as we emerged on the north bank.

"No, you idiot!" the prostitute shouted. "Does she look pregnant to you, simpleton? Gave birth already. Back in Philadelphia."

"Whose baby is it?"

"How am I supposed to know? A dozen babies are born in that house every year. What's one more? Is it yours?" She pointed to Caleb. "Is it his? Or his? Or his? Or any of a hundred other men?"

At least I finally understood what had driven Bess to the brothel in the first place. "Where's the baby?"

"You care an awful lot about this child," she accused, splashing out of the water onto the opposite bank.

"It's probably mine," I said.

Caleb chastised me. "Ephraim! The thought would kill mother. With a prostitute?"

"She wasn't then," I insisted.

The harlot pointed toward the general. "I'd say she's one now."

"And the baby?" I asked. "Where is it?"

Hardened to the everyday goings-on in her world, she shrugged. "Some of the girls raise them in the house. Tend to the critters between their *meetings* with men."

"Did Bess do that?"

"Don't think so. One day she was swollen to the size of a prize pumpkin. That night I heard a lot of shrieking – the kind that comes when a woman freshens. After that, I heard some baby cries. Next day, your dear Bess was back at work. And 'tweren't any baby nibbling at her tit."

"And where do the babies go when they don't stay?" I asked.

"Boy, you don't want to know too much if you don't already have an idea," the harlot warned.

"No," I breathed, fearing the worst.

"Yes," she countered as we dropped into the dark forest on the northern bank. The lighting difference between the river and the woods was stark, I could see nothing but giant dark blobs all around. My eyes had bleached. "Let's just say that there are a lot of deep wells dug in Philadelphia."

"Not Bess!" I said, reining my horse. "She'd never."

"I doubt it," the prostitute admitted. "Ruthless when it comes to her men and her favors. Don't get between her and a man with money and connections. Take the general, for instance. But growing up wealthy made her soft in some ways. Her kid is probably being raised by some rich merchant in town. Maybe one of her customers."

I could take no more. "Keep your eyes and ears peeled," I ordered Caleb.

"What are you going to do?" he asked as I rode back toward the river.

"I need to talk to Bess."

CHAPTER THIRTY-FIVE

"I'm glad you've come back to us, Mr. Weber," Braddock chirped as I approached. He was cheery. His face was of a healthy color. "Ride ahead. I've been thinking about what Father Baron said in his prayer about our morale. And I believe the ladies here could do with some entertainment. No need for drudgery at a joyous time such as this. Inform Colonel Gage and Captain Gates that I want every fife, every drum we have playing from now on. With vigor! I want the French to hear us coming. They must know we are in terrific spirits, a tremendous force brimming with esprit de corps. It will give the Frogs time to reconsider. Might send them into the woods. See what Father Baron thinks of that," he laughed, showing off for Bess. "Oh, how I love the fife!"

"Where's our baby, Bess?" I asked, my beast splashing next to hers in the river. "Why didn't you tell me?"

"Mr. Weber, please," Washington pleaded. "Decorum."

William Shirley, Jr. snickered at my expense.

"Lad, I am ebullient today," warned Braddock, losing none of his merriment. "We are on the cusp of victory. My career, and that of your colonel and all my aides, is secure. Yours, too, if you know what is good for you. Other than when you utter, *yes, sir*, your mouth ought to remain shut."

"The child, Bess?" I insisted.

Bess was dazed. "How do you know?"

"So, it's true?" I surmised.

"Mr. Weber," Washington said. "The general has issued an order. I have always found you to be an asset in the field, if an overly obstinate one. We must be vigilant as we approach Fort Duquesne and have no time for squabbles. Please hold your discourse until this evening."

"The boy is not getting anywhere near my pet to discuss anything this evening," Braddock said, defensively.

"Then I guess right here, right now, will have to do," I barked.

The general's tanned flesh changed to bright red in a snap as his horse padded up the north bank. "Oh, how you people have retained your ancestors' contempt for authority!" he growled.

"My ancestors recognized only the righteous authority of God! That's why they abandoned your shores. And that's the only authority I acknowledge, too. Not some blustering, foul-mouthed coot who disrespects his own wife while in the consort of whores!" It was probably not the best thing to say to a British general with a supreme penchant for spite.

"Mr. Shirley. Mr. Washington," Braddock clipped, his chin jerking upright so that he could peer down his nose at me. "You shall join me this evening in the proceedings against this young man. Insubordination. Disrespect. Disobeying an officer of the army of the crown. I shall add charges as the day passes. When he is found guilty he shall hang in the camp. Let the sight be a lesson to the rest of our enlisted men. Let his swinging in the gallows' breeze be a warning to any Frog foolish enough to hide behind the walls of Duquesne. This general will tolerate nothing but complete submission."

"Yes, general," Shirley said gladly.

"What about you, Washington?" Braddock asked.

"Yes. Of course," Washington said without zeal. He shook his head at me.

"Where, Bess?" I said, returning to my purpose. "The child."

"We'll talk tonight, Ephraim," she said.

"There's to be no tonight!" I shouted. "Don't you get it?"

Bess and the general were all set to erupt, screaming at me. The tears had already begun streaming down her cheeks as we entered the silent wood. His face matched the color of his coat. But Washington spoke up, sharply for a man of such renowned control. "Miss Goode. Mr. Weber. I am certain that this evening, after the judicial proceeding, but immediately before the punishment that is to be meted out, the general, with his Christian upbringing, will allow a few moments of discourse to pass between the two of you – fully supervised discourse." The colonel gave the general a stern, yet beseeching, look.

Braddock grudgingly nodded his approval. His lips were pulled taut. His nose snarled. "Now that I've given you everything you want, boy, I'd rather not put you in irons. Ride ahead. Instruct Captain Gates and Colonel Gage about the music.

Then stay in the van with Croghan. I don't want to lay eyes on you until our hearing. Trust me. It's best for you that I have time to recoup."

I opened my mouth to say something ripe to Braddock, but Washington was quick to fill in the gap. "Thank you, General Braddock. I look forward to seeing justice exercised in His Majesty's army. Mr. Weber thanks you as well for not confining him to shackles for the remainder of what will prove to be these noteworthy daylight hours."

"You're welcome, Mr. Washington," Braddock said with stiff formality. He fixed me with a stare that befitted his hatred of me. "I suppose not everyone in this forsaken land is rubbish. You. Mr. Franklin, perhaps."

And though it wasn't in my nature and I hated to do it, I reached my hand up to the rim of my hat and tipped it to everyone present. Washington had been right to urge caution. I was treading on dangerous earth. A military tribunal was an unforgiving, mercurial beast. Death, more often than not, was the outcome for the accused. I ground my teeth for a fraction of a second, chewing on the choice language I wished to spew. And after masticating the sentiments, I swallowed them down. "Yes, sir, general, sir," I grumbled. "Until this evening, then." When I looked at Bess, she was weeping into a handkerchief, unwilling to glance in my direction.

And I rode ahead into the shadowed forest, not realizing that I would never have to endure the humiliation of a judicial proceeding or the pain of the punishment it brought.

And that would be the worst possible outcome.

For me.

For everyone.

CHAPTER THIRTY-SIX

Fifes trilled. The drummers rapped, pounded, and pattered their calfskin heads. Our colors shone as brightly as they possibly could in the dark wilderness. And though I had many concerns swirling in my mind about Bess and me, not to mention our child, my trial, and my potential hanging; I was inspired by the sharp notes of the musicians. Braddock, the lewd old bastard, had been right. Their song encouraged all of us, stitching stouter hearts within our chests. My horse pranced a little taller, its hooves thudding in tune. The pace of the men in Colonel Gage's vanguard, though dripping wet from fording the Monongahela and the sweat beneath their woolen coats, quickened. Their shoes bubbled and gurgled. They left a wet trail in the dirt as they proudly marched to be the first to see the Frogs flee.

Riding between Croghan and Chief Hendrick, I chuckled to myself. For I had suddenly realized that nothing about my situation was bleak. In my short life, I had already survived far worse predicaments. After all, I was in the midst of the greatest army ever assembled in the New World, by any nation. I decided that even the Mad Scot wasn't so sadistic that he'd have me killed for minor disobedience. This was to be the day of his victory over his country's gravest enemy. And furthermore, Bess would eventually be mine. By the end of the campaign, he'd tire of his so-called pet. She'd be dismissed.

And given what I had learned that very day about her pregnancy and her own problems while I had been away, I knew without a doubt that I would forgive Bess. We'd talk – perhaps shout a little, too – and iron out the past. The future, once the Forks were in the hands of the English, was bright. By Christmas, she'd be my wife. Bess was no longer tied to Williamsburg. She could live anywhere, even on the frontier. In just a matter of days, I could leave the employ of Old Dominion and become a rich trader again working for Croghan. My kit could at last be upgraded.

And I was a father.

I smiled, chuckling to myself. Somewhere in Philadelphia, there was a child with my eyes. I was a father.

"Laughing to yourself like that might make someone think you are a lunatic, Susanna," Tim warned. His beast had not been inspired by the music. He rode a horse's length behind me, his roan plodding along while turning its ears forward, away from the invasive melody.

Moses, who was also in the second row, chirped up in my defense. Turning, I saw that he pointed to Tim. "Who's the lunatic? I've never seen a sane man bring a La Crosse stick to a real battle."

"It saved Susanna's life a few times," Taeheek quipped. "It might do so again."

"Let's hope there'll be no battle," Croghan said, loud enough to be heard over the trilling songs.

"We've seen enough in our time," Hendrick agreed. "I pray the French flee. It will be better for my English brothers and my Delaware children."

"There *will* be a battle," Father Baron said with nonchalance. His borrowed horse grunted like a fat man waddling up a set of stairs. "Monsieur Weber, your prying ears heard what was said between Captain Beaujeu and King Shingas. I have known Hyacinthe Beaujeu his entire life. And he never backs down from a fight. More recently, I have come to know King Shingas. He strikes me as someone equally as determined."

"Aye," I agreed. The Delaware chief was fierce. "But we've got less than eight miles to go. And our scouts haven't come back to report anything yet. I'd say the French are staying behind the walls. Or, they've already run without making a fuss."

Something I had just said worried my more experienced comrades. Chief Hendrick and Croghan leaned forward on their horses and glanced at one another around me. "Your Mingo scouts should have sent word by now," the Mohawk chief said. "No matter what they found."

"True," Croghan agreed, upset with himself. "Guess I was enjoying the music. Lost track of time."

Old Hendrick had lived to a ripened age by being cautious when appropriate, gallant when proper. His many scars told me that he had learned how to tell the difference the hard way. It was time for him to be decisive. "Moses, Taeheek, and Ephraim," he ordered with certain, clipped speech. "Ride your young bones ahead a few miles to make sure the way is clear. If you see trouble, don't be foolish. Come warn us. Our new priest might yet be correct."

"I am," Father Baron assured as the three of us trotted ahead. "I have never had a prayer go unanswered."

A half mile later the beating drums and warbling fifes were no longer even faint whispers carried by the gentle wind that flittered through the woods. Moses, Taeheek, and I had just entered a portion of the forest that was clear. To be precise, it wasn't a clearing. No. The trees, primeval judging by their enormity, grew straight and tall. Their leaves formed a canopy as dense as any we'd traveled beneath since our journey had begun.

"A hunting ground," I whispered as I curbed my mount, senses alert.

The other two men did the same with their horses. Moses nodded. "We have areas of the wilderness where our people burn the underbrush annually," he added. He pointed to a section of ground that had obviously been burned in an orderly manner last year. The base of the healthy trees showed just a touch of black from where the Delaware had temporarily lost control of their fire. "Improves the new fodder for grazing animals."

"And makes it harder for them to hide. Gives our hunting parties more freedom to move before we fall upon the prey," Tim said.

I had slipped down from my saddle and tied the reins to a sapling that grew at the edge of the shaded, yet open area. "But it's also a place that would be ideal for our adversaries to set a trap for our army."

Moses nodded in agreement. He and Tim joined me on the ground. Though we heard only wisps of the indistinct music and saw nothing of note, we crouched, moving deliberately from tree to tree. Soon, I pointed to a short ridge that ran perpendicular to our path. It sat at the far end of the clearing. The trees and foliage on the opposite side of the ridge grew thick and tall, creating a hedge around the open section of forest. "That's where I'd be waiting if I was Shingas," I rasped. "They'd have prime shots at us before we could even see them. A few hundred warriors could hide on the other side of that hill."

"Take a look?" Tim suggested. "If they are hiding, they wouldn't be so foolish to shoot at just three of us and give Braddock an early warning."

Moses tipped his head to the side, listening. "But the general wouldn't hear a few musket blasts over the music. Back in the column where he rides with his woman, it must be louder than one of your concert halls."

Sure enough, the approaching pulse of the drums just began to make itself known. The army would catch up to us in a matter of minutes. And though I understood the general's reasoning, I was beginning to see the drawback to entering enemy territory with fanfare aplenty.

Taeheek peeked around the huge oak against which we leaned. "At least one of us better see what's up there." Without consulting us further, he pushed off from the tree into a running crouch. But I snatched ahold of his belt and yanked him back into place. "Hey!" Tim protested.

"Shh," Moses and I hissed.

I silently tugged on my own ear. Understanding, Tim closed his eyes to drown out the sound of his own breath and the advancing column in order to listen to the forest.

They popped open a second later. "Somebody's up there, on the ridge. I hear them talking. It ain't Croghan's Mingo friends."

Moses strained to lean around the massive trunk and yet stay hidden. "I hear arguing. In French," he said.

I recognized the voices. "Shingas," I said. "And Beaujeu, the Canadian."

"That's the signal!" Beaujeu barked loudly. He was spitting mad. "As plain as day, the English are coming and Father Baron has done his duty, goading the proud goat Braddock. He's gotten them to tell us their exact location at all times."

"We've watched them for days. They are still too many," Shingas said. "Even with your Canadian marines, we are too few. We have no great guns." It sounded like he was getting cold feet.

By now we had each found a safe place from which to view the ridge. Shingas and Beaujeu, hoping to avoid arguing in front of their soldiers, had come to stand on its crest. The French captain was bedecked in the manner I had seen him before, part civilized, part primitive. Shingas was likewise prepared for war. Had I not come of age among men like him, I would have thought he was the most frightening sight I had ever laid eyes upon. Every portion of his exposed flesh was streaked with paint. His face looked like that of a demon.

"If we do this properly, they'll never get their heavy guns set up in time," Beaujeu countered. He stuffed a stiff finger in his comrade's chest. "Outnumbered or not, this is the best place to make a stand or else we race back to the fort and evacuate. Once invested in the Forks, the English will be impossible to pry out. Now, I don't run from a fight. And I don't want to have to come back here in a year with three times as many soldiers to take back what we own today."

"That's just it," Shingas said, using his hand like a hatchet to chop the Frenchman's finger from his chest. "You don't own it. It belongs to my people. The Delaware."

Beaujeu threw his hands up and let them slap his thighs. "King Shingas," he said. "You've got to get something straight. I am with you. I am for you. I am here to sacrifice my life if I must. But you need to understand that these lands can never belong to the Delaware. You were only just settled here in the past few years. Prior to that, these woods were abandoned. They are too big to be held by you and your people. You are too few. But I am here. My king has seen fit to send men to help. Decide now, today, who you'd rather become caretaker, New France or New England."

I didn't need to see the Delaware's face to know he preferred neither master. The merry fife music grew louder. I could make out distinct numbers of instruments. One man in particular was off time. I considered dashing back to my horse and riding to warn the vanguard. But a part of me hoped that Shingas remained stubborn and simply went home, giving Beaujeu no choice but to abandon his gambit.

"You see that, don't you?" the Frenchman said when his Delaware comrade hadn't responded. "You just won't admit it. I don't say these things to anger or frighten you. I speak the truth. The world's powers all have standing armies. They've made alliances with other standing armies. They build, trade, and work with metals. Though you've been exposed to these very same achievements for nearly two hundred years, you choose not to adapt. I want you to live as you will. Hell, I wish to live in that manner. But we cannot! The world will trample us. Decide, damn you! You've already killed the Mingo scouts of that Irish trader. Once and for all, follow me, the one you call your French father, into battle. Do not abandon me today. Your people may decide to remain backward, but advance forward with your men today!"

For a moment, I put myself in the moccasins of Shingas. He was in an unenviable position. There was no good choice. The English powers despised him as evidenced by men like Braddock and Lydius. Onondaga and its Iroquois Alliance scorned him, treating his small tribe worse than a stray pack of dogs to be moved about at its master's will. Even their French fathers, though smaller in number than the English, heaped contempt on his way of life. He could stubbornly or peacefully go home to his lodge, but that would solve nothing. The days of his people were numbered. Or, he could stay on the course set out before him by the Master of Life and at least win glory for his braves, if not ultimate victory.

"We are too few," Shingas repeated. He was a courageous warrior, but not a maniac bent on death.

Beaujeu glanced over our heads toward the sounds of the approaching army. The footsteps of hundreds of marchers and the creak of wagons could be heard. He interrupted the Delaware. "That's why we've brought help. Not only are there Canadians and Shawnee over this ridge, but there are Frenchmen. There are representatives from many of the tribes in the pays d'en haut – Ottawa, Mississauga, Wyandot."

Shingas scoffed. "Those other tribes are here for captives and booty, nothing more. They share nothing in common with my plight. They'd just as soon see me fall today so that they may walk off with my family." His head jerked to look toward the dense forest behind us and beyond the clearing as wagons loudly cracked through brush.

Beaujeu was beside himself with frustration. He shook his head and turned to retreat over the other side of the ridge. "It's over then. We'll barely have time to make it back to the fort and evacuate." His shoulders sank. But after he made a few steps, Beaujeu stopped and turned. "Tell me, if you do not think you have anything to offer today, why have you come?"

Chief Shingas turned his back to us and looked at the captain. A ray of sunlight fell on the Delaware king as he began to speak. "I will tell you something you may view as crazy. I am here because a prophet from my Delaware people, we call him Neolin, has told of a great uprising. All the peoples will join in fighting off the Europeans. In his prophecy we will reject alcohol and material wealth. The Mohawk and other Iroquois tribes have defiled themselves with such things. They've taken the white man's God. Neolin tells us to reject all of it. In return, we will shed much blood. We will enjoy many seasons of victory. We will kill the English and their Iroquois whores." He hesitated, before adding, "But Neolin warns that the season has not yet come for our uprising."

Beaujeu smiled. "Why wait? Why suffer? Why not start today? Many Indian peoples are represented over that ridge, just as your Neolin has foretold." His smile quickly drained away. He'd seen us. The Canadian officer's eyes shot wide and he sprinted the short distance down the ridge toward Shingas. "Enemy scouts!"

And Shingas didn't have a chance to answer the Frenchman's question. Moses had had enough of Shingas disparaging his Iroquois people and their more modern ways. He had hiked up his musket and aimed it at the Delaware's back. "See what your Neolin says about this!" he muttered as he squeezed the trigger.

The ball belched from the muzzle with a burst of noxious smoke. I saw the wadding erratically flutter upwards and then float to the ground. Meanwhile Beaujeu had tackled Shingas. The pair rumbled and rolled through the thin coating of decaying leaves that littered the cleared woods, bouncing off an oak trunk, and coming to rest against a small boulder just a rod away from us. The Delaware instantly hopped to his feet, unwounded, his face darting around to find from where the shot had come. He and I locked eyes, while Moses the Song rapidly reloaded.

I saw a flash in my peripheral vision as Taeheek raised his own musket. "No!" I shouted, ramming my palm into the stock. The gun went off, sending its round crashing into the dirt over Shingas' shoulder.

"What did you do that for?" Tim shouted.

"Get Beaujeu!" I called to Shingas. "Get back to the fort and get out of here."

Shingas looked down at Captain Beaujeu. When the Canadian didn't move on his own, his fellow warrior gathered him up. He slung Beaujeu's limp arm over his shoulder. And then the Delaware clutched around his waist. A large, mangled hole was ripped into the captain's naked chest. Sheets of dark crimson poured down his painted belly. Beaujeu's chin bounced limply against his sternum. He was most certainly dead.

"Thank you, Ephraim Weber," Shingas called. He turned and dragged the captain up the hill, struggling under the additional weight. He shouted over his shoulder. "But Beaujeu gave his life for me. And the captain was right. I have to choose a course. And even if Neolin is wrong. Or he is correct. I have chosen. Today, I will meet you and your whoring general in battle in these woods."

"Damn Delaware," Taeheek cursed, reloading. I could see many painted faces and muskets adorned with feathers popping up above the ridgeline. Their owners were coming to investigate the twin musket blasts. Shingas waved for the newcomers to hold off their attack until our army arrived.

"Damn Delaware savage," Moses growled, leveling his weapon at the chief for a second time.

"Damn you, Weber," I mumbled to myself as I brought my old Brown Bess up to my cheek. I'd saved Shingas again. All so he could try to kill me once more.

Crack. Crack. Moses and I fired up the hill almost simultaneously.

When the smoke cleared, Shingas and his fellow soldier were gone over the ridge.

And they were well prepared to ambush our army in the most opportune place within a hundred miles.

CHAPTER THIRTY-SEVEN

"I smell gunpowder," Croghan shouted over the din of music as he and Hendrick emerged into the clearing. Tim, Moses, and I had raced back to where we'd left our horses. Compared to the relative peace of the forest we'd experienced for the past half hour, the musicians created a deafening cacophony.

"Ambush is coming," I blurted out.

"What about Croghan's Mingo warriors?" Hendrick asked, still advancing on horseback.

"Dead," Moses answered, trotting on foot next to the old Mohawk chief. Moses reached up and forcefully tugged back on Hendrick's reins.

"They were good men," Croghan growled about his dead friends. Like Hendrick, he, too, had not immediately curbed his mount. If the lead element halted every time news of a worrying nature arrived in the vanguard, a marching column would never leave its home town. "They had families," he sighed.

Old Hendrick had grown up in Iroquoia, Mohawk country. He had never been to these parts. As soon as Tim jerked back on the reins, Hendrick's eyes had begun scanning his surroundings with heightened perception. "Hunting grounds," he observed quickly. "A good place for an ambush. For fighting in the Indian manner."

Croghan jerked his reins. His horse, surprised, instantly obeyed and came to a halt. "That ridge is mighty close!" he warned.

A single musket cracked from the hilltop. In the face of our entire army, it was pathetic, really, that we heard but one report. But it was close enough for us all to hear, even above the musical fanfare, and it did cause us to pause. Behind us I heard Colonel Gage shout for his vanguard to halt when the echoing report reached his ears. His men rattled to a stop with perhaps fifty of their number sticking out into the clearing. It took several more screams from Gage to get the musicians to at last quiet down. The fifes and drums in Captain Gates' regiment, which was immediately behind that of Gage, but still in the thick woods, continued on with their merry racket.

Father Baron steadily guided his beast out of the line. After stopping it, he casually slid down from the saddle. Seemingly in no hurry, the missionary walked upright over to a large tree and stooped down in among its huge, snaking roots. "Perhaps your general will believe you from now on, Mr. Weber," he said as he tucked his head down and covered it with his hands. "Our Virgin Mother has answered our calls." Fearing what might next come from the ridgeline, Moses, Taeheek, and I followed suit, scattering to find hiding places.

A heartbeat later it wasn't the soothing voice of Mother Mary that I heard. It was the eruption of two hundred French muskets. Musket balls spit down on us from above. A cloud of smoke formed where a moment earlier the air was thin. Branches snapped over my head. Bark exploded from the trees. Horses dropped to their knees, blood draining from shredded neck wounds. Some whinnied and reared, throwing riders. Wounded beasts bolted in all directions.

Men, however, those brave, well-trained and foolish men, did not run. They should have. I suppose they would, if they could. Those in the vanguard, their bodies slammed instantly by flying hot lead, screamed in agony. In that first hail alone, I saw an ensign and a lieutenant, the youngest officers in the army, crumple to the clearing's soft earth, dead before they hit the ground.

Then all was silent for three, maybe five, seconds.

And the whooping screech of hell's hounds up on the ridge followed thereafter. I had become a man among the tribes and had learned their ways. I had heard, and I had called, the war whoop myself on many occasions. But there was something utterly terrifying about the shrieks I heard that day. Ask any man who was there and fortunate enough to have survived those three bloody hours. He will tell you. Shivers upon shivers raced down our spines. Sweat broke upon my brown. And to the day I die, I'll declare that the devil himself dragged the entire underworld and every cast-off god ever conjured in a man's mind into that clearing along the Monongahela that very afternoon.

And for whatever reason, Providence had fled the field, allowing room for the Indians' Master of Life to make a last gasp. And he was joined by Satan, who was hot, angry, and had an appetite for blood.

CHAPTER THIRTY-EIGHT

From his horse, Colonel Gage used a riding crop to swiftly advance more of his vanguard into place. He swatted the shoulders of the nearest men. The infantry obeyed his violent commands, marching straight toward the ridge while under a terrific hail of fire. They stumbled over fallen corpses and wounded comrades who struggled to crawl away. Still, they valiantly maintained their ranks. On the other hand, Tim, Moses, and I huddled in place awaiting the end of the first great rounds from the ridge. There was a time for heroics, a time for self-preservation.

"Column halt!" Gage shrieked. The hooves of his horse were a mere foot from where I hid. "Deploy the line, Mr. Brown!" he added to a lieutenant who eagerly obliged by jumping over the blanket of death at his feet. Gage then peered down at me, adding, "You'd do well to get yourself in the fight, Mr. Weber."

"Best to wait a bit," I retorted, glancing up from where I cowered. Then I warned, "Might want to break into skirmishers. This ain't gonna be a European fight, colonel."

Gage scoffed as the one-sided fighting continued. "We shall dismantle them in an orderly fashion, Weber." Then he sneered, "Americans! Disobedient even in the thick of combat." His focus quickly returned to his men.

In moments, young Lieutenant Brown had his infantry in a smart line, broken only by the occasional tree. Like teeth in a cog, whenever a man fell away, another redcoat jumped into place. "Fire when ready, Mr. Brown!" Gage called. "Show these savages what disciplined troops can do!"

"Front rank, make ready!" shouted the lieutenant. Those redcoats worked in perfect unison. "Take aim!" Every infantryman dropped his right foot back a perfect six inches and leveled his musket. "Fire!" screeched Brown.

A wall of British lead, propelled by super-heated air, moved from the clearing up to the ridgeline. I don't know if a single enemy was hit, but dirt, bark, limbs, and leaves exploded from the impact of scores of flying shot.

Lieutenant Brown was a good young officer who worked well with his troops. His company of men in the front rank immediately set about reloading their spent muskets without requiring an order. Mr. Brown turned his attention to the second line of soldiers. "Rear rank, make ready!" These men repeated the motions of the first line, except they sidled a perfect six inches to the right to place themselves opposite the interval of the front rank. "Take aim! Fire!"

More flying lead. More devastation of the natural setting and perhaps a few enemy warriors.

"Good, lads," Gage complimented them when the Indian and Canadian guns fell completely silent. "Advance and volley, Mr. Brown."

"Yes, sir," the lieutenant called happily. Just as the words left Mr. Brown's lips, a ball slammed into his shoulder. He stumbled and used one of his men to steady himself upright. It was a natural response to the grievous, but not lethal, wound. The action, however, got him killed. Still swooning, no fewer than three more lead balls ripped into his body which served as a ripe target.

"Damn!" Gage yelled, gnawing on his spittle. He prodded his creature forward, pointing with his sword to where he wanted the line to advance and reform. "Another volley like that will send them from the field!" Colonel Gage encouraged. He then proceeded to call out the orders directly to the vanguard just as Captain Gates and his soldiers emerged from the forest.

From atop his beast, Captain Gates examined the rapidly changing situation. He saw that Hendrick, Croghan, and my comrades all hid in place. He watched as another young officer on foot, who served under Colonel Gage, was cut down. "The colonel needs more firepower!" he called.

"The colonel needs to stop giving the enemy such good targets," I shouted to Gates. I hadn't bothered to move. I suppose some might say I was acting cowardly. To that I say, nonsense! It's easy for a man sitting next to his warm fireplace in Philadelphia and reading about the events of that day from a newspaper to second guess my actions. I had no way of accurately aiming at anyone on that low ridge. Furthermore, I had only so much powder and lead on my person. And from what I could tell, we were setting up to have a real fight. I'd not confuse motion with progress.

"Column! Halt!" Captain Gates told his men after they had streamed into the clearing, walking on their fallen countrymen. "To the right, face!" His warriors snapped to the right. "To the left, wheel! March!" The men who had held the front-most position and now stood at the left, marched in place. The men on the far right took broad steps, swinging the line to face the enemy. "Forward!" Gates screamed when his men were parallel to those of Colonel Gage. "Ensign!" he shrieked to a wide-eyed boy. The ensign had to be younger than I. "Form on the colonel's right flank and take care to fire by company! Control your men!"

"Yes, sir," the ensign said, ducking as a pair of musket balls tore a hole in a maple just over his head. "You heard the captain," the suddenly frightened officer proclaimed. "Quick step!"

I watched as the ensign bravely advanced across the killing ground and deployed his soldiers to the right of Gage's. Six of his men immediately sustained crippling wounds. Captain Gates followed along just behind them, a perfect target for Indian sharpshooters. When a round slammed into his saddle, blasting the leather and wood to bits, he took the hint and climbed down from the beast. With his sword drawn, he organized the remainder of his men. Just one minute after they arrived on the scene, Captain Gates' men began adding steady volleys of their own to the fight.

To my surprise, their combined efforts steadily beat the enemy into submission. The ridge slowly fell silent under the constant barrage from those regulars. For several long moments, only the occasional shot rang out from above as Colonel Gage and Captain Gage methodically advanced their two-ranked lines.

"Fix, bayonets!" screamed the officers. The broken line of redcoats slid and locked their blades in place. "Charge, bayonets!" The soldiers jerked the butts of their muskets under their right arms, holding the swell out front with their left hand. Drummers beat the long roll and the infantry advanced with the quick step.

Moses, Tim, and I took the opportunity to congregate. "Looks like they shut up the turds on the ridge," Tim observed.

"These are big woods," I warned, stating the obvious. Then I pointed in the distance along each flank. "If those Delaware and French are like any other Indians I've fought, they'll circle around. They're not waiting to receive the charge."

Moses nodded. "If they mean to fight it out, that's what they'll do. They're not stupid."

"Lucifer's mittens!" screamed General Braddock as he and his aides trotted into the clearing from their place further back in the column. They brought with them even more regulars. By Braddock's design, most of the provincial soldiers brought up the rearguard and would not arrive for many more minutes.

However, along with the general, a few wagons rolled into the clearing, their drivers hoping for the protection offered by the British regulars. I saw Caleb and motioned for him to set his brake and crawl underneath his cart for protection. He didn't hesitate to follow my instructions. Braun rattled in after. He was smart enough to maneuver his wagon behind the biggest tree he could find. After quickly hobbling his beasts with rope, he hopped into the wagon with his cargo of libations and loaded his musket.

"Still think Lydius and his stink are worth working for?" I asked, goading Braun.

He surveyed the bleeding carcasses of man and beast littering the forest floor. To my surprise, the brute was reflective. "Not my best choice," he admitted, aiming into the gun smoke. "Hell, I was supposed to have killed Chief Hendrick for him by now. Glad I didn't get the chance."

"What kind of scouts do we employ here?" Braddock shouted. The goat was late to his own battle, preferring to cavort with Bess rather than head his army. "I count more than forty dead. We walked into an ambush!"

"The Delaware killed the scouts," I called to the lathered Scotsman.

Braddock's lip curled in anger. He watched Gage and Gates methodically advance near the base of the ridge. While intermittent fire could still be heard in places, the shots returned from the enemy was mostly nonexistent. "The savages and the

Frogs will taste a bitter pill for this." Then he turned to the aide nearest him. "I'll not be outflanked. Take a company of men and support Colonel Gage, Mr. Shirley. Gates has his right. Form on his left."

The son of the Massachusetts governor nodded and gave the sickly Washington a smug look. He then pointed to a captain who had marched in on foot. "Follow me," said Shirley. The captain interpreted the order into a set of proper military commands and about fifty men peeled off to the left.

"I think the Indians are going to fight us in the American way," I warned Braddock.

"How nice of you to share your thoughts. *I* think they're being driven from the field by the most ruthless soldiers on the planet!" Braddock snapped in retort.

"The best supplied, best trained, most ruthless red-coated bastards the world has ever seen!" exclaimed Sir John St. Clair, our quartermaster, as he arrived on the scene. "And they've made the enemy's guns fall silent," he added. "Brilliant! They gobble up shit and blood, they do!"

"Silent for now," Tim said. "The Canadians and Delaware are going to send men around us."

"The odd man can do nothing against a proper line formation!" Braddock mocked. Every gun on the field fell silent, just as Shirly arrived in place on the left. The clearing was anything but clear. A thick sulfur fog hung low. Dr. James came into the clearing immediately bending to the wounded and calling out orders to his fellow physicians and assistants, who feverishly set up an impromptu triage area. Their work was grim, bloody.

Bayonets glistening, Gage's company of men had slowed to a cautious pace on top of the low ridge to investigate the damage they'd done to the enemy. "Here's a dead savage!" one man called triumphantly. "And here's a dead Frenchman dressed like a savage," yelled another.

"Beaujeu," I muttered. "Hope they find more than just two bodies."

"Here's a pack of dead Canadian marines," called one of Gage's men. He turned to face us. We could barely see him through the smoke. "And, General Braddock," he shouted. "The back of the ridge is empty. We've held the field."

Braddock smirked. "Novices," he said. "See there, Mr. Weber. Discipline. Order. Organization. These are the things of a modern army. These are the ways civilized mankind will tame these primitives."

But the battle, thus far, had been a mere prelude.

It was time for the bloody dance to truly begin.

CHAPTER THIRTY-NINE

The proud British regular on the ridge, who had announced our victory to the general, dropped stone dead when the first shot rang out. A second later another musket report occurred on the left flank. It was followed one second later by at least fifty more rounds sent in our direction from all over the battlefield. The captain who had followed after Shirley caught two lead balls in his belly. He double over, clutching his innards and then teetered onto his rump. He collapsed into a fully supine position just as the head of William Shirley, Jr. exploded into a mist of crimson and bone. Twenty of the men in their company were hit in some fashion, falling straight down like heavy rope.

Again, I ducked. "Their targeting the officers!" I called. "Get down, Colonel Washington."

"Mr. Weber," Washington chastised me calmly from atop his beast. "I am a soldier serving His Majesty the king. I believe it is my business to demonstrate conduct befitting an officer. I believe you ought to get into the fight as well."

"I'm not going to stand out in the open so these Delaware boys can use me for target practice," I shouted as the howls from the Indian warriors shrieked from all areas. The right flank, toward Gates, had erupted as well. I saw flashes of Delaware braves dash from tree to tree. Some would pop out and hatchet at our soldiers before melting back into the woods. "At least let us fight fire with fire."

"General Braddock," Washington pleaded, taking up my cause. "Set skirmishing parties. Call up our provincials – the Virginians and any Pennsylvania lads. They know how to fight under these conditions. It is how we settled this country."

"Obviously, nothing has been settled!" the general shouted over the ever-growing din of battle. "And you want me to disband the lines in favor of a desperate strategy employing American greenhorns?" he asked, incredulous as bullets zipped past. "Mr. Washington, this is part of war! I've spent my life training for these infrequent moments. And believe me, victory goes not to the man who panics and abandons what a lifetime of study has taught him. No, man! We stand fast."

Just then, a particularly loud blast of muskets, perhaps as many as three score, exploded from behind nearby trees at once. One of the balls ripped Dr. James to threads, shattering his spectacles, skin, and bones. He died, flopping down on the face of one of his struggling patients. That weak, helpless man, died a few moments later, suffocated by the doctor's immovable body.

The same blast splintered the forelegs of Braddock's handsome, white Arabian. The general toppled out of the saddle over his beast's neck and rolled onto the ground. Stunned, he came to rest against a fern that had managed to sprout in the well-trod hunting grounds. Simultaneously, Washington's horse was pierced by a handful of bullets that tore into its withers and barrel. The colonel firmed his grip on the reins as the poor creature careened sideways. When it was clear to Washington that he'd not be able to keep the beast upright, he flipped his foot from the stirrup and gingerly stepped off. The horse crashed to the ground. Washington tripped briefly, but caught himself before falling.

"Mr. Weber," he said calmly. "Fetch me another horse." The sickly colonel grunted as he retrieved the pillow he was using to protect his raw backside. Clutching the cushion under one arm, he then went to Braddock and helped the general to his feet. "And find one for the general, too."

It was an easy order to obey. So many officers had been killed in those first few minutes of the battle that scores of horses, already saddled, trotted about the clearing. Tim and I snatched their reins and brought them to Braddock and Washington. "Thank you," said the colonel. Lacking his usual energy, he faltered on the first attempt. But eventually, and with a slight groan, he slowly climbed aboard the borrowed beast.

"Washington!" Braddock barked when he was back in the saddle. "Have Gates and Gage form a three-sided square, centered upon our position! Double ranks. Then we'll bring more men into the square. A few minutes of this withering fire is all we'll need to withstand. Trust me."

"Yes, sir," Washington said, without hesitation. I watched quite dumbfoundedly as the colonel trotted ahead with his new horse to convey the general's message. Colonel Washington was a brilliant, huge, and tall target. He seemed oblivious to the hazards as bullets zipped over him. Bark exploded near his head whenever he passed by a tree. Still, by Providence he would say, he suffered not a scratch.

"St. Clair, you runt!" called Braddock. "Act like a proper quartermaster and see the powder wagons brought up here. We're going to use our supplies quickly under these conditions."

"Aye, you bastard!" Sir John called. He seemed to be enjoying the excitement.

"And clear the way for our artillery! Bring the guns forward. This isn't the best place to deploy the 12-pounders, but it is open enough here. Perhaps a few clusters of grape will teach the savages what it is to tangle with a trained army!"

"Yes, sir," St. Clair answered, cheerfully. "I'll see the civilians and women protected from attack, as well. Can't lose the whores!"

"Good," Braddock barked.

"Bess," I grumbled as a curse. I wondered again how she could have thought it was ever a good idea to come on this campaign after all my stories about Fort Necessity and its horrors.

"You forget all about the girl, lad," Braddock warned. From atop his horse he pointed to the right flank where Gates' men were slowly wheeling back the way they'd come, forming the right side of a square. "I want you and your friends on that flank providing skirmishing fire for Captain Gates."

"Three skirmishers?" I asked. "This is the American wilderness, general! Each one of us needs to be a skirmisher!"

"To the flank," the general said calmly. Though I hated him, I took solace from his sanguinity. That's the way it was in battle. Even the most experienced man could have a few moments when his emotions raced, especially at the outset. But Braddock had begun to find his battle cool. He'd suddenly shed his normal blustery exterior and, for the remainder of the fight, he'd be among the most composed men in the forest. "Mr. Weber, we are a people marked by obedience to authority, be that our God or our general. Now, you may not like me. And you don't have to. But you will heed my advice. You will take Moses and Taeheek and go to the flank. You will follow orders or I will forget that I had already forgotten about your pending court martial."

"We have to do something," Tim said, tugging at my collar.

I turned to see that Moses was already obeying the command. He ducked as he ran, leaping over the scattered dead. When Tim jerked on my hunting shirt a second time, I slapped away his hand. He cuffed the side of my head.

"Listen to the Scotsman," Croghan called. He had found a place next to Hendrick, where they themselves acted as detached skirmishers. The pair knelt behind a fallen log, firing rapidly for men of their years. The movements of their arms were efficient, minimal almost, practiced over decades of wilderness warfare. Their two guns did the work of four as they picked out targets on the left, exhaled, and squeezed the triggers. Through the smoke, I watched more than a few Delaware warriors drop. "If two codgers can hold this side well enough, I suppose the right flank will have to do with three young men."

"Alright," I said, sufficiently embarrassed to action by the older men. Tim and I then chased after Moses. Besides, in all honesty, it was high time for me to get in the fight.

"Be careful," Father Baron warned as we passed by where he still huddled among the roots. "The savages are out for blood today."

"And so am I," I said, eyes wild, teeth gritting.

And so, I was.

CHAPTER FORTY

Things had gone from bad to worse for the first thirty minutes of that bloody hell. Shingas and his Delaware, along with the French and Canadians, pressed every advantage they had. They selected officer after officer to kill, decapitating much of the middle command structure. Braddock's, Gage's, and Gates' orders could hardly find their way to the tip of the spear. As a result, these beheaded platoons and companies of regular soldiers were left without direct leadership. They groped and flopped about. They'd been trained to stand firm and follow exact orders, not to think and react on their own, adapting in a cohesive fashion. Therefore, they replied with shot sent in helter-skelter fashion, getting chopped down one-by-one. Even the most elite among Braddock's men found themselves being slaughtered. His burly grenadiers, bedecked with mitre caps that made them appear eight inches taller than most men, were easy for the enemy to pick out amidst the chaos.

But after one full hour of sweating, cursing, and killing, things had settled into what could be considered a battle that favored our superior training. We'd been shoved back from our original position in the middle of the clearing to its edge. During the ordeal, I had watched as Father Baron had taken the opportunity to rise and walk through the disorder to the French lines, never to be seen again.

With the back and forth, some of us still fought in the clearing. Others engaged the enemy from the thicker areas of the forest nearer where we had forded river. The regulars who had survived the opening rounds had congregated into several groups, separated by feet or even many yards. The square ordered by Braddock had long since disintegrated.

"How goes your day, Mr. Weber?" Washington asked.

I was startled by his soft voice. Other than seeing him ride about with Braddock, I hadn't spoken to him since the general sent my cohorts and I to the right flank. "What are you doing way over here?" I asked as I aimed at a Shawnee warrior about two rods away. He descended rapidly on a soldier who had already fired his weapon. My musket sounded, *cra-crack!* The warrior fell and the regular was safe – if only for a second. Another warrior promptly jumped from a bush and rammed a long knife into the man's neck. There was nothing I could do. But several of the regular's comrades hammered their bayonets into the intruder's belly before he could steal a scalp.

"I am not over *here* at all. The right flank has come to visit us in the center, Mr. Weber," Washington informed me.

I knew we had been pushed around, but I had not realized just how thin our supposed square had become. Actually, we now fought in several squares or bunches that dangerously ran the risk of being separated altogether. It was even possible that some groups were already effectively cut off. But the disorder and smoke meant there was no way of knowing who was missing or where they were dispersed.

"Captain Waggener!" Braddock barked over the shrieks of dying men and war whoops. "A platoon of men with you at their head will storm across the clearing and retake the ridge. We need to hold that position. Do that, and we are minutes from success. You shall be the key to opening up the path all the way to Fort Duquesne."

"Yes, sir," Waggener said, eager for swashbuckling glory. We had become quite crowded in that immediate vicinity and so the men he selected were nearly all within an arm's reach. Less than a minute from Braddock's order, the captain had his picked men ready. They knelt with newly loaded guns, bayonets fixed, and ammunition packs resupplied from a nearby toppled wagon. Waggener held a fully cocked pistol and a sword. He squinted, peering through the battle haze at the barely discernable ridge.

"Once you have it, call to us," Braddock ordered from his borrowed horse. "I'll support you with immediate reinforcements."

"And cannons perhaps," Washington added.

"Yes! If only," agreed Braddock. "The ones we have left." Two of our artillery had fallen into the hands of the Delaware after the large guns had been brought to the fore. Fortunately, the enemy, having neither training nor supplies, was not equipped to use them against us. The rest of our field pieces were trapped toward the rear of the battered train and in no place to offer assistance.

Waggener nodded, "I'll shout once we hold the ridge." Then he craned to look his men in their eyes. "We don't stop moving until we reach the top of that hill. Then we form a square and fight like we've trained."

His men said nothing in reply.

"Understand?" the captain asked, growing agitated.

"Yes, sir," came several nervous replies.

"And if I fall, you keep moving," growled Waggener, setting his chin. He punched one of the men in the arm. "He commands if I fall. If he falls, you command," the captain said, pointing to the third man in line. "And so on until none remain. This is a one-way trip, so step lively. Understand?"

"Yes, sir!" they said, with a little more gumption.

Waggener gave no more instruction. He faced into the smoke and jumped to his feet. "Huzzah!" he screamed as he set off. His small column of men popped up after him, adding their own, echoing war cries. The gun-smoke fog swirled as they entered. And while I cannot say it swallowed them whole, for I could still make out the general shapes of the men as they raced across the clearing, dodging trees, fallen soldiers, and enemy, the pungent mist certainly enclosed them.

"Go, lads," Braddock whispered, biting his lip with anticipation.

"Go, lads," I repeated, gaping at their rapid progress.

They had made it halfway across the open forest with increasing momentum. None of them had fallen, though plenty of burning lead had seared the wind about them. "By the devil's britches," Braddock exclaimed, punching a palm with his fist. "They're going to make it. Washington," he added. "Once they're up there, go about retrieving those damn lost cannons and see them dragged above."

"Yes, General Braddock," Washington whispered, unmoving. His eyes were fixed on the running platoon. We all watched Captain Waggener and his swift-footed crew now silently cut their way to the ridge.

"The French are attacking! An entire platoon! Canadians!" came a stark warning from deep within the choking smoke. Alarmed, I peered about, gripping my Brown Bess. But I saw no one other than the occasional Delaware or their allies. No mob of armed Frenchmen descended on our position.

"Fire!" came a command from the same voice who had warned against the looming attack.

More than a dozen guns belched out fire from behind trees halfway up the hillside on our right flank. The power of the blasts sent the smoke, which already hung low, whirling about. At the business end of the barrage, Captain Waggener and half of his men collapsed, crumpling to the left from the impact of the lead.

"That'll teach you, Frogs!" shrieked the unseen Englishman who had ordered the volley.

"Friendly fire, dammit!" Braddock cursed. "Friendly fire! You're killing our own!"

But nobody knew who was calling to whom amidst the chaos. Musket fire was still erupting all around. We fired at Delaware, Shawnee, Wyandot. They fired at us. War whoops and cries in multiple different languages, meant to instill momentary courage, added to the confusion. We stabbed them. The enemy screamed. They stabbed, scalped, or captured us. Our men screeched.

"We've stopped their advance!" shouted the giddy Englishman, whoever he was, from the hillside. "Reload. Send them to hell where they belong!"

Braddock growled from the back of his throat. "I'll have that man's head. Now go, boys. The hill. Take the hill!"

But the survivors of the friendly fire onslaught had lost all their courage. With his comrades in front of him all dead, it was now the sixth man in the original column who should have been in command. However, neither he nor his mates acknowledged that fact. As one, though without the order to do so, they turned leftward and sprinted away from the imminent danger posed by their smoke-blinded colleagues.

"They're running!" the unknown man on the hillside screamed with delight. "Keep your eyes peeled for more of the rascals, boys! There!" he yelled just as I watched a host of

Canadians appear from the far right. A brilliant, clanging clash of arms ensued. At least the mystery soldier now engaged the proper enemy.

But things would get no better.

"Deserters!" screamed an English officer. I recognized Captain Gates' voice, but could not locate his position in the dense fog. "Halt! Or I will open fire! Halt, I say!"

Nothing other than the ruckus on the hillside happened for two more seconds. The men fleeing from the Waggener disaster quickened their pace, now running a straight line to the left, parallel to the ridge and toward the Monongahela.

"Please, sirs. Halt!" Gates pleaded. Another heartbeat passed by, with nothing other than the normal continuing bedlam. "Fire!" Gates ordered reluctantly.

A surge of musket cracks erupted in the face of the remains of Waggener's platoon. To a man, they were mowed down at close range, their torsos being halted by impacting lead before their shoes knew enough to stop running. Their bodies dropped to the forest floor, ending one of the most horrific displays of friendly fire incidents I have ever witnessed in my life – and I have seen a few.

The normal beat of the battle's anarchy renewed itself. Satan's harvesting scythe was sharp that day. His sweeps were broad, gathering ample grain. Braddock's chin slumped to his chest, scraping against his gorget that had begun the day in brilliant condition. Now it looked like its owner felt. "Mr. Washington," the general said quietly.

"Yes, sir," the colonel said, as stunned as the rest of us.

"Hold off gathering our artillery."

"Yes, sir."

With a cocked arm and rigid index finger, the general pointed through the smoke to the ridge. "And Washington, *you* will secure that hill. *You* will hold that hill. Then I will send you support and, by Judas Iscariot's coins, I'll get you those cannons!"

"Yes, sir," Washington said firmly. He extended his neck while sitting up taller in the saddle. "But these are woods like our Virginians and Pennsylvanians are familiar with. Will you place me in command over my fellow provincials so that we may engage the enemy in their own way."

Despite all the carnage and death around me, I remember smiling at that moment. Finally, Braddock would have no choice but to heed Washington's advice. The colonel and others had offered it on numerous occasions since the long march began. But it had been all too easy for the general to dismiss Washington's American ideas as backward when the only thing falling around him had been pleasant sunshine. Now, with metal balls decimating his regulars, Braddock would have to give Washington control and allow him to fight the Indians in the way we'd all learned growing up.

General Braddock cleared his throat, and lifted his chin. Though it was impossible for the smaller man to reach Washington's height in the saddle, he had suddenly blossomed into a more striking military figure. Showing no fear, no malice, no anger, only determination, he answered. "Mr. Washington, I've found you to be a most gallant and honorable gentleman. In such a spirit, I do not take your suggestions as if you hold any unbridled fear or glory-seeking feelings within your breast. I take your ideas for what they are, genuine concern for your fellow countrymen on this day of bloody battle. But they are also laced with inexperience, you see? What we've witnessed just now is part of war. It is evil and inexplicable, inexcusable. Nonetheless," he said, pointing into the smoke and toward a renewed burst of blood-curdling screams. "There it is. Not so plain as day, but real. If you ever hope to command men in battle, you mustn't react to every little setback that occurs, for there will be many – too many to count. Our men are trained for this pandemonium. We are their betters, bred to lead them through such turmoil."

"But sir," interrupted Washington. "We must adapt to the situation, to the enemy, to the terrain. This terrain is best suited to small, maneuverable groups of skirmishers."

"I thank you for your counsel, Mr. Washington," Braddock said. "Your request is denied. You will leave the provincials where they belong, back defending the baggage train with the other women. You will utilize those best equipped to tear the enemy to shreds. And that is these honed men about you."

The muscles of Washington's jaw swelled in anger. They were even more pronounced due to the wasting he'd experienced from his illness. With his rows of teeth gripping each other tightly, he said, "Yes, sir. I shall assemble my platoon, sir. I shall take the hill, sir." He tugged at his reins, directing his horse back.

My smile had long since faded. When a musket ball tore a trench through the earth at my feet, I turned to rejoin Moses and Taeheek in their ferocious battle. "At least we won't have to make the suicide attack on that hill," Tim muttered.

"Poor Washington," added Moses as the colonel slowly maneuvered his beast through the corpses and crouching fighting men to select his platoon for the mission.

"Poor Washington," I repeated, turning to watch him go. The man with the newly levied death sentence had his back facing me. It was straight and strong. I felt a tug, nothing physical, just emotional. Something from deep within compelled me to speak. "Colonel," I called after him.

Washington curbed his horse. "Yes, Mr. Weber?"

"Do you need a hand?" I asked. You might think the offer brave. But it was the most idiotic thing I have ever done.

If Washington ever smiled, he did so then, showing no teeth. "Thank you, Mr. Weber," he said. "But I am required to use regulars for this action." He gave the general a stern look.

Braddock suddenly felt magnanimous. It may have been better for me and my friends had the general retained his outlook that all men from the Mother Country were supreme in their fighting ability. "Request granted," the general said, though no request had been made. "If you think the Pennsylvanian and his savage friends might be of use as a supplement to your British regulars, you may have them."

One corner of Washington's mouth curled up, just a bit more. "Come along Mr. Weber, Moses, Taeheek."

The two Mohawks sighed. Tim said what they both felt. "Thanks, Shit-for-brains." And so, the return of my infamous nickname.

CHAPTER FORTY-ONE

Washington had gathered more than thirty Virginians for his attack toward the hill. No. You didn't read that wrong. The ever-obedient colonel had promptly disobeyed the general's direct order and sent word to the fractured baggage train that they were to send as many provincials as they could spare. The wayward colonel even ordered Alexander Braun to join when we found him bloodied and fighting alone behind an isolated rock.

"I'm not bunching up with the likes of you so I can die like the rest of these redcoats," Braun said, patting the skull of a soldier who had collapsed dead next to him.

Washington would not argue with the brute. He pulled his pistol and aimed it at Braun. "Gather your weapon and fall in line, sir. A man of your size may come in handy. We shall fight in the manner of Americans."

"So, you won't set us up as targets, like those redcoats? We'll actually use our brains?" Braun asked, climbing to his feet while brushing aside the pistol.

"Well," I said. "Those of us who have brains are free to use them."

"That leaves you out, Weber," Taeheek said, knocking his knuckles against my head and making a hollow sound with his tongue and cheek.

Braun laughed. "You ain't bad for a savage."

Tim grinned. "Nor are you," he said pleasantly.

"Thanks," Braun began. Then he said, "Hey!"

"Fellows," Washington interrupted, sliding his gun into his belt. "Should we survive the day, we may resume the bickering at nightfall."

"Then count me in," Braun said eagerly. "But I'd like to survive so I can give Braddock and Lydius a piece of my mind! And fist!" he said balling his mitt into a massive sledge hammer. "Imagine. Upsetting the tribes like that. Ought to know better."

"Kindly refrain from disparaging the commander-in-chief," Washington warned as he led the way. "His task is one few are capable."

We grudgingly gave up our banter, following after our stoic leader. And for once, I was happy to have Braun so close by. As Washington had suggested, his tremendous strength might be the difference between life and death.

The colonel led us at a brisk walk from atop his horse. In a most surreal scene, we cut through isolated, warring clusters of men. Usually, the fighters were content to ignore us, engaged as they were in a primeval battle for survival. But sometimes the enemy took note of us, gallant Canadians or Frenchmen charging at us from the gloom. We responded to their notice in kind, dispatching them to hell where all the Frogs belonged.

The colonel, upon his borrowed horse that had a dirty, dappled coat, made a fine target. Twice, his hat was ripped from his head by whirring bullets. Twice, he reined his horse and waited patiently for me to return it to his hand. He paused a third time when we reached the edge of the clearing on our army's right flank, safely away from the prying eyes of Braddock.

"Seven groups of five of you," he ordered without warning. At his word, the men shuffled, forming their makeshift groups out of those closest to one another. Mine consisted of Moses, Taeheek, Braun, and a Virginian with a slack jaw and deep-set eyes. "Six of our groups will work independently. Your goal is that sycamore tree growing crookedly on the ridge. Spread out. Do not bunch together. If you can get to the hill by stealth, do so. If you must engage the enemy, do so and move on. Mr. Weber, you and your men are with me. Any questions?"

There were none.

"Then steel yourselves. Protect your fellow Virginians. Go. We'll meet you on the ridge."

The six groups raced out, not as one unit, but rather as six separate ones. Some plunged straight ahead, quickly jumping behind a great oak. Others ran further right, assembling among a pile of dead bodies. Slowly, nimbly they all advanced at their own pace – sometimes fighting, other times running, still other times, stalling, or even dying.

"Follow me," Washington ordered our remaining team. "I have a goal in mind that does not involve friendly fire casualties."

The colonel edged his horse into the clearing. We crouched at the beast's rump, making ourselves small.

"Don't you think you should climb down off of there?" Moses asked Washington as we shuffled after him.

He chuckled. You read that right, the colonel chuckled. Leaden shot hammered about us. And he sat up tall, acting as the biggest target in that clearing. Seemingly with no cares in the world, Colonel Washington chuckled. The only times I've ever seen anything like it, were all the other times I witnessed that man face battle. "Mr. Weber will tell you, Moses, that Providence has plans for me. Perhaps it is only to take this hill and then the Good Father will escort me home. So be it. Or, perhaps it is only to draw fire from those other men as they run across the clearing. So be it. Now, I don't wish for death, mind you. But I do not fear it. A soldier, a gentleman, an officer cannot. My first battle I found exhilarating as the bullets sizzled about my ears. But those days seem like decades ago." In truth, it was only the previous year when the colonel had experienced his first taste of war at Jumonville's Glen. "I now understand that it is a task that must be done by men for their country and way of life. War is nothing to revel in. It is my duty. Sober duty." He curbed his horse in a particularly exposed spot. "One of you trot over there and gather up that horse."

The five of us huddling on foot shared confused glances.

"Not ten paces in that direction," Washington encouraged, pointing.

Several near misses scattered debris at our feet. Braun and the Virginian dropped promptly to a knee and returned fire at the set of unseen assailants. Undeterred, Washington added, "It is a good thing I've ridden a horse out here. I can better see the field. Mr. Weber, go retrieve the beast. Be quick."

"Come on," I mumbled to Tim while giving his arm a tug. We crouched and pushed through the choking smoke, prepared to be surprised or attacked at any moment. Behind us Moses and the others suddenly fought off a pair of would-be attackers.

"Keep going," Washington said calmly when Tim and I pivoted to offer assistance. The colonel's eyes darted about the hazy clearing, looking for new dangers as Braun pummeled a

Frenchman to death with his bare hands. "Our Mr. Braun has got this under control."

"What's he want with a horse?" Tim whispered when we continued on, leaving the small clash in our wake.

"I don't know," I said. "Keep looking. I can't see anything."

"He must be crazy, sitting up in the saddle like that," Tim rasped, making himself small while he ran.

A horse nickered. I saw it a moment later when a cloud of smoke drifted away on a wafting current of air. "Easy, girl," I said, taking hold of the reins that draped over its withers. I clicked my cheek and led the creature toward Washington. It grunted, flapping its big lips in frustration. The mare labored to proceed just two steps before pulling up short.

"Wait," Tim offered. He jerked a knife from his belt and moved along the left side of the horse. I hadn't noticed that the original rider's foot was still wrapped in the stirrup. The man's body, along with his heavy gear, was being dragged over the ground. He was clearly dead. For a man cannot long survive with two bullet holes ripped in his waist and his scalp removed. Rather than fumble to free the foot, Tim used his razor-sharp blade to slice through the leather strap. The stirrup and foot plunked to the forest floor with a thump.

"Any trouble?" Washington asked when we returned. He took the reins of the new horse and tied them to his saddle.

"No, sir," I said, stepping over the battered enemy remains of Braun's handiwork. "And you?"

"None that provincials cannot meet head-on. Let's press ahead," the colonel whispered, spurring his beast. "Ephraim, you and the Mohawks take the lead. My fellow Virginians, fall in behind. Be prepared to fire. Once you do, advance without hesitation and seize the cannons."

"Cannons?" Tim asked. We were lost and disoriented from the thick gun smoke.

"Yes," Washington admitted. "But there's no time to chat about it now." In a fluid motion, he ripped the pistol from his belt, cocked it and fired, the muzzle ejecting its foul pellet just an inch over the blaze on his horse's head. The animal reacted with a start, but the colonel fought it vigorously, quickly mastering it once again.

"Conotocarius!" screamed a batch of Delaware Indians that had materialized from the sulfur mist. One of them was buckling under the weight of a wound given by Washington's pistol. I believe they were as surprised to see us as I was to see them.

I managed to pull my old Bess up just a few inches, nowhere near high enough to aim. But the Delaware who hurtled himself at me to close the gap needed to be taught a swift lesson. I fired at him just as Moses and Tim shot at other targets, charging forward. The ball from old Bess struck the warrior higher than I thought it would. Such was the way with a rushed aim. But the blast worked well enough. It struck the top of his sternum, blasting it and the soft tissue of his throat to bits, thereby ending the danger.

"Move, Mr. Weber," Washington rasped. He was spurring around me to meet another threat. "Watch our flanks, my Virginians."

I tore the hatchet from my belt and ran ahead, not certain what I'd find hiding in the thick smoke. One step later sent me tripping over the tongue of one of our pilfered field pieces. I careened forward, dropping into a clumsy roll. When I came to a stop, I looked up to see a Shawnee fumbling with his musket. He meant to aim straight down and shoot me, without ripping off his own toes. His heartbeat worth of hesitation was all I needed. I drove my tomahawk blade into the side of his knee. The joint buckled. He shrieked. His arms jerked, his finger twitched. The gun roared, raining sparks down on me. My face was peppered with burnt powder, a massive cloud of sulfur rushed into my nose. My shirt briefly caught fire. But the ball punched the ground next to my ringing ear. I was unharmed – relatively safe.

Next, I used the hatchet handle like the rung of a ladder and pulled myself up. The warrior fell down, swinging the butt of his musket impotently. Tearing the hatchet free from his limb while scrambling, I gave a short windup, driving the head of the implement into the side of his belly. He wasn't yet dead, but he was incapacitated. I yanked the blade free, bringing a mass of his intestines with it. He whimpered, asking for comfort from his mother in his native tongue. I immediately crouched, ready to receive another attack.

None came.

On his rump, Tim leaned against the spokes of a cannon's wheel, reloading his weapon. A pair of dead Indians lay at his extended feet. I took the opportunity to crawl to my gun and reload it. In the twenty seconds of time that then elapsed, I watched as Washington ran his sword into the chest of a Delaware. Limp, the man slid free as the colonel's wavering arm held the blade out, fully extended.

Washington quickly peered about, panting greatly. His head, like the carved bust of a victorious Caesar crowned with laurel, was wreathed by eddying smoke. "Hitch the horses directly to the piece. The ammunition caisson is destroyed," he ordered, still short of breath.

"We've already taken them?" I asked incredulous.

"We have," Washington allowed guardedly. "But we must hurry." He was now gazing from his place in the saddle up to the ridge. "The first of our men have nearly made it to the crest. We must be there on time. Moses," he called into the smoke. "See the powder and shot for both guns are stacked on the one we'll haul."

"Can't," Moses croaked. "Tim. Ephraim." On my hands and knees, I followed the sound of his voice and rolled a lifeless enemy warrior out of the way. Moses' hand was still clutching the handle of a knife that was rammed into the heart of the dead man. Unfortunately, the dead warrior's hand was gripping his own knife. Its blade was hilt-deep in Moses' quivering, blood-red belly. "Listen to the colonel," he muttered. "Get that cannon up to the ridge."

"We're not going to leave you here," I said.

"You have to," he smiled, crimson pooling in his mouth.

"Come. Hurry," Washington said to the others. He'd backed his beast and the other one so they were on either side of the heavy carriage trail. Tim, Braun, and the Virginian scurried about hoisting the tongue, hitching it to the beasts in a makeshift manner, and transferring extra ammunition.

Five minutes later, the colonel gave the order to move toward the hill. "Get in line, Mr. Weber. We'll return for Moses," Washington promised.

"No, we won't," Braun said marching toward me. "Move," he added as he roughly shoved me out of the way. He then jammed his musket into my chest, telling me to hold it. Finally, as if Moses weighed less than a child, he hiked the Indian up onto his shoulder with one hand. "We can't leave anybody behind," he said as he fell in behind the creaking artillery carriage.

I was stunned, to say the least. "But everyone says you are scum," I said, following after. I ducked, hoping to make myself a smaller target, while carrying the two guns.

"Oh, they're right," Braun answered. He must have been inspired by the colonel. He marched upright, defiantly asking to be challenged by the bands of Indians swirling about the clearing. "I am scum. But I'm not an asshole. You don't leave a friend to die alone on the field."

Moses grunted while he bounced on Braun's shoulder, which was becoming soaked in deep crimson. "So, we're friends now?" the Mohawk asked, forcing a pained laugh.

"Naw," Braun admitted. "I don't have any friends. Mere acquaintances. But you're Shit-for-brain's friend. I suppose that's enough for me."

"And we're not friends," I told Braun.

"Hell, no!" he cackled. "But you've jumped out a window, let me shoot you, and taken a thunderous beating from my fists. You've survived it all. If that don't bond us somehow, I don't know what will."

"Quiet!" Washington ordered. "Maybe we can make it the final length without alerting the entire Delaware nation as to our whereabouts. Are any of you prepared to defend us if we are attacked? Taeheek? Mr. Weber?"

"We've got it," said Taeheek, referring to himself and the slack-jawed Virginian, who had taken the lead. Each had a hand curled around one of the horse's bridles, further encouraging them forward with their heavy load.

"We're alright back here," I added, peering around the cannon as Washington had just begun making his way up the incline. The hill suddenly seemed steeper when I noticed that I trailed behind a couple thousand pounds of bronze. The carriage jerked against its straps. The horses' hooves dug in as they strained against its weight. Washington chatted to the beasts, calmly patting each of them in turn.

"Ephraim?" came a whine not five feet from me. "Ephraim? Is that you?"

The voice was pitiful, beaten, sad. It was the most terrified squeal I'd ever heard.

"What the hell are you doing all the way out here?" I asked the dark silhouette, which was pressed up against a large tree, its arms held out wide so he looked like the Christ at his crucifixion.

"Help." The squeak was short-lived, wavering.

And it was from my brother, Caleb.

CHAPTER FORTY-TWO

"Join the men on the ridge, Mr. Weber!" Washington rasped, his beasts just a rod from the top. "They must hold it."

I again glanced around the cannon, up to the crest. A half score of the Virginians who had originally been dispatched by Washington had made it. They fired madly down the other side at an enemy I could not see. "But it's my brother, Colonel!" I called.

"Braun," Washington snapped without delay. "To the top. Weber, gather your kin and catch up." Having lost so much of his family over the years, especially his dear brother Lawrence, the colonel had a soft place in his heart for siblings.

"Yes, sir!" I called, jumping toward Caleb's pitiful squeak. In a moment, I was on one knee, cutting at the leather thongs secured tightly around his wrists and wrapped around the tree. His face was badly beaten. His shoulder bled from a knife wound. With proper care, he should live.

"Why didn't they just kill me?" he asked weakly, falling into my arms.

"You're lucky," I said. "One of the Delaware must have decided you'd make an obedient captive or slave. They'd retrieve you after the battle and maybe drag you all the way to the pays d'en haut."

"I'm not the only one," he muttered while burrowing his face into my chest like I was our mother. He began sobbing. Caleb was a good boy, not suited at all for the horrors of war. He wasn't weak. His strength was in his faith, true and unsullied. I have always admired him for that.

"We'll worry about the others later," I said, pulling us both upright. "We're sitting ducks out here."

Caleb raised a trembling arm, pointing further north on the hill. "But they're right there."

My gaze followed his finger. Sure enough, I saw more than twenty captives: officers, teamsters, soldiers, wives, and even a few of the harlots strapped to trees awaiting their captors and their horrific new life in the wilderness. I toyed with the idea of setting Caleb down and sprinting along the chain of prisoners, cutting them free. At least they'd have a chance to race to

Washington's side on the ridge or to the main body of the army below.

But I quickly changed my mind and dashed toward Washington. With Caleb's head still nestled against me, his eyes squeezed tightly, he asked, "What are you doing? We have to save them."

"Not yet!" I shouted. Then, lugging mine and Braun's muskets, I forcibly dragged him up the hill. Caleb was pressed against my right hip, trying to help walk. His legs mostly failed as we came closer to the ridge, where Washington commanded the group's actions from atop his beast. The rest of his men were scrambling to set up the field gun or were still firing frantically westward over the hill. I hated to imagine the size of the force they engaged.

It would matter little. Something much deadlier was coming.

"To the right!" I shrieked as I reached Washington's toehold. Moses reclined in the dirt, breathing shallowly, pressing a splattered red hand into the wound that would not stop seeping. "To the right."

Atop his dappled creature, which was now free from the carriage trail of the 12-pounder, the colonel's head jerked right. From this vantage point, I am certain he saw what had driven me from saving the other captives. Still, with our measly force of warriors, none of whom were experienced artillerymen, if Washington was surprised or frightened, he showed none of it. Stoic as the Sphinx, he was.

"Mr. Braun," he said calmly. "Reposition the cannon to fire on our right. Immediately." Washington edged his horse back so that the giant Virginian could maneuver the piece.

Braun, who'd just gotten the cannon set up to fire down the far side of the hill, gasped in frustration. But when he saw the fast-approaching threat from the right, he hoisted the tongue without the slightest hesitation and, using every ounce of strength, whirled it about. The muzzle bashed one of our defenders on the ear. This man began cursing, but when he saw the new threat, he clamped his mouth shut – probably prayed in whatever his manner was – and directed his musket to the right.

"Load the piece, please," Washington ordered to no one in particular. "Grapeshot."

"I can do it!" volunteered one of the Virginians. "With me," he commanded a comrade. They scrambled up from their knees and fell upon the ammunition crates.

"Mr. Weber, set your brother down next to Moses and add your gun to our defense," the colonel ordered, his voice barely audible over the growing chorus of approaching guns. As he had a moment earlier when Braun had swiveled the 12-pounder, he easily shifted his horse to my left and behind me so that I could carry Caleb to a more protected place of rest. As he moved, Washington also reloaded his pistol, aimed it, and fired. "We require every brave fellow at the moment."

Fortunately for the long future of my country, or quite unfortunately for the immediate outcome, I lingered at the colonel's side, glancing again at the coming menace. What I had thought was a score of Delaware warriors ascending the hill on our right flank had quickly grown to include more than fifty fighters making a mad dash. They clearly meant to deprive us of the critical real estate on the hilltop. Several stopped up short now and again, sending their lead ahead of the charge. Bullets tore up the dirt at my feet. They snipped at branches, sending leaves fluttering down among us in a peaceful manner that did nothing to ease the knots that formed in my stomach.

A dense hail of musket balls blazed through the air toward us. Had I not loitered there for those two heartbeats, the shots would have shattered the colonel's leg. Instead, they slammed into Caleb's right side. He, in turn, was rammed against me. I staggered leftward, hitting Washington's leg in the stirrup. With one hand clutching my brother's body, I slapped wildly at the colonel's boot to keep upright. I missed, sharply cracking the horse's ribs. I tumbled down between its legs. The horse jerked forward, kicking my arm free from Caleb. High above, Washington must have reacted by curbing the reins with all his remaining might, for the beast halted before it could bolt.

More blasts, closer this time, sounded from the right. Struggling beneath Caleb, who was heavy and limp, I tried to look up into the chaos. That's when I saw gaping holes ripped into the colonel's dappled horse. Blood spouted. The beast stamped its legs, fighting to stand. A second later it's giant barrel collapsed downward, toward us.

Clutching Caleb, I rolled out the way just as the creature's belly crashed to the ground, grazing the hair of my head.

"Fire the gun!" Washington yelled. I could see the bottom of his boot. His left leg was still in the stirrup, pinned beneath the flailing horse. Its hooves caught me with a pair of whacks as I sat upright with Caleb, who was now sprawled across my legs.

The cannon erupted, bouncing back six feet, nearly taking the bottom half of the inexperienced Virginian holding the botefeux with it. He'd not stand so close next time. Thankfully, the canister shot that leapt into the wind had the desired effect. Not ten paces from us, a half-dozen braves were ripped to pieces. The rest of our defenders poured as much lead at the attackers as they could, breaking the initial assault as the remaining Delaware warriors scattered for the trees.

Washington's dapple had died by then. The colonel struggled to free his foot. "Reload the piece!" he said, sounding calm but exhausted. His breathing was labored. "Single charge, double canister!"

The impromptu gun crew argued for a moment as to the proper order of things, but quickly decided that they didn't have the luxury of time. Unsure, one of them grabbed the wad-screw, twisting out any unknown remains of the last charge. Next, down went the sponge. Then went the powder, followed by two rounds of canister. The match man blew on his slow burning cord to make sure it was ready. For complete novices, the entire process was surprisingly quick. Fear had sufficiently motivated their actions.

And none-too-quickly. The Delaware had waited just long enough for the musket men to deplete their loads. Now, again the enemy raced toward us. "Fire!" Washington said. He had resigned himself to his plight beneath the horse. I no longer heard him struggling to free his foot.

Boom! The cannon belched a cloud of smoke and double the shot. A dozen warriors fell, their sinews shredded. However, this time the survivors were too close to shrink away. Their war whoops pierced the air. Consumed by bloodlust, they gained speed, closing the gap.

At that point, Caleb mumbled, his breath wheezing. "Who's Trudie?" he asked as he lay over my legs. "Is that you?" he added.

"It's the sister you've forgotten all about," I answered hastily, reaching over him.

"Oh, Trudie," he cried weakly.

I grabbed my old Bess from the dirt and fired at an approaching warrior. Down he went, his groin in tatters. I dropped my musket and leaned forward for Braun's gun that I had carried up the hill. My hand instinctively swept the cock into place as the butt fell against my shoulder. I found a target and unleashed the weapon's hell. It barked and jumped. Another warrior dropped. I set Braun's gun aside.

I had not yet really set eyes upon my brother or looked into his condition. A part of me knew what I'd find, but by ignoring the situation for perhaps a minute, I was allowed enough to time to prepare, grieve even. It was because of this extra moment that I did not cry when I saw my little brother's body torn to shreds, pieces of his insides exposed to the outside world in manners that should never be contemplated. It was a gruesome sight. Like the floor of a slovenly butcher's shop.

Patting his sweaty head, I said, "At least Trudie will have another innocent to speak with in Heaven. And when you meet Tahki, giver her my love."

"I remember Trudie now," he said with a smile, his eyes shut to the horrific scene. "Father always told me an older sister was a part of my imagination. But she was real, wasn't she?" That's when his lanky arms quivered for just a second. Then he died.

Screams and clatter brought me back to the battle.

Forgetting about the lesser threat from the west side of the hill, the Virginians, Taeheek, and Braun had rushed ahead to meet our latest attackers. Gun stocks became clubs. Bayonets were wielded by hand. Hatchets were employed with grisly brutality. Tim's game cross vibrated in his hands, bouncing from one skull to another. Between our defenders, they killed two, then six, then perhaps ten of the Delaware and still the Indians came. Many brave Virginians died on that hill, defending the colonel, the cannon, and their fellow soldiers.

I scrambled out from under Caleb, leapt over the belly of the lifeless horse, and reloaded while crouching next to the colonel. He lay on his side, facing away from me. For a moment I feared he had been killed, Providence having successfully brought him to that ridge after all the other misfortunes and near misses in his young adventure-filled life. But you know that the Great Maker had many more plans for George Washington. You know that somehow he survived that battle. But you enjoy perfect hindsight. At the time, remember, I had no idea the god-like presence that would develop in the modestly experienced, often suffering, and failed officer.

"Colonel!" I gasped, setting the muskets down and seizing him by the shoulders.

"Have we held?" he asked, his voice betraying more weakness than usual. His face was bright red. It was not crimson, there was no blood. He was flush with fever. His clothes were soaked with sweat as if he'd just emerged from the Monongahela. He panted. His sickness, the dysentery he'd endured for weeks, was far from leaving him. It was only his tenacity that had gotten him out of the doctor's wagon and up to that ridge. Seeing his current condition, I doubted that same resolve would be enough to see him survive. Then, glancing over the horse and watching our dire predicament, I knew with fair certainty that none of us would live out the day, determination or not.

A Delaware ripped his tomahawk blade from the shattered shoulder of a Virginian. The warrior saw the top of my head peeking over the horse's barrel. He broke off at a sprint directly toward me, shrieking the entire way. I grabbed Braun's gun, leveled it, and killed the man. But the Delaware swarmed like mosquitoes on that ridge. Another warrior saw what had happened and immediately jumped into the fallen man's tracks, racing toward me, a bloody hatchet dripping in one hand, a musket, cocked, in the other. I threw aside Braun's spent weapon and hefted my old Bess. She felt good in my hands. So good.

My eye stared down the barrel, blocking out everything in the world except the tiny foresight that I placed directly in line with the attacker's naked, but painted, chest. He was a dead man. Or, rather, he would have been a dead man had he not done something unexpected. He slowly padded to a stop, hesitated for a heartbeat, then deliberately walked toward me. His gun was leveled at me. Mine at him.

"Ephraim Weber," Shingas said. "This has been a bloody day."

This time I did not lower my weapon. Had I killed him earlier, the motivation of the tribes may have been drained before the battle had begun. "My brother is dead," I growled.

"You had a brother on the field today?" he asked, curious.

"At your feet," I told him.

Shingas took his eyes off me, lowered his musket's butt to the ground and bent to Caleb. I didn't move a muscle. When he again stood tall and in my sights, he said, "Looks like a good boy. Young. So young."

"He was," I agreed.

"Too young," he added. "We, too, have lost many fine young men." His eyes noticed the colonel, who rested peacefully at my side. "Has Conotocarius been killed?"

"No. He's with fever. After I kill you, one of your men will have the honor of killing the Destroyer of Villages," I rasped.

King Shingas peered over his shoulder. Our bold attempt had failed. We were overrun. But Tim, Braun, and three other Virginians fought on madly. "Stop!" Shingas shouted. When the battled continued, the chief turned his back to me and walked among the fighters. I considered shooting him. "Stop!" he commanded. Two of his men and another Virginian were cut down while the fighting slowed and eventually paused. Our tiny band of survivors was surrounded on the smoke-filled hill by dozens of Delaware warriors. We were captives.

Shingas returned to the heavy muzzle of my old Bess that now rested on the dead beast's belly. He bent and grabbed the gun's barrel, lifting. I permitted it, but held my hands firmly in place, my finger brushing the trigger. He pressed the muscled flesh of his chest into the muzzle.

"Ephraim Weber, you may kill me now. I know your Providence has led you to preserve me on several occasions already." He paused and spoke loud enough to be heard by all of us who were on the cloudy hilltop. Below, the battle continued to rage. "If you kill me, my men will continue our assault and take this hill, this cannon. If you lower your weapon, I will permit you and your survivors to return to your lines."

There was really no choice. I mean, we were beaten. But somehow with the battered brows of warriors, friend and foe, all staring at me, I felt a tinge of pride – perhaps it could be dubbed manly pride, or more likely foolish pride. I could shoot the Delaware king and worry about surviving later. I might die. I might survive. But in either case, I'd be a hero to the cause. I'd die within three feet of my younger brother. There was honor in that.

Shingas moved the muzzle to the side, away from his chest. "Take the colonel to receive medicine," he instructed patiently.

I hauled the Brown Bess back, gently lowering the cock.

Chief Shingas smiled, blood splattered all over his face. "Let's see if we can get the colonel onto a horse and get you out of here."

CHAPTER FORTY-THREE

It took three of us, two Delaware and me, to help Washington onto the horse we'd found in the clearing on our approach to the hill. He'd recovered a fraction of his strength, but still wavered in the pillowed saddle.

"You have been a fair man," the colonel said to Shingas. Washington's skin had gone from flush to pale, his skin from balmy to ice. "A gentleman."

The chief patted the horse's rump. "I am a warrior of my people. I would like to call you friend. I tried before all this began. And I know you tried to convince your general, as well. But we are at war, Conotocarius. And we are even," he warned. "When next we meet – today, tomorrow, or thereafter, I am your enemy. I'll give no mercy."

Washington nodded gracefully. "Nor I," he said.

"And I cannot protect you between here and your lines," Shingas warned.

"We can protect ourselves," the colonel answered boldly. But we could not. One of Braun's hands was broken. He'd smashed it on the hard head of an Indian. Only two other Virginians had lived. Tim's broken rib had begun bleeding through his hunting shirt, the wound torn open during the strenuous battle. Moses the Song had expired silently. Washington had no physical strength, only his massive fortitude. It was only I who could defend us. And I had just my old Bess, loaded with one shot.

Shingas smiled, understanding the need for a fellow warrior to end his days with a bit of bravado. "Then may this battle and war be done and over when next we meet," he said.

"May it be so," Washington acknowledged. "Lead the way, Mr. Weber," he added, spurring his third horse of the day.

"May I take Caleb with me?" I asked Shingas.

"Go," the chief warned, sternly. "My warriors have won this attack and deserve trophies. Though you've grown up among the Indians, when the ultimate fate befalls your brother, it will be a sight your English eyes do not want to see."

I swallowed hard. I'd seen how the Indians proved their fighting merit to their loved ones back home. None of the soldiers who'd fallen on that ridge would fade into the dirt as a whole man.

"Down the hill, Mr. Weber," Washington encouraged. "Slow and steady."

I led the way, craning to glance over my shoulder. I should not have. Before the last of our tiny line had even passed off the hill, the victors had begun cutting away their prizes.

As a brother of Ephraim Weber, the scalp of Caleb Weber was prized indeed. His was sliced away first, leaving his bloody pate staring at me as we receded into the smoke. The winners moved on to Moses. And so on.

And still the battle raged.

CHAPTER FORTY-FOUR

"Hold your fire, Mr. Weber," Washington instructed from atop his horse as we cautiously cut our way through the cloud of choking smoke. I've never been a quartermaster, but I'd guess many thousands of pounds of powder were burnt in the forest that day to create that noxious fog. "Englishmen approaching," the sharp-eyed colonel announced.

It was a fortunate thing that he'd warned me. My nerves were frazzled. I was tired and prepared to blast away the first figure that materialized out front. But I held off when six silhouettes emerged from the shroud. "Is that you Colonel Washington?" asked one of the newcomers. "The general sent us looking for you."

"Guide us to the general," Washington ordered.

"Alright," the leader of the group answered. "Follow close. There's a bunch of the savages just over there." He indicated into the thick, smoky fog. "We managed to skirt past them without being seen."

We obeyed, following close. And silently.

"You look like hell," whispered the newcomer. "Couldn't take the hill?"

"We took it," I said. "Even had a cannon up top."

"We heard it roar," he admitted with wonder. "The 12-pounder. But we couldn't make heads or tails of who was shooting it at whom."

"It was us, blasting the living hell out of the Delaware," I said. "But we needed more men. They overtook us." I never even considered admitting that Chief Shingas had repaid a debt or felt pity on us. "We were driven off the ridge. This is all that's left."

He glanced over his shoulder at our shattered force. "How many gone?"

"The rest," I answered wearily. "A lot," I added.

Everyone had lost a lot of friends that day. He nodded in understanding before whistling. "We're coming in," he rasped. "Found the colonel."

In a few moments we had filed through lines of men in red coats or hunting shirts. We were taken to Braddock's current command post, which was next to a tree with a giant limb broken away and hanging above. It was nowhere near the location where we had left the general when we'd gone for the ridge. He and his men had been shoved around some more, giving up ground. But as I glanced around, it was not the worst place to be. The woods were dense, complicating things for us, but the Delaware as well. The regulars and the provincials had been forced closer together. And while it was still not ideal to fight in bunched conditions in the wilderness, at least all of our firepower would be able to work together – for once. Despite our heavy losses of officers and men, we were still a fearsome army, not to be taken lightly by the enemy.

And Braddock was not the kind to give up. "Good, man!" he said, praising Washington. "It would have been a miracle to hold that hill. But you took it, as ordered, and with a cannon." He surveyed our motley, battered band. "We have the women tending to the wounded. Take your men to the train and rest," he instructed.

Washington glanced around. "Your other aide, sir?"

"You saw Shirley killed. The other was wounded," Braddock answered.

"Then you're without any others, sir," Washington said. "I'll remain at your side."

Braddock didn't argue. "You look like a ghost. But, you'll make a fine officer in the regular army one day."

Washington perked up. Perhaps he'd found the British general with enough clout to get him the commission in King George's army that he'd begun to cherish. "Thank you. But what of today?"

The general's upper lip twitched in fiery anger. "Went to piss, didn't it?" he asked, rhetorically. "The men are tired, but trained and know what to do. We're getting a solid defensive position built. I intend to rest what men I can while holding the buggers off the rest of the day."

Washington nodded his approval. "The Indians might disappear overnight, general. They are usually not the kind of warriors to carry on a sustained fight. Unless they are provisioned directly from Fort Duquesne, they don't carry enough supplies."

"That's what I thought. Wait them out. Rest and repair. We'll be upon Duquesne tomorrow night or the next day."

"Or, we back track to join the secondary column, sir," Washington offered, tactfully, as if he'd just thought of the idea he had conveyed to the general more than a dozen times since leaving Wills Creek.

Braddock almost smiled. Almost. But he did acknowledge the suggestion with a terse nod. "I'll consider it. As long as we're back at the Forks within the week. I don't want the Frogs being reinforced from Niagara or the like."

"They can't," I said to the general. "They are extended. We heard as much from Captain Beaujeu. If the Delaware fade away. They'll have to abandon the Forks of Ohio."

I waited for the general to snap at me for inserting myself into his conversation. Apparently, he was tired from the day's events. "Let us hope you are right, Mr. Weber," he sighed. "Now, lead these men to the train and recuperate. I've got your skills in mind for clandestine raid tonight."

"Yes, sir," I mumbled, rather wishing I could sleep tonight and for a hundred more in a row.

"Bring your Mohawk friends when you return," the general said, pointing to Tim with a flick of his thumb.

"Moses is dead," I said.

I expected a condescending response. But punch any man, even a general, even figuratively, for long enough, and he gains some humility. "Gave his life heroically, no doubt. As is the way of his people and ours."

"Yes," I said. It was too bad Braddock hadn't warmed to that opinion a month or two earlier. Maybe he wouldn't have helped add fuel to the fire started by Lydius at Albany.

Ten minutes later I had followed a snaking trail through our column, leaving Colonel Washington at the tip of the spear with Braddock. I led the others through dumped wagons, eviscerated bodies, and dead livestock. Torn flour sacks, shattered water casks, and pots and pans added to the forest litter at our feet. Surrounding us, the battle had settled into a lull. Everyone was tired. The screams had become sporadic. Gunshots echoed about once every two or three minutes. Just over two and a half hours had passed since the clash had begun.

Perhaps Braddock was getting the chance to rest his army that he had desired. And the old goat would be difficult to beat with one full day of experience in Western Wilderness warfare under his belt.

Scores of wounded men lounged and moaned in a large area beneath the dense forest canopy. A total of perhaps six women raced about, their skirts splattered with blood, their hair disheveled, tending to the worst of the lot. They were guarded by a couple hundred provincials who had fanned out in a wide semicircle in the thicket.

I breathed a sigh of relief when I saw Bess kneeling next to a soldier. "Over here," I told Braun and the others who followed behind. Dazed, they made no protest. They did not care where they ended up. Only that they could find a safe place to rest. We plopped down on the matted leaves of the forest floor behind Bess.

"Are you alright?" I asked her.

Startled, she turned. "If that's what you call it," she muttered and returned her attention to her charge. He whimpered like a child following a nightmare.

His hip was torn apart by a musket ball. Bits of bone and mud stuck out of the wound. It no longer bled profusely, though it obviously had at one point. The dirt beneath him was stained black with his blood. Now the injury merely seeped. Or maybe it wept. Most of the soldier's blood had long since departed his body. There wasn't much more remaining.

"He'll be dead soon," I whispered to Bess.

"You think I haven't figured that out," she snapped. She took up his hand in both of hers, clutching it to her chest. "He deserves affection from someone at a time like this."

I suppose he did. He expired a minute later. Bess gently set his hand at his side and crawled through the dirt, sitting next to me. "What's going on out there?" she asked.

"About what you'd expect," I said. "It's a shit-storm. How about here?"

Bess studied the ground, pulling her knees in tight while tucking her skirts under her rump. "About an hour ago we were nearly overrun." She pointed to the young man who had just died. "Boys like that protected us. It wasn't going to be enough. But the Indians were called away. Sounded like they had to attack a threat elsewhere."

Taeheek nodded. "The hill and the cannon," he sighed, groaning as he settled onto his back. "We nearly had it."

"Your ribs," Bess gasped. She stood and rushed to him. Though he was exhausted, she had his shirt stripped and the old bandages removed in a minute's time. She scrubbed the wound with soap and water before wrapping it with fresh bandages. Tim yelped most of the time.

"Can you help with Braun's hand?" I asked when Bess was done caring for Tim. "I think he broke it. Used it in a fight against a swinging musket. Idiot."

Braun chuckled. "Wasn't a musket. I used it to beat a Delaware to death. His head was hard."

"You beat my face to smithereens and you didn't break your hand," I said. "See? There is a benefit to being soft in the head."

Braun and I laughed.

Bess studied us. "You fools are friends now?"

First, the two of us exchanged glances, then shrugs. "I suppose," I said. Fighting side-by-side against a bloodthirsty enemy had a way of uniting former rivals.

"How nice for you," Bess chirped. She descended to Braun and delicately examined his hand. It was about twice the size of the other.

"Don't let the touch of our skin get you all excited," Braun warned her.

Bess rolled her eyes. "Right," she said. Then she jabbed a finger into the back of the swollen hand. Hard. I smiled, remembering why I had fallen in love with her.

"Ouch!" Braun said, recoiling his mitt.

"Yep," Bess said. "It's broken."

"I could tell you that," Braun answered. "Do you know how to fix it?"

"I do. Find a doctor. He'll set it with a splint and advise your course of treatment."

"Doctor James is dead," I informed her.

Bess gave me a disgusted look.

"Oh, you probably already figured that out," I said.

She didn't answer. "Doctor Craik is around here somewhere. I imagine he's busy trying to conjure miracles so a hundred more children don't have be made orphans tonight."

"I'd like to make a few Delaware rats orphans before the day is through," Braun said.

"Well, it's your boss, Lydius who helped turn them against us in the first place," I accused.

Braun cradled his broken hand close to his body. In a second moment of self-reflection that day, he said, "I know it. But taking the job gave me reason to come find you and finish our business." He then looked at Bess and at me. "I'm sorry for all this, this stuff between you." An awkward silence followed before he stood. "I'll go scout for Doctor Craik. And I'll find us some food. I'm starving."

I realized my stomach was growling. "Thanks," I said. Braun walked off into the scattered column to scavenge for food and care.

"So, he's not the brute we all thought?" Bess asked when Braun had gone. Rebandaged, Tim had begun to snore.

"No. He is a brute," I said. "But not a barbarian."

We smiled at one another, briefly, then went about studying our shoes. Bess was filthy and tired. I was exhausted. There was much to discuss. But how can you handle issues of a domestic nature in the middle of a battle with new men being hacked to death or blown to bits with every passing moment? Then I decided that there was no better time or place to profess my love for her. The time may never present itself again.

"Bess."

"Ephraim."

We had said it simultaneously. "Go ahead," I said, nervously.

"I don't really blame you for what happened," she said. "But it was all so much, so fast. One day I'm a silly girl, playing in a well-to-do house in Williamsburg. Driving a few boys crazy with a glance here and there. The next day I'm pregnant. Then homeless. Then running to a big city. Then giving birth in a whorehouse. Then a whore."

"You're not a harlot," I protested.

Her lower lip quivered and a tear streamed down one cheek. "Shut up," she whispered. "I know what you are trying to do, and its commendable. Just shut up."

"No," I insisted.

"Ephraim, please," Bess said.

It went against everything my mind and pride wanted to do at that moment. But I relented. "Go on," I muttered.

She nodded her thanks and gathered her thoughts, getting her emotions in check as well. "You can't just deny that something happened, Ephraim. You can't pretend. We're not children, not after all this."

"I know that," I retorted. Of course. I understood this all-too-well. My parents denied that I had had an older sister who'd been devilishly murdered. They'd repeated the lie so many times that my siblings didn't even know Trudie had ever existed. But I'd never forget. And Bess was so right. I'd never forget what she had done with Braddock and the others.

"So, I want to hear you say it, Ephraim," Bess said.

"Say, what?"

"Admit that I'm a whore." A fresh cacophony of muskets erupted toward the front of the column.

Anger, resentment, sadness rushed at me from all sides. I clamped my mouth shut.

"Then we have nothing more to say to one another," she said after letting me stew for a full minute. Another great volley of musket blasts echoed from the front, followed by screaming.

"That's not fair, Bess," I said. "You say what you have to say, and then we're done? I agree with you, or we're done talking? What? Are you proud of what you've done? You want me to say it so bad?"

Bess rubbed away her tears, smearing grime across her face. She shook her head. "No. I'm not proud of what I did. But it happened. If you ever want it to change, you have to admit it happened."

"Why?"

"Ephraim," she warned. "Just say it."

I ran my fingers through my sweaty hair and then rubbed my dirty palms all over my face, stretching my skin out in exasperation. I again studied my boots. I noticed that I'd worn a new hole in one. "Bess, if it means so much to you, I'll say it. I don't like it one bit. But I'll say it."

The one second pause I had expected to take stretched into ten as I gathered the courage to utter the phrase. But at last I was able to wrestle control over my speech. Very quietly, voice unsteady, I said, "Bess, you're a harlot." Though the words meant the same thing, the one I'd chosen didn't feel so coarse as whore.

When I looked up, Bess was nodding. And crying. "It's true. That's what I did to survive. Maybe I could have found something else. Something better. But it's what I did. But now that you know it, that you admit it, I want to ask you something."

"What?" I asked in a tone that was far from understanding.

"Knowing what you know," she said as a handful of red-coated regulars, fear on their faces, ran through our tiny outpost. They raced each other for the river. Bess and I watched them disappear. Other than more musket fire from the front, nothing more happened. "Will you forgive me of all that? Will you still take me as your wife? And though I wish you to answer in the affirmative, don't do so just to please me. Answer honestly."

"But I thought you said we couldn't be married," I began. Another batch of regulars streamed through the area, panic-stricken. Their gear jangled. They gripped their muskets with whitened knuckles. Something wasn't right, but I was on the verge of something important. To me, anyway.

"I had to know, Ephraim. I don't want to pretend. If we are to do this, I want you to accept me and my past for what it is, flaws and all. I will leave it all behind at this moment. It was wrong, but it is a part of me. You and I will deal with it for the rest of our lives."

She was right about that. "Oh, Bess," I cried, falling into her arms. Sitting in the dirt, a battle of increasing tempo renewed, raging unseen in the forest around us. The two of us embraced. My head was on her shoulder. Hers on mine. "Yes. Yes. Of course, I will. I will."

"Weber!" screamed Braun. Behind me, Tim sat up with a start. "Bess!"

Still enfolded with one another, Bess and I turned to see the giant man. He wore a crude splint on his hand and a sling over his shoulder. He waved his good hand wildly, sprinting toward us. "Time to go! Now!"

"Go where?" I asked. "Does Braddock need us already? He said tonight."

"He don't need us now!" Braun panted. He stopped and yanked Tim to his feet. Then he scrambled around the area, scavenging whatever weapons and ammunition from the dead that he could hold. "Get as much as you can carry," he instructed.

I'd been in the game long enough to know that it was better to move than stop for details. "Come on!" I said to Bess. She and I slung powder horns and ammunition satchels over our shoulders. I hiked up my old musket, loaded Tahki's pistol and latched on to a few more muskets. A dozen provincials came running from the front. They were bloody and frightened.

"Did Braddock order a retreat?" I asked. "The old man is arrogant, but he's not so stupid as to turn his back to the enemy. He's not a total fool."

"Hell no!" Braun snapped. He forcefully shoved us toward the Monongahela. "This ain't no retreat. This is a rout!" He was running. We were running with him. All around us more and more men were running for their lives from an enemy no one saw.

"What's going on?" Tim shouted. He knew enough about warfare to question the sense of racing away out of absolute panic. "Maybe the old sailor here should go talk to his good friend Washington, or even Braddock. To see what they want us to do."

"You don't get it!" Braun exclaimed. War whoops, as renewed and refreshed as those that echoed at the start of the battle three hours earlier, rang from the woods. Musket blasts exploded from the north and from behind, punching shot into fleeing soldiers and beasts. "Braddock is dead! And probably Washington with him!"

CHAPTER FORTY-FIVE

Congestion and disorder reigned supreme as the flying column began its terrified flight. There had been no official order for us to retreat. Instead, the decision had been made by a thousand, frightened minds. Therefore, no planning went into the movements that followed. All of it, every step, every curse, every tumble, was spontaneous. Teamsters unhitched their wagons and rode their horses bareback, scattering through others. Regular infantrymen, who had fought in foolish, but close, order all day, abandoned the unity and cohesion they'd been trained to keep. The phrase, *every man for himself*, comes to my mind whenever I reflect back on that erratic moment of my life. Virginians and Pennsylvanians had defended the train admirably all day. Now, they shoved one another out of the way. Bravery was gone, honor lost. Sense fled. They dropped parcels of food and medicine. With knees pumping high, they poured into the Monongahela to evade the descending Indians and their French and Canadian allies. And for the first time that day, with the resolve of our army vanished, our enemies smelled fear. Fear would beget blood.

"Bess," I shouted as we approached the ford in the river. We found ourselves in the middle of a great mass of others. "Stay with Tim and Alex!"

"I plan on it," she shrieked, hiking her skirts and plunging into the water. "And I'm not leaving you!" To our left, a score of Delaware warriors had jumped into the river further upstream. They whooped as the current carried them rapidly closer to the fleeing men and women.

Despite the coming attack, the decision I had made a moment earlier was steeled in my mind. It was difficult, but necessary. I set my jaw, vowing that I'd not succumb to the panic that had set in all around me. I released Bess' hand. The momentum of the mass exodus propelled her forward. I had to fight against the pulse to stay upright in place. "Take care of her, boys!" I yelled to Braun and Taeheek. They were just ahead of Bess, clearing a path in the center of the swarming bulk of frightened humanity.

"What are you doing?" Tim asked as the Delaware warriors fell upon the outskirts of those fleeing. He and Bess both tried to turn back to see me. But the force of the retreat was too great. It propelled them toward the center of the river, away from immediate danger, and me.

"I have to go get Washington!" I shouted. More than one man cursed me as I struggled against the flow.

"Ephraim! No!" Bess cried. Like a terror-stricken animal, she pawed, trying to climb up and over the man behind her. His head was briefly dunked below the surface from her added weight. When he rose up again, he struck Bess in the chin and tossed her aside. Chivalry was as sparse as courage that day. She was rolled beneath the waters and knocked about between drivers and soldiers, who did nothing to assist her. I watched with breath bated until Tim's firm hand eventually pulled her close.

Relieved, I began elbowing my way back up the bank and toward the deep woods. "Watch her! I'll catch up. Don't stop!"

"Ephraim!" Bess cried.

I waved to her, thinking I had made a terrible decision. But I was determined not to abandon Hendrick, Croghan, and Washington to the fate that had befallen my brother. "I love you!" I shouted. I don't know if she heard me. But it felt good to say. Tim had her slung over a shoulder. She fought wildly against his grip as they splashed up the opposite bank and disappeared into the far woods.

The next five minutes saw me kicked and battered by more terrified souls as I raced against the stream. Eventually, though, as I moved further inland toward the Indian hunting grounds, the flow slowed to a trickle. It decreased so much at one point that I began to think I was the only Englishman left in those woods. Then I wondered if I was the only man left in that vicinity. For even the enemy's bullets had stopped whizzing overhead. Except for the small fighting at the river behind me, even the war whoops had disappeared. I heard the first bird I'd heard in many hours.

"Where's Braddock?" I asked a lone, frightened soldier who sprinted toward me. He wore a drum sling over his shoulder. But his snare was long since gone. He gripped a single drumstick tightly in his pale white hand. The tip of the drumstick was painted red with blood. The musician, it seems, had found temporary use as a spearman.

He pointed over his shoulder with the stick, not hesitating his pace for a second. "Back there! Dead!" he squeaked. I felt a breeze when he shot past. "Must be a couple hundred soldiers stuck back there!"

"Then who is in charge?" I asked his retreating back. "Colonel Gage?"

"Washington, I think!" he chirped.

"Washington?" I asked. "You're crazy!"

A shot from just ten feet away pierced the momentary silence. The terrified musician fell to the ground, rolling to a mangled stop. Bushes rattled and a Mississauga Indian brave jumped out, his musket still smoking. He looked at me brazenly, saw that I was fixed in place for the moment, and bent down. His knife efficiently tore away the young man's flesh and hair. I heard the steel scrape against the skull. Then, when he stood tall, he casually set the butt of his musket to the ground and affixed the scalp to his belt. Warm blood dripped down his naked thigh. Then he noticed the drumstick still clutched in the dead man's hand. Curious, the Indian crouched down. He had to pry open the hand to steal the war trophy.

When he rose again, he looked my way, slipping the red drumstick in his belt. I raised my musket and the warrior grinned, waving with hands red with splattered crimson. He spun 'round, running after all those fleeing, just as I fired. When the shot sailed by his shoulder, striking a sapling, he kept right on running, taunting me with war whoops.

At that point, a large volley of coordinated fire erupted toward the clearing. I quickly reloaded. Resolved to see who was really dead and who was really alive amidst the rumors of war, I put my head down and continued on the way I had been heading.

"Coordination, he says!" screamed Croghan at the top of his lungs. I had only to follow the sounds of muskets and shouts to find him. "Stay together, lads! Keep the lead flying."

"We need to leave now!" Chief Hendrick snapped.

"Need to stay orderly, he says!" Croghan shouted. "You there! Hold that line!" He slapped a soldier, knocking his hat to the ground.

"What happened?" I shouted to my old boss over the terrific noise.

"Half the army panicked when old Braddock was hit!" Croghan barked.

"Are you in command?" I asked, incredulous. He was a good frontiersman, but far from a military general.

"Hell no!" he howled as he marched up and down behind two rows of redcoats. The front line knelt. The second line stood. They rotated with round after round of fire.

"Colonel Gage? Captain Gates?" I asked.

"Ain't seen them in an hour!" Croghan proclaimed. "Might be back sipping tea in Philadelphia by now. No. He's the only gentleman left!" His head jerked to one side.

I followed his direction, turning to see Washington, paler than ever, looking like a twig dressed in rags, sitting atop yet another replacement horse. Somehow, the man who wasn't even officially a part of Braddock's army, the man who had come along as a mere volunteer, had taken over command.

"Good to see you, Mr. Weber," he said. The gun smoke outlined him like the portrait in a cameo, his deathly pale figure against the darker, contrasting plane. Then he slowly moved the beast to Croghan. "Keep them fighting, George. Act as my voice, for I can barely muster the breath," he whispered. "Now that Mr. Weber has arrived, he and Chief Hendrick can lend a hand elsewhere."

"Make it snappy!" Croghan growled. "We don't have much time!" Periodically, a dull thud was followed by a man from his red line falling to the ground. There were fewer and fewer soldiers to take his place with each passing moment.

"We'll need cohesion on the retreat," Washington instructed. "Mr. Weber. Chief Hendrick. Come with me." With careful direction he moved his latest horse. The creature displayed the mannerisms of his new master. It methodically stepped its large hooves among the bodies that littered the forest floor. The smoke was as thick as ever. The air was stifling. The heat was oppressive. Still, the colonel rode about, ignoring the danger in which he placed himself. I expected to see him fall dead, from illness, or more likely, a lead ball, at any moment.

"Don't you think you should climb down off of there?" I asked him.

Like most officers, he ignored me. Unlike most officers, and men in general, Washington had full faith in the care of Providence over his life. "There, gentlemen. One of you gather his legs, the other his shoulders. There's a cart we can use nearby. Be careful."

Looking down, I saw General Braddock. He was helpless, but most certainly not dead. He grunted. His face was snarled in pain. The well-groomed wig he always wore sat in the dirt, stepped on many times since falling from his head. One of his arms was shredded above the elbow. It lay limp and helpless at his side, still attached to his body by a splintered bone and a few sinews. Blood dyed his coat redder by the second. His other arm was wrapped across his chest, the palm wedged tightly between the mangled arm and his body.

"You're younger and stronger," Hendrick stated. "Get the heavy end."

I set my gear down and dug my fingers around the general's epaulettes. We lifted him after a count of three. Braddock let out a great cry of agony. His good arm fell away from where he'd kept it pressed and I saw what he had guarded. The bullet that had so mauled his arm, had punched into his chest wall. It was then that I heard the tell-tale sound of popping and wheezing from his throat. His lung had been struck.

"Get a horse for yourself, Mr. Weber," Washington ordered after we had the general situated.

Had I given it a moment of thought, I would have declined. Instead, I answered, "Yes, sir." There were abandoned horses prancing everywhere. Along with my kit, I was mounted in the blink of an eye.

The colonel wavered in his saddle. But he recovered when he leaned on his horse's neck with long arms extended. "I'll guard the cart," he said. "Chief Hendrick will pilot it. Tell Mr. Croghan to join his Mohawk friend in the wagon. You," Washington panted, exhausted from the act of speaking. "You will convey my orders for an immediate retreat. It shall be organized, tell them. One hundred men will fall back to this wagon upon your word. The remainder shall act as a rearguard. A firing retreat. Do you understand?"

"Perfectly," I said. I was less careful about the path I cut through the gruesome scene than the colonel and his horse. It was not out of disrespect, but haste rather, that compelled me to race my new beast over the bodies of our fallen comrades.

Croghan took to his orders from Washington with vigor. "Keep your head down," he warned as he gladly abandoned his temporary post to join the cart. George then called over his shoulder, giggling, "I don't want to lose you before we win that bet with Taeheek." Though not a coward, the old leprechaun showed surprising agility as he bound away.

Now I had to convey the colonel's orders to the redcoats who remained at the rearmost of our retreat. I had no real idea what commands to give. "Alright!" I shouted above the din of death and battle. My horse's ears scanned the battlefield, racing from one blast to another, looking for the nearest danger. "Starting with you," I called to a man kneeling on the ground. He'd just fired his weapon at an unseen enemy. "And then every second one of you, stand up and walk back to Washington. Form a guard around the cart carrying General Braddock!"

The soldier was likely a veteran of the last war with France. He had that hollow, dark-eyed look that conveyed something along the lines of, *I have experience and you don't know shit.* "Why the hell should we listen to you? I don't want to stay here, but standing my ground and fighting is safer than listening to an American baby. These savages will be whipped soon enough."

I considered diving off my horse and beating sense into his thick skull, or killing him, whichever came first. But something approaching maturity sprung up from within. I wish Washington had seen me at that moment. He might have been proud.

"Sir," I said. "It makes no mind to me whether you live or die, only that you serve with the honor and distinction expected and required of you as an Englishman. You will follow orders."

"I'm from Wales!" he retorted. Welsh, Scot, or Irish, they were still Englishmen to me. "Orders from who?" he added, loading his Brown Bess by touch alone.

"Colonel Washington," I said plainly.

He smirked. "Another American novice." The man turned, pointed his Bess at a figure dashing among the trees, and fired. The Delaware fell to a knee, but soon recovered and limped away, slowly. "See there?" the redcoat asked. "Soon enough." He went through the motions he'd been performing for years, reloading his musket.

"You?" I asked the man next to the first. "Do you recognize Washington's authority?"

He shrugged while glancing at the first man for help. I quickly realized this second man was just the type of man I needed. I lifted the butt of my Bess to my shoulder, pointing the muzzle downward at the first, obstinate soldier.

"Oh, don't think about it, laddy," the first veteran quipped.

"To the wagon, now," I ordered him. My calm exterior belied my nervous interior.

He swung his arm up to swat at the barrel of my old Bess. I promptly shot him in the face. It honestly wasn't my intention to do such a thing at the start. But when you point a gun at someone, you should expect that a likely outcome is they'll receive a musket ball. I'd not make that mistake again. And I was glad Washington did not see such a blunder.

Nonetheless, it worked. Before the second man could do anything foolish, I ripped Tahki's pistol from my belt and jerked back the hammer. "Do you recognize Washington's authority?" I asked him again.

His eyes went to the gaping hole in his former comrade's head. "Yes," said the second man, nodding.

"Then do what I say."

Less than a minute later, and with the assistance of the second man, we had sent the guard ahead to Braddock's makeshift hospital cart. Soon, I heard Croghan's voice conveying Washington's orders to those newcomers. The rattling cart echoed between gun blasts as it rolled away, unseen in the sulfur smoke.

And now I organized the rearguard's retreat. I had never experienced a retreat by an English army. Well, that's not exactly accurate. We had retreated from Fort Necessity, but that had been after a formal, humiliating surrender. After that ill-fated operation a year earlier, we had marched with only the mockery of the Indians chasing us, not bullets. As such, I did not know what a fighting withdrawal looked like in the military manuals. It certainly wasn't meant to resemble the chaos that had happened with Braun and the others at the river. But, during my time trading in the wilderness, I *had* run from an Indian battlefield now and again. And those are the exact tactics I employed to slowly pull us away from the site of our most recent crushing defeat along the Monongahela.

Working in groups of four, I had us maneuver step-wise on Washington's trail. The rearmost men fired at whatever targets they could see. Then they raced over the terrain past the rest of us to another location to reload and wait their turn.

Then the next group fired and did the same. In this manner we withdrew in an orderly manner. It took twenty minutes to reach the winding river. When I saw Washington and Braddock's wagon emerge from the other side, I sent half of my men across. The rest of us protected the northern bank. When the first batch waded out the other side, they turned and fired at anything that moved on the far bank, shooting over our heads as we plodded through the Monongahela.

Dripping, we climbed out and renewed our methods. Our pace was slow, deliberate. We lost ten men as we retreated. And, as I considered myself in command, I felt each casualty as a strike against me. It would be my fault that a wife was a widow or a child became fatherless. But I told myself that every man that perished in the heat and woods sacrificed himself so that others might live. Correction, *I* sacrificed them so that their comrades could live.

Eventually, however, the Indians gave up the chase. The last Delaware face I saw was that of King Shingas, victor. Now mounted on a pony, he trotted along a safe distance behind us, shadowing our movements to make sure he'd driven us off what he still hoped would someday be his lands.

After miles of running, pausing, reloading, firing, and running; of jumping trees and fording creeks and rivers; of sweating and cursing, we at last felt confident enough to organize ourselves into a proper column. I give the redcoats credit (though to admit such a thing in later years would have brought scorn along with tar and feathers). For those men, who had just been whipped something fierce, marched in perfect lines, in perfect step.

But even His Majesty's mightiest of men eventually fade. For the remainder of those daylight hours we marched, shoulders slowly slumping as fatigue set in. For the entirety of that night we marched, our pace as quick as possible. There was no esprit de corps. Our haste sprang from fear, bladder-releasing dread. The column ahead of us paused only occasionally to destroy mortars, ammunition, or any other supplies that had made it across the river. Washington needed space in the few wagons we had remaining for the wounded who could no longer walk. Unrelenting, we marched, staggered mostly, back toward the support column.

Unlike our glorious entry into the Forks, however, this time Braddock's army stepped to the tune of neither fife nor drum. We had only the panicked thump of our hearts and the agonized moans of the dying with which to keep time.

CHAPTER FORTY-SIX

For three days, stragglers who had been cut off or fled the initial battle found their way into the train. As such, Washington made no attempt to make an accurate count of the dead and wounded. The tally was tremendous, that was enough motivation for us to keep driving.

During the early hours of the march, Washington slowly trotted his horse further ahead in the column, leaving the rattling cart which carried the wounded general well-guarded in the center. While trotting, the young colonel, twice defeated in humiliating fashion in his short career, found the courage to utter confidence-lifting words to the bedraggled soldiers. "You've persevered, my fellows," he whispered from atop a horse that appeared as fatigued as Washington. "A few more days of hard march will bring us out of harm's way. Keep the pace."

Eventually, we encountered the support column consisting of supplies, roadbuilders, and a few hundred more provincials. With the additional soldiers, Washington allowed us to pause on the track – if only a few hours. Men flopped by the side of the newly built road. Many of them ate light rations, falling sound asleep within minutes from the impact of the first real food they'd tasted in days.

"Come with me, Mr. Weber," the colonel said. As opposed to Braddock, who had ridden in the center of the column, he had assumed the very first position in the vanguard. "See that adequate scouts are sent out, especially to the rear," Washington instructed the officer who'd been in charge of the support column. "Our protection is in your hands. My officers and men have nothing left to give."

"*Your* officers?" asked the support commander. It did not come across as an arrogant question, like the tone of most of the regular officers. His confusion was more an expression of surprise. "The general? Has he fallen? Killed?" he added, looking at the downcast faces of what had once been termed the flying column.

"Fallen," Washington confirmed. "I go to see if he shall be added to the rolls of the dead – when we tally them. Come,

Ephraim." He turned his horse and began riding back the way we'd just come. The road was mostly open as the men had cleared it. Only the few wagons and carts that had survived the battle and were now filled with wounded, still clogged the center of the shaded road. Flies buzzed over the wounds that were still bare, unbandaged. The insects crawled all over the oozing flesh, laying eggs in the detritus that had been living tissue just a few days earlier. There were not enough physicians, women, and ambulatory men left to care for them.

The colonel and I rode on in silence for several minutes. There was not much to say, even for me. The loss had been catastrophic. We'd been driven from the field, a sure sign of defeat. But we'd also lost a huge portion of the men capable of defending the frontier and the main colonies themselves. If the way had been laid bare by our defeat the previous year at Fort Necessity, it was now paved with smooth stones and decorated with inviting ribbons, virtually beckoning the Indians and French to attack.

"Fitting isn't it," Washington said at last. He'd recovered none of his vibrant, tanned color during our retreat. He remained pale and thin. I remember thinking that there was still a great chance that, though he'd survived a hail of lead shot, with horses blasted away from beneath him, and holes bored through his clothes, he might yet die from dysentery.

"What's fitting, Colonel Washington?" I asked.

He smiled sadly, his eyes half closed. "For three straight years you and I have shared in campaigns along this path."

"Yes," I admitted. None had left a positive impression upon me.

"The first was a near failure," he began. We had survived, but it had been a failure by most measurements. "The second, despite great prospects and early success, ended in total annihilation." There was no other way to put. It had ended thus. "And now this."

"Third times a charm," I mumbled.

The colonel did not grin at my gallows humor. Nor did he frown. "So, it is fitting that less than a mile from the site of last year's calamity, here we sit, defeated."

I had spent years in these woods. But the wide road had changed the scenery. I was exhausted, my thinking cloudy. And I still agonized about the whereabouts of Taeheek, Braun, and Bess. As a result, I hadn't noticed just how close we'd come to the burned out remains of Fort Necessity. "Huh," I muttered. "There's Laurel Hill. That means Great Meadows is just a short way ahead."

"The scene of another defeat," Washington sighed quietly.

"You did all you could with your limited resources," I said. Then I pointed in another direction. "And not five miles in that direction sits Jumonville's Glen, the site of your first military victory."

"Kind of you to remember events in that way," he said. "But let us keep to the truth when we speak with one another." He curbed his beast beside the cart that carried Braddock. Several other officers had congregated there. A young ensign held a strange assortment of the general's personal effects piled in his arms. From our mounts, we peeked over the sideboards. "Has he improved, Dr. Craik?" Washington asked.

The doctor, who sat on a hogshead at the general's side with his sleeves rolled, met Washington's eyes. "It's fortunate that you've come. General Braddock has been asking for you." His tone was heavy.

"I'll leave you and the other officers with privacy," I told the colonel. I didn't want to be a witness to what might turn out to be the last words of the general who would go down in history as one of the worst in British history.

The colonel nodded in agreement. "Very well. Stay nearby."

"The general's asked for you, too, Mr. Weber," the doctor said.

I sighed and returned my horse next to Washington's. "So be it," I said.

Dr. Craik gently shook General Braddock awake. "Colonel Washington is here, sir."

Braddock's eyes flickered open. He focused, not on the doctor's face that hovered above his own, but rather on a point some distance in the sky. "And the others?" he asked.

"All here, just as you've requested," the doctor answered.

"Bring him here," Braddock said, barely lifting his one good arm to wave.

"I'm here, general," Washington said.

"Good," he had begun panting. His words were strained and slow. "I've been told that you properly organized an orderly retreat. Took control when all else was lost. You've saved hundreds of lives, colonel." Since Washington had volunteered to join the march as an aide, Braddock had refused to give him, an American, the honor of addressing him as a colonel. By speaking the rank out loud, I realized then and there that the general was dying, for sure.

"If only I could have done more, sir," Washington lamented.

Braddock smiled. His breathing became regular just a few moments later.

"Let him sleep," Washington said, tugging his reigns.

"No," Doctor Craik said, again shaking the general's shoulders. "He hasn't much time."

"The pistols, the pistols," Braddock said, suddenly awakening. He wiggled the fingers of his good hand, pulling an imaginary trigger.

The young ensign who held the various paraphernalia stepped forward and set a box in the wagon at the general's feet. He unlatched the clasp and tipped open the hinged lid. Inside a red felt-lined case was a pair of highly ornate dueling pistols. "My gift to you, Colonel Washington. For saving what was left of my command."

I noticed that several of the English-born officers, among them Colonel Gage and Captain Gates, scowled at the extra attention received by the foolish American colonel. Sir John, the quartermaster, muttered what each of them were thinking, "Bullshit."

"It's a gesture that is too kind, sir," Washington said. I could tell he considered refusing the gift, but thought better as the general's face fell into a weaker and weaker state. "Thank you."

"The sash," Braddock muttered.

The same ensign closed the lid and set a large swatch of fabric over it. He carefully unfolded it, revealing an elegant silk sash, scarlet red. "An officer in His Majesty's regular army deserves to be properly attired."

Washington's face lit up. Despite the carnage, he seemed to be on the cusp of achieving one of his chief life goals. I suppose Washington believed that he had finally *earned* the love and kindness he had received from his dear departed half-brother, Lawrence, all those years ago. "It's an honor, general. I am hardly worthy of it."

Gage's face and that of Gates told me that they agreed with the colonel's sentiments.

Braddock tried to giggle, but pain cut off any mirth within a second. Instead, he coughed, moaning in pain. "Not yet. I still must pen a letter of recommendation."

Washington's countenance fell. By contrast, those of Gates and Gage sparked to life. It looked like the general wouldn't last long enough to scratch his initials at the bottom of a page, let alone write an entire letter. But the colonel pulled back his shoulders, saying, "Just the fact that you've found merit in me, is reason enough for my heart to swell in pride."

"Very good," Braddock mumbled. "Where's Weber, the German. The Quaker scout who fights like the devil."

"Here, sir," I answered.

The general seemed surprised at the nearness of my voice. He looked in my direction, but through me. "I've been fortunate to linger alive for several days," the general told me. His wound reeked with infection. He stunk with sweat and death. Were it I wounded, I would have preferred to have left this world more quickly. But to each his own. "Bouncing in this wagon, staring at the trees has given me a chance to think." His chest fluttered down and his face settled in peace.

"Is he dead?" I asked.

Doctor Craik leaned over his patient to listen for a heartbeat. He set his ear to the left of Braddock's sternum. "Not yet," Craik answered when he sat up.

"And so," Braddock muttered, beginning where he left off. "I remembered my own wedding to my own wife many years ago. We were so young." He smiled.

"Yes, sir," I said.

"I assume you have already begun to care for, to protect, my pet, Bess, during my illness. I want you to continue, boy. All women are to be cherished, but she is a rarity, even among the fairer sex."

"Yes, sir," I answered. Washington and I exchanged looks.

"Have you?" Braddock barked with as much bluster as he could manage in his state. "Is she safe? Will you make her your wife?"

All eyes fell upon me. Colonel Gage and Captain Gates demonstrated smug joy at the prospect of a pathetic American Quaker lad marrying a former strumpet, whom they may have *known* in the Biblical sense. I wilted under their collective gaze.

Washington, cleared his throat, marshalling to my defense. "Of course, Mr. Weber means to wed the young lady, general. The opportunity has not yet presented itself as we have been in heady retreat. But I assure you that all efforts shall be made to hasten the fine day."

Braddock opened his eyes and for the first time they focused on me. They were moist, deep, saying much. I answered his silent thanks. "You're welcome, General Braddock."

The general switched his focused gaze back to Washington. He had never treated the Virginian with any particular respect, but the young colonel had a way of growing on a man. You see, Washington was honorable in all instances. Of course, at small moments even the big, great man could, himself, be small, even petty. But in almost all essential things, the sometimes awkward, often distrusting planter presented the most admirable qualities. The general's slowly fading eyes and the tight wrinkles at the corners of those orbs conveyed to us that he, too, had noticed those qualities in the colonel.

"And so, we've lost the battle against the French and those savages?" he asked, growing confused.

"I'm afraid it is so," Washington confirmed.

Braddock coughed, blood erupted, volcano-like and splashing frothy pink bubbles all over his chin. "Who would have thought it?" he asked.

The cynic in me answered him silently. You know that several, perhaps many people worried about our potential defeat at the hands of righteously angry Delaware Indians and the Frogs.

"He's dead," Doctor Craik said, rising from where he'd again listened at Braddock's chest. The good doctor's ear was smudged with blood.

All were silent for several long moments. It was Colonel Washington, decisive, who broke the hush. "Doctor Craik, would you please see that the wagon bearing the general's body is taken to the very head of the column? It will give the men who rest by the road the chance to pay their fallen officer final respects."

The doctor nodded his ascent. "And I'll take care of your gifts, colonel," he said, referring to the sash and pistols.

"Thank you, sir," Washington said. He turned to Captain Gates. "Form a company of men. Find them shovels. I should hope there are still ample tools in the support column. See a grave dug for the general's body in the center of the road at the head of the column. I shall arrive later, at the time of his internment, to hold a service."

To Gates' credit, the arrogant ass realized that this was not the time to question Colonel Washington's authority. He didn't even glance toward Gage for his approval. "Sir," he clipped to acknowledge the command and then went off to obey.

"The rest of you shall take the time afforded to us for well-needed rest," Washington said. "When the funeral service is complete, we resume the march to Fort Cumberland. Mr. Weber, come."

Craik stepped to the seat and took up the reins. He soon began moving the wagon forward. The rest of the congregants disbanded, Colonel Gage shaking his head in disgust that a lowly American had somehow found himself in command.

I turned my horse to follow after the slow pace set by Washington. We rode through the rearguard and continued on fifty paces back. Alone, he pulled his mount to a halt. Mine padded next to him. "You need me for something, sir?" I asked.

"Yes," Washington answered, staring off down the empty road that cut through the wilderness. Even that far from the Forks, it was strewn with worn shoes, empty sacks, and a few dead soldiers. Many miles further on, at the path's terminus, sat the bloody remains of our defeat, picked over by Indians and scavenger animals. By now the French would have found Braddock's important documents, which had been abandoned during the chaotic retreat. The papers laid out plans for all the other offensive campaigns that year. They would have already been interpreted and their summaries sent to Quebec. With that one unfortunate, fierce battle, all English hopes in North America seemed to fade.

The colonel said nothing more for a long while. For once, I was happy to allow the uncomfortable silence to linger. Mind and body, I was bone weary.

"Have you found your friends, yet?" he asked.

I sighed. "No sign of Taeheek or Braun since they crossed the Monongahela." He and I both suspected what that meant.

"From what I saw of them, neither would allow themselves to be taken captive. That, at least, can be considered a mercy," the colonel said. The sentiment was uttered without the uninformed bravado offered by men who had never seen combat. He meant it in the sincerest, most agonizing, but also most hopeful way imaginable.

"Uh-huh," I muttered, believing it, but preferring not to dwell on their deaths.

"And Bess?" Washington asked delicately. "I'm told a few women have found their way back to the column."

I shook my head. "Very few women survived. Bess has not come back."

The colonel examined his horse's mane. "I see," he said heavily. He lifted off his hat and poked a finger through one of the bullet holes, pondering the capricious nature of death. "You've lost a wife and now a betrothed."

I had already cried about it for two days while marching and riding. "Won't the entire army walk over the general's grave if we bury him at the head of the column?" I asked, changing the subject.

"Yes," he answered, studying me over his shoulder.

"Humph," I said. "Don't get me wrong, I think Braddock deserves that kind of disrespect after leading us to such an avoidable defeat. But I'd never thought *you* would stoop to my level."

"Mr. Weber," the colonel chirped, slightly louder. I could tell a stern warning was coming my way. "It is out of deep respect for the rank and the man that I bury him at the head of the column. Like him or not, a warrior deserves our admiration. You would be wise to remember that. As to any disrespect that some may infer, they are welcome to their misplaced ignorance. Once we flee, or hobble, I should say, back to Fort Cumberland, we have no way of patrolling the frontier in Virginia, Maryland, or Pennsylvania. Our newly minted Indian enemies will run amok. What better trophy for their barbarism than the body and accoutrements of a British general? None, I say. By burying him at the head and then marching a thousand feet over the site, all traces will be crushed away. His body and soul may find rest for eternity."

My gaze fell, ashamed to meet his eye. "I'm sorry," I mumbled.

"Quite, Mr. Weber," he said, again gazing down the winding path.

At length, I summoned the courage to ask, "What did you need from me, sir?"

"The frontier will erupt into a conflagration of bloodshed," he predicted. "For months, years, I'm afraid, I will be chained up in the administration of forts that I cannot hope to defend. If the legislatures in Williamsburg and Philadelphia have anything to say on the matter, resources may or *may not* ever come my way."

That sounded like a painfully frustrating forecast. "We shall make the best of it, sir." During the monotonous retreat, I had slowly resigned myself to the idea of never marrying, of serving wherever Washington instructed.

"But you are a man whose talents lie, not in shuffling parchment. You are a man of action, with much experience in Indian affairs and battle – more than I, certainly more than our brethren from the Mother Country." That much was made obvious by the miles of debris and bodies that littered our path. At that point, his horse stepped on an abandoned canteen. "I'd like to release you from service."

"What?" I asked, suddenly hurt. "What have I done?"

"Everything," he said, grinning with a thin, toothless smile. "You've done everything I've asked. Pennsylvania should be proud to claim you as a citizen."

"Then why?" I asked, wondering what I could possibly do now that all trade with the Indians would evaporate. With Croghan's trading network in the process of being decimated, a military scout and bush fighter was the only other possible career to which I could lay claim.

"Mr. Johnson and Governor Shirley have campaigns against our French enemies in northern New York and Iroquoia. Either leader would benefit from having a man of your talents along with them and serving at the highest levels. They'll need you especially now that the French will know all about our exact moves."

"Are you recommending me for a commission as an officer?" I asked, not enthused by the prospect of being wedded to the military in a truly official manner. To my young mind it seemed like a constricting prospect for life. How foolish I was! If I was going to serve my country of Pennsylvania with arms, why not do so with the respect and privileges that came along with formal rank? It was a concept I'd not understand until too much time had passed and too many men would always think of Ephraim Weber as a backwoods butcher, not a refined, gentleman officer.

"I'm afraid that after this debacle and with the man who was to be my own patron dead, a recommendation from my hand would fall upon deaf ears," Washington said. "No. I want you to go to them and offer your services as scout and guide. You already know William Johnson. I shall pen a letter of introduction to Governor Shirley. Besides, I owe him a letter describing the patriotic sacrifice of his son on the field."

"Junior's body still rests on the battlefield," I said, his gruesome death still fresh in my mind's eye.

"There were many left behind," the colonel admitted. "But the only way I will release you to those other commanders is if you promise to do one thing first."

"Of course," I said.

Washington stared back down the road. "Go and bring back your Bess. Captive or something other, you deserve to find her. Free her if you are able. A man who has lost as much as you, a brother, a wife, a sister, now this, must know."

I stared down the shady road, too. I had told the colonel about Trudie on several occasions, but had never realized that he had actually listened to my rambling stories of childhood. Knowing that Washington had paid attention and understood my plight, gave me hope.

"Alright," I said. I had been considering doing just that, disappearing into the woods once we had the army back to safety. Only now it was an order.

"I cannot offer any support beyond some rations and ammunition," the colonel warned.

"That's all I need."

"Good," Washington said, turning his horse toward the resting column. "You'll leave after the burial service."

"May I sit here a while?" I requested.

The colonel nodded and trotted off to rejoin his army.

And I stared in silence at the litter-filled road, hypnotized by mental images of the extensive miles of destruction.

EPILOGUE

Two hours later, I sat on the horse that I had now claimed as my own. It's owner, if he had successfully endured the battle and searched for the beast, had not yet found me and asserted ownership. Assuming the man had not survived to demand his property, I meant to keep it. In any case, my best guess was that the horse would find itself wild or owned by an Indian chief very soon after. For I expected to be killed on my impossible mission to recover the remains of Bess and my friends.

Heavy with emotions, I smiled to myself. I never would have thought that Braun and I could become friends. Though we were, I admitted. War meant many horrible deprivations for most. But, in a strange way, it could also bring people together.

My borrowed creature, a dirty palomino, was heavy laden. I had commandeered two extra muskets, a sword, and a pistol to go with my existing panoply. They hung from leather thongs on the saddle along with enough extra gunpowder to bring down a fort's wall made of solid stone and packed earth. Furthermore, I had plenty of food. I would not have to scavenge or hunt for as many as six days, or longer, if I was stingy.

I sat there like a king observing his soldiers of foot. The entire monstrous column streamed by. Even the faces of those who had been in the support column and had experienced nothing of the battle now looked downcast. Defeat had a way of spreading into the minds of everyone, like an infection. The only time their dispositions improved was when they were informed by the men in front of them that they now walked over Braddock's grave. That was when their steps became more pronounced, their knees popping a little higher, their soles firmly pounding down upon Braddock's departed soul. I heard more than one man mutter, "Take that you old goat," as he spat on the dwindling barrow mound. What Washington had meant as way to preserve and respect the general's body from mutilation had at least given the men a harmless way to relieve their tired angst.

When night fell and the column was long gone, none of its surviving musicians so much as whistling, I steered my beast back toward French and Delaware held territory.

It was to be the last peaceful night I'd have for many months.

THE END

(Dear Reader-See Historical Remarks to separate fact from fiction)

HISTORICAL NOTES

I have moved the dates of the Albany Congress to after the events of Fort Necessity so our hero could be in attendance. In reality, they both occurred over the summer of 1754. Furthermore, not every colony, especially the southern ones, sent representatives to the congress. However, the concept of bringing together delegates from all the colonies was new and certainly bold. Heretofore, while the English colonies cooperated on tiny, single issues, there had been no broad coordination of which to speak. In fact, the characters in my tale are not overstating the fact that at the time each colony was viewed as a separate country with a common Mother Country in Great Britain.

As demonstrated in *Savage War*, Benjamin Franklin was a vocal proponent of an official union under the umbrella of London. To support the effort, he created the ominous looking *Join, or Die* political cartoon complete with the severed snake. This illustration would, of course, become a flag and rallying cry in another later, well-known conflict.

Franklin's Plan of Union was officially approved by the Albany Congress delegates. However, they had no authority to bind their respective colonies to its articles. As such, it was sent to each of the colonial legislatures for ratification – where it was summarily ignored in favor of more pressing, local issues.

Like Franklin, London, too, had hoped her far-off colonists would pony up funds and a method to defend themselves against the French. The officials at Westminster knew they would be well-occupied in Europe with the fast-brewing war against France. The failure of the Plan of Union meant that London, if reluctant at first, now felt compelled to send an all-powerful general to take charge of her colonies' defense. Enter General Braddock. The colonists' unwillingness to take matters into their own hands would set up years of growing military intervention from Great Britain.

But the Plan of Union was not the only aspect discussed in Albany. Another outcome of the congress were several transactions negotiated with representatives from the Iroquois. Following the Beaver Wars, the victorious tribes that belonged to the Iroquois Confederacy had named themselves as the chief negotiators with the European powers. They even did so for other non-Iroquois tribes, dictating the terms to them. From Albany came deals to purchase the lands then occupied by tribes which had been considered wards of the powerful Confederacy. Some of the contracts were considered legitimate, like that between Chief Hendrick and Weiser. Others, such as that which was presided over by Lydius, were deemed bald thievery. If the events that took place in *Quaker's War* hadn't already tipped most of the non-Iroquois tribes into the French camp, these treaties, Lydius' in particular, helped.

By all accounts General Braddock was an opinionated man. Upon landing in the New World, he set about upsetting and offending every major official on the continent. He found them to be unhelpful, greedy, and provincial. All of these descriptions may have been accurate. However, Braddock had no restraint on his tongue, pen, or expectations. Governors and legislatures quickly learned that he meant to serve as a master, not a peer.

In a similar vein, his quartermaster, the ever-cursing, Sir John, appears to have been inept. As a result of his failures, it took a fair amount of trickery and flattery for Franklin to successfully gather enough Pennsylvania wagons for the general's monstrous baggage train. This modest success meant that Franklin was one of only two Americans who ever received a word of praise from General Braddock's lips.

The other man was George Washington, who graciously volunteered to serve without rank or pay as one of Braddock's aides. The young Washington was patriotic in causes pertaining to the crown. But he was also motivated by personal ambition. In the mid-1750s Washington still had high hopes of earning a commission in the regular British army. Demonstrating his abilities to a high-ranking officer seemed to Washington the best way of securing the reward.

As in *Quaker's War*, the civilian and trader George Croghan was sent along with the army. His wife was an Indian. He had spent dozens of years traipsing over the wilderness and had favorable relationships with everyone. While Fort Cumberland was being constructed in the spring of 1755 near the site of Croghan's long-time trading post, he sent wampum belts ahead to Delaware, Mingo, and Shawnee chiefs and sachems.

A host of tribal leaders and their families slowly descended on Fort Cumberland at Croghan's invitation. The most vocal had been Chief Shingas, self-proclaimed King of the Delaware. Even though he'd fought on the side of the French a year earlier at Fort Necessity, with the right incentives or respect, Shingas could have easily become an ally of the British.

Enter Braddock's tone-deaf actions with regard to Indian diplomacy. He disrespected the Indians' ability to fight. He disrespected their women, by sending them away after accusing them of causing a commotion among his men in camp. Finally, when Moses the Song, a Mohawk, spirited out a map of Fort Duquesne and presented it to the general along with representatives from the Delaware, Braddock indicated nothing but scorn. In a vast superseding of his authority, he further insisted that the Indians would have no land, no rights. His hubris sealed the fate of the world for much of the next decade.

Braddock's March, as the campaign became known, was marred from the outset. All but a handful of Indians abandoned him. The general assumed they'd go home. He was obliviously undeterred. On the other hand, American officers, Washington among them, worried the Delaware would join the French. They attempted to suggest reconciliation. Braddock had no time for advice.

He did, however, have time for his mistress. In fact, the prevalence of prostitutes among the British officer corps was considered shocking to American sensibilities. Most of the colonists were not as exacting in their faith as some of their Quaker or Puritan ancestors. But the open practice of infidelity on the march was something new and foreign to them. In a bizarre order, Braddock did order every single woman who traveled with the camp to be examined by a doctor to ensure any of his men who visited her would remain in good health.

I've replaced the Iroquois, Scaroudy, with Chief Hendrick on Braddock's March for simplicity's sake. Scaroudy was a new Half King that took the place of Tanaghrisson (see *Quaker's War*).

Since Chief Hendrick will show up in a later tale and Scaroudy has a lessor spotlight, the substitution seemed a logical choice.

Out of frustration of his army's slow pace through the dense wilderness, Braddock split his forces in the manner described. He went against every bit of advice he received from persons who had more experience in the region. However, in an effort to defend his actions, it can be said that none of those men had any experience in a European style war between two powers such as France and Britain. Braddock mistakenly thought his experience was the one to lean upon.

Along the march, skirmishes with the Indians that killed his troops only emboldened the general. He felt that each encounter ended favorably for him. And they did. His flying column made terrific time. They swept away the small bands of warriors sent to disrupt them.

All of that changed after the first column crossed the Monongahela just a few miles from Fort Duquesne and entered a cleared hunting ground. The general's scouts failed to discover that a large force of Delaware, French, and Canadian marines from the Forks had come to meet them. Croghan and Hendrick (Scaroudy) were surprised to meet the lead elements of the enemy. A brief exchange of fire occurred. There was a faltering moment when it appeared like the Indians would disengage in the face of the larger force, but Captain Beaujeu placed himself in harm's way and rallied the men. He was killed, but the momentum he gave his troops would not recede.

Braddock was late to arrive at the front, for even on that day he was in the center of the column enjoying the company of his mistress. Colonel Gage and Captain Gates and their men were the first to meet the enemy. They quickly discovered that the opposition did not fight in a manner to which they were accustomed. Within ten minutes, 15 of the 18 officers in Colonel Gage's command were killed by men hiding behind trees. Cohesion broke down. Confusion reigned. As related in my tale, an entire platoon of 30 men was killed by friendly fire.

Still Braddock mustered his men. By accounts of survivors, he exhibited bravery as he rode his horse through the carnage, ordering troop movements which could not be executed due to the terrain and lack of officers. Multiple horses were shot out from underneath him.

But it was young George Washington who shined amid the defeat. Like scores of other men on the march, he'd been stricken with dysentery. And it is a testament to Washington's innate vigor that he recovered what strength he did in spite of the treatment he had received in the form of Dr. James' Powder. Antimony is now known to be quite toxic.

With a calm that belied his years, he trotted off with the general. When the other aides were killed, Washington was the only one remaining. He had success in retaking lost cannons and in taking a hill. It was at the Battle of the Monongahela that Washington's reputation of having complete calm under fire was cemented. Multiple horses were shot from under him. Washington was so weakened by his condition that it took several men to prop him back up on the last replacement beast.

Despite his bravery, the damage to the army had been done in those first winnowing minutes when the command corps had been decimated. The last straw occurred when Braddock himself was shot. Somehow, notwithstanding more senior men, Washington assumed command and helped stabilize what had become a rout. Braddock's body was buried in the middle of the road near Fort Necessity in order to deprive the enemy from digging it up as a trophy. The hiding spot worked. It wasn't until fifty years later when road workers discovered human remains complete with the buttons of a British officer from the French and Indian War.

The defeat was monumental. Two-thirds of the men in the flying column had been killed or captured. In fact, amidst the battle, dozens of Delaware warriors tied captives to trees in order to return to them at the end and drag them away as slaves or prizes. Almost all of the 50 women in the train were lost during the fighting, with fewer than half of them captured. To put the lopsided nature of the defeat in perspective, it has been estimated that the total loss on the French side was approximately 40.

Not only was the loss costly in soldiers' blood. It also left the western defenses of the English colonies wide open to attack from vengeful Indians. In the twelve months following the fight, the frontier erupted. Over 1,500 American farmers were killed in their homes. Another 1,000 were kidnapped. Some of the captives were never seen again. Others managed to escape or were traded back to white settlements in the coming years. The boundaries of the colonies shrunk closer to the Atlantic coast.

I relied on many terrific works to guide the history of my tale. The most important of those, follow. *Crucible of War*, by Fred Anderson has become the modern-day classic on the French and Indian War. Also by Fred Anderson is *The War that made America*, which is a shortened version, but includes a few interesting details not mentioned in his longer tome. Ron Chernow's *Washington: A Life* was instrumental in fleshing out details of the young man's first journeys westward. I also trusted *Firearms: An Illustrated History* from DK Books. Finally, *The Brown Bess* by Erik Goldstein and Stuart Mowbray was a magnificent reference on the ubiquitous musket. Any errors you spot in the yarn are my own.

If Providence be on my side, like He was for Washington, many more tales of Ephraim Weber's adventures are to come. He has battles to fight – both winning and losing. But first, we must discover whatever became of his beloved Bess and friends. I hope you are willing and able to join him, perhaps even cheer him on as he navigates down the long fuse of liberty.

ABOUT THE AUTHOR

Jason Born is a popular historical novelist. *The Long Fuse* is a chain of novels that thrillingly captures the violent period of America's rise from ragtag colonies to independence. He is the author of *Lions & Devils,* a series which vividly describes the heroes and villains of the monstrous Islamic assault of Western Europe during the Eighth Century. Other works include *The Norseman Chronicles*, a multi-volume set detailing the gritty adventures of the faithful Viking, Halldorr, who desired only peace, but found only war in the Old and New Worlds. *The Wald Chronicles* set of historical novels centers on the rugged conflict and improbable outcome in Germania during the wars between the Roman legionaries and their tribal adversaries over 2,000 years ago. *League of the Lost Fountain* is his first work for kids of all ages. Jason lives in the Midwest with his wife and three children. If you enjoyed this work and would like to see more, Jason asks you to consider doing the following:

1. Please encourage your friends to buy a copy – and read it!

2. Go to his author page (Jason Born – Author) on Facebook and click "Like" so that you may follow GIVEAWAYS or information on his next book.

3. If you think the book deserves praise, please post a five-star review on Amazon and/or a five-star review on Goodreads.com.

4. Follow him on Twitter - @authorjasonborn

5. Visit his website, www.authorjasonborn.com.

Printed in Great Britain
by Amazon